academically yours
best friends book club

jennifer chipman

Copyright © 2022 Jennifer Chipman

All rights reserved.

*Dedicated to anyone who has ever had a crush on their hot professor.
I see you.*

Playlist

1. A Place in this World by Taylor Swift
2. IDK You Yet by Alexander 23
3. Strangers by Jonas Brothers
4. Unsteady by X Ambassadors
5. Crush by Tessa Violet
6. Freaks by Surf Curse
7. The Heart Wants What It Wants by Selena Gomez
8. Drunk by Ed Sheeran
9. Hands to Myself by Selena Gomez
10. Begin Again by Taylor Swift
11. I Like Me Better by Lauv
12. The Fall by Dylan Matthew
13. Give Your Heart a Break by Demi Lovato
14. Call It What You Want by Taylor Swift
15. bad idea by Ariana Grande
16. Wildest Dreams by Taylor Swift
17. Late Night Talking by Harry Styles
18. Can't Remember to Forget You by Shakira
19. Illicit Affairs by Taylor Swift
20. Sometimes by Ariana Grande
21. Never Get to Hold You by Carly Rae Jepsen

22. Softly by Clairo
23. They Don't Know About Us by One Direction
24. Two is Better Than One (ft. Taylor Swift) by Boys Like Girls
25. Cloud 9 by Beach Bunny
26. Close Your Eyes by Michael Bublé
27. Just A Little Bit Of Your Heart by Ariana Grande
28. Thinking Out Loud by Ed Sheeran
29. I'll Keep You Safe by Sleeping At Last
30. You Are The Reason by Calum Scott
31. Are You With Me by nilu
32. Say You Won't Let Go by James Arthur
33. I Won't Give Up by Jason Mraz
34. Stay Stay Stay by Taylor Swift
35. Earned It by The Weeknd
36. Best of Me by Michael Bublé
37. Paper Rings by Taylor Swift
38. Invisible String by Taylor Swift

Table of Contents

1. Noelle	1
2. Matthew	13
3. Noelle	24
4. Matthew	37
5. Noelle	46
6. Matthew	54
7. Noelle	65
8. Matthew	75
9. Noelle	87
10. Matthew	103
11. Noelle	110
12. Matthew	124
13. Noelle	139
14. Matthew	151
15. Noelle	164
16. Matthew	179
17. Noelle	187
18. Matthew	204
19. Noelle	218
20. Matthew	227
21. Noelle	236
22. Matthew	246
23. Noelle	256
24. Matthew	265
25. Noelle	272
26. Matthew	280
27. Noelle	288
28. Matthew	293
29. Noelle	308
30. Matthew	317
31. Noelle	322

32. Matthew	334
33. Noelle	337
34. Matthew	343
35. Noelle	353
36. Noelle	363
Epilogue	374
Extended Epilogue	388
Acknowledgments	397
Also by Jennifer Chipman	399
About the Author	401

CHAPTER 1
Noelle

Do you want to live your dreams? read the poster that was currently at my eye level. I snorted to myself, looking around to make sure no one had heard me before going back to my task.

The printer made an awful noise, and I looked up around me with a start. Thankfully, no one seemed to have heard, or at least, none of them were paying too close attention. That was one thing about campus libraries, I supposed. It didn't really matter if you were being quiet, as long as you weren't being *loud*. I silently cursed at the printer, who had eaten one of the last sheets of paper I was printing to take back to the dorm, simultaneously wishing I had help and being grateful that no one was around to judge me. I should have just used my printer, anyway, but part of my stipend got me free printing, so here I was.

I was frustrated as hell, trying not to hit the stupid piece of university equipment. In that regard, not much had changed over the last almost four years since I attended here as an undergrad.

"Dammit," I said, pulling the crumpled sheet out and disposing of it in the recycling bin. Sometimes I forgot how slow these machines could be, and all I wanted to do right now was meet with Hazel and then get back to my room. A nice nap sounded good. How was it only the first day of school, and I was already exhausted? I had moved in two weeks ago, to train my Resident Assistants—RAs—and get everything ready for the semester, and that was all before *my* classes would actually start—which was tomorrow.

It was crazy—one moment I was walking across the stage of my college graduation, accepting my diploma with a smile, planning out my future with my perfect dream guy, and the next... I looked up from my stack of papers and looked around the library. It somehow didn't feel real, even after all this time, that I *was* back here.

That I was finally doing something I completely loved, every moment of the day. And working towards, well... something. Was it the job I had thought I would have four years out of college? No, absolutely not. But there was something about it that made me happy. That no matter how many struggles I faced with my residents—I enjoyed it. I trudged back from the library to the four-story dorm that I had called home for the last two years as Hall Director. It also came with the perk of the university paying for me to get a master's degree for *free*—something I was almost done with.

Here I was, with just three classes left till I would have my MBA—three nights a week where I would sit in a lecture hall with thirty to forty other graduate students for three hours, before bundling up and getting ready to repeat the same schedule the next day. Sleep. Eat. Work. Class. Finish my assignments. One night a week on duty for the entire campus. Supervising my RAs. And repeat. My final semester of graduate school, and here I was feeling the same excited jitters all over again. If someone had told me four years ago when I graduated and received my diploma that I'd be back, working for the university and getting a master's degree, I never would have believed them. But I couldn't help but be grateful to be here. Especially after everything that had happened in New York.

My eyes drifted back to the dream poster. It could have been about anything, honestly, but the *reason* it caught my eye was so much more than that. Dreams. I couldn't remember the last time I had felt like I had any. What was I searching for? What did I *want* in life? I didn't know.

Hadn't really known what I was going to do since I got back to Portland.

I had moved home and applied for a job with my alma mater, and that was how I found myself here—on the first day of school, a bunch of coloring sheets printed out in my hands. Don't laugh —college students loved to color.

Getting this job on campus where I was able to do the things I excelled at—leadership, mentorship, and yes, the occasional arts and crafts project to help decorate my building—it had surprised me to find it was where I thrived. I loved creating and fostering those relationships with students each year. My residents, my staff —they were like my family. Besides my best friends, they were the people I felt closest to in the world.

Especially since my relationships with my *actual* family were strained, to say the least. But that was what happened when you moved across the country only to come back a year later. Disappointment. I could feel it, too, whenever my mom looked at me. Whenever she called me.

I left the library with a sigh, checking my phone for the time as I trudged over in the drizzle of the day to meet Hazel.

"Noelle!" Hazel, my Assistant Hall Director, waved me over to the table on the patio outside of the student union, which also happened to house the best on-campus coffee shop.

She held up a cup for me. With her brown tight curls piled on top of her hair in a bun, warm brown skin, and a beautiful complexion, she was absolutely gorgeous. I was so envious that it never seemed like she had to try to look good. No matter what she wore—edgy or professional, she always pulled it off. I swore she would look good in a pair of ratty sweats, even.

"You're an angel." I grinned, taking the cup from her. Truthfully, I didn't know what I would do without her. Over three semesters with her, we had grown close—and I tried not to take her for granted for one second. We were a team, and we were friends, and if we also occasionally ended up in the same class together working on our masters, it was just an added perk.

"I know." She smirked before pulling out her phone and frowning. "Looks like it's going to rain most of the evening. Bummer."

I laughed. "Haze, did you really expect anything less during January in Portland?"

"No," Hazel just sighed. "But I thought it'd be fun to do something with our new residents outside on the lawn—like s'mores and bonding."

I just shook my head. "Sounds like the perfect activity for *fall*. You know when school starts in August and it's sunny."

She gave me a resigned look and then nodded. "So... Should we do a movie night in the lounge?"

I loved that she was constantly planning last-minute activities for the dorm—even if it was the beginning of the semester, I had no doubt girls would wander down if they found out there were snacks to be had. Too bad I didn't have time to make cookies. I absolutely loved making them. But I was still trying to get everything set up for the bigger events we had planned for the hall in the next few weeks.

"Sure," I confirmed. "You can pick. But something actually *new* this time."

Hazel laughed. "So... *not Legally Blonde* again?" I just shook my head. It was one of my favorite movies, but we had definitely shown that last semester. We couldn't help it—both of us loved romance movies. I did too, still, even after I had gotten my heart broken. Even after I had sworn off men for a few years, needing the time to just be me.

And there I sat on the patio, taking a deep inhale of the fresh, clean air. The scent of rain still lingered behind—leaving the place smelling so quintessentially *home*. I appreciated my life for what it was for a blissful moment. A fresh clean start of endless possibilities. Even bundled up in the cold, with a caramel latte in my hands, and a list of things I needed to get done for the day, I still felt victorious. Like this was going to be the best semester yet.

Even if I didn't know what was coming next.

"What are you smiling about?" Hazel asked.

"Nothing." I just shook my head with a smile. And then— "Everything. How lucky we are, I guess."

"Yeah?" She asked, but then she nodded her head, her curls bobbing with the movement. "Yeah, I guess we are. We did get the best residents on campus, after all." She cracked a grin. We weren't really at a super large campus—there were a dozen residence halls, and ours was one of the bigger ones, an all-girls dorm with multiple floors. We wouldn't talk about what the girls sometimes nicknamed it around campus.

It was a lot of estrogen in one building, sure, and a lot of hormones, but she was right. We *had* gotten blissfully lucky these two years with good kids.

"I'm gonna get back," I said, gesturing to the stack of papers in my lap. I was grateful for the covered patio and the space heaters outside, but it was still chilly out here, and I wanted to get back to the warmth of the dorm building before it started raining.

"Okay. I'll see you tonight." Hazel picked up her coffee cup. "Oh! And you're still going to go to the staff and faculty mixer at the end of the week, right?"

I nodded. "Oh yeah. Of course, I'm going." I remembered seeing something about it in my inbox, and I really didn't have a good reason to *not go.*

"Good!" She exclaimed. "Maybe this time there will actually be someone exciting there."

"What about Lucas?" I asked with an eyebrow raised. She had been obsessed with this guy who was the Hall Director of the all-guys dorm next to ours *forever.* I wasn't positive he even really knew she existed. Hazel was all bubbly and outgoing until it came to liking someone, and then she was the quietest person I'd ever met. It was almost funny.

If Hazel could have turned red, I thought she might have. Unlike me, with her beautiful brown skin, the only telltale sign of her embarrassment was how sheepish she was acting. "Noelle!" Hazel cried. "I'm *not*... He's... That's not..." She bit her lip.

I gave her a mischievous little grin.

"No." She shook her head vigorously.

I shrugged innocently. "Okay, okay. Sure. Whatever you say."

But I knew how *totally* into the guy she was. He was in his mid-twenties, with thick brown hair and taller than average—he was nice to look at, sure. But he didn't do anything for *me*. I made a mental note to try to push the two together if I saw him at the event. Hopefully, like the rest of us, he would be there.

As I walked back home in the cold, January weather, with my thick hooded pea coat bundled tightly around me to keep out the dampness of the Portland winter, I couldn't help but think of what my mom had said to me when I had moved back home.

After a year of being gone, she looked me straight in the eye and said, *"Noelle, honey, what are you going to do with your life now?"*

I knew she didn't mean it in a *bad* way—despite how she came across sometimes. A little overbearing, a touch too concerned with my wellbeing and how I was living my life.

Such was the curse of being an only child.

"Well, I still have a degree." My mom gave a huff of agreement, and I continued. *"Just because that wasn't the job or place for me doesn't mean there isn't something else I can do with my degree here that I would enjoy."* I sounded much surer than I really was, which turned out to be the exact opposite of the truth.

With an English degree, my mom had always tried to push me toward teaching.

"You'd be a great high school teacher, sweetie," she advised. I wrinkled my nose. Teach *high school*?

What were—perhaps—some of the worst years of my life? I shook my head. *"No thanks,"* I said to her, with as much determination as I could muster. *"I'll find something else."*

But even though I didn't want to become a *teacher*, I had always loved academia, and my college years had been some of my best. So I reached out to some of my old professors and bosses on campus and they all encouraged me to apply for the Assistant Hall Director position that summer. I hadn't been sure if I would get it—but they loved me, I guess. And after a year of that, I got the Hall Director position of Willow Hall. It was a little more responsibility and almost double the salary. Plus the free room and board, which really *did* sweeten the deal.

I couldn't complain too much, except I still had absolutely no idea what path I wanted to take in life. Not one. Did I stay in academia? Did I try to get a job on campus after I finished my master's degree? Or did I finally work on the project I had been fiddling with for the last three years?

Walking towards my dorm building, I had to pause as I entered the academic quad, my bag of papers slung over my shoulder. The sun was shining through the clouds, peeking out as if to say hello, and I had to appreciate the small sliver of sunlight and awe over the beauty of the campus. I had never gotten over it—not in my four years as an undergraduate here, nor in the time since, and even though it seemed a bit silly to love this place so much, I couldn't imagine being anywhere else. It was home.

And this little bit of sun after today's drizzle, and before the sun started to set? It was *magnificent*. I felt a small smile spread across my face, and then hurried off to the dorm that had become my second home.

I couldn't help but play back *his* words in my mind. *Are you happy, Noelle? Because I'm not happy.*

Was I happy *here*? It felt like home, sure, but I still felt like a part of me was missing. Maybe I'd figure out what that was as I finished my last semester of graduate school, even though I felt like it just left me with more questions. What *did* I want my life to be, to look like? I knew what I didn't, sure, but...

I shook my head as I kicked a rock off of the path in front of me. I *was* happy. Yeah. I just needed to repeat it enough times that I would believe it. Absolutely.

I STIRRED the soup cooking on the stove as Charlotte, my best friend, looked at me inquisitively. "What?" I asked her, trying my best not to scowl at her. She had come over after teaching dance lessons for the evening, content to sit in my small dorm apartment as I made us dinner.

"Sometimes I'm still convinced that you're going to disappear again," she sighed.

"Well, you gotta get used to it," I grinned. "Because you're stuck with me forever, I promise."

"Good," Charlotte said, pushing a strand of blonde hair that had fallen into her eyes back as she continued staring at me. "Because I don't want to lose my best friend."

"Geez, Char, you'd think I was thinking about going to an alien planet or something." She looked at me and giggled.

I needed to get her to stop reading those alien romance books. I just sighed.

"I can't help it," she just snickered. And then she made a face. "*Would* you leave me, if there were real aliens?"

I turned to look at my best friend. "Absolutely not." I rolled my eyes at her, and she stuck her tongue out at me. *Not my genre*, I wanted to tell her. Not that she didn't know that already.

We shared a lot of things, and books had always been at the top of that list. I thought it was why we had been such fast friends when we first met. I still couldn't believe how lucky we had got to be placed together that first year. The university had given me my best friend, and I was so grateful that she had never once walked out of my life.

"Well, in any case..." She rested her head on her crossed arms on the counter. "How was the first day of school? Make any new friends?"

"It was good, thanks, *Mom*." Charlotte just grinned at me, and I shook my head. "Honestly, I don't need any more friends. I already have you, Lina, and Gabs. Plus Hazel. Who else could I need?" Deciding the soup was hot enough, I turned off the burner, turning to ladle it into the bowls that were already waiting on the counter.

Angelina and Gabbi were our two other best friends—we all had met during our freshman year of college in our dorm, and the four of us had stuck together like glue. I hadn't known what it meant to find your people until I met them. Despite how different we all were, we had chosen each other and never looked back.

I valued their friendship more than anything, and even when we had been apart, from study abroad programs to my living in NYC, our friendships had never fizzled out. We had even started our little book club; swapping turns on what book to all read together and giving each other recommendations. I loved it, even if it was my mastermind idea to get us all together at least once a week. Gabbi was always on board with me and my crazy book schemes.

Sometimes, I wondered if without me the rest of them would forget to plan anything, but I didn't *mind* being the one to always suggest plans. Sometimes it was exhausting, but it was my role in the group. The ringleader. Or maybe I was just the bossiest one out of all of us. That was my Leo personality coming out.

Whatever it was, I had long since accepted it. Even with that, somehow my best friends had always known just what I needed to distract myself from my breakup and the life I left behind in New York. Because I had lost a piece of myself—and I was working on *finding* it again. Loving myself again. And maybe it just took a little encouragement from the three girls who knew me almost as well as I knew myself. My friends who had been with me through every bump, every accomplishment, every drunken night, and every cry session on the floor of our dorm rooms. *God*, I loved them.

Charlotte was rolling her eyes at me. "Okay, I know we're like, *the best friends ever*, so you can never replace us, but a few more in your life wouldn't hurt, I promise."

"Yeah?" I said, placing a bowl of cheddar broccoli soup in front of her. It was our favorite. I dug out the sliced sourdough loaf I picked up from the store for myself—since I had always liked dipping bread in soup versus eating it with a spoon. Char didn't tend to ask questions about my weird habits anymore—she had seen me eat the same way for the last eight years.

She nodded, grabbing a slice of bread but choosing to slather it in butter before taking a bite. "As long as they don't think they're stealing my maid of honor spot, yeah." Charlotte gave a little scowl to show she was serious. I was pretty sure she wouldn't threaten anyone's life over it, but considering the expression on her face, I wouldn't have put it past her.

"Charlotte," I laughed. "For there to *be* a maid of honor spot for you to occupy, I'd have to be *getting married.*" I held up my left hand, complete with an empty ring finger. "And as you can see, that's not happening." Clearly. Not any time soon.

I didn't miss the expression on her face, but she didn't let up. "I'm not giving up. I have a good feeling about this year. Come on, it's our year. Maybe we'll both meet someone."

I snorted. Ever since I had moved into my dorm freshman year and met my shorter, very blonde roommate, I had never seen her seriously date *anyone*. She had gone out on a few first dates here and there, but hardly anyone had ever made it to date number two. I was pretty sure I could count the number of men she had let *kiss* her on one hand. Which was crazy, because she was gorgeous, and a dancer, and I didn't understand why she didn't have guys falling all over her to date them.

"What?" Charlotte glared at me.

"You, actually dating?" I choked back a laugh. "I'll believe that when I see it."

"Hey! I date, thank you very much."

"Yeah? Who was your last boyfriend?"

She frowned as if she was trying to place a face. Or a name. Maybe both. "Um. Bradley?"

I shook my head. "You don't even remember, do you?" Had she ever let anyone get close enough to call them that? I didn't think so.

Charlotte let her shoulders drop. "*Fine.* I don't date. But that doesn't mean it's not going to happen this year. I'm just waiting for the right guy." She had already met him. I knew it, Angelina knew it, Gabbi knew it—hell, I was fairly sure everyone in our entire dorm had known it. But they were firmly *best friends.* Yeah, right.

I couldn't push that subject more without her getting on *my* case, but hey, at least I had an excuse, didn't I? I wasn't ready to get back out there yet. I wasn't ready to open my heart up—to anyone. And when *would* I be?

I didn't have an answer to that.

We finished the rest of dinner as Charlotte rambled here and there about her job—she was a dance instructor for kids at a dance studio. She always tried to fill the silence, and I didn't mind. I nodded along, trying to stay present in the conversation, but honestly, I wasn't paying that close of attention. Which made me feel like a bad friend.

I was still thinking about, well, everything.

"Noelle?" Charlotte's voice broke through the fog in my head.

I looked up at her and realized I was frowning. I had spaced out without even realizing it. "Uh. Yeah?" I pushed away my bowl as I looked back at her. "Sorry."

Of course, she had noticed me zoning out. "You know... I'm always here if you need to talk. About anything. You've barely talked about New York since you moved back." I raised one shoulder in a shrug. "It's almost been three years, N."

I just shook my head. Did I want to talk about what was bothering me? Did I want to talk about New York? I had given them all minimal details, but they all knew why I moved there—who I had moved to be with.

So, no, I didn't want to talk about it, but I also didn't want to deal with this conversation that Char was going to drag out until she left my tiny apartment. The perks of living alone and on-campus—she'd have to leave eventually.

Instead, I did what I had always done best—deflected the situation. "I'm fine. Just tired, I think. And I have another long day tomorrow." I yawned. Well, I wasn't lying. I *was* exhausted.

Exhausted from the first day of school, exhausted from always trying to be positive and happy all the time, exhausted because I didn't know what I was doing with my life, and I didn't know where I was even going to start figuring that out.

And that night, long after Charlotte had left my apartment and told me she'd see me soon, there was one comment she made that kept replaying over and over in my mind.

And I knew one thing—that I was absolutely, definitely, no way in hell going to fall in love. Not again.

CHAPTER 2
Matthew

TESSA
HAPPY FIRST DAY OF SCHOOL!

My lips curved up into a small smile reading the text from my little sister, Tess. Somehow, she always knew just the right thing to say to brighten my day, and this text made me miss her, and the days we used to spend together—every time I picked her up from *her* first day of school.

It was another rainy day in Portland, a thought that didn't bother me as much as it used to. Over the last two years of living here, I had gotten used to the perpetual gray of the skies.

MATTHEW
Happy Monday.

Getting ready for your last semester, big shot theater girl?

Four years ago, I was a little shocked when she told me she wanted to move to New York and go to drama school there. But I had watched her grow during her High School years and watched her shine on stage, so I knew this was where she would thrive. But

I missed her, living on the opposite coast. It was harder than I thought, being alone here without any sort of family.

But you got used to that, I supposed.

Tessa sent me a thumbs-up emoji and a smiley face.

I was still early, a bit of time till my first class of the day, so I headed off towards the business building to let myself into my office, and to get the cup of coffee I had sorely missed that morning. I should have stopped on my way, but I couldn't explain it—the first day jitters. And why did I have any nerves? It wasn't like this was my first year of teaching.

But there was always a little bit of lingering nervousness and anticipation as the semester began.

"So I heard this rumor—" Another faculty member's voice gossiped as I padded into the kitchen near my office to make a fresh cup of coffee as I waited for my next class to start. One of the perks of the beginning of the semester was that students weren't yet banging down my door to ask for help. I appreciated the quiet and being able to actually hear myself think.

"Oh?" came a second voice. I tried to tune them out. The things the faculty and staff would gossip about never failed to make me roll my eyes.

Like, it was none of my business what Nancy from the English department wore to class today, or what one of their students said in class. I really didn't care.

I peeked my head out the corner after I hit brew on a fresh pot and caught sight of the two female faculty members who were still sharing hushed whispers in the hallway. At least I couldn't hear them now. I just groaned internally. I was glad I hadn't been subjected to their unnecessary gossip—at least, not yet. I hadn't given them anything to gossip about, and I didn't plan on it, either. If the professors gossiped that I was too *boring*, I guessed there were much worse things people could be saying about me.

I'd rather be boring than be the center of everyone's discussions. I had been that before, and I had no desire to do it again.

I ran a hand through my hair, disrupting the gel I had used to slick back my slightly longer-than-usual blonde hair. I knew I should probably get it cut since it was growing over my ears again in a slight curl, but I kind of liked it like this.

And I had been letting my scruff grow out over the winter break, giving me a short beard I hoped made me look a few years older. At least, maybe this way, I would stop getting mistaken as a grad student by some of the older faculty. I had a Ph.D. for crying out loud, and sometimes I still felt like it was my first day as an Investment Banker, right out of college, all jittery and ready to start a brand-new job.

But no—I was in my second year of teaching, and I had multiple diplomas hanging on my wall. I should expect at least some amount of respect for that, I thought. At least my students didn't seem to mind my age.

Finally, I slid out of there, coffee cup in hand. I had just settled back at my desk when a knock sounded on my office door.

"Matthew?" I heard the voice of one of my colleagues through the door, and I tried to pinpoint whose it was. Even after being here for three full semesters and one summer semester, I still didn't know everyone's voices by memory.

"It's open," I called out, relieved when I saw my fellow Finance professor, John Kassidy, walk through the door. I liked John. I wouldn't say we were friends yet—not really—but he had welcomed me to the University with open arms when I started here nearly two years ago, and he was always quick to offer a hand if I needed it. Which had happened more than I cared to admit during my first year of teaching.

And at least he wasn't one of those gossipy women from the hallway who was just trying to find out about university drama. Well, at least I didn't *think* he was.

"What's up, John?" I asked, looking up at him as he clutched an armful of papers in one hand and a cup of coffee in the other.

"Just wanted to check to make sure you were coming to the Staff and Faculty mixer this Friday. Dean Thomas expects us all to be there." He shot me a glare that said *you're not getting out of this.*

Damn. I held back my groan. "John, you know those aren't really my scene..."

I hated them. Despised them, even. They just meant more interactions with the other faculty, half of whom were always trying to figure out if I was dating anyone. And why was everyone so obsessed with my dating life, anyway? The answer was a resounding no, but I suspected some of it was that the younger faculty were trying to figure out if they could make a move, but I always slapped on my best grumpy expression, hoping it would deter them. And if not, ignoring them usually did the trick.

And it had, so far. Well... mostly. Still, I would have rather been anywhere else on a Friday night than at the University. Like at home, with my dog, sitting on the couch and watching television, or reading a book. Goodness knows I'd prefer almost anything than to mingle with a bunch of staff and other faculty members, but apparently, I was fully roped into this shit now.

Great. Simply great. How could I possibly get out of this?

"Please come," John said, almost pleading with me. "They're so boring without good company." Then he flashed a grin at me, and I rolled my eyes.

Yes, I wanted to shout, *that's why I don't want to go!* But John was determined—absolutely determined—to get me there, and I really couldn't think of an excuse. "I—" I opened my mouth to speak, but he cut me off.

"Think good and long about your excuse, *Professor Harper*, because it's the first week of school and I know you don't already have a bunch of assignments to grade," John smirked. "So I better see you there."

I sighed. "Okay, okay, fine. I'll be there." I shot him a little glare. "But don't expect me to stay till the end."

"Good. At least that's something." He nodded to himself like he was proud of his achievement to get me to agree to attend.

I was serious, though. As soon as the event started looking bleak, I would dip right out of there so I could go snuggle with my dog on the couch. At least Snowball didn't ask me any terribly invasive questions about why I didn't have a wife yet or where my girlfriend was that evening (one of these days I was going to just make up a fake one, seriously).

Of course, that may have just been because she was a dog, and couldn't talk, but I digress. I preferred her company to ninety percent of the humans I knew. My sister and best friends were some of the only exceptions.

And I mean, really, it was like people couldn't believe that I wasn't dating anyone. And yeah—everyone else in my life was seeing someone, but what was the point in dating someone I wasn't interested in?

I knew, that once I found the right person, I was going to be in it for the long haul. Once I met her, I was going to do whatever it took to keep her in my life, and make sure she knew that I was hers, forever. And she would be mine. Absolutely, unequivocally, mine.

I was just waiting for her to walk into my life.

ANOTHER SUCCESSFUL FIRST DAY, I thought to myself. I took a deep breath of the clean air, still smelling like rain, and watched the water drip down through the trees from my dry spot on the covered patio.

I had a hot cup of coffee in my hands—my third one of the day, which all things considered could have been much worse—and marveled over how different my life was now versus just a few years ago. In some ways, I couldn't believe I had just begun my fourth semester of teaching full-time. This semester, I had mostly undergraduate classes and one graduate-level finance class. It was crazy to think that after all of the paths that life had led me down, *this* is where I ended up. In a cold, drizzling pocket of the world. It reminded me of home, after all.

My phone buzzed with another text—this time from my group chat with my buddies.

> **BRYAN**
> When are we getting drinks next? First-round on me.

It was from my best friend—Bryan. God, when had we all even gotten together last? I frowned into my cup as I thought about it. It had been too long, even with the holidays. But they all had families and girlfriends, whereas I spent them alone.

More specifically, I spent them traveling, most of the time snowboarding and enjoying the winter season with my snow-loving dog. It wasn't like I had anywhere that I called home to go. And my little sister had opted to stay at school over the break, probably so she could spend time with that new boyfriend of hers, and she was all I had left.

> **MATTHEW**
> I'm game. I just have a late-night class I teach on Wednesdays, otherwise I'm free.

I quickly texted back before shoving my phone back into my pocket.

My best friend Bryan and his wife, Elizabeth, *had* invited me over to their place for Christmas, but I didn't want to feel like the third wheel for the whole week. I loved them both, but sometimes being around all of their love was a little suffocating. Especially since she was expecting their first child. Our other friends, Cole and Tanner, had spent the winter holidays with their parents at a ski resort in Canada.

So, since I had nowhere else to be, I packed up my truck and my dog, and we went to different ski resorts all over Oregon. Ever since I was little, I had always loved traveling, and in the last two years since moving here, sometimes I felt like I needed to escape from Portland. Even though it was a big city, sometimes it could feel so *small*. Ever since I was little, I had always loved the cold and the snow, so it seemed like a logical way to combine both passions. My week in Sunriver had been the best, hitting the slopes of Mt.

Bachelor, and my legs already itched to get back up on the mountain.

But now it all seemed like a distant dream as I settled into the new semester. The breaks in between semesters always went by too fast.

So here I sat, enjoying my cup of coffee before I had to rush to get to teach the next class of the day. Even though it was cold out, the patio was protected from the rain and had a portable heater, leaving me comfortable as I listened to the sounds of the rain hitting the pavement.

Even with keeping myself busy—with work, taking care of my dog, and seeing friends, sometimes I felt like I was missing something in my life. I bit my lip, eyes drifting off towards the center of campus as I pondered the thought. When did I become so discontent with my routine? No matter what I tried, it just felt like it wasn't *enough*. But maybe it wasn't something I was missing—it was someone. Someone to share this life with. Someone to laugh with. Someone to love.

I shook my head. I hadn't ever *had* that before—not with anyone I'd dated or the girls my friends had tried to set me up with. So why was I thinking about it *now*? Why was it that I was wishing for someone to share a life with now?

It had been drizzling outside, but when the rain cleared, just for a moment, the sun came shining through. What caught my eye, though, was the way the rays lit up the red strands of hair on a girl's head. She was standing in the middle of the quad, looking up to the sky: eyes closed, chin tilted up like she was absorbing the few seconds of warmth the sun provided—and then she smiled.

And for some reason, her small smile just did something to me. Because the pure and utter bliss on her face… It stuck with me. I couldn't put it out of my mind, and I went to class that day only thinking about that redhead girl's lips tilted up as she basked in the glow. Because as soon as the ray of sun had come, it was gone, and so was she.

Why couldn't I get her out of my mind? If I was honest with

myself—which I almost always was—something about it unsettled me. I was confused because I felt... *weak*. Like if my feet weren't firmly planted on the floor, the wind could topple me over, just from the sight of the sun shining on a head of red hair. And why was that, anyway? I didn't think I was imagining the rush in my chest as my eyes had settled on her. She just seemed like... warmth. It felt like it oozed from her like she could be the light in any dark, bringing a place to life with just a smile.

Not that I got to see her smile directed at *me*, just at the sun. But for some reason... I wanted it to be. And I couldn't stop thinking that just as I had thought that maybe this life would be better with someone else in it, she appeared. With her red hair and the smile that lit up her face.

I tried to shake the thought away. It wasn't about her, not really—that would be crazy—but this longing that had popped into my mind was making me think crazy things. That was all. And I was too old to have thoughts like this about anyone who could be my baby sister's age. But I couldn't deny that seeing that girl awakened something inside of me, like a little thawing of the frozen heart I had locked up tight behind a fortress of ice.

I sighed, trying to shake off this feeling that had decided to take up residence in my chest. This wasn't like me, to feel an attraction to, well... anyone.

Especially not a girl I had never talked to and whose name I didn't even know. Sure, I had dated a few women here and there, but I had never felt any... desire for any of them. It had almost just been like going through the motions. Went out with women because I felt like I should because our friends set us up because they asked. But it wasn't like I *wanted* them... Nor should I want her. In all my time, I had never found the person I wanted to spend my life with. And I wasn't about to give up everything I had worked towards for a woman who didn't meet every box on my list.

Hello? I wanted to smack my inner self. *Get those thoughts out of your head, Matthew. Don't be an idiot.*

My thoughts kept wandering as I sat in my office, way later than I would normally stay on campus but not wanting to go back to my empty house yet. I had finally gotten my own office this year—one finally opening up after another faculty member had retired—and it was still a little bare. There was a pile of boxes set next to the bookshelf that I needed to put away, filled with old textbooks and volumes as well as a few frames to hang or to prop on the desk: my parents, before they had passed away; one of my white Samoyed, Snowball—named by my little sister, Tessa, whose photo was also in the stack; the framed diplomas from undergrad and my PhD. I grabbed a small plant from the top box and set it next to my computer. It wasn't much, but I would add more as I went.

Either way, at least it was all mine. No more sharing, thank goodness. I didn't think I'd ever be able to describe what had compelled me to leave a good-paying corporate job to become a professor, but I did know that I loved every minute of it. It was fulfilling, even if I felt like there was still a hole in my heart where another person should be.

Despite sometimes getting the reputation of being a bit of a grump, I tried to care for each one of my students. I wanted them to succeed. I was just serious, and I never wanted to mix my personal life into class. It wasn't important, and if being grumpy kept my students from hitting on me or wanting more from me, well, then... It worked.

As the evening wound down, I finished working on some presentations to show in class before finally calling it a night and heading back to my house right off-campus.

Snowball was waiting by the front door, tail wagging as she waited for me to take her out. "Hey pup," I called out as I dropped my briefcase to scratch at her ears. "Give me a moment and then I'll take you out, okay?"

I looked at the time on my watch. Ten-thirty. Enough time to get to sleep and still wake up early for the gym tomorrow with the guys. Luckily, the only class I taught on Fridays was in the afternoon, so I had the morning off to get things done before I had to drive to school. But tomorrow—tomorrow I was going to make plans. I hadn't seen my best friends in weeks, and if I was being honest with myself, I had hardly been present in their lives the last two years while I threw myself into being a full-fledged professor. As the semester started, a lot of my free time that I usually spent with them was dedicated to assignments and lesson plans and grading.

Snowball sat at my feet, her tail wiggling expectantly, and I couldn't help but smile at my dog. "You ready, huh girl?"

I clipped Snowball's leash to her collar and ushered her out the door, around the block of the neighborhood. I purchased a house in University Park this past summer, finally setting down roots somewhere. It was nice to finally have a place I could call my own, no roommates to bother me or anyone to trash the place with parties. It was just me and Snowball in my little starter house. Just like I wanted it, right? That's what I had always thought, at least.

Tessa got Snowball for me a few years ago, delivering her to me on Christmas—adorned with a big red bow around her neck. She simply informed me that I was *sad and needed company besides myself*. Which, to be fair, was *probably* true. During my time in investment banking, I had always been too busy to have a social life. I had barely kept in contact with Bryan, Cole, and Tanner. But my little sister's Christmas gift also presented me with the perfect travel buddy in that little white fluffy puppy, who had since turned into an excessively big white fluff monster, the 40-something pound dog that took up half of my bed every night.

But my sister may have been onto something when she gave her to me because Snowball really had made my life better in more ways than I could have ever expected.

I watched my dog as we walked through the neighborhood, and I pulled my coat tighter against me. It was a chilly night, even for January in Portland, so I was grateful for the extra warmth of my thick jacket and scarf. Snowball didn't seem to mind, though, thanks to her thick fur coat.

"You're lucky, Snowball," I muttered. "You don't have to layer up to stay warm."

I loved having a dog. We had one when I was younger, a husky, but after he passed away when I was fourteen, my parents had never gotten another pet. And then at nineteen, they were gone too, and I had enough on my plate to handle without getting Tessa and me a pet while I was in college and she lived with our grandparents.

But now, as she loved to remind me, I was a *grown-ass adult*, and I could do whatever I wanted. Huh. What was even weirder to me was the realization that she, too, was a grown adult—twenty-two and living on her own. In New York.

I made my way back to the house, letting Snowball guide us through the frosty night air.

And I thought to myself, you know, despite everything, life had a way of surprising you sometimes. Just like how the random ray of sun could bring a smile to her face... This moment made me feel blissfully content, just inhaling the cold, clean air as I stared up at the moon. And it was a reminder that even throughout everything—life could still be good.

CHAPTER 3
Noelle

"Noelle!" Hazel waved at me from in front of the dining hall, and I quickly walked to her side. I had texted her that I was going to be a bit late and to leave without me, but I didn't expect her to be waiting outside for me. I appreciated the gesture though so that we could go in together. She pulled me into a hug, and then surveyed my outfit. "Looking good," she said, giving me a thumbs up.

"Yeah?" I didn't know how formal we were supposed to be, so I was wearing my usual favorite attire: a turtleneck bodysuit with a brown pleated tartan skirt, thigh-high socks, and my favorite ankle booties that added a few extra inches. Not that I would ever call myself short, but sometimes I liked to add on a few extra inches so I could look men straight in the eyes. It made me feel more important. I also added my favorite chunky cardigan on top as well as a long necklace. It was my typical attire around the dorm, and it always made me feel cute and cozy.

Hazel was wearing a pair of tan slacks and a black fitted sweater, but somehow still managed to look perfectly put together. Her tight curls were piled on top of her hair in a bun, and I marveled over the fact that she looked so effortlessly calm and collected. Even without her signature tote bag and the doc marten boots she loved to wear; she was still somehow so very... Hazel.

"How was your day?" I smiled at her. "Did you get everything done that you needed to?" I didn't have to explain further—we always could read each other's minds when it came to dorm stuff. It came in handy more often than I ever would have thought.

Hazel nodded. "Everything is all a go for the semester and looking good." She gave me a quick two thumbs up, which made me laugh. We were trying to work a few months out so that nothing piled up on us. It was our strategy, and it worked pretty well. We had planned out dates for the whole semester at the beginning of the academic year, but we liked to wait a little bit closer to finalize all the details. Thankfully, it was a small enough school that it worked out.

She fluffed her hair absentmindedly as we walked into the building. I could tell she was looking around, trying to see if she could spot Lucas, but I wasn't going to call her out on it. It made me smile.

Normally, I was always early to these kinds of things, but since I had to deal with something for a student, we had been running a bit behind, and I couldn't believe how full the room was. I wasn't sure what I had expected from the staff and faculty mixer, but it certainly wasn't this.

"There's a lot of people here this year," I whispered to Hazel, still standing beside me.

She nodded. "Sounds like a lot of the Deans required all of their faculty to come." Last year, we slipped in and out and were barely there for an hour: just long enough to say hi to our boss, grab a few snacks, and mingle with the other Hall Directors. This year, well...

"I guess they like to keep everyone on their toes." Hazel gave me a big grin. I rolled my eyes.

"Come on, let's go get a drink." I pulled her towards the drink table, hoping they'd have wine. I would have liked something stronger, but, well... I doubted that was an option.

After we had secured our glasses—white for me, red for Hazel—we stood, scanning the room. I saw a lot of professors I had met before standing around—including some of my *current* professors. But instead, I just stood there gawking, like an idiot.

Because at the other end of the room stood the most beautiful man I had ever seen. Not even exaggerating, he was gorgeous. I think my heart skipped a beat.

Holy hell, he looked like he could have been a *painting*. Seriously, I was pretty sure someone had sculpted a god and placed him here on earth: tall, well-built, blond hair that just hit the top of his ears. He was so effortlessly handsome, even wearing a sweater over a collared shirt. Which also somehow still managed to give a glimpse of what I assumed was a very fine muscular body underneath the layers of fabric, probably the whole package contained under that wool and cotton.

And what was he doing here? I didn't mean literally—he was clearly a professor here, just from his attire. His whole attire screamed 'Hello! A hot professor here!' I was positive it should have been illegal for someone that handsome to be standing in front of a classroom, let alone teaching *here*. He should be a model instead. Or an actor. I knew I'd buy something that had his face on it. Or maybe he should be a prince—swooping in to whisk girls right off their feet. *He has the arms for it,* I thought, resisting the urge to giggle as I ogled him from afar.

What does he teach? I wondered to myself as I sipped my wine. I was naturally curious, and I couldn't help it—for some reason, I wanted to know his name.

I wondered if Hazel knew who he was, but I was too embarrassed to ask her and have her realize I was completely transfixed by the guy. Especially after she had heard me rant "all guys are trash" approximately one thousand times over the past few semesters.

Something clicked in my head: suddenly, after all these years, I finally understood what people were talking about when they said they had a hot professor or gossiped in the back row. Wow. Like, *hello.* Eyebrow waggle included. I had never, in all my years of schooling, ever had a hot-for-teacher moment. And it wasn't like I was trying to start now, either—but one look at him standing there, and I was mesmerized by his being. His icy-cold stare seemed to radiate across the room, a grumpy expression settled on his face as he talked to several other faculty members with a cup in his hand. Seriously, this man was *serious*. I could just tell.

I might have been staring at him a little too long, hiding the bottom half of my face in my cup as I sipped on my drink—when I realized he was looking back at *me*.

Our eyes locked across the room. And, oh—I felt my face flush a little under his intense scrutiny, his finely chiseled features not even forming into a smile as his eyes appraised me. I could feel the heat on the back of my neck and my cheeks, the blush blooming on my face, and I resisted the urge to fan myself. After swallowing another drink of wine, I let my eyes drift back to Hazel at my side.

Deep breaths, Noelle, I tried to distract myself. *He wasn't staring at* you; *you were just in his line of sight. Yeah. Absolutely.* Just a completely normal reaction. *You will not let this gorgeous man see what he is doing to you,* I ordered myself as an afterthought. Yeah, that was going to work. Not.

The heated stare we shared from opposite sides of the room made me feel like sparks were lighting all around us. Like the slightest movement would cause the whole room to burst aflame. Yet I couldn't look away—I'm not sure that I even wanted to. All I knew is there was something in his eyes, in the way he was looking at me, that I'd never felt before. And for the first time in my life, I thought to myself, is *this* what it means for fate to exist?

Is there something as beautiful as divine intervention, putting you in the exact right moment that you're meant to be in? Because this moment—the one I was sharing with a stranger, eyes never leaving the others' even as we sipped our drinks, even as people floated around us—this must be one of those moments. It was determined by destiny, here to change your life and sure to make you re-evaluate everything you've ever known. I didn't know how long we were standing there—it could have been seconds, minutes, hours, or days, but finally, I let my gaze drift down to the floor.

But I couldn't ignore the way the air felt charged, though—almost with electricity. Somehow, I knew that nothing would ever be the same again. When I looked back up, as my eyes drew back to his, it felt as if this time I was finally seeing him. For the first time in my life, I was staring straight at him, and I didn't know what would happen when he looked away. It was like there was a fuller picture now, one I didn't have before as if I had learned something unforgettable about this man in less time than it took for me to make a cup of coffee.

And *his* eyes? They hadn't left me, and somehow I knew, without hesitation, that he was settling into the same knowledge that I had—whatever that was. His eyes swept over my red hair and freckled face. I didn't even know what color his eyes were, a thought that seemed so intimate despite the way our gazes remained locked on each other. Light, I thought.

I turned to Hazel to say something when I found her staring at Lucas, who was most definitely on his way over here to say hi. *Oh. Okay.*

I tried to shake the thoughts and intrusive *somethings* from my head—thoughts I wasn't even sure how to process. Hadn't I just sworn off dating and men? Though, maybe I had just sworn off *love*. No one said I couldn't appreciate a man or let him look at me like *that*. I ran my hand through my curls, trying to focus on the strands between my fingers. It wasn't like I was unused to people staring: my frizzy bright red hair had always done that for me.

There was more than just appreciation in his eyes—it was the *zing* that seemed to connect us that truly startled me and shook me off my feet. Still, the way his eyes were focused on me ... Goosebumps trailed up my skin.

But this, watching him as he was taking all of me in—it was

different than when other people looked at me. Maybe it was something about his stare, the way it was so serious, and yet so *captivating*. Finally, he looked away, back to his conversation with the other men, leaning on the mantle of the fireplace that lined the wall. And I definitely couldn't miss the grumpy look on his face as his colleagues talked to him.

Seriously, did the man know how to smile? And why did I want to see it so badly? His smile—I wanted it directed at me. Was there a gas leak in here, or had the wine hit me that much? Either way, there was something very *wrong* with my head. Because I didn't date, and I didn't want to date.

I could just appreciate how fine he was without wanting to date him, anyway. Yeah.

I turned back to Hazel, and she raised an eyebrow at me. "What the *hell* was that?" she whispered under her breath, and I just shook my head.

Voice unsteady, I responded to her. "What?" She just gaped at me. "I don't know?" I tacked on at the end as if that helped at all. How long had we been staring at each other across the room? If Hazel had noticed it... had anyone else? I was a little embarrassed, just thinking about the fact that someone caught me making eyes at a professor. Oh my god.

"You don't know?" Hazel sounded exasperated. "Do you even *know* who that is?" She cursed under her breath again. "Noelle—"

"Think fast," I whispered back, "Look who's coming over to say hi."

Hazel's eyes looked up, and saw Lucas', and then flashed to mine, a little startled. *Save me*, she mouthed.

You're on your own, sister, I mouthed back.

Just then, Lucas came up to join us, and he stood at my other side. "Hey. Good to see two friendly faces," he said. And then he must have followed our gazes to the other side of the room. "What are you all looking at?"

"Nothing," I said, at the same time Hazel uttered, *"Unbelievable."*

I glared at her. "What?"

Hazel seemed to have been ignoring the *man of her literal dreams* beside her, because she exclaimed, "Did you not *see* what just happened, Noelle? Because I saw *it* with my own two eyes, and that—" I cut her off with another pointed look, but Lucas didn't seem to catch it.

"Are you..." He glanced in the direction that Hazel had been gazing at just moments before. "Are you guys looking at Professor Harper?" Lucas finally asked, and I just gave a helpless shrug.

"I think *someone* is." Hazel nudged me in the side, giving me a playful wink.

"Am *not*—" I started to argue back.

And then, in the time it took for me to look over at Hazel, pleading for her to drop this topic of conversation with my eyes, about to change it to something else entirely, I realized he was gone from his spot in the corner of the room. Oh. Okay then. I frowned, turned back to our high-top table, and set my wine glass down so I could balance myself.

"Good luck!" Hazel chirped into my ear, and when I turned around, she was gone, and I was met with a pair of icy blue eyes.

Oh—so that's what color they were. And damn Hazel for abandoning me.

"Hello," he said, with a deep, smooth voice.

"Oh. Hi." I squeaked out. And *oh*. If I had thought he was beautiful from a distance... up close, he was even more so. And with those bright blue eyes?

Suddenly, I wished Hazel had finished her sentence from earlier, about *who* this man was. I looked at her and Lucas smiling together at a table by themselves and narrowed my eyes a little bit at them as she waved with an innocent expression on her face. Oh, I was so going to force it out of her later.

Do I *know* who he is? If he was a complete *sex god* whose gaze had my heart pounding in my chest... Absolutely.

As he stood towering over me, still holding his cup in his hands, I marveled at just how *tall* he was. I was almost close enough to smell his cologne, but I resisted the urge to take a deep inhale to find out just what he smelled like. Pine trees? Musky scents? What on earth was wrong with me that I was *thinking* that? It had been way too long since I had been on a date, that's what. And was I still gaping at him? I really needed to close my mouth and attempt to be a normal human having a normal conversation.

"You looked like you needed a rescue," he said as pushed up the sleeves of his sweater onto his elbows, showing off his arms underneath. A sight I was trying to ignore by reminding myself how he was a professor here. Yep. That arm candy was definitely off-limits.

"Oh," I said again, aware of how much I sounded like a broken record. "Mhm, did I?" I finally asked, looking up at him. A rescue from Hazel and Lucas? *My panicked expression was probably because of you, mister,* I thought to myself.

He just nodded at me, fidgeting with the wine glass in his hands.

"It seems to me like maybe *you* just needed an excuse to get away from *them*," I grinned, tilting my chin towards the group of faculty members he had left behind—or managed to escape from, whatever they had been talking about.

"Maybe so." He frowned, glancing back at them.

"Well, glad I could assist in the save, either way." I smiled at him. His eyes—I couldn't get over how very blue they were—settled back on my face, and even though he didn't return my smile, I could see the way he relaxed a little bit in my presence.

"I'm Matthew." He said, sticking his hand out. "Professor Matthew Harper, to be more specific."

"Noelle," I said with a small smile, still trying to ignore his folded sleeves and exposed forearms. Holy hell—he was beautiful, and what was he doing over here talking to me? *Geez, Noelle, get a grip,* I tried to coach myself. Well, no going back now. What do normal people say when they meet people? Oh. Right. "It's nice to meet you," I nodded in acknowledgment, popping a piece of cheese in my mouth as he continued to stare at me. His eyebrow raised, and I realized what he wanted, oh god—because I hadn't even introduced myself. Yep, I was doing *great*. "Just Noelle Hastings, Hall Director."

Thankfully, this beautiful giant of a man seemed to miss my gawking of him and plowed straight ahead with his topic of conversation. "Well, *Just Noelle Hastings*, it's very nice to meet you."

"What do you teach?" I asked him. "I haven't seen you around before." I felt a little embarrassed to have mentioned that, but oh well. I hadn't had him as my professor in any of my classes, and he definitely hadn't taught here while I was an undergrad. I would have remembered him if I had seen him around before.

"Finance. Do you go here, also?"

"Oh yeah—I'm a grad student." I gave him a little nod. "Getting my master's in student affairs, all set to graduate this spring."

"And do you like it?" His lips tilted up just a little bit, just an almost smile, and I nodded again.

Oh my god, Noelle, my brain yelled at me. *Ask him something instead of just standing here like an idiot.*

"Working here or learning here?" I finally asked, realizing I wasn't sure what he meant, exactly. No one had ever asked me anything like that before—about anything, really. It seemed so much more personal, underlaid with an understanding most people had never given me before.

"Both, I guess." he chuckled.

I just nodded, again. I did like it—I'd always loved learning, loved being surrounded by other people, loved being in a place where I had always thrived before. "I went here for my undergrad, too." It seemed like a good thing to say to stop myself from nodding again.

He was just standing there, peering at me as I fumbled through my thoughts, one hand in his pocket: the picture of composed and elegant. He didn't seem to mind my fumbling because he went back to our earlier topic. "It's only my second year teaching here, so that's probably why we hadn't run into each other before." He tilted his head at me. "Oh, and I hate coming to these things. I got dragged along this time, I normally make an excuse to get out of them." Matthew—*Professor* Harper, I tried to remind myself, even as he ran his hands through his blond hair—said.

"Really?" I resisted the urge to laugh, still wondering why this beautiful specimen of a man was standing here making small talk with me.

He nodded solemnly, leaning down towards me like we were sharing a secret conversation, co-conspirators in some scheme. "The older women are always trying to set me up with their daughters." He shivered.

I laughed, deeply, which also caused me to snort a little. "Oh!" I gasped, embarrassed, slapping a hand over my mouth. After the urge to giggle died, I finally returned my attention to his statement. "And you *don't* want that?"

"No." He shook his head. "I'd much prefer to meet the love of my life in more of a... Unique way."

I raised an eyebrow. "Oh?" I found myself intrigued, even though I didn't quite know why. "And what way is that?"

He shrugged, taking another sip of his drink. "Not sure. I'll let you know when I find out." And then he flashed a little hint of a smile at me, and I realized how badly I wanted to see a real one from this man—a full one.

"You do that." I laughed.

"What about you?" He asked.

I raised an eyebrow. "What about me?"

"Have any crazy coworkers tried to set you up with their sons?"

"No. Heck no. But sometimes the dorm moms." I made a face. It was certainly not attractive, scrunching my nose and all but sticking my tongue out as I shook my head, but I couldn't help it. "I don't need some man-child who still lives in his mother's basement playing video games. Besides," I took a deep breath before biting my lip. "I kind of, ah, swore off dating."

"Hm." Matthew mused as a new reaction spread over his face that I couldn't quite read, and then he chuckled at me again. "You know, it's a shame." A shame? What—that I hadn't been in any of his classes?

And… Was my face on *fire*? And this guy was doing more than just talking with me? This felt like flirting. I could feel the heat rising to the back of my neck, and I tried to keep talking to distract myself from it. "What is?"

Matthew looked at me with the sincerest look in his eyes when he said, "That we hadn't met before." And, oh God—I *blushed*.

I batted my eyes at him. If he was going to fluster me… maybe I could fluster him. "And why is that, Professor?" I asked, feigning innocence.

He laughed. "Touché, Noelle."

"So…" I tried to think of another topic of conversation as I stared at the dessert table. I finally settled on, "Are you from around here?"

He shook his head. "I'm from Seattle, but I worked in Chicago for a few years before I got my PhD."

"So you've moved around a lot?" He nodded. "Has that been hard?" Was that too personal of a question to ask someone you had just met? Maybe it was.

He cleared his throat. "Sometimes."

"I get it." I brushed a piece of hair behind my ear self-consciously. "I lived in New York City for two years. It was… well, I missed home. Hence coming back." I spread my arms as if to gesture that this was home. Because it was, on all accounts. The city, the school, this place… it felt like home.

He nodded. "I understand missing home, believe me." And then he must have caught me eyeing the dessert table again, because he asked, "Did you want one?"

"Oh." I shook my head and then thought better of it. "Well,

yeah. I should have grabbed a brownie earlier." I laughed. "It's fine though."

"I'll get one for you," he said, and then before I could stop him—or tell him I would get it myself—he departed, coming back a moment later with a brownie wrapped in a napkin.

"Thank you," I smiled, taking it from him. "You know, they have the *best* brownies on campus. They're always gooey and just... perfect." Why was I gushing over the desserts? This guy *definitely* didn't care about my obsession with the sweets on campus, and he was going to think I was just rambling. So much for an intellectual conversation.

He chuckled. "I'll keep that in mind." I noticed he watched me as I took a bite, and I resisted the slight moan I felt as I tasted it for the first time—they really were the best—before my eyes darted back up to his.

We spent the rest of the event in an easy flowing conversation, sharing our experiences working in Chicago and New York, how different it was to live in big cities versus the small ones we had grown up in, the hustle and bustle of life and how it never stopped, and any other topic that came to mind. It all just poured out of me, and I found myself pleasantly surprised about the course of the evening. I hadn't even realized that I hadn't looked for Hazel or Lucas in a while when I looked away from Dr. Harper and frowned, seeing that everyone had started to pack up around us.

"Oh," Professor Harper looked down at his watch. "Wow. Look at the time. I didn't realize it had gotten so late."

"They probably want us to get out so they can finish cleaning up," I whispered to him like I was sharing some big secret, and we both headed towards the door.

"It was really nice chatting with you tonight, Dr. Harper." I gave him a small smile.

"It was my pleasure," he said, and then added, "Thanks again for the save." He smirked. "I enjoyed this more than I thought I would." At my confused expression, Professor Harper looked at me with an emotion on his face that I couldn't quite place before continuing. "This was... honestly the best conversation I've had at one of these things in a while." He leaned in close to my ear and murmured, "The rest of the faculty is rather boring, I'm afraid."

I couldn't help the blush that crept over my cheeks. "Oh, uh... I appreciate it. Well, I should get going," I said, looking down at the time on my watch, "I have an early day at work tomorrow. Maybe I'll see you around." I gave him a small smile before readjusting my purse strap on my shoulder.

"Good night, Miss Hastings," he murmured under his breath, so low I barely caught it as I turned to leave, and then I was out the door, into the quiet of the hallway, pacing towards the quiet of the night outside of the business building on campus.

"Goodnight," I whispered to the night as I felt the flush rush back to my cheeks, thinking about how long we had stood in each other's company, just chatting. When was the last time I had done that with someone like him?

And why could I not get him out of my mind for the rest of the night?

CHAPTER 4
Matthew

I couldn't stop picturing Noelle at that mixer last Friday, so imagine my surprise when the redheaded girl I saw the first day of classes turned out to be her. It almost felt like fate, which was crazy. The sight of her there was like a shock to my system. And as soon as our eyes had met—as I caught her staring at me across the room—I knew that she was someone special.

I wanted to meet her—wanted to know her name. No... I had to know her name. I escaped the boring conversation the other professors were having (though, if you asked me, I couldn't have told you what they were saying, anyway), and found myself wandering over to her. She was like a magnet, and I was being pulled in her direction.

And suddenly, with her fiery red hair radiating around her, there she was. Noelle Hastings, in my life. I knew I would never forget it. It had been so sweet on her lips, her voice warm and friendly as we talked all through the night. And what was wrong with me that I was enthralled just by Noelle's presence? It wasn't like she was wearing anything out of the ordinary: a pleated, skirt with a white turtleneck, complete with a chunky sweater and those damn thigh-high socks, but it took everything not to let my jaw drop open when I saw her, gazing my way, and not even realizing she had been staring at me.

I hadn't even been able to pull my eyes away from her to say hi to the other faculty or staff members at the event. All I knew was that she was in front of me, and for the first time in my life, I thought, *what if?*

And when she had asked me how I wanted to meet someone, I almost said it. *Just like this.*

I couldn't stop staring at her beautiful, freckled face. I knew that I shouldn't be so attracted, so captivated by her—it was crazy. I had never been before. But there was something in me that wanted to hear Noelle's laughs fill the room, to see her warm face smile at me.

I couldn't stop replaying the moment I had gone up to introduce myself to her in my mind. The way she was speechless staring back at me and didn't even introduce herself at first. And my God, what *had* I been thinking? I hadn't been, seriously. But she was all I could think about as I got back to my house that night.

And that *what if* bubbled up in my mind, even as I told myself no—you can't have this. You can't have *her*.

Because having someone meant having someone I could lose. I closed my eyes, sighing in frustration as I sat at my desk at home the next day. I stood with a yawn, grabbing Snowball's leash so I could take a walk around the block to distract myself. The cold air sounded like a good idea.

But even then, as we started our walk, I briefly saw a flash of red hair from my neighbor's front lawn, and it made me think of Noelle.

Deciding that she had already occupied way too much of my thoughts lately, I picked up my phone and dialed my sister's phone number. Even though we were close, she *was* still in college, and I never wanted to text or call her too much to bother her and feel like I was a burden on her already busy life.

I knew what it was like to try to juggle all of that as well as your relationship with your sibling—I had balanced it throughout my last two years of college, trying to juggle the grief and the newfound responsibility of being my little sister's sole caretaker as I tried to graduate from college.

I had never wanted to push her too far because I didn't want to lose her from my life entirely. And living on the opposite side of the country from her, I couldn't help but worry that I had allowed too much distance to grow between the two of us. Maybe it was time to change that, especially with her graduating soon.

"Hello?" Tessa's voice answered as she picked up on the fourth ring.

"Hi, Tess."

"Hey, big bro, what's up? You don't normally call this time of day." I looked at the clock. It was still pretty early in the afternoon there, especially for the weekend.

"Does a brother need a reason to call his baby sister?" I smiled at the phone. "I know we haven't talked too much lately, and I know your semester just started, but I thought I'd check on you and how you were doing."

"I gotta be honest, Matt, the senioritis is real," she started, "but it's not all bad. My theater program here just keeps getting better, and I'll honestly be sad to say goodbye to the department at the end of the year. Plus, I am definitely not looking forward to the job hunt."

"Have you given any more thought about moving here?" I asked hopefully. I really missed having her around. These last four years of her studying in New York City had been quiet, and I didn't want us to grow apart anymore. She was the only family I had left, after all.

"Honestly? I don't know what I'd do there. I mean, I know I love what I'm doing..." She trailed off.

My sister had always loved theater and performing—I always knew it was what made her soul tick. And now she was in New York, studying Acting and Theater. I totally understood it was her dream. For me, that passion came from teaching, of all things, so I wasn't about to tell my little sister to not follow her dreams.

"But?" I said, hopefully.

"But I still don't really know *what* I want to do. Honestly, I've been feeling a bit overwhelmed with all of my options lately."

"You can always come and spend the summer here. I have the guest room." I suggested. "Your lease in NYC ends in June after graduation, anyway, doesn't it?"

"Yeah." She agreed with me, and I could almost feel her nodding over the line. "It *does*, but..."

"Whatever you want. You can stay with me until you've figured out what you want to do—you know I'll support you with whatever you decide. Plus, it means one last summer with the two of us together before you get your big break and decide to leave your big brother forever."

It was her turn to laugh. "I'll never *leave* you, Matthew. Seriously, I owe you everything. After Mom and Dad..." I swallowed as her voice trailed off. "Well, I don't know what I would have done if you hadn't stepped up and taken such good care of me. I'm sure I wouldn't be where I am today."

"You don't have to thank me. I would do anything for you, sis. Even if you drive me crazy sometimes."

"Well, even so." She sighed. "I never realized everything you sacrificed for me. And I feel like it's my fault that you're still all alone and haven't gotten married yet. Like maybe if you hadn't had to take care of your kid sister, you would have already met the love of your life and gotten married."

"Tess," I said, furrowing my brow even though I knew she couldn't see me. "No. I didn't stop dating people because I was taking care of you. I promise. I just didn't have anyone I was interested in back then."

"And now?" She asked, and I could almost hear her grin through the phone.

Did I? I was attracted to Noelle, sure, but that didn't mean that I wanted to date her. Just that I wanted to get to know her. Maybe in more than one sense of the word.

"*Tessa,*" I said, rolling my eyes as I sighed in exasperation. "I promise I'll tell you if I meet someone. Okay?"

"Okay. *Maybe* this year? I'd really like a sister-in-law, you know."

I groaned, rubbing my hand over my face. "It'll happen when it happens."

"That's what you *always* say."

"Well, it's true."

"Well, try a little bit harder, bro. You're not getting any younger, and I want a niece or a nephew before you're in a walker," she teased me and then paused. There was some chatter in the background of the call, and I could tell she had pulled the phone away from her ear to listen to it. "Listen, Matthew, I gotta go, but take care of yourself, okay? And even if summer doesn't work out, maybe I'll come to visit for Spring Break. I know our weeks are different, but I'd still love to come out if you're okay with it?"

"Of course, Tess. We have a bit to figure it out. Just let me know."

"I will." She sounded happy. "I love you, big bro. Miss you lots."

"Miss you too, baby sis. Take care of yourself. Don't let those silly NYC boys forget how kick-ass you are, okay? Keep that boyfriend of yours in line."

Tess giggled into the line. "Never. I'm keeping him on his toes, I promise."

"Okay, bye. Talk to you soon."

"Bye!" She exclaimed, and then promptly hung up the phone, leaving me somehow even more homesick for my little sister's presence than I had been 20 minutes ago before calling her.

I made a note on my phone about spring break, reminding me to check in with her about flights in a few weeks. Hopefully, she wouldn't change her mind and want to stay in NYC or take a trip with her best friends or boyfriend and would come here.

I could use some sister time.

Also, and I wasn't sure I wanted to admit this to myself, but I could use something else to get excited about that wasn't the thought of seeing Noelle around campus. Yeah, something was *definitely* wrong with my brain for me to be thinking about that little redhead this much.

But could I see more with her? A future, a life? I thought about what Tessa said about kids and frowned. It wasn't like I hadn't thought about it before—having a family, settling down, having two kids, the white picket fence, and the big house. Yet I couldn't help but worry because I knew the truth: once you had everything, you could also lose it, just like that. And I didn't think I could survive losing everything. Not again.

∽

AS IF MY mind had manifested her, on Wednesday, I finally saw her again—bundled up in a burnt-orange turtleneck sweater dress and her winter coat back on top, walking towards the coffee shop on campus as class got out.

The coffee shop where I was currently sitting.

I had tried to go about my way on campus the rest of the week without thinking about her too much, without looking for her everywhere I went, but it was impossible. It was like now that I had seen her, my mind was specifically tuned to her frequency, and all it wanted to do was seek her out.

And God, if knowing she was out in the cold without someone to warm her hands did something to me, I wasn't going to show it. Nope, nope, absolutely not. Because why the hell was I thinking these thoughts? She wasn't *mine*, and what she did or didn't do had no impact on my life. Absolutely none.

A moment later, with her sweater dress and leggings and with her long hair pulled into a ponytail on top of her head, there she was. Had I manifested her? Had I somehow made myself see the girl of my dreams wherever I went? But no, she was there, that tiny smile of hers and all as she ordered a cup of coffee and pointed to something in the pastry case.

Girl of your dreams? Oh god, Matthew. You need to rein it in buddy, I tried to scold myself. And so, I did what any normal, sane person would do when they saw the girl they had spent an entire evening talking to standing at a coffee shop (not). I called her name.

"Noelle?"

"Oh, my God." Her hand flew over her heart. "Professor Harper. I'm sorry, you startled me."

"Sorry." I frowned. "My bad. I didn't mean to scare you," I shook my head.

"Oh, it's okay." Noelle gave me a tight smile. "I didn't expect to see you here."

I raised an eyebrow. Because we were standing in the middle of the coffee shop on campus. Where we were both employed. "Because professors can't order coffee?"

She snorted, and her hands flew over her mouth as she flushed a little. "No, I didn't mean that. It's just..." She tilted her head as she looked at me, and then shrugged.

"Well, here I am." I gestured with my cup of coffee. "It's better than the stuff they serve in the offices upstairs." I looked down at her table—laptop perched on the edge along with her coffee cup and muffin. "Do you mind if I sit?" I asked. Hoping she wasn't going to think I was some sort of creep, or that I was stalking her. God, I hoped not. I just wanted to get to know her better.

Noelle nodded, turning her attention back to her laptop. "Sure, go ahead."

I pulled the bagel with cream cheese out of the paper wrapping. This place always served the best bagels, warm and fresh, and I liked the way they slathered them in cream cheese.

"So... Not a sweets guy, Professor?" she gave a small chuckle as she picked up her sugary muffin.

I shook my head. "Most of the time, no."

"Hmm," Noelle said to herself as she took a giant bite of the chocolate concoction.

"What?"

"I'm just thinking you're full of surprises, that's all," she smirked.

"I'm sure there's a lot more of those when you get to know me." I winked at her.

Noelle's cheeks flushed. I thought I heard her mumble under her breath, "I'm sure there is," but I wasn't positive, so I didn't say anything back.

She turned back to her laptop, typing something into a document as she continued to nibble on her muffin.

Even after most of the blush on her face had faded, she still had a slight pink tinge to her cheeks, and I wondered if I had ever thought someone's blush was beautiful before. If there had ever been a girl that I had seen just once and been so easily... *bewitched* by before. It wasn't like she was even trying to cast this spell over me; she just *was*. The curve of her hips, the tilt of her lips when she smiled, the way her voice sounded when she laughed... it was transfixing. I was mesmerized, and I couldn't keep my eyes off of her. She carried herself as if the very world depended on her light, the warmth of her smile. Maybe it did.

I smiled into my coffee as I thought, maybe *mine* did.

We sat there for a while, me as I ate my bagel, Noelle as she hummed to herself and typed on her computer. Neither one of us broke the bubble of silence that we had somehow entered.

I didn't know how to explain it, even as she peeked her head over her laptop and peered up at me. There was just this sense of... rightness sitting here with her. I caught her eye, and I loved the way she looked away shyly. I couldn't help but wish I could count all of the freckles that swept across her face.

I cleared my throat. "So, uh, busy day today?"

She nodded. "I have to finish this presentation on Leadership I'm giving later this week, and then I have class at four." Noelle peeped at me. "When's your last class of the day?"

"Well," I started, taking a sip of my coffee, "Wednesday nights are the one night a week I teach late. We get out at ten."

She winced. "Those are always rough."

I shook my head. "It's not so bad, honestly."

"Lucky you. Sometimes I have to load up on caffeine just to stay awake for my night classes." She rubbed her eyes. "It's a miracle I've almost finished my degree."

I chuckled. "And what are your plans after graduation?"

"I'm not sure yet." Noelle shrugged. "I might stay on another year as Hall Director, and then… we'll see."

"I'm sure whatever you pick, you'll excel at it."

"Stop," she said, brushing me off but I could see her smile. "You don't even know me. How do you know I'm not absolutely lousy?"

I just raised my shoulders. "I can just tell. I have a good feeling about you, Noelle Hastings."

"Well, Professor Harper, I hope I prove you right."

"I'm sure you will." I winked at her, and she laughed.

"I should get going, but thank you so much for the company. It was really nice." She gave me a smile, but from her comment I wondered if she was surprised at how good of a time we had together. But maybe it wasn't so surprising, was it?

"Anytime." I got up from the table as she packed up her belongings.

Noelle gave me another look as she flitted through the doorway, back out into the cold. I watched her go as she walked through the quad, back to being all bundled up in her coat.

It was all I thought about as I got in my truck after class that night and settled into the silence as I drove the short way home. I wondered what it was about her that I found so compelling. Because, really, I was being *insane*. Over a girl that I didn't even know. And that just wasn't like me.

CHAPTER 5
Noelle

"Earth to Noelle," Gabrielle called out, waving her hand in front of my face as we gathered around the table at our favorite coffee shop off-campus. The four of us – Angelina, Gabrielle, Charlotte, and I had been coming here for years, even during undergrad and when I'd come home to visit while I lived in New York. I was lucky, in that regard, that all of them had decided to stay in Portland after graduating. It meant I didn't have to say goodbye or worry about when the next time I'd see them would be. There were enough people in my life that I'd had to say goodbye to—I didn't think I could stomach losing these three.

We had simply moved our on-campus hangs to a minimum once weekly date at the little coffee shop, or sometimes a café for breakfast. And then we would catch each other up on our lives: just the little things, but it beat texting. Sometimes we would talk about who we were dating (a conversation I had not participated in for a while), and the annoying things happening at our jobs—Gabbi and Ang had it the best because they worked for the biggest tech company in the city and could talk at work—and whatever book we were currently reading.

Our *Best Friends Book Club*, as I had lovingly dubbed us the first chance I got. They all hated it—of course—but it stuck. I wanted to get matching t-shirts, but Angelina had just rolled her eyes and gave me a firm *no*. I was still thinking maybe I could get away with matching tote bags, however. Maybe bookmarks.

"Sorry," I finally said, coming back from my space-out moment and back into the conversation. "I'm just a little distracted."

"Why?" Charlotte asked, stirring her hot chocolate with a spoon, "Did you finally end up meeting a hot teacher on campus?" she wiggled her eyebrows at me.

"Char!" My face turned bright red. *Failed, once again, by my ginger genes.* Any time I was even the slightest bit embarrassed, my whole face flushed. And of course, none of them would miss this detail – they all knew me way too well for that after almost eight years of friendship.

"Oh my god, she totally *did*," Angelina laughed. "Come on, girl, you gotta give us more details than that. Who's your eye candy for the semester? Does he have a name? It's been so long since you broke up with Jake—"

"No, no, no." I threw my hands up. "We're not going to do this. I am not hot for a teacher." Technically, that was true—he was a professor, after all. "And absolutely nothing is going to happen. With anyone." I narrowed my eyes at them.

Charlotte grinned. "Please, there totally is someone! You're never this vocal about denying things unless they're true." She licked a dollop of whipped cream off the top of her cup in total Char fashion, and I couldn't help but roll my eyes. Geez, did I have to be such an easy book to read to all of my friends?

"We never said anything *was* going to happen, Elle, but come on, let us have a little bit of fun," Gabbi pleaded with me. "We're all single right now anyway, so give us something exciting to talk about. There's gotta be something better than vicariously living through romance novels, I swear." She held up the book we had been reading this past week as if to further emphasize her point. If only it was so easy.

"Guys..." I sighed. "There's nothing really to say, I swear. He's..." *the most beautiful man I've ever seen, an absolutely fine male specimen, a gift from God*, all came to mind. But I knew I'd never hear the end of it, so instead, I lamely went with, "Well—he's just a professor. And before you get any other ideas, I've barely even talked to him, he's not *my* professor. I'm really not interested, and I doubt I'll see much of him, regardless." I shrugged at them and gulped my drink.

"Ugh, fine," Gabbi admitted in defeat. "Don't tell us the specifics. But I think there's something there." She gave me a sly smile.

Yeah, I wanted to say, *just the most handsome man on campus coming over to talk to* me *at the staff/faculty mixer. No biggie.* But I didn't say it, and she continued. "Don't forget, we know you, Noelle. I know what that little blush on your cheeks means." She took a sip of her coffee as she stared at me, and I just shook my head.

Yep, there were some negatives of your best friends knowing you almost better than you know yourself. Just a few. "Like I said, just forget about it, because nothing's going to happen. I'm not dating anyone."

The rest of the girls rolled their eyes at me, and then we were back on a different topic, and Charlotte had pulled a new book out of her bag, babbling on about how much she loved it. That girl burned through books, I swear—even with her part-time job at the dance studio and her side business making dresses, she still always seemed to have her nose in a book. We were all talking about book recommendations for next week and discussing our favorite moments from the one we just read, the earlier conversation finally long forgotten. At least I hoped it was because I had no desire to spend any more time talking about something that was not anything.

"Oh!" Charlotte exclaimed after the conversation had settled again and we were all just sipping on our drinks. "I gotta tell you about this thing that happened last week to Daniel and me—"

Angelina rolled her eyes like she hadn't heard the same sentence numerous times over the last almost decade. "You know I've never understood how you are *best friends* with my older brother." I wanted to laugh. I had witnessed their friendship begin in college just as ours had. It seemed like wherever Charlotte was, Daniel wasn't far behind her. I really didn't mind, because he was always nice to me—and had always helped me with my math homework when I needed it. It was one perk of him always hanging around our dorm room in college.

Charlotte stuck her tongue out at her. "Look, he just gets me. Besides, you're all my best friends too."

As much as she protested, I knew Angelina and her older brother were super close—she had followed him to the same college, after all, and they had spent a lot more time together over the years than most siblings I knew.

"You know," Gabbi elbowed her, "You haven't dated anyone in a while, and you and Daniel are both still single. Why don't you give *that* a shot? He's got to be better than all the other losers you've dated."

Charlotte made a face. "We don't like each other like *that*, Gabs. You know this. Sure, I love him, but like, as a *brother*, not someone I'm going to marry and have babies with—"

"Okay, *okay!*" Angelina exclaimed. "Enough talk about my brother and *anyone* having babies. That's a concept I have no desire to think about right now."

She was right. It hadn't even been four years yet since we graduated college—it was crazy to think that just a few short years ago we had all walked across that stage together. Marriage and kids still felt like the last thing on each of our minds. It felt like we were all too busy trying to make something of our lives first to worry about who we were going to spend them with. I *certainly* didn't have time for any sort of relationship right now. Going to school and working full time as a Hall Director, leading my RAs plus being there for my students was enough. Not to mention the untouched word document that had been sitting on my computer for ages. One day I would have time to work on it again.

Not anytime soon, though, because let's face it—I was swamped. I definitely didn't have time to fall in love with someone. I made a face as I took another drink of my coffee. Yeah, there was no chance in hell of that happening. Not again.

I laughed. "I can't even imagine dating anyone right now. Like, my life is a mess enough without trying to add another person into it." I had already tried to live my life with another person, and see how well that ended up? Honestly, I was better off alone.

"Well," Charlotte just smiled, "I think it sounds nice. Meeting *the one*, being swept off your feet, falling madly in love, and living happily ever after. Where do I sign up?"

"That's a *fairytale*, Char," Angelina said. "Not real life. Like, do you really think someone's going to swoop you up and ask you to get married to them tomorrow?"

Charlotte just frowned and mumbled under her breath, "Well, it *could* happen."

Angelina just scoffed. "I think it's more likely that I'll fall into bed with my enemy than you getting married just like that." She snapped her fingers.

Gabbi frowned at her, and I wondered what was going on in her head. I knew she wanted to find her person just as much as Charlotte did, even if she didn't say it. Angelina always said she was too busy for a relationship, but Gabbi had slowly given up on online dating after a few failed relationships. *"Anyway."* Gabbi finally changed the subject. "I think we're all *vastly* overdue for a girl's night. Should we make plans soon?"

"Ooooh, yeah, drinks would be fun," I agreed. "Just not a night where I'm on duty. Maybe a Monday?"

"I have a dance thing for my kids this Monday, but maybe the next one?" Charlotte loved those girls she taught so much–you could see it on her face.

"Good with me," Angelina nodded.

After we all agreed on drinks, we settled back into our book conversation, and after we had all finished our drinks and said our goodbyes, we were off, back to our normal—if not boring—lives.

∼

As it happened, on Monday morning I was typing away at the coffee shop, working on a paper for class, when in walked the one and only Professor Matthew Harper. Again. If seeing him for the last week had been a shock, it was even more so seeing him again. I was sure it was a coincidence; but why did it make my heart flutter a little to see him here?

I watched him go up to the counter and order his coffee while I sat, quietly, sipping on my caramel mocha.

Figuring what the hell, I went over to say hi as he waited for his order. "Hi, Professor Harper," I smiled at him.

"Oh. Noelle." He gave me a little nod. "Hello. How's it going today?"

"Good." I gestured to my table, wondering if it was too forward to invite him to sit with me again.

I couldn't explain it, but I felt comfortable around him, and I liked talking to him. Yeah—this beautiful, tall, blonde man, who I seemed to run into everywhere I went on campus—I had to admit that he fascinated me. "I'm sitting over there if you want to join me."

"Hmm," he mused, looking down at me. "Do you want me to join you, Noelle?" His beautiful blue eyes lit up and I had to wonder—was he teasing me? Or was he flirting with me?

I nodded and flushed a little. "If you want." And then I remembered exactly what he said to me last time, about how much more there was to him under the surface. And I wanted to know it. God, I wanted to know everything about him. What he liked, what he disliked... I couldn't help but wonder and be curious—it was just in my nature. That was all.

He peered at me curiously and then smirked. "Go sit down. I'll come and join you."

I left with a nod and was only slightly relieved when he slid into the chair across from me a few moments later. "How was your weekend?"

"Good. I just stayed at home and worked on grading. The weather was awful this weekend."

I nodded along. Were we *seriously* going to make small talk about the weather right now, of all things? "It really was." I frowned, and then thought, screw it, because who cared if I had an actual conversation with him instead of us talking about the rain?

"And how was yours?" he asked as I took another sip of my coffee.

"Oh." I tried to think of what I had done after leaving my best friends on Saturday. "It was good, I guess. I got to see my best friends."

"That's always nice. I'm beginning to think mine are ignoring me," he said, and I laughed.

"Ignoring *you*?" I scoffed. "Who could ever?"

He gave me a small laugh, and then returned his attention to his coffee. "I think they're all too busy for me. I'm sure our plans will pan out soon."

"Yeah." I nodded, sure that his friends would come through soon. How could they not? Though, then again, I had never seen him with anyone else. He seemed like a loner. I couldn't imagine him smiling and laughing with anyone—which only made me want to see it more.

My phone buzzed on the table, and I looked down and saw that my mom was calling me. I cursed internally. I knew I had to stop putting her off and talk to her, but there was a part of me that just didn't want to. I wasn't sure I could take her advice on my life right now. As confused as I was about what I wanted, about my dreams... I just wasn't ready to talk to her about it again.

"What?" he asked, peering at me as if I was making a weird face. Oh—maybe I was.

"Hmm?" I said, realizing I had been staring at him for maybe a beat too long. "Oh. Nothing. Just thinking."

Matthew tilted his head towards me as he took another sip of his coffee. "Do you do that a lot?"

"What?"

He chuckled. "Get lost in your thoughts."

"Oh. I guess so." I bit my lip. "Feels like I've been doing it a lot more lately."

"What's on your mind?"

Besides my future? *You*. The thought came faster than it should have. But I couldn't say it, so I settled for, "Everything, I guess. You know how the beginning of the semester is."

"Somehow both severely boring and insanely busy?"

I laughed. "Yes. That."

He looked down at his watch as if he realized he needed to check the time. "Shoot, Noelle, I'm sorry to cut this short, but I gotta run. It was nice to see you."

"You too," I responded, and then gave him a small smile as he headed out of the coffee shop, giving me a little wave before he walked out the door.

And what was my heart doing—or my brain for that matter? I wasn't going to think about how just talking with him gave me little butterflies.

I rolled my eyes as I went back to my laptop. I needed to stop thinking about him. Jake had backfired on me enough without me getting involved with a professor and ruining my entire reputation at my university, or worse.

So no... I wasn't going to keep having those thoughts. Absolutely not.

CHAPTER 6
Matthew

I knew I had been thinking about Noelle Hastings more than I should have been, but as I looked up as I walked into my night class that Wednesday, I couldn't believe my eyes. There she was. Sitting in the back row, coffee cup in hand, smirking at me. And what was Noelle doing here? She wasn't enrolled in my class, but she was there anyway, with a mischievous look in her eyes.

Seriously... What were the odds she would end up *here*? Was this... was she here on purpose?

"Hello class," I said, clearing my throat. "I hope you all did the assigned reading from last week—as you know, we have our first quiz at the beginning of the next class, and I expect you all to do well on it. Like we discussed, the only thing you're allowed to use is the formula sheet that I provided last week, but don't forget you'll have to know how to apply it correctly to pass."

I watched the heads bob in the room, agreeing with me, and I watched Noelle stare at me with interest. I was... enthralled, simply by her being, and I couldn't help but want to smile as I watched her pull out a notebook like she was going to take notes in my class. My graduate-level finance class had no impact on her and I was sure wouldn't interest her at all. Yet, it made me stand a little taller, and speak a little more confidently just knowing she was in the room, watching me. I tried to ignore her as I lectured my class on the topic of the day, but every once in a while my eyes drifted over to hers in the crowded room. I knew she had a busy schedule—she had told me she had a night class on Wednesday nights as well, but she was here.

As class wrapped up, I wished all my students a good night and reminded them about our plans for class next week. I didn't even see her approaching, too busy putting my laptop and books into my bag and getting ready to leave for the night.

But the sound of footsteps and the clearing of a throat distracted me, and by the time I heard, "Professor Harper?" I was looking up into her chocolate brown eyes and at her lovely, freckled face.

Shit. Had my head jolted up at the sound of her voice too quickly? Had I been staring at her too long? Hopefully, she didn't notice. Was that weird? Was I overthinking all of this? Probably.

I cleared my throat. "Noelle. Hello," I finally said, trying not to seem inane. Probably wouldn't be good to outright admit that all I could do was think about her... *yeah*. So instead, I said probably the dumbest thing I could think of, considering she'd shown up to my class randomly. "Did you enjoy the lecture?"

She nodded, pursing her lips slightly. "I have to admit, I wasn't planning on sneaking in, but then my class finished next door, and I saw you inside last week... And my curiosity got the better of me."

"Well, I'm glad you did," I said, again—like an *idiot*—because I was happy to see her, and then further dug myself into this hole because I wasn't able to use my rational brain when it came to this girl. "It was nice to see you." When had I ever said something like that to a student? Ugh. But she wasn't a student—not really, and she wasn't mine, anyway.

And she blushed. I loved it when she did that, watching it spread over her freckled cheeks. Oh, God. I was totally obsessed with this girl, wasn't I? "Learn anything interesting?" I asked, hoping to distract her back into her talkative self and not let her slip into that over-thinking brain of hers.

"Oh yeah." she grinned. "That I was absolutely not made to be a finance person."

I smirked. "Some people tell me it's an acquired taste."

"And what do you say?" she asked me, looking so sincere as she held her book bag in front of her.

"I like numbers," I finally said. "They make sense to me."

"That's how I've always felt about words." Noelle laughed. "I guess that's why I majored in English the first time around."

"Do you write?"

She nodded. "When I have time. I... I've been thinking about it a lot." When I raised an eyebrow, she continued. "Writing. Maybe trying to publish something."

"I think that would be incredible, Noelle. I'm sure you're an incredible writer."

Noelle's lips tilted up in a small smile and I delighted in it—making her smile. She gripped her bag a little tighter and then bit her lip. "I should... I better get going." She looked down at her watch. "I have an early day tomorrow. I'll see you around?" She laughed a little to herself, and then she settled her bag back over her shoulder before turning to leave.

"Good night, Miss Hastings," I murmured as she walked out of the door and away from me. I couldn't decide if I hated the sight or loved it. And had my eyes been glued on her back the entire time until she was out of my sight? Maybe. The way her sweater dress hugged her curves, her hips... *Fuck.*

I needed my best friends to smack some sense into me. I needed them to tell me to cut it out, to set me up with another woman who would maybe last a date or three so I could get Noelle out of my head and make it through this semester intact.

Two weeks. I had known her for two weeks. Two weeks that somehow felt like an eternity, because I didn't *want* to go back to a time when I had never laid eyes on Noelle Hastings. And I couldn't get the image of her blushing out of my mind. Dear

Lord, seeing her face flame red was… wow. Watching it spread over the freckles on her nose and cheekbones…

I frowned as I sat in my truck after class, hitting my head against the steering wheel of my truck. God. Seriously, it was like someone possessed my body and had taken control of my mouth. That seemed to be the only acceptable option for me to say such stupid things.

Yup. I was definitely way in over my head here.

∽

"Matthew. Dude. Get out of your head," Cole barked at me from the weight machine next to me. "You've been super distracted all day, dude."

Tanner, spotting for his brother, chimed in. "Yeah, what's up with you?"

"Nothing," I said, frowning, dropping my legs to the floor as I focused on the two guys in front of me.

They were twins, both of them sporting identical shades of brown hair, complete with identical hazel eyes and tall, muscular builds. We played basketball together in college and had been close ever since. Even though I hadn't pursued it professionally, they both had, and I always enjoyed watching them thrive in their careers.

Well, shit. If they could tell that I wasn't mentally there, I was doing a terrible job of keeping my thoughts of Noelle at bay. I should be thinking of other things, like the research I was supposed to be doing or working towards getting tenure at the university, not to mention I *really* needed to get a social life again. The only people I ever talked to outside of work were Tessa, the guys, and their significant others. Did I need more friends? Sheesh. I probably had spent too many nights working and reading over the last few years, and I could tell I had neglected my friendship with the guys.

But here I was, working out with them for the second time in a week, feeling better about finally putting the effort in again. Because I *had* missed this. Even if it was too easy to shut everyone out and wrap myself up in my own life. Something inside of me was telling me that it was time to really start *living* again. I just couldn't put my finger on exactly what was calling me to do so.

I had to remember what it was like to share details of my life with people, instead of keeping everything bottled up inside. I wasn't sure I was particularly good at that, anymore. It had been so long since I shared anything with anyone besides Tessa. She was the only one who knew what I went through after our parents passed away. How much it had hurt me. How hard it still was, knowing they would never be there for all of our big milestones. How they had missed our college graduations. They would miss our weddings, the birth of our children, if either of us even had any. I hoped Tessa would fall in love and get married eventually, not wrapping herself up in her career as I had. Me? Sometimes I wondered if it was a lost cause. Not that I was too old to meet the right person, but... I sighed. I had never found anyone that I especially wanted to be with either. I didn't want dating to feel like a chore, something I should do. I wanted to find that person who made me feel like it was something I had to do because I couldn't live without her.

I liked to think it was what my parents would have wanted for me. Would have wanted for us. It still hit me like a ton of bricks even almost ten years later, and I had never even talked about it with my best friends. Was that when I started shutting them out? Sophomore year of college, when I had withdrawn myself into the icy exterior I built for myself. Because maybe, if I was grumpy and off-putting, people wouldn't want to dig deeper.

But these guys—Bryan, Cole, and Tanner—they had never given up on me, not for one bit. We had lived together our last two years of college, renting a house off campus, and even when we were all in different cities, we had stayed in contact. They had simply not allowed me to fall off the face of the earth.

And for some reason, now felt like the time. To let them in, to give back to them after all the years they had been there for me. Twelve years of friendship, and I still didn't know what I would do without them. Tessa was my heart, but these guys? They were my backbone. They were the ones who had helped me keep going when the world was dark and bleak.

I sighed, deciding that I would try to open up, to share a little bit, at the very least. Not about the redheaded girl though, or my strange fascination with her. The way I couldn't help but look for her. The way I had randomly wandered into the coffee shop she worked at and then couldn't stop myself from going back, every single day. As if I couldn't make coffee at home. The way I had started looking forward to the faculty events, on the off chance she might be there. I wasn't sure I'd ever be ready to share those little tidbits with, well... anyone. My infatuation with her needed to remain just that. A little crush, some physical attraction that I never acted on. Because I barely knew her, and she was a grad student, even if she also worked for the university. That meant... Well, we couldn't happen.

I cleared my thoughts, turning back to the conversation at hand. Why was I so distracted? I held back a snort. All of my answers and thoughts circled one girl. "I've just been exhausted from working a lot lately," I finally said. "Working towards tenure and just—all of this, being a full-fledged professor—it's a lot more than I realized it would be. A lot more responsibility than just teaching a class or two a term." I knew the guys wouldn't understand the teaching aspect—they were professional basketball players, both playing for the Portland Trail Blazers after a few trades had finally landed them back on the same team together. It was nice to have them both in the same city as me again. But they surprised me by nodding.

"We get it, man. But you can always share what's bothering you with us, you know? We're here for ya." Tanner said as Cole stood up from the machine and they swapped places.

"You know," Cole laughed, "just because your students call you grumpy and icy doesn't mean you have to be cold with us."

I still sat on my bench, hands running through my hair as the two of them resumed their workout. "Thanks, guys. I promise I'll work on opening up more." I nodded, then continued after a pause: "You know, it's just been me and Tess for so long that sometimes I forget that I have other people I can open up to—and with her not even on the same coast as me anymore..." I shook my head, shrugging my shoulders as I stood to give up my equipment to another guy. "I'll work on not bottling up so much." Well, it was something, at least.

"Despite all that," I added as the corners of my mouth tipped up slightly—almost a smile. "I love it. Teaching. Helping these kids figure out what they want to do with their lives. I know I appreciated my professors in college who took the time to help me."

"Do you think you'd do it any differently if you had to do it all over?" Cole asked.

I shook my head. "Nah. Investment banking might not have been for me—I know I was good at it, and I made decent money for those years—but I think I needed to learn that I wasn't looking for a desk job. I think I needed something different. And this..." I took a deep breath. "It feels right, you know?"

The guys nodded. "I'm happy for you, man," Tanner said, slapping me on the back.

"If you had to do it all over, do you think you'd still choose careers in basketball?"

"Oh yeah," Cole laughed. "I love it. The games, the adrenaline as I'm running around the court, the way I feel when we win a game... It's all worth it."

"Plus," Tanner grinned, "it's what brought us our girls, so." He grinned. Kelly had been a dancer on the Trail Blazers team when Cole started, and one thing led to another, and both brothers had found themselves on a double date with both sisters. Tanner sang Cole's praises every day for setting him up on that date.

"Yeah. And knowing how we'd end up, that we'd be back on

the same team after six years apart? I wouldn't trade getting to do what we love together. Not one single day."

I couldn't help cracking a small smile while looking at my two friends. "I'm really glad we all ended up here."

"Yeah," Cole grumbled, faking a little pout as he held back his laughter. "Because otherwise, you'd have no friends."

"Hey!" I frowned.

"You can't tell me you're going to argue with him right now, Matthew?" Tanner said. "You know he's right."

"Maybe," I mumbled, but I didn't say much more. They knew letting people in was hard for me. Letting someone see underneath the wall of ice I had built up to protect myself, to keep my feelings bottled down inside? That was *hard*, even with them, and we had known each other since I was a baby-faced Freshman with braces. But I didn't need other friends—these guys were enough for me. Our friendship was rock solid, and even when we had gone periods without talking much, it had never lessened our bond.

As we finished our workout I knew it, too—no matter what, these guys had my back. They would always have my back. And that feeling, that bond? It was stronger than friendship. It was what I had always imagined having a brother would be like.

So maybe it *was* about time I opened myself up to them.

∼

I WANTED to stop this obsession—I really did. To stop thinking about her, stop picturing her anytime I closed my eyes. I hated the reaction she invoked in me, for making me want to be around her even more. And if it wasn't bad enough that I was struggling with these completely ridiculous thoughts, I kept seeing her *everywhere*.

The coffee shop. The library. Asleep on a couch tucked into one of the corners of the business building. Eating a salad at the cafeteria on campus. But this? I kept myself from groaning as I watched her from afar, wearing a pair of leggings and a giant crewneck hoodie. Noelle bit her lip as she stared at the display of cookies.

I almost thought she was standing there debating whether or not she should get them. It made me smile. A lot of the things this girl did had that effect on me. I didn't want to take the time to analyze *why* that might be, why I'm so entranced by her presence. Even with her hair up in a messy bun and no makeup on, it hit me once again how beautiful she was. It wasn't even in a sexy way, just the way her freckles were splattered all over her nose and cheekbones and the glow her bare skin had—she just lit up any space she was in. And somehow whenever she was around, I was always noticing the little things she did.

She always had some kind of sweets on her. Seriously, I'd known her for a little over two weeks, and I think I'd seen her eat almost every dessert or pastry I could imagine. Muffins, scones, coffee cake, cinnamon rolls, cupcakes, those little chocolate pastries she liked to sneak at the coffee shop when she thought no one was looking. *Maybe no one else is, but I am,* I thought. I couldn't help myself from noticing the little way she scrunched her nose when she was focused, or the way she laughed when she was genuinely amused. Her little snorts, and then the way she giggled when they caught her by surprise.

I couldn't explain what those things did to me because I didn't understand it myself. All I knew is it made me want to know *more*, want to get to know the girl behind all of those things. I wanted to know her coffee order, her music tastes, and the trivial things I could never know just by observing her.

I stared at her deliberating on the cookies for so long that I realized she might catch me and think I'm a creep, so I made my way over to her, basket in hand. I hadn't needed that much when I stopped at the grocery store that night—just picking up a few things for dinner for the upcoming week—so it was fairly easy to glide quietly up behind her.

"I can tell you want them," I finally said.

"Oh!" Noelle exclaimed, a little startled as she dropped the package in her hand back on the pile before turning to me. "Oh. It's you." She bit her lip, and then picked back up the package of red velvet cookies.

"Get the cookies," I urged her again. "You know you want them."

She laughed. "You're right. I do." Noelle looked at me and then she sighed. "It's just... a lot of people in my life have told me I need to stop eating so much sugar." She looked down at her cart and shrugged. "I mean... maybe they're right."

I shook my head. "That's stupid, and you know it." I tried to keep my eyes from roaming down her body, appreciating her ample curves and lovely form. When she went to protest, I stopped her. "I promise, you don't need to worry about that. Seriously."

She blushed. A little red tint spread over her nose and cheekbones, but I could see the color creeping up her neck, as well. "Um, thanks." She looked at my basket, at the veggies, meat, and the few healthy snacks it contained. "Wow, you seriously weren't kidding when you said you didn't eat sweets." She twisted up her face, like she was contemplating how that was possible, and then looked at me.

I snickered at her expression. She was so serious. "I wasn't." It wasn't like her cart was just junk—it was clear she fed herself healthy food too, and it wasn't like I hadn't seen her eating a salad before. But something about her eating desserts and sweet food was exactly *right*, and it warmed my soul.

"What?" Noelle asked, one eyebrow arched as I chuckled to myself.

"You're just different from so many people I've met, Noelle," I murmured, as we still stood talking over the cookies.

Her voice dropped lower to meet the same register as mine. "In a good way?" I could hear her breath catch. When had we moved so close together? We were only a breath apart, enough distance for my hand to reach out and grab hers. But I didn't—

didn't let myself touch her. I couldn't because it was going to end me if I did. Just like she already had just by showing up in my life.

"Yeah. In a good way," I confirmed. She just stood there, gnawing on her bottom lip, and I wanted to know what was going on inside her head, but I didn't have the right to ask. We weren't friends, after all. Just a little bit more than acquaintances. She still called me Professor Harper, for goodness' sake. I shouldn't ask her what's on her mind. I shouldn't have wanted to follow her around the store to ask her what all of her favorite foods were. What was I going to do with that information? Cook her dinner? No. Absolutely not.

"Right," she nodded, finally putting the cookies in her cart.

"Well..." I trailed off. What else could I possibly say to her? How could I possibly keep her talking? It was crazy: during the last fifteen years, there were less than ten people who I liked enough to want to sit around and talk to all day—and two of them were gone. But something about being around her just felt right. Like something had clicked into place inside of me.

I didn't know what to do with that, but I also knew I couldn't admit those things. Couldn't ask her for more time. Because it was *crazy*—all of this was.

Noelle gave me one last smile before she glanced at her cart and said, "I guess I should probably get home now. Goodbye, Professor Harper. It was good to see you."

"Yeah. It was good to see you too." And it really was.

CHAPTER 7
Noelle

Was fate trying to tell me something? I was pretty sure the number of times I had run into Matthew Harper in the past two weeks couldn't have been a coincidence. I was wondering if I should just hole myself in my dorm room just so I didn't *keep* seeing him. Because every time I did... This crush of mine was growing.

I swear, showing up at his class lecture had been an accident. It was just that, well... My classes had been over for the evening, and I had seen him in the classroom next to mine as I walked out the week before, and I couldn't help myself. I snuck in the back, sat in the last row, and I enjoyed just listening to him teach Finance. It wasn't something I had ever really learned about, just the basics, but I was quickly enthralled by the amount of passion with which he talked. Yes, he was a little grumpier than he was with me and didn't light up the way he did when we talked, but I could see his passion for teaching.

Not to mention the way he would look around the room as he talked, looking over all of the students, but his eyes always settled back on me. And I knew, the first time our gazes had connected, that I was *caught*, but I was enjoying listening to him too much to care.

He'd ran his hand through his combed-back hair as he looked over his slides, coming to the end of the presentation. My eyes had trailed back up, meeting his. He was so serious and focused, but even then, I could tell that this was his thing. The thing that set his soul on fire. I was still trying to find mine.

The realization sank in me that as attracted as I was to him, I also really genuinely respected him. He seemed to care about his students, even with his grumpy mask, and he did seem interested when he asked me all those questions about myself at the mixer the other day.

It was... surprising to me, how good it felt to know that someone wanted to talk to me. And when he looked up at me sitting in his classroom... Well, I think my heart skipped a few beats at his expression. I couldn't help it. He was beautiful. Seriously.

And then running into Matthew at the grocery store last weekend had been weird, but... normal, somehow. And for some reason, he had recognized my cookie dilemma and talked me right out of it. I hadn't even felt guilty about eating them, or the countless other sweets I found myself munching on, day after day. I didn't care if I watched my figure. I didn't care if the weight went to my thighs, my butt, or my hips. That wasn't to say I was against eating healthy, or physical activity—although, let's be honest, I detested working out with every fiber of my being. It just meant that I wasn't going to let people's jokes about me only eating sweets bother me anymore. Because even though he didn't say flat out that he appreciated my body, I had seen the way his heated gaze swept over my curves. Oh god. Just thinking about it made me warm all over. And he had said *You don't need to worry about that, seriously.* It was so matter of fact. So certain.

My ex had never treated me like that—it was quite the opposite. That's why it was such a relief to talk with Matthew like that. Because I knew the most important people in my life—Angelina, Charlotte, and Gabrielle—they had never once judged me for it either. Had never once rolled their eyes when I showed up with cake, muffins, or a sweet treat. They had always appeased me when I tried a new cookie recipe by tasting it for me. So, what Matthew said and how he made me feel, it just felt... right.

I was still lost in my thoughts when I almost ran into someone on the sidewalk. When I looked up, I saw the same icy blue eyes that had come to my mind a few more times than I would like to admit over the last few days. Seriously, was our campus that small?

"Oh, hi, Professor Harper," I smiled, taking a step back so we weren't almost touching.

"Hello, Noelle," he returned, shuffling a stack of papers in his arms.

"You look like you're in a rush," I said, gesturing at his pile. "I'll let you go."

He shook his head. "I'm just on my way to class. Care to walk with me? I still have a few minutes."

I wasn't sure what compelled me to say yes, but I did. And then we were off, slowly walking across campus in the gray haze of the day.

"So." He looked over at me. "Crashed any other unsuspecting professor's classes today?"

I grimaced. "I'm sorry if that was inappropriate of me—"

"Noelle." He gave me a look, and I shut up. "It was fine. Don't worry. I was just surprised to see you, that's all. Like I told you, it was nice to see you." I tried to ignore the burn on my cheeks, burying my face in my scarf, when he looked over at me. "You're welcome in any of my classes, any time." He nodded to himself. "Just maybe don't tell the Dean, because I don't think he'd support someone taking a course for free." Matthew chuckled.

"Right. Of course." I nodded along, "I probably shouldn't though... I wouldn't want people to get the wrong idea."

"About what, Noelle?" He looked at me.

I cleared my throat. "Um. You and me."

"You and me?" He asked, tilting his head in amusement. "I don't think you have to worry about that."

"Right." I forced out a laugh as we came to a stop in front of the building his class had to be in. "Well, I'll see you around."

"Goodbye, Noelle," he gave me a warm smile. "Have a good day."

"Thank you," I mumbled as I left, only realizing later that I hadn't even given him a proper *goodbye* back. Ah. Did this man understand what he was doing to me? He was constantly showing up everywhere and confusing my brain. I didn't know what to do with the thoughts I was putting in my head, but I certainly wasn't going to act on any of them. Nope.

Not. Happening.

I went back to my dorm and stared at that blank document on my computer again. When was the last time I had felt the desire to write? When had I last been creative and put words onto paper? It felt like years, and maybe it was. In college, I had been so jazzed about writing. Had come up with a binder full of characters and ideas. And then I had gotten so caught up in my relationship, in my move, that I had lost sight of what mattered to me.

And the word document had just blinked back at me every day since our disastrous end. Because if you didn't believe in love, in a happy ending, how could you write it, right? I sighed and shut my computer lid again. I wasn't ready. Not yet.

But one day soon, I'd tell the story I wanted to tell. Maybe I just had to sort out the rest of my life first.

∼

Monday night had finally arrived—when the girls and I had agreed to go to the bar together. It felt like it had been eons since we had all gone out, so despite my normal objections, and any intentions I had to stay home and study, I found myself at our old bar off-campus at six pm, surrounded by Gabbi, Charlotte, and Angelina. Wearing a tight black dress with tights underneath and knee-high boots might not have been the *best* call—it was honestly a little sparse for a cold January night in Portland, but thankfully it was warm in here. Plus, after a drink or two, I would be even warmer. And maybe some dancing would help, though I doubted I could drag anyone else out on the floor with me. Maybe Gabbi, if she didn't find a guy—or girl—to flirt with at the bar.

I had been responsible and took an uber there, not wanting to risk driving home after drinking, especially considering that sometimes when the four of us got together in one room it got a little... crazy. And was it so bad that I wanted to let loose a little bit anyway? Between my hall director duties and classes, I was working on a myriad of projects. I had earned a little break. Plus, the distraction from Matthew Harper would be good for me. Absolutely. I had been thinking more and more about it—and him, and I was firmly convinced that the universe was just out to get me. Why else would it dangle a man so fine in front of me like a bunny with a carrot?

I was standing in front of the sign outside, staring at the newly painted sign that said Dusk, before wandering my way inside to find the girls standing at the bar, drinks already in hand. Gabbi pushed over a cider in my direction, knowing my tastes in alcohol, and I thanked her before taking a sip. It was sweet and tart, just like I liked it. The perks of a years-long friendship: they could order for you and know exactly what you wanted.

Angelina had already started her rant as I sat down. "*Ugh*. Today was awful. There's this asshole at work who keeps pestering me over emails. I haven't even *met* him in person, and I already hate him. It's always *Ms. Bradford* this, Ms. Bradford that. Can't he just use my first name instead of treating me so formally? Ugh. I hate him."

Gabbi, Charlotte and I just looked at each other before laughing.

"What?" Angelina asked, crossing her arms over her chest. "He makes my life a living hell. And, again, *I haven't even met the dude.* I think my anger is warranted."

I shrugged. I wasn't going to say anything about her annoyance with the man, but Charlotte, always the peacekeeper, said something instead. "You know, maybe he's just addressing you formally because he respects you. That's the way you should be treated in the office, you know."

Angelina raised an eyebrow. "No. That's not it. His emails are the *opposite* of respectful. He's always talking down to me, discrediting my work, telling me what I do isn't important—"

Gabbi frowned. "This is Benjamin we're talking about, right? Benjamin Sullivan?"

"Yeah," Angelina huffed. "It's only getting worse, not better." Gabbi shook her head, taking a sip of her beer. The rest of us followed suit, letting Angelina stew in her grumpiness for a moment.

"What exactly does he say in these emails?" I asked, wondering how this guy could get so easily under Angelina's skin. She was always so confident, and I knew how hard she worked. She had been at the top of our class, always working her butt off in college, and that showed even now in her role at the tech firm she worked at.

Ang just bit her lip. "Oh, the usual. *You forgot a comma in this report*, or *that sentence stops abruptly or—*"

"Maybe he's just trying to help," Gabbi suggested.

"*Help*?!" Angelina threw her hands up in the air. "You think this arrogant man wants to *help* me?"

"Or he likes you," I smirked.

"No way in hell. He hates me. And I absolutely hate him."

"*Okay*," I sang, but I shared a small, secret smile with Gabbi. It seemed like Angelina was so worked up over this man she hadn't even met, and I couldn't help but wonder why.

"Well, come on!" Angelina said, raising her voice so we could hear her among the noise of the bar. "We should let loose a little. Let's get some shots." And then she was waving over the bartender, ordering before we could stop her, and once the tray of tequila shots was placed in front of us, she passed them out to each of us. Was she just trying to get drunk to forget about her problems? Maybe, but for once I was sort of okay with that. I didn't want to think about my life or all of the things I had to figure out at this moment either.

I downed the first shot, and then we ordered another, the buzz finally sinking into my system as I finished the second one.

Charlotte and I were chatting, rambling on about some book we had read, Charlotte bemoaning the fact that she was alone and single and was never going to find anyone—much to the rest of our amusements because we were *all* single and twenty-five and probably weren't where we thought we would be in our lives at this point either. Well, except for maybe Angelina, who had managed to be a fairly high-up marketing manager for the firm she worked at. And Gabbi, who had recently got promoted to the manager of HR at the same firm.

"At least fictional men don't let you down," Charlotte complained. "I went on this date last week, and this guy was so *nice*."

"He was nice, and you're complaining?" I raised an eyebrow. We were a little tipsy, and sometimes Char liked to complain even more when we were. I didn't care though—I was happy to sit and listen to her.

"Yeah. Aren't you paying attention to me?" She frowned. "He was so nice it was boring. I swear, he hardly had anything to say. We spent most of the evening talking about me." Charlotte moaned.

"But..." Angelina popped in. "Don't you love talking about yourself?"

"Yes!" Charlotte groaned, burying her head into the crook of her elbow on the bar. "That's what was so boring," she said, a little muffled into the wood surface.

We laughed. "There, there, Char," I said. "It was just one date. There will be others. You'll find the right person eventually, I promise." I patted the back of her head soothingly before turning back to the bartender.

"Another round, please," I asked the bartender with a smile, before nudging Gabbi with my shoulder. "So, Gabbi, how was your day?"

She shook her head. "I dealt with a bunch of idiots all day." I didn't miss the look she shot Angelina. "But other than that... it was fine, I guess."

"You guess?" I frowned. "What about that girl you had a date with last weekend?"

She shook her head again before downing her next shot. "God, doesn't anyone have a brother I could date? It's gotta be easier than this."

"Sorry, Gabs, I'm afraid *mine* is already spoken for," Angelina said, sipping her water and glancing at Charlotte.

Char rolled her eyes, but she didn't comment further. I on the other hand, couldn't stop giggling.

Sometime after our third shot, a guy sat on the empty stool next to me and started chatting me up. I was only half paying attention because there was a part of me who couldn't help but wish he was someone else.

Which was weird because I had always loved flirting before. It was fun. It made me feel special.

And sure, this guy was attractive, in a subjective way, but he didn't do it for me. None of it did. I couldn't get a certain blond man and his grumpy expression out of my mind. I frowned as I picked up the glass in front of me, taking a swig of whatever alcohol the girls had ordered last.

Despite the constant chatter around me, I looked up to realize my friends were no longer sitting at the bar. *Fuck. Where had they gone?* I knew I hadn't seen them sliding into a booth, but I didn't think I had spaced out so much as to not hear them say they were leaving. Huh.

"Did you see where my friends went?" I asked the bartender, but he just shook his head.

Maybe they had gone to the bathroom. Goodness knows we had drunk enough liquid to warrant it. I moved to go find them, planning on making my way there myself. I was feeling a little dizzy, and when I stood up, I found the guy from the bar *right* there next to me. Like, just a few inches from my face. Had I said anything to make him think I might be interested? I didn't think so.

"Um, excuse me." I tried to push away from him, only teetering a little bit in my heeled boots.

Was I *that* drunk? I unlocked my phone to text my friends and look at the time. How long had we been here, anyway? I was still trying to figure out how this guy had gotten so close to me without me noticing.

There was one thing I was sure of: my alcohol tolerance had definitely gone down since college. *Fuck.* I lost count of how many shots I had done—it had just seemed like a good idea at the time. But I had been drinking water, hadn't I? Normally us all being together, we kept count and kept each other from drinking too much, but...

The guy caught my wrist with his hand, and I was pretty sure I was looking at him like he was insane. "I thought we were having a good time, princess," he drawled, pulling me in closer. I squirmed, trying to get my wrist out of his hand, but it was no use.

"Let me go," I said. "I need to find my friends."

Fuck, I thought again, still surveying the bar for my friends. I couldn't see them, and all I wanted was to leave, to slip my arm in Gabbi's and Charlotte's and have them help me walk out of here with my dignity intact. And I wanted this asshole to leave me alone. I hadn't even given him any indication that I was interested, anyway. He had been talking to me, but I had barely acknowledged him.

So what the hell was wrong with him?

"Please," I said again, using my other hand to try to free my wrist.

I was starting to panic when I looked up for help and saw the other man who had walked to the other side of me. Even through my drunken haze, I could tell who it was. Jake. The asshole who left me. Why was he here? My blood boiled in my veins as I gaped at him, trying to wish him away with my brain.

Maybe I was hallucinating. But I couldn't be that lucky, could I? And I was sure I had never been *that* drunk, but it sounded much more preferable to reality. Which consisted of him standing in front of me, saying things to me that sounded a lot like, "I missed you."

I couldn't even process the words, just watching his lips move as I stared at him in shock.

Asshole number one dropped my hand, though he looked increasingly pissed, and I thought for a moment I was free—until he wrapped his arm around my waist and pulled me into his side.

"What the hell are you doing?" I cried, trying to push away from him.

That was when I heard a familiar voice—loud and growling—say, "Everything okay over here, gentlemen?"

And I was pretty sure I swayed on my feet at the sight of *him* standing there.

CHAPTER 8
Matthew

She was upset. And drunk. I could tell that much from the back of the bar where I sat in a booth with Bryan, his wife Elizabeth, Cole, Tanner, and the blonde twins they had been going out with for the last two months. Kelly and Kaitlin, or something like that. They were bubbly and had way too much energy for my liking, but the guys seemed really into them, so I kept my mouth shut. It wasn't my place to say anything about who they were dating when I had snubbed every attempt of theirs to set me up with someone over the last eight years.

When they had invited me out to the bar tonight, I really couldn't find a good excuse *not* to come, so there I was, sitting at the bar with an IPA in hand, watching Noelle Hastings stumble onto a stool, drink in hand, laughing with her friends. Her little dress and those little knee-high boots, damn. Of course, my friends had picked a bar off campus to go to, and of course, it had been the same freaking one that Noelle and her friends chose to come to. Was this a form of torture designed specifically for me?

"So, Matt," Elizabeth distracted me as I stared towards the bar while sipping my beer. "Any updates in the romance department? Are you going to bring a girl to one of these get-togethers any time soon?" A glass of water sat in front of her, and she rested one hand on her stomach, while one of Bryan's arms was draped around her and rested on her shoulder. The way they leaned into each other, drawing from each other's warmth, reveling in each other's presence... Yes, okay, it made me want that too.

"Still looking for the right girl, I'm afraid," I said, giving her a small smile and willing myself not to look back towards Noelle in her little black dress.

Fuck, I couldn't help it. She was giggling and pushing at her blonde friend's shoulder, while the guy behind her was looking a little *too* closely at her ass. Nope. Not okay, dude. And if he touched her without permission... *Woah.* I scowled. That thought came out of nowhere.

"Well, if you're looking, I have a friend who might be interested. I could set you up?" Liz sounded hopeful, and I could see Bryan nodding along with her. I knew he wanted me to get married and settle down soon as he had. He had a nice comfortable job as a pharmacist, a nice house, and a gorgeous wife. I was seriously envious of them. For having it all together, having their lives all figured out. Mine was a mess in comparison.

"Maybe?" I offered her a small shrug, eyes darting between her and the bar. To Noelle, cheeks flushed as she finished another drink.

Bryan's eyes must have tracked mine because he was glancing in the direction of the bar, too, and I could tell he was trying to figure out what—or who—I kept staring at. "Everything good, man?"

"Yeah," I answered too quickly and waved him off. "All good. I just know... someone over there."

"You know, if you want to go say hi, it's alright," chimed in Cole's girl, Kelly. Or was it Kaitlin? It was hard to tell them apart unless they were sitting with their guys, and sometimes I could barely tell the two of *them* apart. Two sets of identical twins dating each other—sometimes it confused my brain. I couldn't imagine being them and being constantly confused for each other.

"Nah, that's okay, really. She doesn't even know I'm here."

"Oh, *she*, huh?" Tanner interjected, wiggling his eyebrows at me.

"Fuck off." I punched his shoulder from his side. "It's not like that."

"But it *could* be?" Bryan asked, taking a bite of the fries we had ordered. Out of solidarity for his pregnant wife, he hadn't ordered a drink tonight either, so he was simply munching away on all our appetizers.

"No." I narrowed my eyes. "She works at my university too, guys. Rest assured; absolutely nothing will be happening there."

"Oh, but I bet you could *teach* her some things," Cole smirked, and Tanner high-fived him.

"Hey," Elizabeth said, giving her best mom stare at the twins. Geez, her kid wasn't even born yet, and she already had it down perfectly. "Don't joke about that kind of thing. Still, you could go say hi if you wanted. What does she do?"

I just shook my head. "It's fine. I'm here with all of you. And she's the hall director of one of the dorms." I frowned because I realized I didn't even know which one. "And she's also a grad student." I looked over at her again, now seemingly talking to the man who had been ogling her ass. Jerk. I wanted to go and tell him off, but I bit my tongue instead.

"Oh, and does this *grad student* have a name?" Bryan asked, and then winced in pain. Elizabeth had probably just kneed him under the table, which made me laugh.

I waited for a beat before responding, "Noelle." And then went back to sipping my beer, choosing to look straight ahead instead of watching her flirt with some guy. And why was I so jealous, anyway? Hadn't I just told my friends that nothing would ever happen between us? "Doesn't anyone else have anything exciting happening in their life that we could talk about instead?" I asked, trying to deflect the conversation off of me.

"Well, I just got a promotion at work." Kaitlin smiled, "I'm the new Head Nurse of the Pediatric Ward."

"At OHSU?" Elizabeth looked at the blonde girl with pride.

"Yeah!" she exclaimed. "I'm excited because it means I get to work more closely with my favorite doctor, and he's—"

Tanner groaned. "Babe, you know I hate when you talk about how excited you are to work with other men."

"I can't help it if you're jealous, sweetie, but really, I have a super-hot basketball boyfriend. And I'm not interested in Hunter, I promise." Kaitlin patted Tanner's bicep, and then shifted in her seat to place a peck on his cheek. Again, I needed all of my friends to stop being so... sweet and happy, because it was making me feel a heck of a lot lonelier than I had been before. "Besides, he works too much," she added, scrunching up her nose. "I've never seen him make time for anyone. Not like you do for me." Kaitlin interlaced her fingers with Tanner's hand.

"Working in a hospital must be intense sometimes, huh?" I asked Kaitlin, trying to remain present in the conversation as Noelle began dancing with the asshole.

"It can be challenging working with infants and kids, but at the end of the day, I wouldn't trade it for any other job in the world. I love helping those families, and knowing what a difference I make in their lives... That's what's important to me, you know?"

I nodded. "I feel the same way about my students. Not that I save their lives, but you know, I hope I make a difference in them."

"I'm sure you do," Kelly popped in from Cole's lap. Huh. I hadn't even noticed her moving to sit on him, but most of my attention had been focused on Noelle since I noticed her at the bar, anyway.

It was then that I saw another man approaching Noelle, and I saw the way her eyes got big, and her stance instantly went on the defensive. What was going on? Who was this guy to her?

I couldn't hear what she was saying, but she tried to pry the guy's hand off of her. She looked around her nervously, as if to try and locate someone—most likely her friends.

"I'll be right back," I muttered to my friends, and before I could fully process what I was doing, I was chugging down the rest of my drink, standing up from my seat at the edge of the booth, and walking over to the bar. Right to Noelle, still stuck in the middle of the two men.

"Please," she said, trying to push the guy off of her. The asshole was trying to wrap his arm around her like he was asserting his territory, and while she tried to squirm out of his grip, the newcomer was saying something to her that made Noelle frown.

"What the hell are you doing," she cried, and I knew I had to swoop in. Because nope. Nope. *Nope.* Fuck this, I was getting her out of there.

I stepped up between the three of them, leaning my arm on the bar as if I was going to order a drink. "Everything okay over here, gentlemen?"

"Yeah, we're just fine," the asshole hissed. "The little lady was just talking with me, and this guy came over here to try and cut in."

I looked at Noelle, who looked pissed off and also scared, although she was trying to cover it up. "Hm. Well, I think maybe the *little lady* might not be interested in talking to you anymore, pal. So, I suggest you let her go, and we won't have any further problems."

"No way. She's mine, dude. I'm not giving her up like that."

"She's not your *anything,*" I growled, "and she's drunk, so she's certainly not going home with *you.*" Noelle was pale but nodded at me. The way she looked at the other guy, though... it seemed haunted, that was the only way to describe her expression.

"And who are you to stop me?" he countered back. I was seriously only five seconds away from punching this guy in the jaw. He deserved it.

I looked around. Her friends hadn't come back from the bathroom. I didn't want to risk them all being too drunk to help the situation either, so I said the only thing that came to my mind.

"I'm her friend." Noelle still said nothing, eyes a little misty as she stared at the man who wasn't saying anything, and I couldn't help how protective I felt over her. I couldn't control it either.

"Listen, asshole, if you don't let her go in the next three seconds, you and I are going to have some serious problems." I stood up to my full height, towering over the guy who stood at maybe five ten, and gave him my fiercest scowl.

Finally, he unwrapped his arm from her. "Fine, whatever. You can have her." He stalked off, adding, "Not worth fighting over some girl. Have fun with her," over his shoulder, and then he disappeared into the crowd. Noelle was left standing, looking especially wobbly on her heeled boots, and I helped her onto the nearest stool.

As if she was just some girl to me? Someone who I would want to just have my way with and then abandon, instead of the woman who haunted all of my dreams. As *if*. I couldn't help but look at the guy's back in disgust as he left. "Fucking jerk," I muttered under my breath, then I addressed Noelle directly for the first time all night. "Are you okay, Noelle?"

She nodded; her voice quiet as a whisper as she replied, "Yes. Thank you. He wouldn't let go of me." She bit her lip as she looked up at me, and all I wanted to do was pick her up in my arms and hold her tight.

The other guy who had seemed to make Noelle upset was still lingering around, and I glared at him. "Dude. Leave her alone. I don't know what you said to her, but she's clearly upset, so—"

"What the fuck do you even know about her?" he sneered back at me, which made me even more furious. "She's *my* ex-girlfriend, man, I think I know more about how she feels than you do."

I narrowed my eyes at him, then looked at Noelle—the sight of her, looking like she had seen a ghost, made my heart ache. Clenching my jaw, I focused on her asshole of ex-boyfriend again. "Look, if any of my exes were almost in tears at the sight of me, I think I would assume I had seriously fucked up, so if you care at all about keeping your face intact, I'd leave." I would do it. I totally would punch him, right here in the middle of the bar to take care of her.

It was then that I noticed her friends coming back from the bathroom, the three of them huddled together speaking in hushed tones. When they finally saw Noelle sitting between me and the asshole, still a bit paler than usual, they rushed over.

"What's going on?" the brunette girl asked. "Are you okay, Elle? Is he bothering you?" And then she turned to the ex. "How dare you show up here, Jake. Leave her alone, you already did enough damage to her life without showing back up here again."

"Gabrielle—" the man, Jake, started.

"No. No, we're not doing this tonight. Leave our friend alone and *don't* contact her again. Or show up anywhere around here. You left her, and none of us are interested in seeing Noelle heartbroken over you for a second time. Leave." Her amber eyes were lit up like fire, and her body language screamed *don't fuck with me, man.*

Noelle's other two friends were bent over her as she sat on the stool, sharing a whispered conversation I couldn't quite hear. I took a step toward her ex and raised my eyebrow one last time.

"This isn't over," Jake said, addressing Noelle, "I just want to talk, Ellie. We were so good together, and I want another chance."

"Fuck you," she said, calmly, though the tears that had started spilling from her eyes. "Just go, Jake. Please. Leave me alone."

He opened his mouth like he was going to say something else but just shook his head as he turned around and walked back out the entrance of the bar, disappearing into the night.

Noelle finally stood up from the barstool, stepping towards me, and I took a deep breath. "So, um... I'm sorry you had to see that," she said, sniffling. "Thank you again for the help." She just blinked, and I could tell that even though she had sobered up a little bit, she hadn't fully processed what had just happened.

"No problem," I nodded. "Are you sure you're okay?"

Noelle's eyes bore into mine for a long moment. "Did you mean what you said?" she said eventually. "Are we friends?"

Oh, God. In that moment, I forgot how drunk she was, and I noticed how her voice wobbled as she spoke; little tears still trickling down her face. She sniffled again, and I resisted the urge to wipe away her tears.

"You tell me, Noelle," I said softly.

"Well, I've never been friends with any professors before, but I think I might like to give it a try—" She swayed on her heels, and I darted forward to catch her, ending up with her in my arms, peering up at me with her huge eyes.

I was touching her. *Holy shit*, I was touching her, and I couldn't help but notice how right she felt in my arms. I wanted to tuck her in and pull her in tight to a hug, but I knew we weren't there *yet*, so I loosened my hold and guided her backward.

"Woah there, sweetheart," I said, placing her back on the stool. "I think it's time for you to get home."

Her blonde friend nodded and dug through her purse to get her car keys out. "I can take her home, the rest of you can stay here—"

"Oh, no," I said, surprised by the sudden calmness in my voice. "I think you've all had a little too much to drink. I can take Noelle home; I live right near campus." They all raised an eyebrow at me, but I insisted: "I only had one beer tonight, and I'm not going to do anything, I promise." I held my hands up. "I just want to see Noelle back home safe. So, you all stay and have fun, or get yourselves home *safely*, but I'm going to get her home."

I watched Noelle as she continued gnawing on her bottom lip. "Is that okay with you, Noelle?" I asked her, waiting for her nod of confirmation before I turned back to her friends, daring them to say anything else. As long as she was okay with it, that was enough for me.

I knelt in front of her on the barstool, slowly placing my palm on her knee. *Goddamn*, I was touching her again. Why could I not stop myself from touching her? "Noelle, what dorm are you in so I can get you home?" She nodded, leaning in to whisper the name into my ear.

"What was your name again?" her black-haired friend asked me as I focused on Noelle in front of me. On her tear-stained, freckled face, and brown eyes swimming with emotion. On her ginger locks, that were spilling onto her face. I had to resist pushing them back behind her ear. And of that damned black dress, which gave the other assholes in the bar insight into a little too much of her curves, her cleavage almost spilling out the top.

"I'm Matthew," I said, addressing the three other girls. "I'm a professor at UP."

"*Oh*, you're—" the blonde one exclaimed, before the brunette one, Gabrielle, elbowed her.

"Sorry about her," Gabrielle apologized. "This is Charlotte." She indicated to the blonde. "And Angelina." She waved towards the black-haired girl. "We're Noelle's best friends. If you're going to take her home—" I nodded, and she acknowledged that I wasn't going to budge on this— "Can you text us when she's home safe? Normally she doesn't get this drunk, but you're right, I think she had just a little too much tonight…"

"Sure, of course. I'll text you from her phone when she's back safe."

"Don't fuck with our best friend, or we'll find you," Angelina added, crossing her arms over her chest. She was kind of intimidating, but I liked that she cared that much about Noelle.

"I don't plan on it," I assured them, and then I offered Noelle, still way too drunk and very clearly out of it, my hand. And when she slipped her hand into mine, leaning onto my arm and letting me steer her out of the bar? Well… it just felt like this was exactly the place I was supposed to be tonight.

I helped her into the front seat of my truck and buckled her in. Before I had even crossed back over to the driver's side, her head was resting against the window, eyes closed. I chuckled and began driving to campus. I left the music off as Noelle slept quietly and drove in silence to her dorm building, which was luckily only a few short miles from the bar.

"Noelle," I called as I pulled into the spot in front of her dorm building—an all-girls dorm, several floors high—and tried to gently rouse her awake. When she didn't stir, I got out and went around to open the passenger side door. "Noelle," I said, trying to resist my urge to touch her again to wake her up. She mumbled a little under her breath, but I soon came to the realization that she was not going to wake up, so I did the only thing left to do. I scooped her into my arms. Feeling like I was violating a bit of her privacy, I dug through her purse till I found her university ID card, her phone, and her keys inside. I very well wasn't going to be able to let myself into the dorm with my ID, after all.

As I walked across the grass towards her building, she stirred in my arms slightly, only to bury her head further in my chest. "You're so warm," she murmured into my shirt. "Can I stay here forever? Feels like heaven."

I laughed, hoping she wouldn't remember this in the morning, because I was quite sure she would die of embarrassment knowing she said that to me. But I couldn't help but think about the beautiful blush she would have if she did realize it, and it made me smile.

As I got to the door, I brushed a piece of hair off her cheek, tucking it behind her ear, and placed a small kiss on her forehead. "I know, sweetheart," I said, feeling it too. "I know."

Goddamn. When she had asked me if I was her friend at the bar, all I wanted to say was yes. Yes, I wanted to be her friend. I wanted to be so much more than that because I couldn't deny how attracted I was to her. But a relationship, was I even ready for that? I didn't know. I just knew that I wanted to be with her, to get to know her, to see her every day, and have her smile at me. And for her to never let another man touch her again.

As I slipped inside the front door, the dorm was decorated just how I imagined it would be—somehow, I could feel Noelle's influence in all of the displays around the lobby—I was grateful for the girl who sat at the desk and noticed me holding Noelle.

Because I honestly had no idea where I was taking her or where her room was.

"Oh!" the girl exclaimed.

"Hi," I said, sheepishly, making sure to keep my voice low. "Can you point me to Noelle's apartment? She had a little too much to drink, and well…" I did my best imitation of a shrug, unable to raise my shoulders fully with Noelle in my arms still.

The brown-skinned girl nodded. "Right. I'll take you there." She eyed Noelle in my arms. "I'm Hazel, by the way. Noelle's Assistant Hall Director."

I gave her a little nod. "Nice to meet you, Hazel."

"It's right here," she said, coming to a stop in front of the door. "You have her key, right?" I held it up in my hand.

"Thank you," I whispered. "I'll see you on the way out."

Hearing that seemed to have made her a whole lot more comfortable with me leaving Noelle in her room, so she gave me a nod of approval before turning around and going back to the desk.

I sighed as I looked around the small apartment. Honestly, it was bigger than I thought: a living room, a small kitchen, and then what I assumed was her bedroom and bathroom off to the side. Looking around, I knew how much it screamed *Noelle*: trendy but with stacks of books everywhere—she just seemed like that kind of girl, especially after she told me *I like words*. As I tucked her in, I wondered at the implications. At how weird it felt to be in her bedroom, like this. Before I left I made sure she was laying on her side and put a trash can by her bedside on the floor in case she had to throw up during the night.

I quickly opened up her phone in my hand, thankful that it didn't have a passcode, and sent a quick message to the group chat that included Gabrielle, Charlotte, and Angelina.

> Hey, it's Matthew. Got Noelle home safe and all tucked into bed. I'm leaving now, if one of you wants to come to check on her in the morning.

The name was *Best Friends Book Club,* and I had to admit, it made me smile. It was so very Noelle. Finally, I plugged her phone into the cord on the nightstand, reading the response as the screen lit up.

> GABBI
> thank you so much, matthew.

I dropped a small kiss on Noelle's forehead as I whispered good night, shutting the door behind me as I walked out and waved goodbye to Hazel at the front desk.

It wasn't until long after I had left the dorm building that I realized I had forgotten to tell *my* friends why I was leaving. Oh well. They'd understand.

I hoped.

On second thought, this was probably not going to end well.

CHAPTER 9
Noelle

I wasn't sure how I managed to drag myself to the library the next morning. All I knew is that I felt like utter crap. I was pretty sure the pounding migraine was my punishment for all of the shots I did the night before. I reached up to rub at my throbbing temples before taking another big gulp of water.

I wasn't just embarrassed—I was *mortified*. When Hazel had knocked on my door in the morning, checking in on me and making sure I was okay, I just blinked at her. And then it all came rushing back. I groaned into the pillow for a long minute, before I reluctantly dragged myself into the shower to try and wash off the shame and humiliation of the night before, and ordered myself straight to the library so I could get work done before my night class.

But of course, despite all of that, I was still staring at a blank document on my laptop as I chewed on the top of a pen cap. I wanted to crawl back into bed and not come out for a week. No, a month. No—the rest of the school year. No—

"You look confused," a strong voice called out, pulling me from the fog I had found myself in.

There, standing in front of me, peering down at the book in

my hands, he stood. Matthew Harper, who saw me drunk off my ass last night. *Great.*

Not only that, but he had carried me into my room. Which meant two things. One: this beautiful, attractive man had seen my bedroom. And two: I had been in his arms.

Yeah, I couldn't forget the fact that he had seen me at my most vulnerable and then had taken me all the way home either. No biggie. Or that Hazel saw all of it and gave me a *look* in the morning when she knocked on my door. Why had I never asked her what she was about to say at that mixer a few weeks ago? It suddenly popped into my mind now.

Was I still staring at him without saying anything? Oh—yeah.

He cleared his throat. "Hey, Noelle. How are you feeling?" He crouched down next to my chair.

"Hi, Professor Harper."

"Please," he insisted. "We're friends now, aren't we? You can call me Matthew."

Oh—*right*. The other declaration I hadn't even begun to unpack yet. Him saying—no, asking, if we were friends. I think I told him I'd like to be. I wanted to bury my face in my hands. Could this be any more mortifying?

"I..." I looked into his eyes—his beautiful, blue eyes—and then I blushed, remembering the way I had buried my face into his chest as he carried me. "Oh god, I'm so sorry about last night. I didn't realize how much I had to drink, and I was completely inappropriate."

"Noelle. Please, don't worry about it. I was happy to help."

"But I—"

He scowled at me, and I didn't finish that thought, closing my mouth and mumbling, "Thank you," under my breath as I awkwardly fumbled with the book in my lap.

"How much do you remember from last night?"

Everything, I wanted to say. How right it felt in your arms, most definitely.

"Not *that* much," I said, timidly, before lowering my voice into a whisper. "Just... you almost got in a fight over me. I didn't dream that up, did I? Oh, and I think I *may* have fallen asleep in your truck." I winced. I wanted to apologize for it again, but I didn't think he'd let me.

I didn't mention how when I had woken up, I had been secure in his arms, almost sure I was dreaming. Or how I hoped that I hadn't said out loud what I thought I'd said out loud. Either way, the damage was done. Despite all of that, despite everything he had seen, me drunk and freaked out, Matthew was still here, checking on me.

How did he know I was here, anyway?

"Are you checking up on me?" I asked with a raised eyebrow, "How did you know I was here?"

He chuckled. "Noelle. I'm not stalking you; I promise. One of my undergrad classes was in the library today so we could do research. I just happened to see you hard at work as I was heading out, and I figured I'd see how you were doing." His hand moved like he was going to reach out towards me, but he didn't, and I kept my hands in my lap, holding onto the book.

"Oh. Okay. Well, I'm all right. Feel free to continue on your way then," I said, waving him away, thinking for some reason that he would actually leave.

He didn't. Of course. Instead, he slid into the seat next to me, peering at my laptop screen. "What are you working on?" Matthew asked, looking closely like he was trying to read the words on my laptop screen. If there had been any—which there weren't because I was still staring at a blank document— "You looked like you were spacing out. Is there anything I can help with?"

"You... you want to help me?" I asked, shocked even though it shouldn't have surprised me.

"Sure," he shrugged. "Why not? I don't have anywhere to be for a while."

"Okay then," I said, surprising myself. I hardly ever asked for help, and normally wouldn't accept it. But there was something about this man that I found myself *wanting* to say yes to. Why? I couldn't explain it.

He tapped the book in my hands. "So, what is it that you're working on?" Matthew asked me again.

"Part of my job as Hall Director is to teach a class on leadership to the RAs, so I'm just trying to get my lesson planned out for this week. I just haven't figured out exactly what I want to talk about yet." I fixed a thoughtful expression on my face. "I mean, I guess I know what I'm supposed to talk about." I pulled up the general overview for the class, pointing at that week's topic on the document.

"Okay, sounds fun," he announced. "Want to walk me through your ideas? I can help you narrow it down if that helps."

"Well..." I hesitated.

Matthew, who I was finding I was quickly growing comfortable being around, gave me a small, comforting smile. "What do you have to lose, right?"

"You're right," I said, feeling surprised at how easily he reassured me and calmed my nerves. I went over my few ideas, and he nodded along, listening with rapt interest, never once taking his eyes off me. I couldn't believe how present he was in the moment. Asked me questions, supplying me with other topics that were related, things that would help flesh out the presentation.

Once I finished talking, he sat back in the chair and flashed me a grin. "Do you know what you want to talk about now?"

I couldn't help the smile that spread over my face. "Yeah. I do. Thanks." I looked at him thoughtfully. "You're surprisingly good at this, you know."

"At what?" he chuckled. "Giving advice? I do it all the time. I still work as a consultant for businesses, you know."

"Oh." That made sense. "But no, I meant—you told me once that you were good with numbers. But you're good with words, too."

Matthew gave me a little smirk. "I read a lot as a kid."

"I see," I said, wondering why that surprised me. It wasn't like

I knew much about him. Sure, we had talked for little bits of time, here and there, but I didn't really *know* him. But I wanted to. Because underneath the beautiful exterior and the athletic build, he was witty, brilliant, and seemed to really *care*. Matthew could have been a professional athlete, even, based on his height and body tone, but instead, here he was... as an academic. And he was always surprising me.

"Don't look so surprised, Noelle."

"Who said I was surprised?" I fixed a little scowl on my face, but I didn't mean it. It just seemed like more fun to mess with him.

He reached over and touched the tip of my nose. "That little expression of yours did."

And *oh my God*, did he just touch my nose? "I—" I just looked at him, a little too stunned to speak.

"I loved to read growing up. I still do. I read a lot more academic journals now, of course, but I like to read a good novel when I can. Mostly science fiction and fantasy, but I branch out occasionally too."

"It's just—I *love* to read." I gushed. "I love fantasy," I blurted out, wondering if we were close enough friends for me to give him book recommendations. He probably didn't want to read the things that I did, anyway. Although... "And romance." I blushed a little.

"I know," he said, with that deep voice of his.

"What?" I squeaked.

"I saw your piles of books and your bookshelves—plus your group chat name is cute. I'm guessing you came up with it?"

Right. I forgot he saw my room. Geez, I needed to purge some books to get rid of those stacks. I nodded. "I did. The girls hated it at first, but I made it stick." I flashed him a grin. "That's what they get for starting a book club with me." I shrugged.

He laughed. "Of course they did. What books do you normally read with them?"

I looked around the room, like, *Am I being punked right now?*

Does this beautiful man want to talk about books with me? He raised an eyebrow. I cleared my throat with a cough. "Mostly romances, honestly. The last one was about two rival novelists." I nodded.

He signaled at me to keep going. "We don't have to talk about books. Really," I insisted, waving my hands at him in dismissal, "I'm sure you're busy, and I don't want to take the time from your schedule—"

"I'll always make time for you." And damn if that statement didn't make me feel all warm inside.

I could feel the warmth rushing to my face, creeping up my neck. "Are you sure?"

"Yeah." He stretched, flexing his muscles, and then placing his hands behind his head. I watched as his biceps pulled against his sweater-clad arms and willed myself to not visibly react to his body. "That's what friends do, right?"

I flushed. "About that—"

"No takebacks." He grinned. "You said you wanted to try it, this friendship thing."

"Professor Harper—"

"Matthew."

"Matthew," I repeated. Why did I like saying his name so much? "I just don't want..."

"Don't want?"

"People getting the wrong idea. Or think that something is going on when it's not. Or that we're—"

He shook his head. "I told you before, Noelle, you don't have to worry about that. You're safe with me."

I was, wasn't I?

I believed him. And a sense of calmness swept through my body at that conviction. Besides, I really did want him in my life —and even if I couldn't give in to the physical attraction I felt to him, the way my eyes always found him in a room as if I could physically feel when he entered the building—maybe I could have this. Because being around him felt right in a way that none of my relationships ever had before. "You're right." I finally said, quietly, under my breath.

"I always am."

I wanted to punch him in the shoulder for that comment, but instead, I just furrowed my brows and gave him a little glare. He laughed.

"You know, if you need help with any of the other aspects of your class, I'm always willing to help," he said as I started placing stuff back in my laptop bag in preparation for heading to class. I looked up at him.

"Really?"

"Really. I like spending time with you. And if I can help make sure you do well... well that's a reward in and of itself, isn't it?" His usually stoic-grumpy face formed into a cocky grin.

Who was this man and what had he done with his grumpy professor self? Ever since last night at the bar, he was different with me. He had called me sweetheart and cared enough about me to almost start a fight with my ex-boyfriend. And I had been drunk enough that I hadn't even noticed him at the bar till he had interjected between me and the guy who had groped my ass. Gross.

Yeesh. How had I gotten so drunk that I had even allowed that? I was normally never so crazy, so brazen, or bold. But alcohol had lowered my inhibitions and when my friends had gone to the bathroom, I had kind of... spaced out. And I was so grateful Matthew had been there to rescue me. Even more so indebted to him when he and Gabbi got Jake to leave without me having to talk to him. The whole experience was hazy in my mind, but I remembered him placing me on a barstool and the tears that spilled out of my eyes. *How embarrassing*. God.

I had to get out of there before I did or said something else as stupid as I had done yesterday. "Well, I better get to my class," I said, breaking the silence that had grown between us as I stared at him. Why was I always doing that? "I'll see you later?"

Matthew's lips tilted up into a small smile, and he nodded at me. "Sure, Noelle."

He watched as I finished stuffing all of my belongings into my tote bag, and then offered me a hand up from the table we were sitting at. "Oh. Thank you." I took his hand, readjusting my skirt as I stood.

"See you soon." He grinned.

And if his smile wasn't the best damn thing that I had seen all day.

∞

FRIENDS. I liked the sound of that more than I could properly express. I couldn't help but think about all the ways this man had gone out of his way to help me. And why? I had to face the truth: he must have liked spending time with me as much as I did with him. Those little conversations in the coffee shop, randomly seeing him all over campus—it was always the best part of my day. I couldn't stop thinking about it. About him. Because... damn it, I wanted to spend more time with him. I wanted to get to know him and hear his stories; wanted to see his face light up as he talked about things he was passionate about.

I wanted to talk with him about the book I was reading and the things I liked about it as well as the things I didn't. I wanted to share stories about the dumb things that my residents had done that day with him and have him share stories about his students with me. I wanted to feel his hand in mine, holding on tight as we walked through the cold. I wanted to know what his lips would feel like, how it would feel for him to carry me into his—

Woah, Noelle, screamed my head. *Stop getting ahead of yourself.* Friends. That's it. *You don't even want to be in a relationship, remember? No dating.* I remembered, but I felt like my once very solid reasons were slipping away. For the life of me, I couldn't figure out *why*. Maybe we could just have a physical relationship and not an emotional one, anyway? Nothing was stopping us from doing that. That didn't count as falling in love, after all.

There was also this invisible line I felt like we were toeing. I was a student, and he was a professor, no matter if I wasn't in his class or that I was also university staff, the administration would frown on it, wouldn't they?

Except... I thought about how sincere he looked when he talked to me. There was no way Matthew Harper could ever settle for a no-strings-attached relationship. That much, I was sure.

After my class, I hurried back to the dorm and found Hazel sitting at the front desk, like a cat waiting to pounce.

"Hi," I said, with what was the guiltiest expression ever to exist on my face, I was sure.

"I think," Hazel started, getting up from the desk and pacing over towards me, "that it is time for us to talk, young lady."

I scoffed. "You know I'm older than you, right?"

She narrowed her eyes. "Not. The. Point."

I sighed. "Okay. Let me have it."

Hazel glanced around, making sure that there were no girls around when she pulled me into the chair next to hers behind the desk. "Professor Harper?!" She exclaimed.

I shrugged.

"Noelle. He literally *carried* you home last night, and all you're giving me is a shrug?? What happened?"

"Well..." Fuck. I had to tell her the whole story, didn't I? "I may have drunk more than I should have last night." I rubbed my temple as if it was still throbbing. "And Matthew just happened to be at the bar, and he kind of... swooped in and helped me. And then I wasn't feeling too great, so he offered to bring me home." I knew I was blushing, but I trudged on anyway. "I sort of fell asleep in his car, hence why he carried me inside." I buried my face in my hands. "Oh, Hazel, I'm so embarrassed."

"Don't be," she laughed. "You've done the impossible."

"What?" I jerked my head up, looking at her. "What *impossible*?"

"You've broken Matthew Harper's icy reputation."

I raised an eyebrow. "He's always been nice to me—"

"Exactly. But do you know how he is around other people?"

I shook my head. I hadn't seen it, had I?

"Cold. Distant. Grumpy."

"Oh. Well, I knew the last one. Sometimes it takes a bit to get him to smile." But it hadn't been as hard lately...

"He hasn't dated a single woman since he started teaching here, Noelle. Seriously, he's never shown interest in anyone." Hazel smirked at me, and I had the urge to tug on one of her tight curls. "Not till *you*."

"Oh my god. Nothing is going on, seriously. We're just friends. We've just been running into each other a lot around campus, I promise."

"Is that all you want to be, though? Just friends?"

I nodded. "Yeah." It was, wasn't it?

"Okay," she said, but it was clear she didn't believe me.

"What?"

"It's just... I saw you two at that mixer. There were literal sparks. I think you should give him a shot."

I made a face. "I don't even know that he's interested."

"Oh, believe me," she grinned, her whole face lighting up with a mischievous expression. "He's interested."

"Well." I shrugged, pretending I wasn't feeling anything out of the ordinary.

"When are you seeing him next?"

"Oh. Um. I'm not sure. We didn't really talk about it. I don't even have his number."

Hazel just gave me a look. "Please, *please* tell me you're going to do something about that."

"I—maybe. I don't know, I haven't thought that far yet, Haze. I'm still freaking out over him finding me feeling like crap in the library today."

"Oh my god," she squealed, "he what?!"

I proceeded to explain to her exactly what happened earlier in the day, and she couldn't stop grinning.

"Oh, Elle. That man is down for you *bad*."

"What? No."

"Yes." She nodded, vigorously.

I sighed and sat there, defeated, till I finally mumbled something and got up to trudge towards my room. I had things to work on, sure—but I couldn't get him out of my mind.

And for some reason, I knew it needed to be me. That he wouldn't push me, that I had to make the first move.

There were so many reasons I wanted this. Because I couldn't help the way my heart fluttered when I saw him walk through the door—always wearing his sweater and button-up combo. I needed to just plunge into the icy waters. My heart had been broken in the past, sure, but this? This was friendship. And it wasn't too forward to give him my number the next time I saw him, right? That wouldn't be *weird*. It would be... normal.

For us to talk more—to *really* be friends.

Would it change everything?

But then I realized, who cares? I had never felt this way before, and all I knew was that I didn't want this to end. He *had* said we were friends. And friends did swap phone numbers.

I tried to remember how everything started with Jake. But I had been young, ignorant, and naive back then. We had class together, friends in common, and when he asked me out one day, I had just said yes. And I fell into something with him that felt... comfortable. Until it didn't, and I ran back to Portland with my tail between my legs.

But... It shouldn't have been long enough for Matthew's smile to affect me like this, I thought with a frown. For his conversations to have meant so much to me. I clutched the collar of my sweater and inhaled deeply, trying to bring myself back to my senses. Trying to reign in my heart, beating way faster than it should have been. Stressing about what I had just done, and how terribly this could go if I had read everything wrong.

It seemed like the one time I was actually desperate to run into Matthew, I hadn't seen him around. And since the last week had been so swamped with classes, I hadn't even been able to stop by his office to say hi.

And then, suddenly, it was Friday, and I was staring at my white board, where *lunch with mom* was written in big red letters. Oh, yeah. I tugged on a nice dress, already dreading the event. You see, I *loved* my mom. She was great—really. A huge support system in my life, especially considering it was just her. But still... she was constantly second-guessing my choices, and sometimes it just wore me down.

Because as much as she was glad I was back in Portland, she also didn't understand why I hadn't gotten married and settled down yet, and it wasn't like I could explain to her that I wasn't sure I was ready—wasn't sure I would ever be ready, honestly—to date again after Jake so *thoughtfully* and thoroughly broke my heart. I had tried to put the jagged pieces of my heart back together as best I could, and I had come to accept that I didn't want to be loved like that again. I didn't want to be vulnerable enough to let someone have enough of me that I could feel that level of devastation ever again.

Yep. I stabbed my fork into the pile of noodles as I listened to my mom. "You know, Noelle, sweetie, you can always be a teacher —" she started to ramble. This again? I groaned. "What? I've always told you that you would make a good teacher."

"Mom, I got a degree in English for a reason. I don't want to *teach*; I've never wanted to teach. And I'm sorry that has always been your dream for me, but it isn't mine, okay?" I frowned. And I definitely didn't want to teach middle or high school. I resisted making a face.

Why did I agree to this, again? I was trying to wrack my brain to remember, but I had definietly been bamboozled into it. There was no sound reason that I would have agreed to a lunch date from hell with my mother if I was in my right mind.

See, here's the thing. As I said, I loved her. I really did. She was a great mom growing up, and she cared about me, I knew she did. I'd never had to question that. And she went through hell raising me on her own, so sometimes I found myself forgiving her little transgressions. Like her insistence on knowing best what I wanted for *my* life.

"I'm sorry," she said, directing my thoughts back to her. "I know. I just worry about you, you know?" My mother, Christina, frowned at me. "And ever since you came back from New York, it's like... You won't open up to me anymore. Are you still working on your book? How's that going?"

I shrugged. How did I explain that between my job as hall director, all the other little things I juggled on campus and the classes I was taking for my masters, I hardly had time to do anything fun? To even breathe, let alone work on a book. Sure, there was a word document on my computer that I opened and worked on every so often, but I couldn't have even told her when the last time I wrote 5 words on it was. "Honestly, it's on pause right now. I haven't had time, and I've been trying to focus all of my efforts on the new semester with grad school—it's my last, you know?"

She nodded, sipping her wine glass as she took another bite of the salmon on her plate. "That makes sense. Are you enjoying your last few classes?"

I felt relieved. This line of questioning I could handle. "I really am," I smiled. "It's been... really good so far." I trailed off. It was more than just a good semester or good classes. It was also... Him. And where did I start? I wasn't going to share with my mom the little butterflies that I got when I saw him with her. Because she would take it the wrong way and wouldn't understand. Honestly, I still wasn't sure I even understood it. "Everything is really great. I've got Hazel still, and she's awesome, and I feel like maybe things are finally looking up for me." I continued babbling on about some of the things I was learning, but I couldn't help the smile that spread across my face.

And what if some of it was Matthew? I bit my lip as I thought about it. Sitting in his class had been more than just interesting. Did I know what was going on? Absolutely not, but it had made me realize how kind and genuine he was as a professor, even under the grumpy exterior he wore during class. And so what? Was there something wrong with that? Or how he had taken me home when I was drunk and then made sure I was feeling okay the next day?

"And did you meet someone, hm?" My mom cut into my thoughts.

"What?" I stammered, feeling like my tongue was caught in my throat.

"Noelle. I think I know my daughter enough to know what that blush on your cheeks means." God damn—I needed to get these cheeks of mine under control. Was I that easy to read, like a book? It seemed like everyone in my life knew what I was thinking lately.

I held up my hand to my face, indeed finding my cheeks warm. Oh, God. I groaned. "You can't be serious right now, Mom." I wished I could bury myself in the pasta dish that I had ordered, instead of having to stare down at my mom and try to deny that I was thinking about him.

And suddenly, lunch just got a whole lot more fun. For someone. Just not for me.

"Well? Who is he? Is he nice? And attractive?" My mom was never one to beat around the bush.

"I, well... erm... yes?" I diverted my eyes away from her into my lap, staring down at my textured tights and the heeled boots I had chosen for the occasion.

"And?"

"And what, Mom? I'm not looking to date. Nothing's going to happen with anyone." Maybe ever. No matter how good-looking Matthew Harper and his stupid rolled-up sleeves were.

"You never know," she shrugged at me with a smile on her

face. "Stranger things have happened. When I met your dad, he—"

Oh, here we go again. "Mom." I cut her off before she could retell me the same story I had heard a million times during my life. "I know, Mom, I know. You never expected him to walk into your life or your college dorm room, and even though he was a senior and graduating that year, you just knew—"

My mom shot me her best mom look, the one that said *shut up, I'm trying to make a point here.* "I'm just saying, Noelle. Expect the unexpected and sometimes things will happen that you don't expect. And it's not like you're an eighteen-year-old with your whole life in front of you. You're twenty-five, sweetie. Don't you want to settle down and get married soon? Sometimes I think you're not even trying to put yourself out there!"

"Maybe I *don't* want to," I muttered under my breath. It didn't even feel like she treated me like I was an adult most of the time.

"What?" she said. "You still have your whole life to look forward to, I promise, even with a husband. You have plenty of time to figure everything out. Even if you don't want to be a teacher—" I shot her a look, and she promptly changed gears. "I'm sure you'll figure out what you *do* want to do soon. And then you'll find a nice man, settle down, and give me some grandkids, okay?"

"Mom," I groaned. "After Jake… I just don't think I'm ready to date anyone right now. And I'm not getting married. I don't think love is for me." I didn't want to go through that heartbreak again. I just couldn't let someone else have my heart just to rip it out of my chest cavity.

"Nonsense." My mother just scoffed at me. "Love is for everyone. And you never know… maybe you've already met the right person and you just don't know it yet." I raised an eyebrow at her, and she smirked. I could see the wheels turning in her head, and I opened my mouth to shut her down, but she waved me off.

"I don't... I can't get left again." I said quietly, under my breath so I wasn't sure if my mom even heard.

No matter what she said, no matter what I was even feeling... yeah, that wasn't going to happen. So I wasn't going to tell her about Professor Matthew Harper and my stupid crush on the man. Because no matter how gorgeous he was and how much I wanted to see him smile at me all the time, he and I weren't going to be some crazy love story, some fated pair who fell in love.

So what if I thought he was attractive? I bet the whole school did.

But I certainly wasn't going to act on it.

Not ever.

CHAPTER 10
Matthew

"Bryan?" I asked, picking up my phone as it rang. My scantrons were done, I had taught my class for the day, and I was finally settling back down at my desk to answer some emails before I went home for the day.

"Hey, Matt." As soon as I heard his voice, I realized I had forgotten to call him after everything that happened.

"Sorry for leaving without telling you the other night, I just—"

"Don't worry about it, man. We all saw what happened at the bar. She got home safe?"

I closed my eyes. "Yeah. She had a little too much to drink, and I don't think her friends realized how much until it was too late."

"Good thing you were there to swoop in like her knight in shining armor."

I scoffed. "She's not some princess from a book, Bryan." And I'm wasn't her knight. Or her prince. Just her friend.

"Sure. Anyway, drinks got cut off early, but Cole and Tanner got us all tickets to one of the home games next month if you can come. They got you an extra ticket, too, so you can bring a date if you want and not be the third wheel, like always. If you want to bring that girl—"

"We'll see," I interrupted with a grunt. When was the last time I had taken someone out on a real date? I had been so busy the last few years. And had there been anyone I even wanted to take on a date, anyway? Not in a long time. But now... "And I'm not your third wheel. Geez. Way to rub it in that all my best friends are in serious relationships but me."

"Hey man," he laughed, "I'm just saying. If you had a girlfriend, it would make all of our hangouts a hell of a lot more fun for everyone. Elizabeth keeps wanting to do couples shit, but I hate planning stuff without my best friend. So..." I didn't mention the fact that she was seven months pregnant, which had severely limited our group activities these days. It's not like we did much besides hang out and watch sports games or go get meals, anyway.

"Yeah, yeah, yeah. Don't hold your breath. Anyway, life's been so crazy these last few years, and I haven't had time to date."

"It's always something with you," Bryan wheezed into the phone like he couldn't believe my excuse. Maybe he was right. It was a rather lousy one. "Next, you're going to tell me you're going to wait until you have tenure before you try to find someone. You're gonna be like thirty-five before you get married at this rate."

"Whatever." I rolled my eyes. "I can't help it if I haven't found the right person yet. And... I can't help it if I want what my parents had."

They had been so in love with each other, and my sister and I had always known it. I had always felt their love for each other and us, every day. And then... they were ripped from us way too soon, and Tessa had to grow up without them. It still hurt to think of all the milestones of ours they missed, but at least now it was a dull ache instead of a constant sharp pain. And I didn't want to love someone, to get so attached to them, just to have my entire life ripped away in one moment. It was a risk I wasn't sure I wanted to take.

Except maybe, with Noelle... my brain seemed to whisper to me. *What if?* Was she worth the risk? No one had ever been before.

"I know, man," Bryan's voice lowered. "And I know how much you miss them, too. Listen, you never talk about it..."

"It's okay." I tried to brush it off. Even after all this time, it still hurt to talk about. Even with Tessa, we hardly mentioned our parents. And after our grandparents died, we were all we had left. And it was just another reminder of the hole in our hearts that would never be repaired every time someone brought it up.

"We're always here if you want to. All of us," he offered, and I knew it was true, but I just shook my head, even though he couldn't see me through the phone. I chose to bottle those emotions up inside. In some ways, I had to—I really didn't know what would happen when they all spilled out.

"I appreciate it, man. Listen, I gotta get some work done, but I'll talk to you soon, okay? We can plan dinner soon. You could all come over here, I've got almost everything set up at the new house. And I'm sure Snowball would appreciate someone besides me to give her some love too."

"Sure," Bryan chuckled. "We'll figure out a day soon. I'll text you."

"Talk to you later," I said, hanging up the phone and slumping back against my desk chair, thinking about everything Bryan had said.

About the basketball game. And bringing a date. I needed to *find* a date. But fuck if there wasn't only one woman who popped up in my mind. Was it crossing the line entirely to ask her to come with me?

It wasn't weird to ask your friend to go to a game like that with you, was it? Because that's what we were—friends. Yeah.

I took a deep breath as I refocused my attention on the computer.

Friends. But was that all I wanted us to be?

∽

Somehow, over the last three weeks, I'd gotten used to seeing Noelle everywhere. And now, every flash of red hair, every cup of coffee, and pastry reminded me of her.

And it had been days since I saw her in the library. Days since I talked to her, and I thought I might be losing my mind.

Had I scared her off? I didn't think so, but then here I was, going out of my mind thinking about her.

And then—finally. There she was, in all her glory, standing in the middle of the quad and squinting up at the sky, as if she was trying to decide if it was going to rain or not today.

"Noelle!" I almost shouted, finding myself walking quickly to catch up with her.

She gave me a warm smile. "Matthew. Hi."

"Hi." I grinned back. "It's been a few days."

"Missed me that much, huh? I mean I know I'm *unforgettable*, but..." Noelle laughed.

It was good to see her like this. Flirting and laughing. Had she gotten more comfortable being around me? Normally she was always blushing, and while I liked that, I thought I liked this version of her even more. I wasn't going to look too much into it, because all I knew was, she was here, standing in front of me, and looking absolutely gorgeous even in her t-shirt dress and a long, chunky cardigan.

So I couldn't be faulted for going for it, really. "Do you want to—Do you want to have dinner with me tomorrow?"

She smiled. And then her smile dimmed. "*Oh*. Oh no, I can't."

"What?" I frowned.

Noelle bit her lip, looking up at me as she played with her hands. "You see, I sort of already have plans."

I just blinked at her. "Oh." A date? Why was I so worried she was going to tell me she was going on a date?

"I kind of... promised my residents that we'd take a field trip —" She stopped and thought to herself. "Well, maybe field trip isn't the best word, but anyway, we rented a bus and I'm taking a whole bunch of my girls to the zoo." Noelle pushed a wavy strand of her red hair behind her ear and peered up at me as if she was wondering what I would say.

Hell, I was wondering what I was going to say. The *zoo*? I raised an eyebrow. A bunch of college students wanted to go to the zoo? And why did I... "What if I..." It came out before I could stop myself.

Noelle looked at me expectantly.

"What if I come with you? I'll be good company, I promise." I would have gotten down on my knees and begged, but she didn't need to know that. I just wanted to spend more time with her, even if it was crazy. Although I found that I didn't care. Even if she was still a student here, there was something there that I couldn't explain. A need to be with her.

"You... you actually want to come with me?" Noelle raised her eyebrow. "To the zoo. With a bunch of underclassmen?"

I nodded. What the hell—I really did.

"Has anyone ever told you you're insane?" she asked me.

I couldn't help but laugh. "No. I think you'd be the first."

"Well, in that case..." she grinned at me.

"So, do you have room for one more?"

She blinked. "Oh, you were serious. Well... um. Yeah. I think we can squeeze you in." Then she considered something. "If all of my girls spend the whole time ogling you, though, we might have a problem." Noelle winked.

Were my cheeks warm? I thought they might be. I hoped the back of my neck wasn't all splotchy in the way that it got when I was embarrassed, but from the way she was looking at me, well... I rather thought that it was.

"Oh my god," Noelle gasped. "Are you blushing?"

"Shut up," I mumbled, shoving my hands in my jacket, and trying not to make eye contact with her. But I couldn't help it, because this was Noelle, and all of my senses were attuned to her.

And I knew my eyes had dropped down to her lips—pink and full and totally kissable, but I didn't move from the spot where I was very rooted into the ground. I couldn't.

I cleared my throat. "Yes, I would very much like to accompany you and your residents this weekend. If it's okay with you."

Noelle beamed. And that was when I realized—this girl was the sun. And I wanted to bathe in her warmth. "I'd love that. But seriously, fair warning, they can get a little... loud sometimes." She winced, and a small laugh escaped from my lips.

"I think I'd like to see that," I said, lips tilted up in a smile.

"What?" She put her hands on her hips. "A bunch of crazy undergrads?"

"No," I shook my head, stepping closer to her, almost to the point where I'd be whispering in her ear. "You in action." I said, and when she looked up at me, that lovely grin affixed on her face, I knew this was going to be fun. "It's only fair, you know, after you crashed my class."

"I didn't—" she huffed. "Okay, well. Bus leaves at nine am sharp tomorrow morning. We'll meet in front of the dorm." She pointed a finger at my chest. "Don't be late."

I nodded. "I won't be."

"For some reason, I believe you." She then pulled something out of her pocket and handed it to me.

I looked down at the slip of paper, at the writing that was on it. "In case you need it, or whatever," Noelle said.

"Had you already..."

She looked sheepish. "Look—it's normal to give friends your phone number. So. I may have been planning on coming to find you if I didn't see you." Noelle shrugged. "Don't make a big deal about this. It's not like I was going to *stalk* you."

I laughed. "No, because I'm the one who always does the stalking, right?"

She nodded solemnly like this was a very serious topic. "Exactly."

"I'm glad I ran into you," I smiled.

"Me too." Noelle flashed me another one of her sunshine-filled smiles. "I'll see you in the morning, alright? Bundle up, sounds like it's going to be chilly tomorrow. But hopefully it won't rain." She crossed her fingers.

"Alright," I nodded in response, and then she was off, shouting a quick, "Bye!"

And that was when I realized, standing in the middle of the quad, what exactly I had signed myself up for tomorrow.

A day with Noelle, sure—but also a day with dozens of her residents. And, potentially, students.

Hopefully none of *mine*.

CHAPTER 11
Noelle

Hazel was going to kill me. There was absolutely no way of getting around that. Because I had just sat in front of her, only a few days before, telling her there was absolutely no way anything was going to happen between Matthew Harper and myself... And now he was coming on our little zoo trip with us.

I groaned as I walked back to the dorm, already hitting myself for saying yes. I was going to spend eight-plus hours with the man and a few dozen freshmen and sophomores.

"Hey, Noelle," Hazel greeted me, looking up from the textbook in her lap as I plopped down next to her on a couch in the lobby area.

"Hi." I sank into the cushions, letting my bag fall to the carpet at my feet.

She eyed me rather suspiciously. "What's up with you?"

"Well. Uh." I bit my lip. "I may or may not have invited someone along for the zoo trip tomorrow."

"Noelle!" Hazel exclaimed. "The bus is already full—"

"I know, I know. And it's fine, that's not a problem. He can just share my seat, it's just that—"

"Wait a sec." She narrowed her eyes at me. "*He*? Oh, Noelle, who did you invite?"

I muttered his name under my breath.

"What was that?"

"Matthew Harper," I said, giving her my best innocent smile.

"Noelle! You little minx!"

"It wasn't my *goal*. I was just going to give him my number, and then he asked if I wanted to get dinner tomorrow, and then I told him I had plans, and he sort of... asked if he could come."

"You're bringing a *date* on our field trip?"

"It's not a date!"

"And what did you tell him about dinner, anyway?"

"Oh." I shook my head. "It didn't come up again."

"But do you... you know." She raised an eyebrow. "Want to?"

"Get dinner with him?"

Hazel nodded.

I ran my hands through my hair, separating the wavy strands. I hadn't styled it today, so it was wavy and frizzy, all-natural. "I don't know, Haze. I feel like there are some things in life that once you do them... you can't quite go back." She looked at me, the question evident on her face. I just sighed. "I think going out with Matthew Harper is one of them." I picked at the hem of my t-shirt dress, thankful that the weather was warming up slightly so I could wear a little bit more of my wardrobe.

"What do you mean?"

"You know those people, who you like—like, you really like, but you know that they'll ruin you for all other men?" Hazel gave a little helpless roll of her shoulders and I continued. "Well, he's like that."

"And that's bad because...?"

"Because I'm not looking to fall in love," I waved my hand in the air like this was some wild concept. "Because we can't."

She buried her head in a pillow and groaned. "You are the most stubborn girl I have ever met."

"I'm not stubborn!" I protested, and Hazel just gave me that look. I threw a pillow at her head.

And stuck out my tongue at her, for good measure.

Who said twenty-five-year-olds had to act dignified?

Not me.

∽

IN WHAT MAY or may not have been the very best decision of my life (the jury was still out), at eight forty-five the next morning Matthew Harper came strolling into the lobby of the building, carrying what very suspiciously looked like a to-go container and two coffee cups. I raised my eyebrows at him as I stood in the middle of the room, clipboard in hand and ready to usher my 50-some-odd residents onto the bus we had rented.

"Hey." Matthew smiled at me as he approached. I handed the clipboard to one of my RAs and gave him my full attention.

"Hi. You're early."

"Well, someone said I couldn't be late, so..." he winked. And then he held out the container and the coffee cup. "I brought you breakfast. I figured you probably didn't have time to eat."

"You'd be right." I laughed. I took the box from him and then smiled as I looked inside. It was one of the cinnamon rolls from the cafeteria, covered in icing. "Thank you."

"You're always eating sweets, so I figured you'd like it," he mumbled. "And one caramel mocha." He placed the cup in my hands.

I raised an eyebrow. How had he known my coffee order?

"I pay attention," he said, defensively.

"Come on then, you," I said with a grin as I held the warm cup up to my face to take a sip. "Let's get on the bus."

After careful maneuvering, only one girl forgetting her phone in her room, and only missing three students (which could probably be attributed to oversleeping, too much homework, or deciding not to come at the last minute), we were finally on the road.

Hazel and I normally sat in the very front when we took our residents on little outings like this, but the seats next to us usually housed our bags. Today, the seat next to mine was very full—of one very tall blonde man, who was currently watching me as I drank my coffee.

"What?" I asked, looking up at him. Most of the girls on the bus were either talking to their seatmates or listening to music—including Hazel across from us—so I didn't have to worry too much about someone listening to what we were talking about.

"Nothing. I just like the way you did your hair today." Matthew smiled, and then he reached over and tugged on a strand of hair in my ponytail.

"Oh. Thank you," I said. I had done a little half-up, half-down hairdo, partially because I knew we'd be outside most of the day and I wanted to keep it out of my eyes, but also because I wanted to do something cute since I knew I'd be seeing him. And if I had also done my makeup and worn something a *little* nicer than what I normally would have worn to something like this, well, that was between me and myself.

"You know," I mused, "it almost seems unfair."

"What?"

"That you know my coffee order, but I don't know yours." I frowned. He just chuckled. "What. Don't tell me—you just drink boring old black coffee?"

Matthew laughed. "Sorry to disappoint, Noelle."

"Oh, come on. Not even milk? Or sugar?" I looked at him in disbelief, shaking my head. "Of course not, because you don't like sweets, so why would you put sugar in your coffee?" I mumbled aloud.

He chuckled, taking another sip of his drink.

I narrowed my eyes. "I just don't get what you have against cake."

"Noelle, did I ever say I was *against* cake?" I shook my head.

Matthew had that smirk on his face again, like he was enjoying this. "I do like cake. I just don't eat it regularly."

"Oh."

"But I like watching you eat sweets." He mumbled under his breath, "I think it's cute." Just quiet enough that I almost couldn't hear him—but I did.

"What's that?" I beamed. Why did his compliment, calling me cute, send a rush down my body?

"Nothing," he grumbled, turning his head towards the front of the bus.

But I didn't miss the tiniest smile on the corners of his lips or the way we were sitting so close to each other—almost touching, but not quite. If either one of us moved just a fraction of an inch closer, our thighs would be touching, and I could almost feel his warmth through my jeans.

Luckily the zoo wasn't too far from campus, and we pulled in just a few minutes later, saving me from potentially embarrassing myself even further.

Yeah, like that wasn't going to happen anyway.

After everyone assembled outside of the bus, I turned to the girls. "Alright, the zoo closes at five today, and the bus is scheduled to leave at five-thirty, so we'll meet back here at five twenty. Have fun, and if you need anything, feel free to text Rachel or Jessica." I looked at the two RAs that came with us. "I think you all should have their numbers."

We waved goodbye to everyone, and then I turned to Matthew. "What do you want to see first?"

He laughed. "I can't tell you the last time I went to the zoo."

"Wellllll," I said, tapping my index finger on my jaw as if I was thinking. "What was your favorite animal as a kid? We could start there?"

And that was how we found ourselves in the arctic exhibit, staring at the polar bears. I snapped a few photos of them rolling on the ice and swimming, and I couldn't help but look up at the big man next to me.

"They remind me of you," I giggled.

"Hm?" He said absentmindedly, tearing his eye away from the bear who was swimming through the water.

I gave him a little fake pout. "They're grumpy. And big."

He chuckled, and then he leaned down next to my ear and whispered into it, "I think I'm more like a wolf." Matthew gave me a devilish grin.

"Oh, yeah? And if you're a wolf, what am I?"

He stepped back to look over me, appraising me, and then he nodded. "A little red fox."

I laughed. "Too bad they don't have those here, huh?"

"Yeah," he nodded and then turned his head back towards the polar bears. I couldn't help but notice the grim look on his face.

"What's wrong?" I asked, placing my hand on the railing next to his. Not quite touching, but—

Matthew just shook his head, and then plastered a fake smile back on his face. "Nothing. Come on, let's go to the next one."

His hand slipped into mine, and I pulled him towards the next exhibit. Even as we looked at the penguins and I guided him around the zoo, our hands didn't drop again. It was like they were glued together. And I wondered if he was thinking what I was: was it supposed to feel so right to have his hand in mine? Had the spaces in between my fingers been made perfectly for his to slip between?

We pulled to a stop in front of the otters, and I gasped. "Oh my God. I have to send a picture to Gabbi." I looked at Matthew, trying to offer a bit of explanation. "The brunette you met at the bar? She *loves* otters. They're her favorite animal."

He nodded at me silently and watched as I snapped a few photos of the otters running around and then diving into the water, over and over, as they slid down their little slide.

"They're so cute," I said as I typed in a message to Gabbi on my phone.

> The otters say hi!

I attached a photo and a short video of them playing in the water. I was hoping if we stood here long enough, we could see them floating and holding hands. But no such luck.

"Yeah," Matthew said, but when I looked up, he was looking at *me*. "Here, give me that," Matthew said, reaching for my phone.

"What?"

He pried it out of my hands, and then surprised me by opening up the camera... and taking a selfie of us. I just kind of stared at it as he placed my phone back in my hand.

Huh? "There. Now you have a photo for my contact on your phone."

"You know," I said, putting my hands on my hips, "that does require me to actually *have* your phone number, Mr. Harper."

"Well, Miss Hastings, I think I can solve that," he said, whipping out his phone and typing something in.

My phone buzzed, and I wasn't at all surprised when I read:

> Now you have it.

I looked back up at him, and he smirked.

"Where to next, sweetheart?" Matthew asked with a smile in his eyes. I interlocked our hands again as we headed towards the African Savanna habitat, home to—among other things—the Giraffes.

We watched them from the railing together, and I squeezed Matthew's hand. I could tell he'd been in his head all day, but I didn't know why. I didn't really know that much about him when it came down to it, so I had no idea what was bothering him, I just knew I wanted to make him smile again.

I nudged him with my shoulder. "Come on, I know something I think you'll like," I said, my face breaking out into a wicked smile.

"Oh?" he asked, and when I led him in front of the Dippin'

Dots booth, he laughed. "You want to get ice cream in 50-degree weather?"

"Come on, it's like the zoo *experience*. You have to get Dippin' Dots at the zoo." I narrowed my eyes at him. "Do you even know how to have fun?"

"Of course, I know how to have fun!"

I crossed my arms. "Prove it."

He got vanilla, which I made fun of him for being boring, and I got the Birthday Cake flavor. "Mm," I said as we sat down on a bench, side by side, our thighs touching. "See, wasn't this a good idea?"

He ate a spoonful, and then looked at me with a funny face. "These are weird."

"No way." I looked at him, hand over my heart in shock. "Have you never had Dippin' Dots before? Are you sure you're from here?" I pointed my spoon at him, all serious.

He laughed. "Yes, Noelle. My family always just got regular ice cream. Like normal people."

I narrowed my eyes. "Are you implying that I'm not *normal?*" I asked, pretending to be offended. But this teasing, this playful banter... it felt right. And it was good to not have Matthew looking so sullen.

He changed the topic, spoon resting in his cup as he looked out across the zoo from where we were sitting. "You really love it here, huh?"

"Yeah. My Mom used to bring me here when I was younger," I said, looking over at him. "It's always felt a little like home to me because of it."

"And what about your dad?" he asked, and it took a moment for me to respond.

"I didn't..."

"Oh." His hand found mine and gave me a little squeeze. "I'm sorry for bringing it up. We don't have to talk about it if you don't want to."

I shook my head. "It's not that. It's just... I never got to have these moments with him." I bit my lip. "It was always just me and mom."

"I'm sorry," he said after a few beats. "That must have been hard."

"It was, and it wasn't at the same time. Like... when I was younger, I didn't know what I was missing, you know? I didn't remember having a dad to miss him. And then I guess when I got older..." I shrugged, holding my ice cream cup between both of my hands, trying not to shiver from the cold.

He just nodded, and when I finished eating my Dippin' Dots—it probably was too cold for them, but I wasn't about to admit that to him—he pulled me up to my feet, grabbed my hand, and we were back on the path again, wandering around the zoo. Lions, tigers, and bears, oh my!

"You know they have red pandas here?" I said, steering him towards the exhibit, grateful for the distraction from talking about my dad. There was so much more I wanted to say, but I didn't know if I was ready—didn't know if my heart was ready to reveal those things to him.

We walked along, and I couldn't help but smile as we watched the red pandas play; those things were so freaking *cute,* and if I audibly said *aww* a few too many times out loud, well. *Sorry.* I couldn't help it. I had always loved cute things.

As the day wound down, and after we made one final loop, leaning against each other as we watched the sunset, I couldn't help this feeling of rightness that spread through me. Like I was supposed to be here, today, with him.

We had seen some of my residents around during the day and had always awkwardly separated as I gave them a wave or stopped when they came up to ask me a question. But even then, it felt so natural. Even when two of the sophomores who had come up to us had recognized Matthew and told him that they were in his Introduction to Finance course. I may have giggled at his reaction after they left—he looked mortified. And a little pale, too, but I just pinched his side and pulled him towards the flamingos.

We stood by the gift shop, facing each other, far enough apart that we weren't touching but close enough that I could study his face, the lines of his throat, the scruff on his jaw. I had the strange urge to reach out and run my fingers over it, to trace the rough edge of his face with my hand. But I didn't, and we just stood there, transfixed. Staring at each other.

Breathing each other in.

He cleared his throat. "Thank you for today. The last time I went to the zoo, well… It's been a long time." He paused before saying, "About earlier, I want to—" but he got choked up.

"It's okay," I insisted. "You don't have to."

Matthew sighed, seeming almost frustrated with himself. "I *want* to share it with you. All of it. I'm just…" He looked so lost, eyes full of hurt and confusion and I knew whatever he felt, it was buried deep inside. I wanted him to feel comfortable sharing his fears and worries with me, but not before he was ready. Not before he realized that I wanted to keep his heart safe, that I wouldn't let anything happen to him.

"When you're ready." I hoped I reassured him with a warm smile, resisting the urge to wrap my arms around him and hug him right here in front of the zoo's gift shop.

He nodded, and when he blinked, those bright blue eyes seemed a little clearer. Matthew squeezed my shoulder in a reassuring firm grip, and I was pretty sure my insides were going to melt when he said, "You've made today so special."

Did I imagine it? Did I imagine the way his eyes darted down to my lips?

If I had been breathing deeper, if I had run my tongue across my bottom lip, dampening it—I wasn't sure I would have noticed it. Wasn't sure I would have noticed anything at that moment. Not one of my residents coming up to me, not a storm pouring down on us, not the world ending.

Because it was just Matthew and me, staring into each other's eyes, and for a wonderful moment, that was all that mattered. His beautiful, icy blue eyes, like a glacier pool, somehow told me everything I needed to know.

And I hoped mine communicated those feelings back to him. *You're safe. You're cared for. You're wanted.*

I wasn't sure why those were the feelings I had felt so strongly —because wasn't this insane? But looking into Matthew's eyes, I *felt* it.

And then I blinked, and it was over, and we were corralling all of the students back onto the bus and settling back in for our ride back to campus. Where I sat, thigh to thigh with Matthew Harper, our hands dangerously close to touching between us.

It should have been a short ride, except we hit traffic, and before I knew it, I must have dozed off against his shoulder, because his lips were brushing against my forehead as he whispered, "Noelle, we're back."

I sat up with a start, almost hitting my head against the headrest.

"Sorry," he murmured.

I shook my head, rubbing the back of my head. "It's fine." I looked at him and dropped my voice low. "I have a hard head." And then I winked at him.

What did that even mean?

I was so stupid. I could have slapped myself in the face. I sighed instead and got off the bus behind Matthew.

And if I watched his ass in those jeans as we got off... Well, no one could fault me for looking, right? His body was objectively incredible. Toned and fit and everything.

He reached out his hand as I hit the bottom step, helping me to the ground, and then the moment had finally come. Standing on the grass outside my building, where I would have to say goodnight, and our magical day would end.

I sighed again. I really didn't want it to end.

"I had fun today," he smiled. "I don't think I'll ever see Red Pandas again and not think of you."

"And do you?" I asked. He just blinked at me.

"What?"

My face split into a grin. "Think of me." I gave a wink.

He shook his head and flicked my nose. "You're so..."

"Charming? Alluring? Momentous?" I did a little flip of my hair and stood with my hands on my hips. *Beautiful? Lovely? Incredible?* I wanted to know what word was on the tip of his tongue. I wanted to hear him say it, to let it fill me with warmth from my head to my toes.

But he only shook his head and chuckled to himself. "Goodnight, Noelle. Thank you again for letting me come."

"Don't tell Hazel, but I think I had more fun with you than I would have with her," I whispered. Matthew smiled at me before he turned around and walked toward his truck.

"And Matthew?" I said, and he turned around, looking back at me. His hands were shoved in his coat pockets, and I loved the way his hair was a little windswept, a little tousled from the day we spent outside. "About dinner..."

He stiffened as if he was fearing the worst. Like I was going to reject him. Like I would actually do that. Especially after everything we had shared today.

"I'd love to." I smiled. And then, very businesslike, I stood to my full height (which was not much compared to his 6'4 stature) and said, "Tomorrow night. Pick me up at seven."

He let out a relieved breath, and the left corner of his mouth tilted up. "See you tomorrow, Miss Hastings." His eyes sparkled with amusement.

I stepped in closer, and he pulled me into his arms. And then—we were hugging. I was hugging Matthew Harper, here, in front of my residence hall. I couldn't help myself as I wrapped my arms around him and buried my face in his chest though. I took in the scent of him, like pine trees and man and something that was just *him*. It felt right in his arms, a feeling of rightness I didn't want to end yet. I didn't want to step out of his powerful hold, even as I sighed against his tall frame.

"Goodnight, Noelle," he murmured into my hair.

"Goodnight, Professor Harper," I said against his chest before he finally pulled away, taking the heat of his body with him.

Despite how cold I already felt in his absence, I didn't want to show my disappointment with our lost connection, so I just winked at him again—what the hell was wrong with me—and then spun on my heels, almost skipping back into the building.

Even when I was lying in bed later that night, I couldn't stop smiling. I was just repeating the day in my mind, every glorious moment with him. Even with all of my residents who we had seen, who had said hello to us, somehow the day just felt like ours. Like maybe it meant something more.

Just holding hands had sent a rush through my body, sparks that lit up every inch of my being. I couldn't stop thinking about what it might feel like to feel his lips against mine. The desire curled in my stomach; a want that was driving me crazy with need. Where did it come from? I hadn't been with anyone—romantically *or* sexually—in three years. And when I had tried to scratch the itch, to give into my body's needs, it hadn't felt *right*. I had never gone further than kissing, and even then, it felt wrong.

A betrayal of something I didn't even understand back then.

But now, it felt like I did. It felt like my whole life, I had been waiting for someone. Waiting for this. Waiting for him. Because when he touched me... He set my soul on fire. He filled me with warmth, and happiness, and somehow... a belief that maybe, everything might be okay again. That I could lose myself in him and never let go.

That he would never leave me.

I buried my face into the pillow, wishing I could inhale his scent one more time. I was remembering the way he had hugged me as we said goodbye, how he held me tight like I was treasured. The way I pressed myself to his chest, taking in the scent of him. The strength of him. I couldn't get over the feeling of him holding me against his body. It was like I was on fire, and I needed his touch to cool me down. Or maybe I'd let him burn me, and we could bask in this warmth together.

My phone buzzed, and I sat up to pick it up from the nightstand.

It was a text from Hazel, a little winky face emoji, and a photo attached. I opened it, and I think my breath caught in my throat. "Oh, Hazel, you sly dog."

It was us—Matthew and I—from behind. We were holding hands, completely oblivious to Hazel behind us, and I was laughing at something he said. And the look on Matthew's face? I couldn't ignore the warmth in his eyes, the smile as he looked at me that communicated things that words did not. It was beautiful, and I knew I would treasure the memory forever.

I was speechless and *breathless*, and I knew that if I wasn't careful, I was going to fall hopelessly for this man.

Maybe I already was.

CHAPTER 12
Matthew

I wanted to hold her again. Wanted to take her in my arms and never let her go.

It seemed like even if I was determined to get this girl out of my head, she was all I could think about. About the little redhead who was beautiful and passionate and whose eyes lit up when she smiled. And after we spent the day together, after she had opened herself up to me, told me about her past... I couldn't bring myself to stop it. In over a month, I had come to enjoy seeing her smile. And I was positive that I liked her in every way that I shouldn't.

I had never considered myself a very observant person, but over the last few weeks, somehow I had learned Noelle's schedule. And I couldn't help myself from going to the coffee shop in the mornings when I knew she would be there, sitting at a table, working on her laptop as she sipped her coffee and ate her morning treat. I loved sitting there, across from her, watching her work. I couldn't help it. I loved watching the way her eyes lit up when she talked with others.

She was loud, opinionated, and sometimes, a bit of a brat—but she never held back. She was never scared of asking questions or speaking her mind. And she was caring, and always went out of her way to help people. I had seen her talking to her residents, and it was so unmistakably there how much she cared for them. Noelle always seemed to know just what someone needed, and it always made me smile when you could tell someone made her day. It was almost like she was floating. Noelle just had this... joyful magic to her, and I enjoyed it more than I could describe.

That was what I liked about her so much. How she was not only beautiful but thoughtful. One-of-a-kind.

And... *then* there was her body, the sight that had driven me mad with lust from the first day. I wanted to have her, wanted to touch her. I hated how much I wanted her. God, I hated that I liked it, how every time I closed my eyes at night all I could see was her curvy body and her throwing that perfect red hair over her shoulder. The truth was, I didn't hate it at all. I loved the way she dressed—every garment hugging her curves, showing off her perfect hourglass figure, even underneath the sweaters or turtlenecks she had so often worn due to the cold climate of winter in Oregon. I loved how beautiful she was—enchanting. She was absolutely, breathtakingly, enchanting.

I knew there was something there—that she was attracted to me, that this spark between us went both ways... I could feel it. But we hadn't talked about it. And... was she even interested in me like that, anyway? I was beginning to wonder what I wanted with her, but I couldn't have any of that if she didn't want it with me.

She was still in her twenties, too young to want to be tied down to someone like me, right? To a thirty-year-old who sought stability, who couldn't help but think about settling down. Finding a wife. Noelle had her whole life ahead of her to figure out what she wanted, and well... I was pretty sure that I wasn't it.

And it was crazy, wasn't it? That I was even thinking this way because for so long, I'd been so resolutely against the idea of being with someone. I was still worried, of course, because loving someone meant that you could lose them, but the closer I got to

Noelle, the more I wondered. If this would be the one. If she was the one girl who was worth it.

But where did I even start? I hated to admit that I didn't have very much experience with this kind of thing—with relationships. Sure, I had a few casual relationships. I had been with enough women to know what I was doing in bed, but other than that, I hadn't felt like I needed to go and seek out women. I always had one excuse or another why it wouldn't work out.

And I didn't want that to happen with Noelle.

After my parents died my sophomore year of college, I just buried myself in my studies, and over time I wondered if I was simply finding reasons to not risk getting my heart broken, or if I just *wasn't interested* in the girls I met.

But then there was Noelle, standing in front of me, and I didn't think there had ever been a woman in my life that I had wanted *more* than I wanted her. Was I just interested in her because of the thrill of the chase? Or was it something more that had caused her image to be burned into my mind?

As we said goodbye, after I had hugged her and thanked her for the day, she had turned to walk back into her dorm. And I hadn't moved from my spot, just watching her walk away, until —*About dinner*, she had said.

And I didn't know why my stomach had dropped, but it had. My eyes had dropped to my feet on the pavement before I felt her stare boring into my soul. *I'd love to.* My eyes had drifted back up to hers, and the smile on her face was so big, that I almost staggered in response. Even now, I still felt what that smile did to me.

She had lifted her hand to give me a wave, and then slipped back inside her dorm.

I wished I could convince her to give me more time in the day than just these small meetings, these small instances running into her around campus that fueled me. I wanted more days like we had in the coffee shop and then on our walk afterwards. I wanted to have all of her days and all her nights, because I always, always wanted to be surrounded by her bright smile and warm demeanor.

And I wasn't sure which thought scared me more. That I wanted her by my side or that I was going to have to come up with more excuses to have her close. Something had changed that night at the bar—a newfound protectiveness, even if this girl wasn't mine. *But she felt like it!* My brain screamed.

She felt like mine *in my arms.* Something I had never—not in my thirty years of life—ever experienced. A true, genuine connection with someone. Little sparks that you felt when you touched. It was all there, for the first time, with Noelle.

Now, I just had to figure out how I could keep it. How I could have her—and keep her. Because I didn't want to let it go or give up on it.

I wanted her. No. I needed her.

∽

At seven pm sharp, I stood leaning against my truck, waiting for Noelle to walk out the door and into the chilly night air.

I couldn't wait to see her. I knew I sounded like a teenager, like all of these hormones pounding through my system must be controlling my brain, but I couldn't help it. For the first time in my life, I wasn't ignoring what my body was telling me. And it was telling me that it very much did want Noelle.

And dinner—we were going to dinner. Nothing could dim the grin taking up my face, even as I rubbed at the slight stubble on my jaw.

I probably should have specified that this was a date. Did I need to? Fuck. I was wearing a pair of nice slacks, and a button-up, and had even put on a suit jacket, but I hadn't told Noelle this was anything other than a meal, had I?

Hadn't I implied it? Hadn't *she?*

My panicking was interrupted when she came out of the

building, dressed in a tight white turtleneck sweater dress paired with tan ankle boots, and—*wow*.

"Hi." She gave me a little wave.

"Noelle. Hey." I ran my hands through my hair. I couldn't stop staring. Lord. She was so beautiful. And if I could be looking at her, why would I want to look at anything else?

She clutched the chain of her purse as she came to a stop in front of me. "So, where to, prof?" She tilted her head at me.

I cleared my throat and offered her my hand. "You'll see. Shall we?"

I hoped Noelle would like the place I had chosen to take her. I didn't know *why* it mattered, but suddenly it did. The split-second realization hit me like lightning: everything mattered to me when it came to this girl and making her happy. It was like it hadn't even occurred to my brain that there was anything I could do except to make her smile.

"Matthew." She stopped in the parking lot next to my truck. "Is this... a *date*? What are we doing here?" She gestured between the two of us.

"Do you want it to be a date?" At her hesitation, I stepped towards her, leaning in close to her ear. "Believe me, sweetheart. You'll know when it's a date, okay?" I stepped back, flashed a smile at her, and opened the door for her.

Noelle just stared up at me for a moment, cheeks a little flushed and lips looking completely kissable.

After I helped her into the passenger seat, I closed her door and then slipped into the driver's side. The whole way there, Noelle babbled about her day, her residents, and how she had gotten so much feedback that her girls had loved zoo day yesterday. I smiled to myself as I looked straight ahead—because I had to. Normally, idle chatter like this would annoy me. Small talk, inconsequential conversations—I had never really bothered with them before. I had always wanted to get down to business, get to the point.

But with Noelle? I found that I wanted to hear about every

second of her day when I wasn't with her. I was enthralled with every conversation, every meaningless story, every grin and giggle that she gave me.

I hadn't had that much time to plan—twenty-four hours had never felt so long and so short simultaneously—but I had known, for a while, where I would want to take her if anything like this ever happened.

Her eyes drifted over and met mine, and then she burrowed her face in her thick sweater, suddenly bashful. I chuckled but just kept driving silently.

Finally, we pulled up to the restaurant: my favorite little Italian place, still family-run. The atmosphere was so different from a chain restaurant: small, warm, and cozy. The lights were lit up outside and with all of the lights strung up in the trees, it felt almost romantic.

I offered Noelle my hand as I opened the door, grateful to be touching her when she slipped her hand into mine.ABishing I could do more as I helped her down, like put my hands around her waist and *lift* her. And then, maybe I would spin her around before kissing her senseless. And then—*only then*—would we go to dinner.

But it was too soon for any of that. And I thought... Even if she had noticed me staring at her lips, even if she had wanted to kiss me like I had wanted to kiss her, I didn't want to scare her off. I didn't want her to tuck her tail between her legs and run away from me.

She made a little awed sound as she observed the lights and the small restaurant that sat in the middle of the neighborhood. "This is so cute."

I kept her hand firmly in mine as we walked in and asked for a table for two. I didn't want to stop touching her. After yesterday, at the zoo... I didn't think either one of us wanted to lose this connection between us. I couldn't help it. Everything felt so right with her hand in mine. And maybe it was a little bit too soon to feel that way—I hadn't even known her for a full month. But here and now... For the first time, it was just the two of us.

When we got to the table, I reluctantly surrendered her hand, sliding into the booth across from her.

After we had placed our orders with the waitress, Noelle leaned back into the seat and gave me one of her best inquisitive stares as she crossed her arms and leaned them on the table. "So..."

I smirked back at her, mirroring her posture. "So?"

She held up her hand, holding up one finger.

"What are you doing?" I raised an eyebrow.

"I'm going over all of the things I know about you. Now shush." Noelle narrowed her eyes at me playfully, and I couldn't help the look that I gave her. Because really.

"Noelle—"

"Come on. It'll be fun. And then you can tell me more things I don't know." She grinned.

"One. You used to live in Seattle." I nodded. "Two." She held up another finger. "You don't like sweets. Or put any sugar in your coffee. Which is boring, honestly. Three, you like wolves." I gestured for her to continue. "Hmmm, what else." She pretended to wrack her brain.

"I used to play basketball in college," I said.

"That makes sense," she said, eying my torso.

I laughed. "Why?"

"Because," she said, eyes opening wide. "You're *so tall.*"

"Unlike you, who are so little."

"Hey," Noelle frowned, "I'm not *little.*"

"You're little to me," I smirked.

"I'll have you know that I am taller than average height, thank you very much. I can't help it if you're a giant."

The waiter brought over bread, interrupting us before I could rebut the statement.

Noelle picked up the bread and tore off a piece. I couldn't help but smile as I watched her eat, knowing how much she enjoyed food. It was weird, wasn't it, to notice something like that about someone? But I did. Every time I watched her eat, it was obvious how much pleasure she derived from eating. She slathered her bread in butter before plopping it in her mouth.

I had this urge—to want to cook for her, to see that look on her face as she ate *my* food. To take care of her like that, the way she deserved. I knew it was possessive, the way I felt for her, but I couldn't help it.

"What?" She asked me after swallowing her bite.

"Nothing." I shook my head, trying to play off my staring at her. How I was always transfixed by her. Maybe I needed to get my head checked.

Or get the guys to knock some sense into me.

"Alright, back to the questions. What do you want to know about me, Noelle?"

She shrugged. "I don't know. The important things. Do you have any siblings? Do you love your mom? Are you going to steal me away into the night so I never see my friends or family again? How old were you when you had your first kiss? Do you think this is crazy? I mean… it's a little bit crazy, right?"

"Noelle." I laughed. "You're so…" *Beautiful. Enchanting. Incredible. Sexy. Honest. Loud. Ridiculously and unabashedly you.*

"Oh, not this again," she groaned.

"You're so much more than I could have ever expected," I said honestly.

She only paused for a beat, as if she was digesting my words before she waggled her eyebrows at me. "And what exactly *did* you expect, *Professor?*"

"Noelle." *God.* Back to that. I hated it when she called me that.

Except… I *didn't*. It felt like this game between us, part of the line that was between us that was taut. I just didn't know what either one of us would do when it snapped.

She just giggled at me as she took a sip of the Italian soda she had ordered. Damn, this girl and her never-ending sweet tooth.

"Not sure," I chuckled. "Certainly not this feisty *little*

redhead who's sitting in front of me though." I thought back to the first time we met when I saw her standing across the room.

How did I explain to her that her presence had always had some sort of magnetic pull on me? Like she was the *sun*, and I was destined to orbit around her for the rest of my life. And maybe I just needed her sunlight in my life. *You're like the sunshine,* I wanted to tell her. *And I can't help but want to be around you and absorb every bit of it.*

But she didn't press on the matter further, and then the waitress came over with our food, and I watched Noelle's eyes light up as she took the first bite of cheesy pasta on her plate.

Note to self: Noelle loves pasta. I didn't know why it surprised me, why I found it pertinent, but I filed that knowledge away for later consideration.

"You never finished answering my questions." She finally said, frowning at me as she looked up.

"Finish your food before it gets cold." I pointed my fork at her plate. "And then I will answer your questions."

"And then... Can we get dessert?" Her eyes twinkled like a kid in a candy store.

Yep, I was down *bad* for her because my instant response was, "Of course. We can get whatever you want."

And the smile that spread over her face? Worth it. It was all so, so worth it.

∼

AFTER WE FINISHED with dessert and I paid the bill—at my insistence, I wouldn't let Noelle pay for hers, since I had been the one to ask her to dinner in the first place—I got up from my chair and extended a hand to her. I couldn't explain what made me want to hold her hand again, but all I knew was that ever since the trip to the zoo, since taking her home from the bar, maybe even before *that*, it was all I wanted to do.

I didn't drop her hand outside. She didn't release it from my grip either.

"So…" she began, finally breaking her gaze away from her heeled boots and looking into my eyes. Like this, I could appreciate our height difference. Her shoes added a couple of inches, but she was still short enough that I had to lean down a little bit to look at her, but not so much that I couldn't lean my head forward—just a little—to place a kiss on her head.

Not that I was going to. That would be weird, considering the state of our current relationship. Which was… Friendship? Yeah. That's what we had agreed on. Even though it felt like something more could come of it, neither one of us had mentioned it. Not yet. Even though she had agreed to *dinner* and this entire night had felt like so much more.

But there were so many things I needed to tell her before we got to that point—if we ever got to it.

"Okay. You had questions," I said, as we strolled past the trees with the twinkling lights. It was strange to me, how even in the cold, all I could feel was the warmth from holding Noelle's hand.

She nodded, and I began to think about what she asked me earlier.

Do you have any siblings? Do you love your mom? Are you going to steal me away into the night, so I never see my friends or family again? How old were you when you had your first kiss? Do you think this is crazy?

"I have a sister. My mom is the best woman I've ever known. I have no intentions of kidnapping you, sunshine. I was sixteen when I had my first kiss, but it was awful, so I think it shouldn't count. And yes," I concluded, leaning in closer to her, lips almost at the crown of her head. "I do think this is crazy."

She beamed, and God, I loved seeing her smile directed at me. Just from my truths revealed to her. And yeah, maybe it wasn't everything I needed to tell her, but it was a start.

"Okay. Now my turn."

I didn't need any time to think about it. "Why'd you decide to be a Hall Director? What was your favorite thing about living in New York? What's your favorite dessert of all time? Can you tell me the best Christmas gift you've ever gotten? And lastly... do you know how amazing you are?"

She blushed, and I couldn't help but tip her chin up to look at me with the hand that wasn't holding hers. "You are quite incredible, Noelle; do you know that?"

"Sometimes it's nice to be reminded," she murmured under her breath, and I knew, right then, that she hadn't been told how special she was enough, and I vowed to do everything in my power to make her believe it. To make her see what I saw in her. A strong, brave woman who was doing everything she could to pursue her dreams.

As I said nothing, just watching her.

She took a deep breath before answering my questions. "When I moved back from New York... I knew I needed a change. I still had a lot of connections back here, and I've always loved the campus. It always felt like home. So when someone told me they thought I'd make a good Hall Director, and that it came with housing and food and a salary, I jumped. My favorite thing about living in New York..." She twisted up her face as if she was thinking. "Maybe Broadway. I don't know, I expected to like to live there more than I actually did. My favorite dessert is red velvet cheesecake, and I think the best Christmas gift I've ever gotten must be my typewriter." She beamed. "I know they're impractical, but it's so cool. And to maintain some modicum of self-preservation, I will not answer the last one."

We stopped at the end of the street, by a little park, in between two of the lit-up trees. I brushed a hair back behind her ear.

"Any other questions for me?"

She shook her head. And then she sighed, and I wanted to scoop her up in my arms and tell her everything was going to be okay. But I couldn't, so I just stood there, running my fingers over the back of her hand, trying to tell her with my eyes what my words couldn't.

It was too soon to comfort her like I wanted to, and I managed to pick the exact opposite of the right thing to ask when I said, "What happened… with your dad? You mentioned him at the zoo…"

The frown on her face was instant, and I wished I could take it back, but it was already out there. "My dad… died when I was three."

"Oh, Noelle, I'm sorry—"

"Don't worry. You didn't know. I didn't say it before. And I… I barely knew him, anyway. My mom was the one who lost the love of her life, you know? There was an accident at his work and suddenly, he was gone. Ever since, it's just been my mom and I."

"I understand," I said softly. She looked at me, and I wondered if she knew how deeply I understood the pain that I knew she carried under the surface, even if she didn't show it.

The thoughts that I had carried with me all day at the zoo. Because I remembered the last time I was at one, standing in front of the gray wolves at the Zoo in Seattle. The animals I had always loved, always felt a kinship with that I couldn't quite describe.

"Noelle—"

She shook her head. "You don't have to say anything. You don't have to apologize. I… I've had a long time to get used to it."

I had wanted to tell her then, standing in front of the red pandas, but I hadn't been able to find the words. But today—I knew what I needed to say. Felt in my heart, the words that she needed to hear. So I took a deep breath and plunged feet first into the depths of my grief.

"I lost my parents when I was in college. Car accident. There was black ice on the roads, and their car slipped, and rolled… Luckily my sister was at a friend's house that night, but I… It never really gets easier, does it?"

"No…" Noelle shook her head. "Oh. Matthew. Is that, why, at the zoo—"

I nodded, the words tight in my throat. "My sister is eight

years younger than me. The last time my family went to the zoo, I must have been... sixteen?"

"And it made you think about your parents." Noelle's voice was wobbly. "Matthew, I'm so sorry if I made you sad going there. If, because of me—"

"I wasn't sad," I assured her, brushing my thumb over her cheek. "I just miss them sometimes."

She leaned into my touch. "I always wonder what my dad would think of me if he was still here. If he would be proud of me." Her eyes sparkled with unshed tears, and I wanted to comfort her, but I stayed still.

"Oh, Noelle," I whispered. "He would be so proud of you. I know he would. How could he not, with how bright and strong you are?" Did she not know how impressive she was? God, even the way she lit up a room... "You're just... sunshine, Noelle."

"Matthew," she breathed, and God, when she said my name like *that*... My heart stopped for a beat every time. She must have noticed because she stilled. "What?"

"I just... I like it when you call me Matthew."

"Well, that's your name, isn't it, dummy?" She crinkled her nose, and I loved that look on her. "I thought you said we were friends now. That's what friends do, right? Call each other by their first names? Or do you prefer *Professor? Sir?*" She smirked mischievously.

You're a brat, I wanted to say.

"We are." I nodded instead. How could we not be, after we had started opening up and sharing our pasts? "We're friends, Noelle."

"Yeah," she smiled, eyes looking at our combined hands in between the two of us. "I guess we are." Our fingers were interlocked, and her small hand felt perfect in mine. It wasn't the first time I had come to that conclusion. "I'm glad we're friends, Matthew."

"Me too, Noelle," I murmured under my breath.

Her eyes dropped down to my lips as we stood there, just

staring at each other, faces mere inches apart. Either one of us could have leaned in, just an inch, and our lips would have connected. That was how easy it was to kiss her—and I wanted to. So badly. But instead, I just looked at her, breathing as steadily as I could as I tried to ignore the idea of how her lips would feel against mine. What she would taste like.

The lights twinkled on the street; strands of white lights wrapped around the trees. I was looking at her, face lit from the warm glow and the moonlight, and I couldn't help but think about how beautiful she was. And the way she was looking at me...

We said we were friends, but she was looking at me like I was so much more. Maybe friendship wasn't all that there was between us anymore. With all we had shared, the time we had spent together—maybe I didn't *want* just friendship with Noelle. Not anymore. But did she? Whatever the case was, my eyes darted down to *her* lips, and then back up to her eyes. Even with her full hips and curves, she seemed so much shorter than me, her head landing at the top of my chest, and I tilted my head down towards her as Noelle brought her chin up to mine.

"Matthew," Noelle whispered as she continued to stare at me, her palms reaching up and landing flat against my chest. "What are you thinking about?"

"I'm thinking that I really want to kiss you right now," I breathed, as my hand wrapped around the back of her neck and the other wrapped around her waist, pulling her closer.

"So why don't you?" Noelle tipped her head up and stood on her toes.

"Because I..." I swallowed. "I don't want to take advantage of you." *And there's a voice in my head screaming that this is wrong, even if it feels so right.*

"You're not," she breathed against my lips. "Kiss me, please?"

And I could never deny her. I closed the distance between us as my lips found hers. It was our first kiss—just a soft, chaste thing —but somehow it felt like I had been waiting my entire life for this. For her. Nothing more than a peck, which immediately made me want more. I placed another kiss at the edge of her mouth, and then my hands were cupping her face as I kissed her harder, with fervor and adoration and—

And then she was so soft and pliant in my arms, and I felt her sigh into my mouth as she opened herself up to me: my tongue swiping into her mouth, tasting the chocolate cheesecake she had after dinner, and I was lost in our kiss.

When Noelle pulled away, her cheeks were pink and she was a little breathless—we both were. I pulled her in closer to me, and I rested my head on top of hers, relishing how perfectly her head fit under my chin. I closed my eyes, inhaling the sweet scent of her hair—like vanilla—and then she sighed, wrapping her arms around me.

"Matthew—" she started, her voice a bit higher than normal, which made me frown and pull away.

"Sweetheart, what's wrong?"

She just shook her head and tugged at the lapels of my jacket to bring my lips down to hers. My arms curled around her back, pulling her in tighter, every inch of our bodies connecting, and it was everything—*everything*.

And I *knew* then. I was obsessed with her and every bit of her being, and it was all I could do to hold myself back. No matter how much I felt this spark between us.

Because I wasn't going to rush it. I wasn't going to let myself ruin this.

I couldn't risk losing her.

CHAPTER 13
Noelle

Kiss me, please? I whispered, and suddenly my whole life had changed. In an instant, in a flash. Because Matthew Harper's lips were against mine—his hands gently holding my face, kissing me like I was someone who he *cherished*, who was worthy of it—I wanted to sink into it.

And when he pulled away, asking me if something was wrong, it was all I could do to pull him back to me. To kiss him back with everything I had. And when he tugged me and lifted me off the ground, allowing me to wrap my legs around his waist so I could kiss him with more ease—as he pressed my back into the tree with its beautiful twinkly lights, I thought, *this is it. How could I come back from this?*

A moan escaped from my lips, and I knew he could feel it—how much he was affecting me. I could feel how much I was affecting *him*. Every delicious, beautiful inch of him was currently pressed up against me. All hard, no soft bits to Matthew. Especially not the one that was positioned right over my—

"Matthew," I murmured, tugging at the hair at the nape of his neck. I wanted to kiss him again. I knew that, and yet... "Matthew, we shouldn't..."

His lips were swollen when he pulled back, hands still curled under me to support me, and when he realized where we were—what we were so close to doing, his cheeks pinked.

Matthew Harper was *blushing*.

"Oh, you beautiful man," I cooed, and he set me down gently onto the ground.

I wasn't sure if the sound that escaped my mouth was a giggle, a disappointed sigh, or somewhere in the middle, but it didn't matter.

Because the spell was broken.

And did Matthew look a little mortified over our kiss, or was that my imagination?

Oh. Had he not been enjoying it? Because I thought he had. I had *felt* him, after all. If we had gone on for just a few moments longer, he would have been grinding against me. I frowned up at him, just staring at his blue eyes.

Matthew just shook his head, his fingers trailing over his lips like he couldn't believe what we had just done. "Come on," he said. "Let's get you back to campus and get you home."

I took in a deep inhale of breath and bit my lip as he slipped his hand back in mine, the feeling finally tethering me back down to earth. But I couldn't ignore the butterflies in my stomach, or the heat that had blossomed inside of me.

I had to ignore it, though, or else I was going to lose my mind just from being around him. This physical pull I felt in his presence—the way I felt when our hands connected, or when we touched, when he held me... it was all too much to try to resist.

And when we got back to the truck, it seemed like Matthew couldn't resist either—not when his hands went around my waist to help me get in, not as we drove back and his palm rested on my thigh, like he couldn't stop touching me. Like he would die if he had to.

Once at my dorm building, I stared up at him, leaning against the front door and wondered if I could get him to kiss me again. Watching his eyes as they darted down to my lips once more. But even though my tongue ran over my lips, moistening them, he didn't move in any closer.

"Goodnight, Matthew," I whispered.

"Goodnight, Noelle," he responded, placing a kiss on the crown of my head, before moving away from me and back towards his truck.

I stood there, on the sidewalk, watching as he drove away.

And when I got back to my room, I collapsed against my bed thinking only of one thing. His lips on mine, and how badly I wanted more.

No—needed more.

So much for your, no men rule, Noelle, I scolded myself.

But maybe he was different.

Maybe he would stay.

∽

I TOSSED and turned all night, and when I pulled myself out of bed on Monday morning, I had barely gotten a wink of sleep. Still, I dragged myself to the coffee shop, desperately needing the caffeine, the familiar routine to keep me awake, keep me from thinking about Matthew and his touch.

But I was barely able to keep my eyes open, and the longer I sat there, the more my eyes drooped as I typed on my laptop. I didn't even realize I had dozed off until I felt a strong hand reach out and lightly shake my shoulder. My eyes flew open, and to my surprise, there he was—standing in front of me in the flesh. Matthew Harper.

"Noelle." His quiet voice dragged me from my thoughts before I could even open my mouth to explain. Well. I guess that wasn't happening. I could see the concern in his eyes, and I felt bad. Was he... worried about me? "Is everything okay?"

I rubbed my eyes as I looked up at him, as if he was a hallucination I could just blink away, before closing my laptop lid and staring at him. At this good man who seemed to care about me for reasons that I couldn't begin to fathom. Finally, I nodded. "Erm. I'm fine." A lie, but who was I lying to, anyway? Myself?

He certainly didn't buy it.

"Noelle," he said again.

"I'm just—I couldn't sleep last night." I gave him a sheepish smile. And then, since I was already lying, I figured I'd just keep up the ruse. "I'm trying to juggle everything, but between assignments and my hall director responsibilities and everything, I guess one thing had to give." I yawned. "I guess it was sleep, but here we are."

"And my sanity," he grumbled under his breath. "Noelle. You need to get some sleep," Matthew ordered, giving me a stern stare. "You shouldn't be falling asleep in here. And I definitely don't want you falling asleep in one of your classes."

As if I wanted to be dozing in a public space. I was embarrassed enough about this, let alone the fact that he was standing here concerned about my sleep schedule. Even though I hadn't been able to get a wink of sleep in because of him. Because my body was on fire, and I couldn't stop my heart from racing at the mere thought of his presence.

"I know..." I frowned. "I'll try. But I still have a million things to work on and—" I was just making excuses, I knew, because I completely realized the fact that I needed to get some sleep, but I didn't want to admit that to him as he stood, arms crossed over his chest as he... worried about me? What was happening here?

"Noelle," he sighed. "I just want you to take care of yourself."

"You do?" I whispered, and that was when I noticed we were only a breath's distance apart. Just a little closer and I would be touching him again. If I shifted my body slightly, if I extended my fingers... I could brush them over his arm, could give in to this irresistible pull my body felt whenever I was around this man. "Why?" I asked, not sure if I wanted to hear the answer. Not sure I even would hear his response with the way my body was so focused on him.

"Why?" Matthew repeated back to me, though my eyes were

still engrossed with his forearms and his delicious rolled-up shirt-sleeves. My eyes flickered back up to his. *Right*. We were having a conversation here.

"Y-Yes," I mumbled. "Why do you worry about me?" His eyes were focused on me as he uncrossed his arms from his chest—making me frown at the loss of his sleeves bunched up and his muscles flexing, and I inhaled deeply as I stared at him.

"You're really asking me why Noelle? You're going to make me say it? After last night?" He shook his head at me.

I felt my body trembling as I nodded at him. Before I could do anything, he was brushing my arm, the lightest of touch as he dragged the tips of his fingers along my skin. "I... what?"

"I don't know what you're doing to me," he whispered, one of his other fingers coming up to my hair and wrapping around a strand. "How could I not care about you, sweetheart?"

"Matthew..."

"Go home," he said, more determinedly, tucking the hair behind my ear, fingers lingering on my jaw. "Get some rest, Noelle. I'll talk to you later," Matthew promised. "And if you can't sleep... Will you call me?"

"Okay." I agreed, and his hands ghosted down my side before landing back on his.

I couldn't help myself as I reached out and squeezed his hand once before dropping my hand back to my side and turning towards the door. When I turned around to say something else, I saw him shaking his head, muttering something unintelligible under his breath. I thought it sounded a lot like "I didn't get any sleep either," but I didn't want to press the matter. And then he was brushing his big hands through his hair and my brain short-circuited again.

It was such an automatic, involuntary gesture: the way he ran his fingers through his blond locks as he shook his head. Yet I couldn't quite describe what it was doing to my heart. What *he* was doing to my heart, showing concern for me where hardly anyone outside my small circle of friends ever had.

"I'll see you later?" I asked, barely a whisper. He nodded.

"Sweet dreams, Noelle."

Oh, they'd be sweet, indeed. And... Wicked. Very, very *wicked*.

I turned and walked out without looking back, bag swung over my shoulder, wondering how long I could go without succumbing to this want that was burning in my bones.

∾

"NOELLE?" Charlotte waved her hand in front of my face as I zoned out—yet again—during lunch. I had to cancel on Saturday because of the zoo field trip, but Charlotte and I always tried to make extra time during the week to hang out, so she had agreed to meet me at the campus cafeteria that Wednesday. Perks of her usually working in the evenings at the dance studio.

"Ugh. I'm sorry." I rubbed a hand over my face, careful not to ruin my eye makeup. "I'm just tired. I haven't been sleeping well this week."

She raised an eyebrow. "That's not like you. Does this have anything to do with the handsome professor who rescued you from the bar the other night?"

"*What?*" I asked, maybe a little too quickly. "No." *Maybe. Yes, because you see, I'm pretty sure I'm dating him now, because after I took him with me to the zoo—the zoo! —we had dinner together, and we talked about our dead parents, and now I'm not sure where we stand.*

And I haven't been sleeping enough because I keep lying in bed at night thinking about him, and wishing his hands were—Nope. Not going there.

"The fun part about having known you for the last seven years is that I can tell when you're lying, Noelle."

"Like *you're* lying to yourself about Daniel?" I muttered under my breath.

She looked confused and then narrowed her eyes. "What's

that supposed to mean?" She asked it as a question, but it fell flat like a statement, a challenge, a dare.

"Never mind. Look. No, nothing's going on with Matthew." Another lie, but I was on a roll with them at this point. "I'm just swamped with hall director stuff and assignments for class. Once I get through this next week it should be better." Again, not technically true, but I wasn't going to tell her that.

"Sure, *sure*. Whatever you say." Char grinned.

I glared at her, but chose to change the subject. "How's the dress business going?"

Charlotte was an amazing seamstress. She had designed and created some of the most spectacular gowns I'd ever seen. She was trying to make a living off of it, but due to the amount of time it took to make each one and relying on custom orders, she had kept her part-time job at the dance studio as an instructor. For a few months, she'd also worked as a barista at the coffee shop down the street from her apartment.

If I was crazy busy, I didn't even know what to call Charlotte. Her life seemed a little too insane, even to me, juggling all of these things and still managing to keep up with all her best friends. But little miss social butterfly over here never went a week without talking to me.

"It's... well, I wish I had more time to just work on orders. Sometimes it's like I can't keep up, you know. But I got this wedding dress order in today, and oh my gosh, Noelle, it's going to be beautiful."

"I'm so happy for you," I smiled. "That's amazing, Charlotte."

Charlotte beamed. "Thanks, N. One day, hopefully, I can take it full time, but until then..."

I nodded. "I get it." My phone buzzed, and I realized what time it was. "Oh, shoot, I gotta go, Char. Class calls. See you next week, yeah?"

"We'll make plans," she smiled. "The girls want to make up

for you missing Saturday. Plus, we still need a do-over of bar night."

I groaned. "Don't ever let me drink that much again. I barely remember anything from that night." Probably for the best though.

"Of course not." Charlotte frowned at me. "Honestly, I didn't even realize how drunk you were until we went to the bathroom and came back to all of that... mess. Luckily that hot-as-fuck professor was there to save you, huh?"

"Oh my god," I said, burying my flushed cheeks in my thick blanket scarf. "Can you *please* not call him that?"

"Nope." Charlotte laughed and I scowled at her. "Come on, Noelle, this may be the most exciting thing to happen to you. Like, ever."

"You can't be serious right now." Groaning, I ran my hand over my forehead. "Seriously, Char. I swear, nothing's happening there." But even with my protestations, it felt less and less true. And when was I going to admit to her, and *myself*, that there was something there?

"Okay, okay. But for real, get outta here. I'll text you."

"See you soon, C." I picked up my bag, gave her a wave, and walked out of the cafeteria towards my classroom.

PART of me acknowledged that the more I talked to him, the worse my little infatuation I was harboring for him was getting, but I couldn't stop. Or maybe I just didn't want to stop. Hazel was so going to chide me for this. Ugh, why did she always have to be right? And why did I have to like him so much?

I had surprised myself when I got back from hall director duties and class that day by sitting down in front of my blank document—the one that would eventually hold the words that would make up my very own book, and I began.

I didn't know how it would end up, or where I was going

with it, but I had written almost a thousand words without even really thinking about it, and even if it was terrible (quite possibly), it felt good that I had begun.

Like maybe all of the ideas sitting in that binder collecting dust might finally see the light. It felt like I'd found something to dream about again. Potentially even somethings to dream about, if the man I couldn't get off of my mind was any indication.

Even with everything that had happened, I couldn't help my thoughts—I was a hopeless romantic at heart, and this was always where they drifted. But suddenly, for the first time in a long time, I felt hopeful again. Like maybe I could make my mom proud and make myself happy at the same time. And somehow... I could dream without limits again.

And maybe it was because I had been thinking about him all night, of all the wonderful things he had done for me, that as I slid into bed and settled under the covers, I finally crossed that one line I hadn't yet.

I texted him.

NOELLE
Hi. I can't sleep.

His response came through a moment later.

MATTHEW
Did you try counting sheep?

Haha. Very funny.

I was too riled up to sleep. Even after my conversation with Charlotte, all week, when I had closed my eyes, his face was all I could see.

Luckily, I didn't have to wait long before he texted back.

Noelle.

Matthew.

I imagined him scowling from his side of the phone. For some reason, the thought brought a smile to my face now. Maybe because I felt like his smiles were saved, only to be given to me.

> You can't keep running on fumes, sweetheart. You're going to collapse if you keep running on empty.

For some reason, I liked taunting him, but I wasn't going to look into that any deeper.

> I'll just drink some coffee, it's fine.

As I was drafting another text, my phone rang. When I saw his name on the screen, my heart skipped a few beats. Sure, we had been texting... but this? Talking on the phone?

"Hi?" I squeaked.

"Noelle," he addressed me, not bothering with the formalities of saying hello. I guess we'd already been having a conversation anyway, so what did that matter? "You need to sleep."

"Do you ever lay in bed, staring at the ceiling, trying to force yourself to sleep but you just can't? Like, every time I close my eyes, I just..." I trailed off. I couldn't tell him I was thinking about him. Fantasizing about him. Replaying that kiss over and over in my mind. Nope. Absolutely not. I didn't finish my thought, but Matthew didn't seem to notice.

"Please. You're killing me here. What can I do to help you get some sleep? I'll help you with your projects or whatever so you can get some actual sleep tomorrow night."

You could come over here, I thought, *and maybe put that mouth of yours to use*—God. He wanted to help me? Didn't he know my problem was him? *I'll help you so you can get some actual sleep tomorrow night* shouldn't sound so dirty. But I was pretty sure if he helped me like that...

I shut my eyes. "I—"

"And before you say no, just know there is absolutely no way

I'm letting you out of this until you get some sleep. So tell me what I can do to help or I'm showing up at your place and figuring it out myself." I could almost hear him nodding to himself through the phone.

I knew that I should find his behavior *concerning*, the way he was going all alpha male on me, but really, I knew how sweet and caring this man was. How this came from a place of concern. And even though I would have hated it on someone else, I loved it on him. And it was fair because it wasn't like I was telling him what was wrong with me.

Could I? I pushed the thought away. No. We couldn't cross that line. It would be disastrous for both of us if we did, wouldn't it? I figured the university would frown on it, and if there was a chance we could put either of our jobs at risk... No. I shouldn't jeopardize either one of our careers just because I wanted him.

"Pushy, huh, Matthew?" I snickered. He was wearing me down too easily, because I knew there was no way in hell I was going to say no to this man's offer, no matter what he asked. Well, maybe the one to come over to my place. I glanced around my somewhat-messy dorm apartment. It was too soon for *that,* and my face flushed at the thought of him over here. Maybe I should clean up tomorrow.

But seeing him? I wanted that—more than anything in the world.

"Noelle." He sounded like he was gritting his teeth. "I'm serious."

I giggled. I liked pushing his buttons. Because as much as I didn't want to admit it, it was *nice* to have this with him. Something more than just the physical response my body was having to him, that couldn't get my mind to settle. Or maybe it was something more than that, thinking about what it would be like to have him here.

On my couch. On top of me. In my bed. In—*Dammit.* I needed to keep these images at bay. Because ever since he had held my hand, touched my arm, tucked the hair behind my ear, all I could think about was the wicked things I wanted him to do to me. Nope, nope, nope. We weren't going there while I was on the phone with him. Not thinking about his finely sculpted arms picking me up or his fingers running over my bare skin. Nope.

My breath hitched a little as I thought about being pressed up against his erection as my back rested on the tree bark.

"So? What'll it be?" He finally said, breaking the silence I hadn't even realized I created fantasizing about him.

"What?" I asked, spell broken.

"Did you want to get dinner?" Oh. *Oh.* I had spaced out, and he expected an answer. And I didn't trust myself inviting him over to my house, knowing what direction my brain was going in.

"When?" I tried not to stutter.

"You have class tomorrow night, right? So, I'd say on Friday. Now, seriously. Get some sleep."

"Okay, okay. Good night, Matthew."

"Good night, Noelle."

As soon as I hung up, I swear, honest to goodness, the butterflies were back. Damn him.

Because when I finally did fall asleep that night, it was with the thought of me kissing him again. After dinner.

On our date.

And... What was this, anyway? I didn't think we could classify as just friends anymore. Were we, though? Dating?

And maybe, more importantly... Did I want us to be?

CHAPTER 14
Matthew

"Matthew!" Bryan fist-bumped me, leaning against the bar where we chose to meet that night. Just me and the guys—Elizabeth had opted to stay home, and Kaitlin was on the night shift at the hospital, which left Kelly, who decidedly did *not* want to crash guys' night. Not that I blamed her.

"What's on the agenda for tonight?" Cole asked, sipping on his beer. "Another bar fight breakup from this one?" He jerked a thumb at me.

"Very funny. That will not be happening again." *I hoped.* Because this time, I *would* do way more than I had before. This time, Noelle had weaseled her way into a corner of my heart, and I wanted to protect her, take care of her.

"How is your girl, anyway, Harper?" Tanner asked, nudging me in the side.

"She's not *my* girl," I sighed. *Not yet. Not until I figured out how to banish her demons and make her mine. Not until I figured out how to kiss her without aching to be inside of her.* Damn, I was a mess, wasn't I? I gripped my beer tighter, thinking about her. Maybe it *had* been too long since I had been with a woman.

Changing the subject, I turned to them, "How are *your* girlfriends? You know, the ones that actually exist. As opposed to my imaginary one."

Cole scoffed. "She's not imaginary just because you haven't asked her out, Matt."

I rolled my eyes. I hadn't told them about our dinner yet. I wanted our kiss to remain just that—ours—for a little while longer.

"Our girls are good," Tanner added, "since this one over here isn't inclined to say that." Cole just shrugged at his twin before taking another gulp.

"How's Liz?" I asked, looking at Bryan as I nursed my beer.

"She's good, just hating her swollen ankles," he laughed. "No matter how much I rub them, she still complains the next morning." He sighed like a lovesick puppy. It was, surprisingly, a good look on him. We could joke about how much he did for her all we wanted, but it was obvious how much he loved his wife. "Not that I'm complaining. I love her."

I smiled. "Yeah. I know."

"Anyways, have you figured out if you're bringing the little redhead to the game next week?" Tanner asked.

I almost choked hearing someone else call her that. "She's not that little," I grumbled. Because *I* could call her little, thinking about how tiny she was as I held her in my arms, couldn't I? But when someone else did it, it was weird. I didn't like it. "And no, I haven't asked her yet. I'll let you know. We're... I don't know what we are." I ran a hand through my hair. It wasn't like we had labeled it.

"But you like her?"

I nodded. "I tried not to, but I do. I really do."

"So what are you going to do about it?"

"I don't know." I took another sip of my beer as the guys stared at me with vacant expressions. "I'm freaking out a little bit, okay? It's... It's been a long time. And I just... can't."

"Dude. Is this about your parents?" Bryan asked, and I could feel the ache in my heart just thinking about them.

"No." I narrowed my eyes. "This has nothing to do with them. I don't want to talk about them." But it *was*, wasn't it? Everything was always about them. They'd never even get to meet her.

"Well, we want to meet her, Matt. That's all we're saying." My friends returned to their conversation about the basketball season, but I was too distracted with thoughts of my parents—and Noelle—to pay attention.

What would *they* think of her? I wished they were here. I knew they would have given me excellent advice. Pointed me in the right direction; assured me I wasn't *crazy* for being head over heels for her. Helped me work through the way I felt for her.

And I knew, when I introduced them one day, to the girl I was going to marry, that they would have been so excited for me. Happy, elated even. They would have been looking forward to the idea of grandkids that they could spoil. But when I looked at the future right now? It felt bleak, empty. Because I was going to have all of this with someone, one day, and my parents wouldn't be here to see it. To tell me how proud of me they were. To love their grandchildren. The feeling hit me like a ton of bricks.

I'd never get that back. I sighed.

Pushing those thoughts away, I did what I always did—buried them deep down. Hid it behind a wall and bricked it up behind me. Focused on what was *here*, what was now, instead of all of the emotions I had encased in ice at the tender age of nineteen.

All of those thoughts and feelings I had never quite confronted.

And what would happen when I let someone in? When those walls came melting down? Would I survive the tidal wave of emotions that were sure to come? Would they still choose to stay by my side when they realized that I was just a broken boy, still missing his parents almost twelve years later?

I didn't know, and I wasn't sure I wanted to find out.

Was asking Noelle out—being with her—worth the risk of giving my heart away and letting someone else in?

Maybe it was. Maybe I was just terrified. Or maybe I was just being a coward. Too scared to lose someone to even try. Maybe. Maybe. Maybe. My mind was running a thousand miles a minute.

But there was only one thing that calmed the storm that was my mind. That got the winds to quiet and not rage in my ears.

And that was thinking about Noelle, in my arms, smiling up at me as I kissed her forehead.

And I knew what I wanted—maybe even needed to do. I had to try,

And when she called me that night, when I was sitting there, thinking about her, staring at the ceiling, I asked her out again without a second thought.

To dinner. *On Valentine's Day.* No big deal.

∽

I HUNG UP THE PHONE, pinching my brow between my fingers.

Had I caught her that off guard that she hadn't even realized what Friday was? I knew Valentine's Day had crept up on us, but I thought asking her to get dinner on the day would have been a little more... shocking. For the first time in my life, I couldn't help but want to have someone by my side for the holiday. Even if it was just invented for Greeting Cards. It was something more to me now.

And there was only one person I was thinking of. That I had been thinking of all week. I was trying to keep my distance because now that I had tasted her, it was all I wanted to do again. I wanted to bury my hands in her soft body, run my fingers over her thighs, and kiss her senseless until she was begging for more.

I didn't know how to explain it—I just knew that it was inevitable.

And she had agreed to dinner. *Tomorrow.* On Valentine's Day.

Were we dating? Was that... was that what this was?

But we hadn't even *discussed* the topic, so even as I pondered over our options for our *date*, I didn't want to do anything that would freak her out. And I needed a place where I had to keep my hands off of her. My house was out of the question, of course, but I had this idea of a spot she would really love.

On Thursdays, Noelle had a late-night class. I had her schedule down pat: she would come to the coffee shop on campus for a few hours to get some work done, and it was always in the time between my classes, so that's where I was.

Staring at her, wearing a white sweater covered in red hearts and a matching red skirt. My heart skipped a few beats. We had settled into this routine—it was comfortable, really—and when I slid into the chair across from her, she didn't comment.

I raised an eyebrow at her attire. "Valentine's Day is tomorrow."

"I am aware, yes."

"So... You are celebrating early?" She shook her head. "You *love* love?" I was teasing her, but even as she gave me another shake of her head, her lips tipped up in a smile.

"If you *must* know," she sighed. "I can't wear my usual Valentine's outfit tomorrow, because someone asked me out on a date."

I gasped. "Wow. The gall."

She nodded, all solemn, and pulled out a saran-wrapped package of heart-shaped cookies from her bag. "I know you don't like sweets," she said bashfully. "But I made these, and I wanted you to have one."

"You made these?" I asked, surprised, looking at the sugar cookies in my hand. I glanced down at the icing on the top and noticed what it said: *Will you be my Valentine?*

Oh, this girl. She was definitely after my heart. And if I wasn't careful, I was pretty sure I was going to give it to her.

"Thank you. I'm sure they're incredible."

She grinned. "It's my grandma's recipe. On my dad's side."

I nodded. "And are you going to share any of these with your... *date*? Tomorrow?"

Noelle paused like she was pondering the thought, and then

shook her head. "No. I think he'll have to earn his cookies."

"Oh, yeah?"

She bobbed her head. "I'm afraid so."

"I think your date is wondering if you might like Chinese food," I asked. I didn't know what we were doing here, not really, but I was enjoying it. And I wanted to ask her to *be* my Valentine—in *every* sense of the word. I wanted to kiss her and pour out every bit of my soul to her. *Yep.* I wanted that, even if it was crazy. And it wasn't just the heated glances we shared or the little looks, even her smiles, and the waves over the last month. It wasn't even that kiss we had shared. It was the way I wanted to know everything about her, to get to know her inside and out. To share the things I had never told anyone before with her, and only her. It was *everything* about her.

She nodded. "You can tell my date that I do like Chinese food. But only on one condition." I raised an eyebrow. "Surprise me."

I laughed, and she turned her attention back to the cookies that sat on the table in front of me. "You'll have to tell me if you like them. I'm a little famous for my sugar cookies, you know?" She grinned. "But don't tell everyone else," she glanced around the coffee shop like she was guarding a precious secret. "Can't have anyone else think I'm playing favorites, you know?"

Oh. I couldn't help it—the corners of my lips tilted up. I wanted to kiss her. I wanted to kiss her so *fucking* bad. "Well, I better go make sure everything is all set up for said date tomorrow." I picked up my coffee cup from the table—she had ordered it for me— and spun it around in my hand as I fumbled with something else to say to her, and that was when I noticed a red kiss mark on the side of the cup. I glanced back up at Noelle's face, noticing her matching red lipstick, and she blushed shyly. This girl. I swear.

Her cookies were incredible—and that was coming from me, a guy who hardly ate sweets. They all had a little saying on top, icing in reds, pinks, and whites that spelled out different phrases just like those disgusting candy hearts. I liked the one that said *kiss me* because it made me think of her glossy, red lips—totally kissable. Which made me think about how I wanted to kiss her again. I had been wanting to kiss her again since the last time. Why couldn't I get her out of my mind?

I saved the final cookie for when I got home that night—one that read *text me*—and I couldn't help taking a picture of it on my counter, sitting next to a cup of coffee, and sending it off to Noelle.

> Your wish is my command, sweetheart.
>
> Thanks again for the cookies, I loved them.

NOELLE
Well, of course, you did. I made them, after all.

> See you tomorrow, Noelle.

See you tomorrow, handsome.

∽

"Hey, Noelle," I said, noticing the way the very tip of her nose was reddened from the cold, and the top of her head and hair was slightly damp from the constant Portland drizzle. I had asked her to meet me in my office, and I watched her eyes look around the room as she entered.

I was glad I had finally gotten around to unpacking all of my boxes and hanging my frames. It was still fairly sparse in here, but I had the bare minimum of decorations at least.

"Hi, prof." I laughed at her insistence on calling me the ridiculous nickname. Noelle gave me one of her warm smiles, and I was so happy to have it all for myself. To have her all to myself, even if it was just like this.

"Why do you call me that?" I wanted to reach over and run my fingers through her damp curls. Needed to touch her, but I knew that I had to wait. *Just a little longer.*

"Have you considered that maybe I like calling you prof, Matthew?" I didn't miss the way she added a little *pop* to the word or a little emphasis over my name. Honestly, I loved the way it sounded coming from her lips. "Maybe I like seeing the way it gets under your skin?" She grinned.

I was beginning to think she loved torturing me. I didn't think she missed the red that was creeping up my neck. I just hoped my face didn't show it as much as the rest of my body did.

Noelle sat her stuff down in the chair across from me and then she shed her coat, revealing her long-sleeved red dress and the heart-printed tights she was wearing underneath it.

"You look incredible," I said, and I meant it. "So *this* is the infamous Valentine's Day outfit, huh?"

She shook her head. "No, this is my *special* occasion Valentine's Day outfit," Noelle declared, with a nod. "So... what's the plan? You promised me Chinese food if you didn't forget."

I laughed. "I did not, don't worry."

"Okay, sweep me off my feet," she said, kicking her feet up on the edge of my desk. "I am ready to be wowed."

"Grab your coat," I whispered in her ear, brushing the hair off of her neck. "We'll go eat." I lifted the picnic basket I had packed as a surprise. I *had* gotten us Chinese food—and red velvet cheesecake for dessert and even slipped a bottle of wine into the basket.

"Oh. We're—we're having a picnic?" She slipped her arms into her coat before looking up at me, expectantly. "But... It's like forty-something degrees outside right now. It's freezing." She narrowed her eyes. "Where are we going to have a picnic in this weather, Matthew?"

"Come on," I said, steering her out the door. "I have a place."

She probably thought I was crazy as I led her, hand in hand, down the path that led to one of my favorite spots on campus.

A hidden gem. It was a gazebo, nestled at the edge, overlooking the river and the city beyond it.

I had already come here earlier, putting out a blanket, a lantern, and a space heater.

She gasped. "You did all of this?"

I nodded. "I wanted to have you all to myself," I grinned.

I guided her down onto one of the blankets before piling another over her legs, nestling beside her and pulling the food out of the basket.

Noelle inhaled deeply. "This all smells amazing, oh my god. And I've been dying to come here, it's been forever." She piled some food onto the plate that I gave her, and I poured some wine into one of the cups I'd brought.

"Glad to be of service," I said, waving my chopsticks in the air before pointing at her food. "Now eat, so I can stop worrying about you starving in that tiny dorm apartment of yours."

"Hey!" she protested. "It's not that small."

I raised an eyebrow. "Noelle. I've been inside. Your bedroom barely has room for your bed, or did you think I didn't notice when I carried you upstairs and placed you in it?"

She flushed red. "Oh god, can we please never bring that night up again? I'm beyond mortified, and I can't believe you saw my apartment like that."

It might not have been the cleanest apartment I had ever seen, but it certainly hadn't been the messiest, either. And who was I to hold that against her? I leaned over to brush her hair back behind her ear to keep it out of her food. "I'm not sure I'll ever forget it," I said, trying to hide my grin as I thought about that night. About how perfectly Noelle fit inside my arms. About her mumbling into my chest how warm I was. About how hard it had been to leave her on her bed and walk away, and not stay there all night making sure she was okay.

"Well, you should." Noelle frowned. "Because I did."

I leaned in closer, my lips next to her ear, and I spoke slowly against her skin. "I don't *want* to forget how you feel in my arms, Noelle."

And even though she continued to flush—creeping up her neck this time, her whole face already red, I could see this tiny expression in her eyes as she remembered me carrying her back into her house that night. That she didn't want to forget how it felt in my arms either. And maybe we were tiptoeing the line between friends and something more, whatever this thing was between us, but I didn't care.

She looked back down at her food as she continued to eat, and I took a bite of the dumplings. "Oh, these are good," I confirmed, taking another bite.

Noelle's nose crinkled as she laughed at me, eating another bite of noodles, and I waited until we had both finished the majority of our food before we continued our conversation. For some reason, I didn't want it to end, never seemed to want to stop talking to her, but primarily, I wanted her to eat.

"What?" she asked, a forkful of food paused in the air.

I shook my head, running a hand through the strands of my blonde hair. "Nothing," I chuckled. "I just love how much you love food."

She turned red all over again. "Ah. Yes. I believe you called it 'cute' at the zoo."

"It is. But you're always cute, Noelle." I grinned a little sheepishly. Why did I sound like I was talking to my eighth-grade crush?

"Well..." She tilted her head, looking at me as if she wanted to confess something too but didn't know how to say it. "You're not so bad yourself," she mumbled, finally taking her bite and chewing.

I smirked. "Oh?"

"Don't get all cocky on me now," she frowned, pointing her fork in the air at me. "Guys are not attractive when they turn into arrogant assholes."

I held my hands up. "Don't be an arrogant asshole. Got it."

"Good." My favorite smile of Noelle's spread across her face —a warm one, that made her brown eyes light up. "Because I like you just the way you are."

Me too, Noelle. Me too.

"So. Tell me about your friends," I said, long after we had

finished our food, as we both sat, nestled together, one blanket spread over both of our laps.

"Gabbi, Angelina, and Charlotte?" She asked. "The ones you met?"

I nodded. "How'd you meet?"

"In my freshman year of college. Charlotte and I were roommates, and then Daniel made sure we met Gabbi and Angelina—they lived in the room directly across the hall from us. We were fast friends, and once we stuck together... You know what they say about bonding for life? I feel like that's us. They're like my family at this point." She was rambling now, but I didn't care to stop her. "The sisters I always wished I had."

Daniel? Why was this the first time I was hearing about him? I needed to find out who he was—and why was I jealous of some guy I didn't even know? Honestly, what *was* wrong with me that I was thinking about her like some sort of weird possessive guy anyways?

"So, who's Daniel?" I couldn't help myself from asking.

She frowned. "Oh, he's my best friend Charlotte's—well, they're not dating, but I guess he's her best friend too?" Noelle shrugged. "She has both of us, you know. He's Angelina's older brother. He met Charlotte on move-in day and the rest... well, as they say." She rolled her shoulders. "That's history. I'm fairly sure he's never had a girlfriend since he met her. But they're both too stubborn to see the other person right in front of them."

"Oh." I sighed in relief. "So you've never...?"

She raised an eyebrow, and I gave her a sheepish grin. "Are you asking me if I was ever *interested* in Daniel, Matthew?"

"No," I said quickly, and *yeah*, that was a little more defensive than I meant for it to sound. "I know you've probably dated other people, Noelle—"

"Sure..." She raised one eyebrow at me. *Shit*. What was I implying here? That I was jealous of a potential man in her life? That anyone who she had ever harbored affections for was somehow now my competition? I wasn't sure if she even harbored any affections for me or if she was feeling the same way I was any time my knee brushed hers or the back of my hand bumped into hers.

I just shook my head. "Sorry. I don't want to be a crazy guy. It's just that, thinking about you with another man..." I winced, looking at her guiltily.

"And what about you?" Noelle asked. "Have you had anyone you've been interested in here?"

"On-campus?"

She nodded, popping another forkful of the red velvet cheesecake in her mouth as I bit my lip.

"Just one," I said as our gazes connected. She licked the icing off the fork. "You might know her," I said. That got her attention, and her eyes narrowed. "She's about... uh, this tall, and has gorgeous fiery red hair, and the biggest sweet tooth of anyone I know."

Her eyes lit up, widening. "Really? There hasn't been anyone else?"

I shook my head. "Remember when I told you about needing to escape my crazy coworkers who were always trying to set me up with their daughters or relatives?"

"Right. Well... I'm glad you didn't let them set you up," Noelle said with a singular bob of her head before turning back to the skyline and the dark river below.

"I know we haven't..." she sighed. "I know we haven't put a label on this, and I don't want to rush into things here—" I nodded, even though the one thing I wanted was her tongue back in my mouth. "But I just need you to know that there's no one else. Okay?" she bit her lip. "And there hasn't been... in a while."

Did she look nervous? Hell, I didn't want to know what 'a while' was for her, because it had been *forever* for me.

I placed a kiss on her forehead. "There's no one else for me either, sweetheart."

"Guess that means you've earned the cookies, then," she said with a grin.

And I know she meant the literal cookies—the ones she gave me yesterday, but I couldn't help but think of the metaphorical cookies. I leaned over and ran my thumb over her jaw. "I'll remember that, Noelle."

She paused for a moment before turning to whisper in my ear, "I hope it's worth the wait." And then—she winked.

Fuck me. Was I red, again? How did her words always manage to affect me like this?

"Let's go," I said, holding out a hand to her after I collected our things.

She frowned. "Already?"

I couldn't tell her the truth—that if we were out here for one moment more, I was going to find a way to make that wait increasingly shorter. Because I needed to take my time. Tread lightly.

Because I wasn't going to accept anything less than forever, and I wasn't sure yet what Noelle was willing to give me.

I tucked her underneath my arm as we walked back to her dorm, and she kept the blanket we had been cozying up underneath all night as she turned to go inside.

Before she could go, I caught her wrist, spinning her back towards me. "Happy Valentine's Day, Noelle."

And then—I kissed her. Long, hard, and passionately, and probably with more longing than I should have because when she pulled away, I was breathing deeply and it was all I could do to let her go.

"Happy Valentine's Day, Matthew." She wrapped the blanket around herself. "Thank you—for tonight. It was perfect."

"Yeah?"

She nodded. I kissed her once more, on the tip of her nose.

"Goodnight."

"Night." I grinned, and watched her retreat inside, warm and bundled up in our shared energy.

My life had never felt as full as it did at this moment.

I just needed to figure out how to keep it that way.

CHAPTER 15
Noelle

Saturday morning, I once again found myself surrounded by my best friends at our favorite coffee shop, with a stack of books on the table as well as a plate of pastries and our four coffees.

"I hope you all know I had absolutely *no* time last week to read," I frowned. "So I didn't get to reading our last picks—but I will, I promise."

"It's fine, Elle," Gabbi nodded. "We know you've been swamped with everything going on. We wouldn't hold that against you."

"I just can't wait for this semester to be over."

"How are your classes?" Angelina asked, popping a grape in her mouth.

If I was being honest, I was *envious* of her. Ang had known what she wanted to do in college, had gotten her marketing degree, and now was working for a prestigious tech software company—and was well on her way to her next job promotion, climbing the ladder through sheer will and determination. She was, as I lovingly referred to her—a boss bitch.

Even Gabbi seemed like she had it all figured out, working at the same firm as Angelina as a human resources manager and dabbling in photography on the side. It was nice that they had their lives together. Me, on the other hand... I was happy for them, I was, I just hoped that realizing my dream would be enough for me. Whenever that happened.

"Classes are okay." I lifted my shoulders in a shrug. Charlotte must have told them about last week. "I'm just swamped, and with spring break coming up it feels like everyone's piling on extra work. But it's okay because Ma—." Shit, I had to stop myself from mentioning Matthew. Again. How was his name slipping out so easily now? "Because I have it under control," I said a little bit louder. I gave a sheepish grin.

Why couldn't I tell them? I wanted to, didn't I? But also... maybe I wanted to be in this cocoon with Matthew, warm and secure, nestled under that blanket together, and not have anyone asking me questions. Not have to think about where we were going, what the future held. Right now it was just us, trying to toe this line of something more.

The cord was going to snap at some point. It was frayed, and I knew I couldn't resist him for much longer. Knew I needed more than kisses and holding hands and small touches. Last night when I sat next to him—I hadn't mistaken the charged energy in the air. Or the way our eyes would catch, and hold, for a little too long without either one of us saying anything.

I sighed, just thinking about it. It seemed like even if I was ready for that next step—towards whatever it was—he just kept pulling away. But as much as I knew I wanted that—wanted to give in to my physical desires, with him, I wasn't sure I could do anything more than sex. Did I want to be in a relationship?

Charlotte nodded over her bowl of pineapple. "I swear, you guys, she's hardly sleeping."

They all narrowed their eyes at me, and if Matthew had been here, I knew he would have agreed with them. "Honestly, I'm fine," I said to all of them. I appreciated that they cared, I did, but it wasn't like I could just get him out of my system. I needed him—he was like a drug.

A drug that was keeping me from sleeping. Well, maybe it wasn't a very *good* drug. Or maybe I just needed to get f—

"Okay, Noelle," Gabbi said with a frown, the mom friend of our group through and through. "But if you need something, anything... you'll tell us, right?"

"Right." Or I'd tell Matthew, but that was beside the point. And the way my brain jumped to him to ask for help before anyone else... What was up with me that I was thinking this way? I knew what it was, but I still... didn't want to talk about it with them.

"Okay then," she nodded. "Now, who has a book they want to talk about?" Gabbi grinned, and we launched into my favorite discussions we shared: the ones about books. I had read some of the ones they were reading or had just finished before, and I was glad to be able to join in parts of the conversations, despite having been too busy to read anything this last week.

"Anyone do anything fun yesterday?" Angelina asked, and I looked up at her in confusion. Did she know... somehow?

"Huh?" My mind had immediately gone to the gazebo with Matthew.

"Valentine's Day?" she said, a more matter of fact, how-did-you-forget kind of tone.

"Oh. No. It's not like any of us had dates anyway," I muttered under my breath.

"Well... someone sent me flowers at work," Angelina said, narrowing her eyes. "And they didn't even attach a card, so I have no idea who they were from. Just a dozen red roses, sitting on my desk. Weird."

Gabbi was just looking at her, and Ang just raised a shoulder. "What?"

"Nothing." Gabbi just shook her head.

The rest of them ignored me, and then Charlotte launched a discussion about how Valentine's Day is stupid and how society should reject the norms and just celebrate *Galentine's Day* instead. Sometimes, I thought that girl watched a little too many episodes of Parks and Rec, but I wasn't going to say that to her. No, if she wanted to worship Leslie Knope and eat a lot of breakfast food, who was I to say anything? We all had our things.

And... my heart fluttered a little bit, just thinking about last night. I fumbled with my hands as I sought a way to distract myself from the conversation. Before last night, when was the last time I had done anything for Valentine's Day? Maybe before Jake and I broke up because I didn't remember following any of my traditions last year, or the two years before that.

I used to love spreading joy through seemingly insignificant things—candy, cookies, cards of appreciation. Spreading them out to my professors and friends in college made me feel so warm and appreciated inside, and I missed that feeling.

And this year—maybe it was how I was feeling about Matthew, maybe it was that it had been long enough since things had ended with Jake—but I had woken up on Wednesday and baked four dozen heart-shaped cookies. Most of them had been devoured by the girls in the hall—I had left them by the reception desk—and I had kept a few for me, sure, but then there had been that bundle for Matthew.

It felt like... maybe I was finally ready to accept love in my life again. I felt that in my *soul*. Was I in the position to let my heart get broken again? Absolutely not. I'd protect my own heart no matter what. But to give and receive love—wasn't that one of life's biggest miracles?

I took another bite of my cinnamon roll, pondering all of that when I felt Charlotte's eyes on me again. She leaned in close, whispering in my ear, "So how's it going with Professor Hottie?"

"Char." I groaned. "It's Professor Harper, and don't call him *that*." Was my face red? Was I flushing, just over a simple question about him? No. Fuck.

"So what do *you* call him?" Charlotte smirked.

"Matthew," I mumbled.

"Matthew?" Gabbi raised an eyebrow. Fuck, we hadn't kept our voices low enough.

"Oh, uh, yeah. He asked me to call him by his first name. That's not that weird, I've had professors in tons of classes tell us to do that."

"Is this the same professor that took you home from the bar that night?" Angelina gave me a look, which I promptly shot back with my best shut-up-now face. But they didn't. Of course, they didn't.

"Are you the *only* one who he lets call Matthew, Noelle?"

I wracked my brain. Really pondered it. Tried to remember if I had heard any of the students, undergraduate or grad level, call him by his first name. When we were at the zoo... those girls had called him Professor Harper, hadn't they? I wondered if he instructed his classes to call him by his first name, or if it was only me. But I couldn't think of a single moment where anyone had called him anything but Professor Harper or Dr. Harper, so I had to concede that yes, I may have been the only one calling him Matthew. Because all along, he had asked me to.

Because he had never wanted that kind of relationship with me. The professor/student relationship. That wasn't who I was to him, and it wasn't who he was to me. I was lying to myself if I pretended it was anything else. And I knew I was the only one. The only one who had kissed him outside of a restaurant after dinner. The only one who he had packed a Valentine's Day picnic for. Certainly the only one he was showing up to the campus coffee shop every day just to see.

And, well... I couldn't deny it to myself anymore. It was one hundred percent, way more than just friends.

"I—"

"Oh my gosh," Gabbi's eyes lit up. "You're absolutely *smitten* with him, aren't you?"

"Smitten?" I said, raising my voice as I started to protest. "I'm not *smitten* with him! I don't even have a little teeny-tiny crush on him or anything. Nope."

"So if I told you that he was standing in line at the counter, you wouldn't turn around as fast as possible to see him?"

I shook my head. "No, of course not." Was my voice a little too high and breathy.

"You're the worst," Angelina sang, and the other girls joined in laughing.

Maybe I was just in denial. Because... If he had been here, at my favorite coffee shop with my best friends, I would have turned around. And after our Valentine's dinner... What would I do if he *was*? I felt like my feelings were all tangled up inside, and I didn't even know what I wanted. There were still so many unknowns between the two of us.

And would I tell him I'd been thinking about him every minute of every day since he had kissed me the first time? Ask him if it meant for him what it meant for me? No—I couldn't do *that*. Because I wasn't ready for the inevitable heartbreak when he told me that I wasn't enough for him. That I didn't mean enough to him.

Because I was easy to leave. Because I wasn't noteworthy enough for someone to stay.

And dammit, I wanted him to stay.

∼

THE NEXT WEEK passed like usual—coffee shop dates, lingering glances, the brush of our hands when we saw each other. But we didn't kiss again. We hadn't even held hands again since Valentine's Day. And if I was being honest, I didn't know what to do with myself.

Didn't know how to be around him without asking him what we were anymore.

It was all I could do to chip away at the word document on my computer to distract myself. I surprised myself by typing another ten thousand words here and there over the week

My phone buzzed, and I unlocked it to find a text from Matthew. I couldn't help the racing of my heart when I saw his name on the screen—especially not after everything that had happened between us.

MATTHEW
Hey, are you free tonight?

I chuckled at my phone. He knew that I was. I wasn't on duty tonight as Hall Director, had pretty much got everything done in preparation for spring break in two weeks, and was currently just sitting on my couch, scrolling through my computer.

Pretending like I was going to type on my book document, but this sounded much more promising.

NOELLE
Well, prof. I don't have class tonight, but I'm sure you already know that.

You know that wasn't why I was asking, Noelle.

Okay... Well, I don't have any specific plans.

Good. Do you want to go to the Blazer's game with me? I have an extra ticket.

I wasn't sure how to feel: on one hand, I was a little giddy that he was inviting me somewhere again, but on the other hand, I wasn't even his first choice. But it wasn't like we were dating, right? Nor were we even *best* friends... So why was there this sinking feeling in my stomach that there was someone else that he would have rather had come with him? Maybe one of his buddies. Especially since he was asking me at the last minute.

Sure, sounds like fun.

I finally typed a response back, and then leaned against the couch, shutting my eyes as I waited for his reply to come through.

> Okay. I'll pick you up at 5:00?

> Yeah. You know where I live.

> See you soon, sweetheart.

I was getting increasingly used to being around Matthew, just *having* him around in general, but was I going to admit to him that I have barely seen any sports games and my knowledge of sports was slim at best? Absolutely not. Especially not when I thought about the fact that he told me he played basketball in college.

I groaned. I was so in over my head.

When he picked me up, I was dressed in a cute black turtleneck bodysuit and a pair of skinny jeans—what did one wear to a basketball game, anyway? I paired it with my favorite long gold necklace and a pair of ankle booties, and after surveying myself in the mirror for about the hundredth time, deciding to apply a quick coat of eye makeup and lipstick, I was finally ready when his knock came at the door.

"Hi." I smiled, leaning on the door frame as I opened it up.

"You look beautiful."

I blushed. Why was it that the sweet things this man would say to me were the ones that made me feel so treasured, and appreciated? I felt like I was constantly flushing red around him. "Thank you. I didn't know what one normally wears to a basketball game, so I just guessed."

"Well, you look great." Matthew smiled, and I grabbed my coat and purse off the side table. "Ready to go?" he asked.

"Yep." I pulled the door shut behind me and locked it with my keys.

~

"Wait, wait, wait." I pulled at his arm, coming to a stop in the middle of the stadium. Because I was staring at him, at the tickets, and our seats, and I was sure my jaw was on the floor. He hadn't told me that the seats were courtside at the freaking game, and I felt grossly unprepared for watching the game right on the floor. We were there early after Matthew had secured us some snacks—I suspected he figured out that I hadn't eaten in a few hours, because he seemed to have some sort of radar for food with me—and then he guided us to our seats, not even a hint of hesitation as he walked through the rows of benches.

"Matthew," I hissed at him, "You didn't tell me you got us court-side tickets."

"Oh, I didn't?" he said, holding back a laugh, a twinkle of amusement in his eyes.

"No! You didn't!" I whisper-yelled back, and that was when he took my hand in his free one, and I tried to ignore the sparks up my arm as our hands connected. The heat that bloomed in my chest at the warmth of his palm in mine.

After we settled into our seats, I had hardly put a piece of popcorn in my mouth when two extremely tall brunette players walked up to us.

"Um, hello?" I said, peering in between them and Matthew, catching all of the goofy grins on their faces.

What the hell was he up to?

"Noelle," Matthew finally said, "these are my friends, Cole and Tanner."

"You're... what? You *know* them?" Oh my god, I hadn't realized tonight involved a meet and greet with two of the actual players. I didn't even know much about sports, but the two guys standing in front of me were tall and unmistakably handsome.

I tried to take a break from my mini-freak-out (because, hello?) and turned back to them. "Hi." I gave a sheepish wave. "I'm Noelle."

"It's good to finally meet Matthew's girl." One of the twins drawled, and I was fairly sure if my jaw wasn't already opened, it would have been at that.

His girl? Why did I want to squeal over that? It was possessive, but I liked the sound of it, surprisingly.

"Yeah, he's been *super* secretive about you, but we all can't wait to get to know you better." The other twin laughed.

I glanced over at Matthew, who looked a little sheepish, one hand still holding the popcorn he had bought and the other one draped over the back of my chair. He leaned in closer to whisper in my ear. "Sorry for not telling you. I thought it'd be a fun surprise. And—oh, look! They made it!"

Matthew glanced up, and it was then that I noticed the couple he must have been talking about heading to the seats next to us: a beautiful, dark-haired pregnant woman and the man whose palm was against her back, guiding her towards our chairs.

"Bryan! Elizabeth!" One of the twins exclaimed as they settled into the bench beside us. "Glad you could all make it." The woman—Elizabeth—settled in next to me, and her husband sat beside her. I gave her a small smile as I waited for Matthew to introduce us.

"These are our other best friends, Bryan and Elizabeth." Matthew gestured to the two of them, and then his free hand was slipping into mine again, squeezing it. "This is Noelle."

"Hi," I gave a sheepish smile, looking around at the group. "It's nice to meet you all." We all exchanged hellos before he turned back to the twins. "Are your girls coming tonight?" Matthew asked Cole and Tanner, who just shook their heads.

"I'm sorry, hold up a moment," I said, interrupting the conversation while looking at Matthew, "I'm still trying to get over the fact that you're friends with two of the Blazers?" I was pretty sure my jaw was still on the ground.

Matthew shrugged. "We all went to college together." He grinned at me. "They offered me tickets tonight and I couldn't turn them down." And when he had said everyone else was busy... it seemed like all his closest friends were right here. *Oh.*

So maybe I was the first person to cross his mind. After all, his friends had called me his girl. I sat a little straighter, feeling the warmth and pride from the idea flowing through me.

"Matthew has told us so much about you," Elizabeth gushed from my side. She was gorgeous, with her tanned skin and dark hair and a glow to her that was radiant.

He *had*? "I wish I could say the same," I fake glared at him, though I was really trying to hold in a smile that he had been talking about me with his friends. Why did that make me... happy? "But I'm afraid Matthew hasn't shared much about any of you with me. He's somewhat of an enigma." He just looked back at me with the most adorable feigning-ignorance eyes.

Bryan, from Elizabeth's side, chuckled. "You have no idea, Noelle. I've known him for over twelve *years*, and I still haven't quite figured him out."

"Oh, well." I locked eyes with Matthew, unable to pull myself away from the icy blue of his eyes. I was always getting lost in them. "Hopefully one day I'll understand the whole of Matthew Harper, huh?"

"If anyone can do it, you can," Elizabeth said, nudging me in the side. I think I flushed a little, the red spreading over my freckled cheekbones at that declaration.

And... what? What did he tell all of his friends about me that they were so sure I was going to crack Matthew's perfectly crafted interior? What made me so special that they thought I alone could melt the ice around his heart?

But... maybe I already had, considering how much he did for me. Considering how much he had shared with me in the last two weeks.

I muttered something unintelligible under my breath, and then Cole and Tanner were departing, and everyone was wishing them good luck on the game, and I was pretty sure I was still just *staring* at Matthew.

As the game began, all of the players from both teams ran out onto the court as they were announced, and I lost myself in it. Did I know what was going on most of the time? Absolutely not. Did

I still stand up with the others and cheer when our team made a basket? Yeah, I did. (I was trying, here, especially after Matthew told me he played in college. I hadn't wanted to seem like an idiot.)

Halfway through the game, they started the *dreaded* Kiss Cam up. I groaned when I saw it, burying my face into Matthew's shoulder, and sighed in relief as it almost stopped on us several times but moved to someone else. Finally, it focused on Bryan and Elizabeth, who got a loving peck on the lips from her husband.

And then up on the screen—there were our faces. Yep, that *was* us, on the kiss cam. I didn't know when I had gotten so terrified of public displays of affection—it may have been because I guessed that Matthew didn't like them, but I didn't want either one of us to be comfortable. And it felt like if we did this, if we kissed here, in front of all of his friends, we couldn't go back from it.

Maybe we didn't want to, not anymore.

"Matthew—" I started to protest, looking at him. I knew we had kissed before, but this—in public? I was trying not to freak out.

"Hey. Breathe. Just don't think about them. Focus on me," he breathed, hand resting on my thigh as he leaned in closer.

But yeah... I *wanted* to kiss him again, didn't I?

Before I could say anything else, his lips were on mine, softly at first, and then he wrapped his hand around my neck, bringing me closer to him and deepening the kiss. His tongue was pushing against my lips, seeking entrance, and I couldn't help but let him in. God, this kiss... It was full of passion, longing. Our tongues joined together as our mouths connected, and I was *melting* underneath his touch. My hands were in his hair—w*hen had they gotten there?* —digging in tight to his wavy blonde locks. Pulling myself closer to him.

The crowd *erupted* with cheers as Matthew full-on kissed me right there, in front of everyone. *Oh*. Oh, *God*. I pulled away, breaking the kiss, and my face flushed as he stared at me, his hands finding my face, lingering there, thumb caressing my cheekbone over and over as he looked in my eyes.

And... What did a kiss like *that* between us even mean? Because I could tell, from the way he kissed me, that he wanted me as much as I wanted him. I knew it, fundamentally in my bones, from the way I lit up just from his touch. The way his hand lingered on my neck sent little fireworks down my body, even as his lips pulled away. I was on fire, heated just from the simplest of touches, but all I wanted was more, more, more.

Somehow though, at that moment... He made me feel *comfortable*, even with all the people who were watching us. And all I wanted was his lips on mine again. I couldn't deny the way he had made me feel. Comforted, wanted, and always cared for.

"You good?" he breathed. I nodded into his hand that was still cupping my cheek, trying to pretend like I wasn't nuzzling into his large palm. But I couldn't find it in myself to be embarrassed, even when he pulled away and tucked me underneath his arm. I cuddled into his side, resting my head against his chest.

For the rest of the game, his hand never left my shoulder, that thumb rubbing circles against my bicep, holding me into his side maybe just a little *too* closely. I couldn't bring myself to care, though, not when it felt so right to be tucked into his body. To absorb the warmth from him down to my bones. I was so close that when I inhaled, the smell of his cologne—a wonderful, masculine scent, with woodsy notes of pine and fresh air layered on top—flooded through my senses.

It was like my whole body had come alive. Just from his touch, his smell, and the thoughtful expression that didn't leave his face as I leaned into him further.

"Thank you," I breathed, so quietly I didn't think he had heard me, even as his fingers dragged against my leg and I interwound our fingers.

"For what?" Matthew murmured back into my hair a few moments later, and I smiled.

"For *this*. For always making me feel comfortable." I felt like it was just the two of us in this bubble, and nothing could pop it.

I didn't want to leave this moment. Wanted to stay here, nestled into him, absorbing his warmth, feeling his hand in mine.

"Anything for you," I thought I heard him mumble before I felt a kiss on the crown of my head. I blushed a little, turning my eyes back to Matthew's friends on the court.

After the game, the twins, Cole and Tanner, said hi to us in the hallway near the locker rooms, and then Matthew was guiding me out of the Moda Center, towards his truck, and it was only when he stopped abruptly in front of a bench that I gave him a puzzling stare.

"Matthew—" I started, right as he cleared his throat and said, "Noelle."

"Oh," I said.

He waved me off. "You can go first."

"Um." I bit my lip. "I'm just wondering, Matthew. Because now I've met your friends, and we spent Valentine's Day together, and now this, and I just... What are we?"

"What do you want us to be?" he asked.

"Well, we're friends, right?" The words felt...wrong, somehow, coming out of my mouth now. Even though we were, we had started to feel like something more, too.

His blonde brows furrowed on his forehead as he looked at me. "Do you think friends normally kiss like that, Noelle?"

That kiss—that spinning, dizzying kiss he had given me for the kiss cam. The kind that set my soul on fire and had me aching for him, aching for more. I'd take whatever he'd be willing to give me. Could I tell him that what I wanted was him, all of him?

I began walking towards the parking garage again when he reached out a hand, grabbing my wrists and holding me in place.

"Noelle—" his voice was pained as if it hurt him to say it. "I just—"

"It doesn't have to mean anything," I confirmed. "Not unless you want it to." And friends could kiss, surely? Maybe I hadn't ever kissed any of my friends—didn't want to, for that matter. I had hardly ever found myself this intimately connected with anyone else... But surely, there was logical reasoning for these kisses beside the one thing I was trying so hard to deny.

"Do you think *I* kiss my friends like that?" He gripped my chin, tilting my head up to look at him.

I think I swallowed. I might have licked my lips. All I knew for sure was the next thing to slip out of my mouth was "No."

No. I don't think you would kiss a friend like that. I just don't know how to deal with all of my feelings for you. Because what will I do if I get attached and then you decide this isn't worth it? How will I deal with that, then?

Looking up into his eyes, I realized I wanted things that I hadn't wanted since Jake. Things I maybe hadn't even wanted with Jake.

Love. A future. A life together.

Fuck. When did I begin to want those things again? Had this man somehow made me yearn for the love and appreciation I hadn't felt in years? All because he... what? Cared for me? Made me feel protected, even safe? Because he kissed me like if he didn't, the world was going to end?

I was really in over my head here.

Maybe I needed to sit down.

Because there was no way I was thinking all of these things—not for him. I tried to remind myself that no matter what I felt, we shouldn't...

I couldn't listen to that part of my brain anymore, though. Not when he was looking at me like this.

Like I was everything.

CHAPTER 16
Matthew

We were standing outside of the Blazers Stadium—inches apart—and I thought if I didn't kiss her again I might lose my mind. And...just *friends*? Was that all she wanted us to be? All she thought I wanted us to be?

I didn't kiss my friends like that. In truth, I hadn't kissed anyone like that—ever—not until Noelle, but I didn't want to freak her out by telling her that. The passion and intensity I felt for her... I had never experienced anything like this with *anyone*. But if all she wanted was for us to be friends, then I guessed I would take what I could get to continue to be around her. I enjoyed her presence too much to risk that. Every conversation, every laugh, every smile... I was convinced that Noelle was the most captivating woman I had ever met.

But I couldn't help myself, standing this close to her. I could smell her perfume, like sweet-smelling roses, and she was right there. And I wanted more of her. "Do you... think I kiss my friends like that?" I asked, voice a little hoarser than I had hoped.

Noelle just looked at me, and then I caught her face. Our gazes connected and I could feel the sparks as we just stared at each other, inches apart, and finally—Noelle shook her head. "No." Her voice was all breathless. I watched her run her tongue over her bottom lip, and then I leaned in closer to her, close enough that she would be able to feel my breath on her skin when I spoke.

"How about we try again?" I murmured, running a finger across her jawbone. "And you can tell me if I kiss you like a friend, sweetheart."

Noelle sucked in a deep breath, brown eyes connecting straight with mine, and then she nodded. Permission.

I closed the distance between our lips in a heartbeat. I did what I had wanted to do since the kiss cam had left us. This kiss was slow, at first, just a few gentle presses to her mouth. Exploratory pecks. And then, I kissed her harder as she parted her lips for me. And we were losing ourselves in each other, in this kiss. Her hands found my chest, clutching onto my shirt, fists in tiny little balls as both of mine cupped her face.

Kissing her—*ah*. Kissing her made me feel like everything was right in the world. Tasting the sweetness on her tongue, feeling her body pressed up against mine as she moaned into my mouth... Was there any experience in the world that was as good as this? If I could be kissing her... Why would I bother doing anything else?

By the time we broke apart, we were both breathing heavily, lips swollen and I knew—I could see it in her eyes. The *lust*. Her lust, for me. The thing that had been *building*, growing, and festering since the very first time we saw each other, the first time we spoke. I had known, even then, that I wanted her. And I couldn't ignore it anymore, couldn't ignore the way my body responded to hers, the way she made me feel things I didn't even know I could feel. Things I hadn't ever felt for anyone, ever.

She ran a finger over her pink lips and frowned at me, the desire and lust slowly disappearing from her eyes as she seemed to remember where we were.

"Fuck," I groaned, looking down at the ground. "Noelle—"

"Don't apologize," came Noelle's response. And then she blinked a few times before meeting my eyes again. "Matthew, I—"

"We should get you home, Noelle," I said as I tucked her hand into mine and headed towards the parking garage.

Before I do something stupid and ask you to stay the night at my house. Before we let our lust rush us into bed with each other.

Noelle nestled into the warmth of my body heat and held onto the arm I had wrapped around her. I couldn't help it—touching her was second nature at this point, and it felt so right to have her here, like this. We drove the truck in silence, the only noise you could hear was the cars on the busy roads, and I just wished I could have her like this, forever.

I had to find a way to make her mine, really mine, and hold on tight.

Because I wanted to keep her.

∼

NOELLE WAS beautiful as she stood outside her dorm building, wrapped up in the sweatshirt she had found in my car. It was huge on her, but I liked seeing her in it—it made me feel a touch possessive, but I decided right then and there that there was nothing that I liked more than the sight of her in my clothes.

"How long are we going to ignore this thing between us?" Noelle whispered to me, stepping in closer as we stood by the truck. Not leaving. I didn't want to say goodbye, and I could tell she didn't want to go inside either. "Do you not... Are you not interested in me like that?" She bit her lip, looking more insecure than I had ever seen her.

"Not interested in you?" I muttered, a low growl coming from my diaphragm.

She blinked back in surprise. "I—what?"

In all of the time we had spent together, up till now, we had never talked about it, this thing that I knew was between us.

I wrapped an arm around her waist and tilted her head towards me. "How can you even think I wouldn't be interested in you like that, Noelle?" I shook my head. It was maddening how much I wanted this girl. How attracted I was, had always been, to her.

"Well—every time we kiss, you stop it before it can go any further."

"Because we're always in *public*. Because I'm trying not to fuck this up before it's even started. Because I like you so much, I think I would die if I did something to scare you away."

"I just thought..." Noelle closed her eyes. She looked a little mortified, and I hated it. Hated that I had created any doubt for her. "That you didn't think I was pretty enough." She mumbled under her breath. There was something else, too, but I didn't catch it.

"Noelle. You're... You don't even know what you do to me, sweetheart. How much I want you, all the time. How much I want to take you inside right now and fuck you all night long." I cupped my hands over her cheeks. "Tell me you feel this too, Noelle."

We were almost pressed completely together, and I wondered if she looked down if she'd be able to *see* how much I wanted her. My growing desire, just from touching her. From thinking about going inside her apartment and slipping underneath the sheets with her.

"*This*," I repeated, and I tried to ignore the thump-thump-thump of my heart. Wondered if she could feel it beating against her chest. "This... attraction. Sometimes I think it's going to *drown* me, Noelle, the pull I feel to you. I *know* you know what I'm talking about. I know you feel it."

"And what if I do?" Her voice was hoarse, barely above a whisper. "What if I do want that? All of it?"

"Then we should stop resisting it," I said as I pulled her in closer to me, as every inch of me pressed up against every curve of her.

"*Can* we?"

"Noelle..." I sighed, and brushed my thumb against her cheek, smoothing her soft skin under my touch. She shuddered a little, and I knew she was as affected by me as I was by her.

"This thing between us," She started, eyes locked onto mine, our lips only centimeters apart. "I... I don't *want* to ignore it. Not anymore." She blinked up at me, and her beautiful brown eyes were hypnotizing.

"So?" I asked. I wondered if I sounded as breathless as I felt, with her lips hovering right below mine.

"So kiss me again, Matthew," she said, intertwining her fingers through the hair at the base of my skull. "And tell me how much you want me," she pleaded. "Ask me to come inside."

"I think about you all the damn time, baby," I said, and then my lips were on hers, finally, *finally*.

And *this kiss*—this one was passionate, caring, both of us giving in to the lust in our blood when we looked at each other. But it was more than that, with Noelle, and maybe it always had been.

But I couldn't think about that—about anything. Not with her lips on mine. Not as she had twisted her hands in my hair, pulling herself closer to me, pressing our bodies further together. My arms wrapped around her thighs, lifting her hips, hoisting her up onto my body—which pressed her right up against my erection. I groaned at the contact, hoping she couldn't feel how hard I was through my jeans.

She let out a small noise of surprise before wrapping her legs around my waist, locking herself in place on my body as I kissed her again. As I let my tongue slip into her mouth and hers into mine.

I was well aware we were making out in front of the dorm she worked at, but I couldn't find it in me to care, not when I was feeling so much. And I hated it because the sight of her building sobered me up. Made me think about where we were.

"I can't come inside," I whispered when we pulled away from each other. Noelle almost seemed transfixed as she ran her hands over my face, cupping my jaw as we continued to hold our gaze.

"I know," she sighed, looking at the building. It was a line that we couldn't cross. "But..."

"I want to make you so happy," I said, a whispered promise on a sweet reverent breath. She pushed the hair off of my forehead and kissed my jaw. "Let me make you happy, Noelle," I murmured, "please?"

She gave me a small smile, nodding. It was all I wanted, to make her happy.

"I should go," I added, needing to pull away before I did something stupid. I cupped her face once more with my palm. "I'll see you Monday." I needed to go home and take care of my problem down there before I went mad, but I knew I couldn't let my urges get the better of me.

I needed to go slow and take my time with her. I dropped a final kiss on her lips before I watched her walk away.

It was Monday—the beginning of the last week before Spring Break. And for some reason... I knew I needed to make the next week count. And maybe... Maybe she would *want* to spend her Spring Break with me. At my house.

Where she'd let me worship her all night long.

~

"So." Bryan raised an eyebrow as I pushed around the eggs on my plate. I was currently trying to remember why I had agreed to go to breakfast with them in the first place. Seemed like a bad idea now, as I was about to get interrogated by them.

"So," I said back, not feeling like playing this game. I directed a glower right at him. "Get on with it."

"Just friends, huh?" He smirked. Elizabeth rolled her eyes as she leaned against her husband.

"We're just—" I shrugged. "I don't know what we *are*, you guys." I groaned. "I just like being around her."

"We could tell," Elizabeth smiled. "She seemed nice. I'm glad you brought her." I looked back down at my plate as I waited for the classic *I told you so.*

Because hadn't they both said something in the bar not that long ago? And suddenly, I was grateful that it was just the three of us getting breakfast—Cole and Tanner had chosen to spend the day with their girlfriends. Bryan and Liz might have been relentless about me being happy and finding someone to settle down with, but I knew it was only because they wanted me to be as happy as they were. Cole and Tanner, on the other hand? They just loved to tease me. Never mind that I was older than them, they always loved finding ways to get under my skin.

"I think she's good for you," Liz said, pulling me from my thoughts as she sipped her decaffeinated tea. "You smile more around her."

I tried to ponder that thought. "Yeah," I muttered, frowning at her being right, "I guess I do."

"Cheer up, you sap," Bryan grinned at me. "You like her. We could tell from the way she was looking at you last night that she likes you. And she certainly let you kiss her—"

I flushed. Like, my neck and ears were red, and I knew that they could see it if I could feel it. Great. Now we were going to talk about me shoving my tongue down her throat at the game. Lovely. A grown man, basically blushing over kissing a girl.

"It's not like I haven't caught the two of you sticking your tongues down each other's throats a few dozen times over the years."

"Well, that's different," Elizabeth insisted, looking at her husband as I raised an eyebrow. "We ended up getting married," she grinned at me as she picked up her breakfast sandwich.

Bryan rolled his eyes at his wife, before turning back to me. "We also never tried to hide us from you. Once we realized we liked each other, that was it. We were together." My best friend smiled smugly, looping his arm around his wife. And maybe I was a little envious of their college romance, and how easy it had been for them.

"It's not that easy," I finally said, shaking my head.

"Isn't it? Just man up and tell her you want more with her, dumbass."

"It's—"

"Don't you dare tell me *it's not that simple* or *it's too hard* or anything like that. Matt. I've known you since we were eighteen. Since we were stupid freshmen walking into our dorm rooms. I've never seen you act this stupid over a girl before. So can you just... I dunno, tell her how you feel?"

"What if..." I said, and then I paused. Saying the words out loud seemed like I was dooming myself. But, when Bryan raised an eyebrow and Elizabeth just sighed at me, I knew I had to keep going. "What if I tell her, and she doesn't want me like that? What if... she rejects me?" Could I handle that? I didn't know.

Elizabeth shook her head. "Don't let your fear of losing her keep you from going after what you want, Matthew. And if that's her... just tell her." She glanced at Bryan, and then looked back at me.

"What?" I asked her, suspicious over the look she shared with her husband.

"I have an idea. But you have to trust me."

I did. Of course, I did—she was one of my closest friends. She married my best friend, for goodness' sake. I would do almost anything she asked because that was how much I trusted and respected her. So I nodded.

And then she told me her idea, and I knew what I had to do.

I took a big gulp of water, hoping I wasn't making the dumbest decision—or biggest mistake—of my life.

Hoping that the girl I wanted more than anything wanted me back. Hoping that there was a future in front of me that didn't involve me, alone.

It was all I wanted, and suddenly—all I needed. Her, just her.

CHAPTER 17
Noelle

I couldn't help replaying our kiss over and over in my mind for the rest of the weekend. Not the one at the game, but the one after. When he asked me if I thought he normally kissed his friends like that, and then he showed me. And my body—every bit of me—was on fire. Every time he touched me, it was like something awakened in me, and I didn't know if I could go back anymore. Didn't know if I wanted to. Because even thinking about it now, my pulse was thrumming, and my heart was pounding in my chest.

I couldn't help but replay the moment when he stood on my doorstep as he dropped me off after the game, and I had looked up at him, just staring into his eyes. Neither one of us pulling away, only inches apart, not moving closer.

But putting it into words, talking about how I had *never* felt anything like this before in my entire life, even for the man I had once thought I would marry? It terrified me. Being that open and honest with him was like giving him a piece of my heart. Dazed and distracted, I had turned my focus back to him. To his skin touching mine. To the sparks that ignited in my blood at his touch.

This thing that was between us? I felt it, so strongly, every day

—the pull to him. The magnetic attraction snapped into place the moment we locked eyes across a crowded room. And there was this feeling that somehow this was *right*. Like out of everything in my life, it was *him* that made sense to my brain. Every other decision faded away until it was just him and me standing in an empty room, sparks flying between us as his eyes caught mine. And I knew—one of us would cave. One of us would stop running, and we would give into this thing. It was inevitable. Because I craved his touch and his kisses and so much more, and I couldn't keep telling myself I didn't want it or couldn't have it anymore.

I needed it—needed him.

I wanted to plead with the universe. Ask them—God, or the fates, or whoever was in charge—to give us our happy ending. Tell them that if this *was* fate, if we were meant to be, then I needed to know we would be okay. That we could be happy.

Because if I let Matthew Harper have my heart, there was no getting it back.

As much as I couldn't deny the physical connection we shared, the butterflies in my gut, or the spatial awareness I felt in his presence—it was the way he had shown me, over and over, how much he cared for me that really mattered. Someone who just wanted my body, wanted to sleep with me and discard me, would never look at me this reverently, right?

Not like the way Matthew had looked at me last night. Like I was his damnation, but also his savior. He looked at me in a way I hoped he had never looked at anyone before, because I wanted this—him—to be all mine. For this feeling, these moments, to be just ours. And the heated expression in his eyes right before he finally pressed his lips to mine... I knew there was no going back from this moment. For either of us.

I wondered, for only a moment, if I should worry about that. Because as much as I was sure Matthew Harper could, and *had*, repaired my shattered heart, I also knew he could just as easily leave it broken on the ground once again. But I couldn't think about that, not *now*.

Not while I was sitting with my friends. I couldn't keep the truth from them anymore. Not when I had been this close to begging him to take me back to his house, making him give me what he promised me. *Fuck you all night long* was on a loop in my brain right now. The words sounded so absolutely filthy coming out of his mouth. But I loved it. And I wanted it.

So I told them it... All of it. Well—except for his comment about what he wanted to do to me in my bedroom. They didn't need to know *that*.

"You guys *kissed*!?" Gabrielle cried out, gaping at me as I pushed around the eggs on my plate at our favorite breakfast place on Saturday morning.

"Shhh," I said, looking around as I bit into my croissant sandwich. "Don't say it so loud!"

"Noelle," Angelina rolled her eyes. "I don't think anyone in here is going to care about your relationship." She dropped her voice into a conspiratorial whisper. "Not even if he's a smoking hot professor."

"It's not that," I protested. I just didn't want to share the details with the whole world. Especially not at our coffee shop, the one we came to almost every weekend, where the baristas knew our names and orders.

Gabbi frowned. "Honestly, what exactly are you holding back for, Noelle? You want him, right? And it sounds like you want him. So what's the problem?"

"I just—" What *was* holding me back? The truth was, I *did* want him. Had wanted him since he kissed me the first time, really. Would have let him do me against the tree, right then and there, if we hadn't been out in the open. Why were we constantly having this happen to us in public places?

I couldn't get him out of my mind. Couldn't get the way he had held me after the Blazers game to stop feeling like an imprint on my brain. It was like kissing him had rewired my entire brain, and all I knew was I didn't want to run away from it—didn't want to run away from him anymore.

"I don't know what I'll do if it ends badly, you guys. Jake... he broke me."

"And since you met Matthew, you've finally been smiling again, Noelle. Do you know how long it's been since we've seen you genuinely happy? Because in all the time since you moved back from New York, I don't think I've ever seen you smile as much as you have this past month." Charlotte said, somehow always knowing exactly what I needed to hear.

And I realized she was right.

I *had* been smiling again. Not because of him, necessarily, but because the wounds Jake had left in me felt like they were growing smaller. Because the weight of the grief had lessened since this big grumpy professor had walked into my life and showed me how much he cared about me in so many different ways. So many ways I had never even known, even when I had someone I called my own. Someone who I *thought* had loved me.

And last night, when I kissed him as we said goodbye, our bodies pressed together... I knew. It was an undeniable truth. I wanted this man. My *body* wanted this man. I was so tired of dancing around, not knowing quite what we were. He had kissed me, taken me to dinner, spent time with me... but what *were* we?

It was safe to say I knew we were *friends* now. But it was more than that. There was this... energy when we were around each other. I could tell he felt an attraction to me as strongly as I did to him. The way he reacted when he touched me, was like it zapped his skin. How his eyes drooped lower as his hand brushed against mine—yeah, I wasn't imagining it. And I wanted to hold his hand through *life*. So badly.

"You're right." I sighed. "I think I really like him."

"You *think*?" Angelina snorted. "Ging, we know you do. And we get it. Truly. So go get your man."

I groaned into my arm as I laid my head against the table. "But how?" I asked, rhetorically, but when I lifted my head I found shared wicked expressions on all three of my friends' faces.

"I have an idea," Gabbi smirked.

If last night was any indication, the way Matthew had pressed against me, the way I knew he wanted to come inside my apartment...

But at least, after *this*, neither one of us could say we were just friends.

~

I KNOCKED on the door to his office. I knew his last class of the day had already gotten out, and I hoped that he was there.

He'd been on my mind all weekend, even more so after I left lunch with my friends on Saturday. And now, here I was, standing outside his door on Monday afternoon because I thought I might go crazy if I had to go one more day without seeing him.

"Come in," his voice came through the door, and I took a deep breath before opening it.

As I slipped into his office, the short heels of my boots clicked against the tile floor. For a moment I just stood there, hand still on the doorknob as I stared at him from the doorway. Then I cleared my throat, enjoying the way his eyes trailed up and down my body, and smiled at him. "*Professor Harper.*"

"*Miss Hastings?*" Matthew raised an eyebrow in question at me.

I finally closed the door behind me and flipped the lock. There was no point in risking anyone catching us in here alone together. I leaned against the door as I watched him.

Matthew, no longer sitting, was leaning against the desk, arms crossed over his chest. He looked perfectly relaxed, the complete picture of comfortable and confident all at once. His blonde hair was combed back today, just a single piece falling onto his forehead. A little single curl that I wanted to reach out and brush back.

Patience, Noelle, I tried to give myself a pep talk. *You have a plan.* A plan that involved a red lacy underwear set, but I didn't argue that back with the wisest part of my conscience. I snorted at the thought, and Matthew just stared at me as I resisted laughing at myself. Instead, I just admired how good he looked leaning against his desk.

"And what can I help you with today, Miss Hastings?"

"Oh. Well, you see, Professor..." I smirked at him and played with the hem of my skirt. My very, very short skirt. "I seem to have a problem, and as it turns out, only you can solve it."

He raised an eyebrow and rose off the desk to take a step toward me. "And what might this problem be?" He trailed off, looking straight at me.

We had grown closer over the last two months, and after all of those possibilities of *something*, all of that *want*, well... I was tired of fighting this.

"*You.*" I breathed.

"Noelle..." I looked at him with a tilt of my head. "Me?" he simply asked, and I just smiled sweetly, looking up at him while batting my eyelashes.

"Yes, Matthew," I repeated. "*You* are my problem." I could feel the warmth creep through my body, my pulse racing as he took another step toward me.

I needed this. Needed him.

He hummed. "And do you... have a solution to this problem of yours, sweetheart?"

"I have a few ideas, but I'm open to suggestions... *Sir.*"

I took a step back as he took another forward, finally ending with my back pressed up against the door as his body was now only a breath apart from mine. I was close enough to catch a whiff of his cologne, the strong and masculine scent so seemingly *him* that it filled all of my senses.

"My sweet little Noelle. Did you come here just to tempt me?"

"I have no idea what you're talking about," I breathed, hand moving towards his body. I wanted to touch him. He was so close. I just wanted to taste his lips again, to feel his breath on my neck. I wanted all of him, every last thing he would give me. I would let him have whatever he wanted if he only asked for it.

"Sweetheart," he said, lips only inches from my forehead. "My little temptress. Do you know how much I think about you? I can't get you out of my goddamned mind."

I tilted my head up as his hand found my face, cupping my chin. "No," I breathed. "Tell me. Tell me how much you think about me."

"You *vex* me," Matthew said, and then he crashed his lips onto mine, once again giving in to the pull we felt between us. "You *enchant* me." He placed a kiss on my lips. "I think you've placed a curse on me because all I want is *you*." I thought again how strange it was that his lips against mine just felt so *right*. I tried to remind myself who he was to me, that he was a professor, but all I could see was the warm and kind man who had helped me with my project, taken care of me when I was drunk and made sure I was getting enough sleep. None of that mattered anymore, because we were here, and he wanted me. I knew he wanted me.

"I couldn't sleep," I said, pulling back as my hands grasped the collar of his shirt. "Ask me why I couldn't sleep, Matthew."

"Why couldn't you sleep, Noelle?"

"I would lay in my bed at night and think about you, Matthew. About your kisses. Your hands. What it would feel like when you touched me. Wishing that you were in my bed *with me*." I ran my lips over my mouth. "I want you," I breathed. "So much, Matthew."

"I told you, I'm not going to fight this anymore," he said against my ear, before placing a kiss there. Nibbling at my earlobe. "I can't. I can't ignore what I feel for you, Noelle."

We were still against the door, me trapped within his big arms, and I once again appreciated his height. Even though I wasn't exactly short at 5'6, I loved the way he completely towered over me, and how his tall frame dwarfed mine. And God, with his head, tilted into mine as he held my face with his big, strong hands, I thought that there was nowhere else in the world that I'd rather be than in his arms. I shifted beneath him, still pushed up against the door, the wooden grain rough on my back, the door handle cutting into my back as he pressed me roughly against it.

His lips were back on mine, and the way he was kissing me—like perhaps he would die without it, without my touch under his—it completely derailed me from any other logical thought. All I could focus on was the feeling of his lips against mine, soft lips in stark contrast to the scruff of his not-yet-shaved beard against my cheeks. His tongue pushed against my lips, begging for entrance, and I opened for him, letting him in, feeling a little dizzy as our tongues swirled together.

Matthew's hands moved from my face to my back, simply holding me closer to him. I couldn't help but bury my fingers in his hair, messing up his perfectly styled strands in the process. I took pleasure in how I ruffled through them even as he kissed me harder, with more passion and intensity.

This kiss. It wasn't soft, like the kiss we had shared after dinner. It was hard, commanding, maybe even a little sloppy, and full of desire. I couldn't help but let out a small moan into his mouth as his tongue explored mine even further. I fumbled with the hem of his shirt, wanting more of him, wanting to touch the bare skin he always kept hidden away, wanting to memorize the lines of his body with my hands.

"Do you—" he asked, pulling away as his tongue, wet with saliva from both his mouth and mine, trailed across his lips.

The words hadn't even left his mouth when I uttered, "Yes." I realized that I would agree to anything this man asked of me.

"You're sure?"

I nodded frantically. "Just *shut u*p and take my clothes off," I growled, tugging on the bottom of his sweater, pulling it off in one, fluid motion. Then I tugged at the buttons on his shirt, finally leaving it open against his skin.

And *hell*, maybe I was in heaven? Because the abs on his body were not what you ever expected to see on any professor. He was beautiful and sexy and, at this moment, at least for now, he was *mine*. I ran my hands down his chest, trailing over his nipples and down to his finely chiseled stomach.

He shrugged the rest of the shirt off of him, leaving it in a pile on the floor with his sweater. And then, *finally,* his hands were on me, tangling in the buttons of my blouse, pulling it open to display the red, lacy bra I had worn today.

"Did you wear this for me, baby?" He *tsked,* hands running over the straps, admiring the curve of my breast. "Pretty thing."

"Yes, *sir,*" I groaned as he ran a thumb over my nipple, exposed even underneath the layer of lace. "Just for you."

"Not sir," he whispered into my ear, breath hot against my neck. "If we're doing this—and we are—it's just us. Noelle and Matthew, not anyone or anything. Okay?" I nodded, and he snapped one of the bra straps against my skin, causing me to gasp at the sudden sting.

"Okay," I nodded.

He bent down, lips finding my neck as he placed open-mouthed kisses on it. I tilted my head to give him a better angle, to appreciate the way he sucked at my skin—the way he trailed down, sucking my covered nipple into his mouth.

"Oh, God—Matthew…" I closed my eyes. No one had ever done this to me before.

He leaned into me further, so close now that his breath was again on my cheek, and his fingers found the clasp of my bra in the back, quickly undoing it and letting the undergarment fall to the floor. Then I was bare in front of him, wearing only my skirt and thigh-high socks, feeling shyer than I ever had around this man.

"God, baby, you're absolutely *stunning*," Matthew said, although his tone was light and playful as he cupped my breasts with his hands. "You wore this outfit just for me, hm? Noelle—" God, this beautiful man who looked at me like he wanted me more than he wanted air to breathe.

His hands were so large, but even they couldn't fit all of my breasts in them. He massaged them before rubbing his thumbs over my nipples.

"Matthew, please—" I pushed my hands up his chest. "More, I need—I need more."

When he dropped his hands and put them on my waist, I pushed myself closer to him. I was so close that I could feel the bulge in his slacks against my thigh—God, the way he was already hard for me. I reached my hands out, palm cupping him through his pants. Matthew gave a sharp intake of breath as I also pressed my hard nipples against his chest.

"God, Noelle. Can you feel what you've done to me, sweetheart?" he murmured into my ear. And then Matthew tugged on the hem of my skirt, pushing it up, bringing into full view my lacy panties, red ones that were a matching set with my bra. "Am I going to find you all soaked and wet for me, sweetheart?"

"Yes," I moaned, and he placed a finger against the fabric, dragging it up over my folds, already sensitive yearning for him. Wet for *him,* just thinking about all the things I wanted him to do to me. Just from him touching me.

"Tell me who did this to you," he said, placing his hand over me, cupping my sex as his thumb brushed over the hem of my panties.

"Y-you." I rocked my hips into his hand, needing more pressure, more contact, *something.* "Just you. Only you."

He hummed, seemingly satisfied with my declaration, hooked one finger around the waistband of my underwear, and gently pulled them off of me. I couldn't help but notice the devilish grin spreading across his face as I trembled under his touch. When Matthew's fingers reached my feet, I moved to kick the panties off, but he put up a hand, and I froze. "Matthew, I need—"

"Shh, sweetheart. I got you. Let me take care of you, Noelle."

My eyes were on him, watching intently as he knelt before me, pulled the underwear the rest of the way off, and then stuffed them into his pocket before I could even open my mouth to protest. I raised an eyebrow but determinedly said nothing as he looked up at me, light blue eyes shining with *want*.

"Now, my sweet little temptress, what do you think your punishment should be for coming to my office like this, *hm?*" I whimpered, and Matthew's tongue clicked against the roof of his mouth. "Use your words, baby."

"Touch me," I begged. I needed him to touch me, to whisper sweet nothings into my ear, and to rock into me until I came. I didn't just want it, God, I needed it. "*Please* touch me, Matthew."

His hand slipped down between my thighs, fingers ghosting over my entrance before his thumb began circling my clit.

Fuck, I thought, closing my eyes as he began to pick up the pace.

And then he slipped one finger inside of me, exploring my wet folds, and I had to clasp my hand over my mouth to muffle the cries that threatened to escape. I tried to remind myself where we were—that we were in his office, that this hot-as-fuck Professor was the one crouched before me fingering me, but all I could think about was how good his finger felt inside of me.

"Fuck, you're so wet for me, Noelle."

"*Matthew*—" I moaned, and he increased the pressure, crooking his finger into me before slipping in a second one, working me with such intent that I had to grip the door frame, to stop myself from trembling. "Right there," I squeaked when he hit a particularly good spot, one that was sending waves of pleasure through my whole body. I was so close—

He pulled his fingers out, eliciting a deep whine from me. But his icy blue stare never left me as he licked me clean off of them. "*Please*," I moaned, trying to grab his hand to put it back where I wanted it, but he simply shook his head.

"I want to taste your sweet little cunt first, Noelle. But you have to be quiet," he urged. "Or someone's going to find us."

My nod was followed by a gasp as he gripped my thighs, spreading them apart. Matthew hoisted one leg over his shoulder as my thigh-high socks rolled down. I couldn't focus on any of it though, not when his lips were kissing up the inside of my legs, and then my whole brain went fuzzy when his tongue licked a line up my entrance.

And *oh God* when he dipped his tongue inside of me—I moaned, deeply. If it wasn't for his tight grip on my thighs, I probably would have lost the ability to stand.

One of his hands released its hold of me and his thumb found my clit, rubbing it in circles while he continued to feast on me with his tongue, lapping at my folds and exploring every inch of me. I again buried my hands in his blonde hair, tugging on the strands to pull him closer into me. "Matthew, *please*, I'm so close—"

He pulled away, thumb stilling as he looked up. "Shh, my good girl, we don't want everyone to hear you when I make you come." I could do this. I could be quiet. I removed the hand from the door frame to cover my mouth. But then he put his lips on me again, licking me all over, and I couldn't help the cry that I let out into my palm.

He was good with his tongue—God, how was it possible to be too good— and I wondered how many other girls he had taken just like this, with one leg over his shoulder and his mouth on them.

The thought made me suddenly angry, like my blood would boil over at just the idea of his mouth on someone else, but then he pressed his tongue down against my clit again, and any thought of other women was gone from my brain, leaving only thoughts of *good, so good, fuck, harder please, oh god.*

He lapped at my sex, sucking and kissing my most sensitive parts, and between it and him slipping two fingers back inside of me, working me fully, I could feel my body clenching around him, the pleasure building and peaking as Matthew worked me senseless with his tongue. "I—*Oh*—Matthew. I'm going to come," I cried into my hand. And it wasn't long before my back arched against the door and I reached my climax, and then I was *soaring*, muscles tightening as the feeling overtook me.

A few moments passed before I could catch my breath, and when he looked up at me, my body still awash with pleasure from the orgasm he had given me, the intensity in his eyes made me shiver. He slowly dropped my leg down as I let myself rest against the door frame, still heavily panting.

Matthew stood from the floor and his hand caught my chin, tilting my head up to look at him fully.

"Did you like that, wicked girl?" he asked, bringing his lips onto mine, letting me taste myself on him and I hummed into his mouth in agreement.

My fingers grasped his belt loops as I stared up at him, but before I could get another word in, he was scooping me up and placing me on the desk, still wearing only my skirt and socks.

I watched as he undid his belt and slid off his pants, kicking them away from him, and then his briefs followed quickly behind. Suddenly, the entirety of him was exposed in front of me—and he was *big,* so big.

I could feel my eyes growing wide. I wasn't a virgin in any sense of the word, but no one I had been with had ever been as big as he was. "Oh my *god,*" I balked, "You're—you're not gonna fit, you're so—"

"Shh, my sweet girl. You're gonna take me so well, I promise," he soothed, stepping towards me, running his hands over my bare shoulder. "I'm gonna take care of you, baby. I promise." He waited for me to take a breath and nod before he used his knee to push my legs open, stepping all the way in, his dick standing between us, against my stomach. "I'm going to take you right here, Noelle. On this desk. Spread those pretty legs wide for me, honey."

"Matthew—please..."

"I'm going to fuck you now, Noelle, and when I do, you're going to be *mine,* okay? So, you can't charm anyone else with those big brown eyes of yours—cause I'm the only one who gets to see you like this, who gets to feel your pussy clenching around me, hm?" I nodded in agreement, hands drifting down towards him, running a finger over the precum that dripped from the top of him.

He leaned back, opened a desk drawer, and pulled out a shiny square package, and I wondered at the implications of him having condoms in his desk. Had he been expecting this, *here*?

Wanting to take me in his office, to fuck me senseless till I couldn't think anymore? And if he had... Why did that make me *more* turned on?

I took the package from his hands, unwrapping it and pumping him once, twice, before I pushed it down on him.

"Good girl," he rumbled and then moved closer to me, his eyes clouded in a haze of lust. I moved my hips closer to the edge of the desk, gripping the wood tightly. "You're sure, right, Noelle?"

I nodded. He notched himself at my entrance, guiding his hard length into me, even as I was still sensitive from the previous orgasm.

"*Matthew*," I gritted through bared teeth as I tried not to cry out at the pressure of him against me as his tip entered me. Matthew pushed in slowly at first, giving my body time to adjust to the feeling of him, and even with how wet I was, it was still a tight fit. I tilted my hips up to try to accommodate his length better.

"Noelle, *fuck*," he growled back, thrusting into me, fully this time, causing me to give a small shriek at the feeling when he hit *just* the right spot.

"Goddamn." I didn't even know what I was saying anymore, I just knew that I was being filled up, fully, completely—and if he didn't move soon, I was going to *fall apart*—

"I'm going to move now, okay?"

Oh my god. He hasn't even moved yet and I'm already on the verge of another orgasm.

I nodded as Matthew used his hands to position me even better, the new angle filling me even fuller before he started to thrust his hips against me. I bit my lip to try to stop from crying out at his movement. In the silence of the room, there were only the noises of our bodies melding together, the occasional whimper I gave, or the grunt Matthew made as he pressed further into me.

"So big," I moaned. 'S—fuck, Matthew."

"You're taking me so good, pretty girl," he said, "like you were made for me."

His hands moved from my waist to my breasts, covering them, fingers pinching my nipples as I cried out from the sheer pleasure of it, the pain leading to a warmth that spread through me, and I felt like I was absolutely floating on air.

"Yes—yes—*fuck*—"

He closed his mouth around my nipple as he rocked into me, tongue lapping at it before his teeth grazed over my breast, and then he was biting, licking, and soothing, and I thought I might *break* if he gave me anymore, his thumb still brushing over the other side as he continued to pound into me. I moaned, deeply, throwing my head back, and he halted inside of me, breath ghosting over my neck as he leaned into me. "What do you want, sweet girl?"

"I need to come, please, *please,*" I begged, pulling my lip in between my teeth, and inhaling deeply, fingers digging into his skin as my bare ass moved on the desk, wrapping my legs around him to push him into me deeper.

"God, Noelle. Fuck. You feel so good," he said, and then his thumb was back on my clit, rubbing it in circles, and I sighed under his touch, his big strong hands coaxing me into another orgasm as he pulled out and rammed back into me. He continued his pace through my orgasm, whispering pretty things into my ear that had me moaning under his touch, and God, I needed to be quiet, because *if someone heard*—

Matthew's big hand wrapped over my mouth, and I squealed against him for a moment before I regulated my breathing through my nose, eyes locking with his as he thrust into me. "Shh, sweetheart, what did we say?" I just shook my head. If he was fucking me like this, I thought I would forget my *name*, let alone whatever *command* he had given me. Still, he grunted as he pulled out completely once more and then pushed all the way to the hilt — "Fuck, Noelle. I'm gonna come."

With his free hand he gripped my waist, roughly, and as his eyes rolled back, he lost himself inside of me. As he grew still, the grinding of his hips startling to a stop, I peeled his hand off of my mouth. I was panting heavily from the way he had fucked me, hard but so delicious.

I could have stayed there forever, like that, with the way he was holding me and looking at me so reverently, but then Matthew pulled out of me, and I whimpered—actually whimpered, despite myself. I was already feeling the absence of him, a lack of the pressure I had grown used to. He tied off the condom and threw it in the trash, and God if the sight of him like that didn't make me lose my breath all over again.

"That was... wow." I hopped off the desk, found my shirt on the floor and picked it up, watching as he tucked himself back into his pants.

"Noelle, I—"

"I *know*," I said, standing and buttoning my blouse, adjusting my skirt around my hips, and pulling the socks back up my calves.

"I—This—But we shouldn't do this again... not in here." He looked around his office with a grimace before pulling me closer to him. "I don't want anyone to hear you."

And if we got caught—both of our lives, our jobs—would be in jeopardy. I knew that, but still...

I sagged a little against his body, hating that he was right, that we could so easily be discovered if we did this again in his office. Even if it was the hottest sex I had ever had, it couldn't happen again. "You're right."

He sighed. "But... when can we—"

"God, Matthew. Are you already asking me when we can fuck again? Because I know that was *good*, but..." I stuck my tongue out at him. *As if it wasn't the best damn sex I had ever had.*

"Noelle," he groaned. "I was just going to ask when I could see you again." He smoothed his hand over my hair. "Not seeing you this weekend was torture."

He was breathing deeply as I leaned against his body. I curled my hand against his chest, my fist balling into his shirt. "Whenever you want, babe." I got up on my tiptoes and placed a kiss on his lips. When I pulled away, his eyes were still closed. He chuckled then, and I couldn't help the warmth that I felt spreading across my chest. Whatever this was, whatever we were... even if it was sort of wrong, I loved spending time with him. "We still have the whole week until Spring Break, after all."

"Sure," he mumbled, one of his signature grumpy glowers taking over his face. I wanted to kiss it off of him, but I did have to go, so I settled for a kiss on his cheek, and then I was off, leaving Matthew standing in his doorway. I didn't look back to see the smile on his face, the way he ran his hands through his long, blonde hair, ran his hands over the short beard.

But God, if I had seen it... he was the most beautiful man I had ever seen, especially when he smiled, and I knew that was true.

I couldn't stop replaying the moment as I walked to my car in the dark. Us, together on his desk. The way he wanted me. The way he called me baby. And... he said, *you're mine,* hadn't he? Had he meant that or was it just an in-the-moment, caught up in the good sex kind of thing? I didn't know. Was there any way this was going to end well for either of us though?

As I hopped into my car, I realized that *dammit,* I had forgotten my underwear. In his pocket. *He kept my panties.* I groaned, hitting my head against the steering wheel.

CHAPTER 18
Matthew

Holy fuck. My chest was still heaving as I sat at my desk, cheeks flushed as I thought about what I had done to Noelle, right here. In my office.

Damn. It turned out I didn't even need Elizabeth's help or advice. I certainly hadn't expected Noelle to show up at my office, wearing that tiny little skirt and those *frustrating* lace panties. That were still in my pocket.

Hell. I was going to hell, most definitely.

I had tried not to watch as her retreating figure left the room, tried not to dwell on the emptiness that settled in my chest as she left me after I had just fucked her senseless on my desk.

And what the hell was that?

Who was I doing something like this at my place of employment? But she had gotten into my brain, and all I could see, hear, and feel was *her*. Her in my arms the night I had carried her into her apartment, drunk as hell; her falling asleep in the bus after the zoo; her when we had kissed; her nipples under my hands—

I groaned out loud. "What the hell is wrong with you, Matthew Harper?"

We hadn't even been able to keep quiet. I knew we could have been caught, that one of my colleagues could have been there working late or leaving after a late class, but I hadn't been able to bring myself to care, because the girl I wanted was *there*, and she wanted *me*, and that's all I had ever thought for days. Weeks, really. Maybe since I had first seen her on the quad.

And maybe she only wanted to hook up—maybe she wanted something casual. But I *had* her, and I knew I was going to have to hold on tight to keep her. Because I wanted her in any way I could, and I was terrified she was going to retreat into that big brain of hers and pull away from me. I just had to remind her what was good about us, so that she wouldn't.

I had to make her realize she couldn't live without me, just like I had realized I couldn't live without her.

And fuck if I knew how to do that, I just couldn't bear the thought of losing her. Of someone else kissing her, touching her, holding her tight at night. Hearing those breathy little sounds she gave off when I was inside of her.

I hadn't even left my office yet, but I couldn't keep my mind from thinking about her. I hadn't even told her what I wanted, but I had called her mine.

But she *was* mine, wasn't she? She felt like mine. Any time I wrapped her up in my arms, the world felt calm. Like everything was going to be okay. Like as long as I had her in my life, the sun would keep shining down on my face. It would be fine. It had to be.

Because there was no way I was going to let her go.

∽

THERE WAS one thing I did know, however, and that was that I was quite sure there was nothing I enjoyed more than watching Noelle just *be*. It felt like pure sunshine every time she smiled, every time she shared it with me. Even getting to see it, getting to witness it... I was simply happy to be there in the moment with her.

And every so often, the way she glanced up at me, and I

would catch this look in her eyes... She would glance at my lips, and I couldn't mistake the longing there, the heat in her warm brown gaze, and I wondered if she could see it back in the way I had always caught myself staring at her, admiring her bravery and her tenacity.

It was like the universe had plans for us. Like there was some invisible force, even now, still nudging us together. Even now, after we had slept together. I was a mess inside the whole next day, and it seemed like every time I left my office I just kept wanting to see her. *Everywhere* I went; even more so than I did *before* all of this. Everywhere I turned, there she was. Us at the library. Me rescuing her at the bar. At our gazebo. Every kiss we had shared in front of her dorm.

And then, like an answer to some unspoken request, a miracle answered and granted, there she was: typing away furiously at the cafeteria on campus as a plate of food sat next to her, untouched.

Had I ever spent a day at work so entirely distracted and utterly useless? I didn't think so. I was surprised I made it through my lectures without stumbling on my words or losing my train of thought. I had been way less patient with everyone today, though, and I thought I knew why. I hadn't heard from her.

Not one peep—no text, no call, no *Hi, Matthew, I know I had your dick inside me yesterday, but I can't stop thinking about you.* Nothing.

After I had finished all my classes and office hours on campus for the day, I couldn't help it anymore. I hoped that she wasn't on duty tonight, and I gave in to the voice in my head. The one that was still screaming at me that the one thing it wanted to do was fucking talk to this girl. I listened to the part of me that was telling me to just do it because I wanted to. Because I'd been thinking the same thing for months. And even though we had kissed, even though I had been inside of her... I wanted *more* than just lingering stares and accidental brushes of our hands and a few kisses underneath the stars. This redhead who filled my thoughts and whose small smile I hadn't been able to get out of my brain since the first day of classes—I wanted all of it with her. I wanted a lifetime of kisses. A lifetime of laughter.

So, fuck it. I texted her.

> **MATTHEW**
> Noelle. Did you eat anything yet today?

> **NOELLE**
> No. I've been too busy with work.

> Where are you at? We're going to dinner.

> Matthew.

> You're not even giving me a choice??

> Noelle, seriously. You need to eat. I saw you at the cafeteria today.

> Stalking me again, huh?

I rolled my eyes as I laughed at my phone; this girl never failed to bring a smile to my face even when she accused me of following her around. It might not have been my intention, but I loved seeing her everywhere anyway.

> Where are you? I'll pick you up, just tell me where to get you.

> I'm at the dorm. Really, it's fine, I can just make something.

> For some reason, I don't believe you. I'll be by in fifteen minutes.

I got in my truck with Snowball in tow, and we both drove to her building. I was determined to distract her from all of the things she was working on and get her fed at the same time. I liked taking care of her. I didn't care if it fulfilled some primal possessive urge in me to make sure she was fed, cared for, and happy—I just needed it.

And I wanted to share something else from my life with her. I looked over behind my shoulder, at the big white fluffball who sat in my backseat. Had I even told Noelle I had a dog? I shook my head, realizing there were still so many things she didn't know about me that I wanted to share with her.

And after sleeping together, I figured it wouldn't hurt if I took her out. Luckily, it was almost March, and it was finally warming up a little bit even though it was still drizzly out.

Promptly fifteen minutes later, I knocked on her door, trying to hold in a smile as she opened it up. And... wow. Even in her tight-fitting teal sweater dress, I couldn't help but admire how beautiful she was. Or notice the way the sweater dress hugged her curves. She readjusted her hair clip holding back half of her curls, and then her entire body seemed to glow with the way her eyes crinkled, and her lips tilted up at the corners.

"Ready?" I asked her, trying to distract myself from staring at her even more.

"Is my outfit okay? I wasn't quite sure where we were going, and I didn't want to be too casual—" She picked up her coat off of the table by the door and held it in her arms.

"You look perfect." I smiled because I meant it. And I hadn't planned some crazy dinner date anyway—just a visit to the food carts. I had no doubt Noelle would love it—she *loved* food.

She glanced down at herself again and then nodded. "Okay." I held out my hand, grateful for the warmth of hers when she interlaced our fingers, and we walked towards the parking lot.

"Come on," I said, urging her towards the truck. "I have someone I want you to meet."

She raised an eyebrow at me but didn't ask any other questions. As soon as we got to my truck and Snowball's fluffy white head popped up in the window, though, Noelle gasped in surprise.

"Oh my gosh," she cooed at my dog, "She's so beautiful—she is a girl, right?" I nodded, trying to hide the corners of my mouth tipping up—a smile, just from how amused I was by her presence.

"What kind of dog is she?" Noelle opened the door to the backseat where Snowball was sitting and petted her on the head.

"This is Snowball. She's Samoyed." My dog was wagging her tail like crazy, obviously pleased to have attention from another human besides me. I couldn't stop the smile on my face as Noelle pet her.

"Snowball!" she exclaimed, letting off a beautiful, pure laugh that I loved. "That's such a fitting name for you, huh girl? A big white ball of fluff." Noelle scratched between Snowball's ears one more time and then looked up at me. "I should have guessed."

"What?" I asked, scratching the hair behind my ears.

"That you'd have a big wolf-like dog." Noelle's face split into a grin. "You're so very predictable, prof."

"Hey, I'll have you know she was a *gift*."

Noelle snorted. "Whoever got her for you must have known you really well."

"Yeah," I nodded, thinking fondly of Tess. "She does."

Noelle's mouth formed into a line, but she just kept loving on my dog. I realized she might have taken that the wrong way, thinking an ex got her for me or something, and I quickly fixed the misunderstanding. "Tessa," I choked out. "She was a Christmas present from my little sister."

"Where are we going to eat so that we can take a dog with us?" Noelle changed the subject on me, but I could see the little bits of pink on her cheek.

"You'll see," I smiled.

"Oh yeah?" she snorted "It's always gotta be a mystery with you, doesn't it?

"Maybe." I held open the door for her, locking eyes as I ushered her inside the truck and let her buckle herself in before I closed the door and walked around to the other side. "Maybe I just like surprising you," I mumbled to myself as I hopped onto the drivers seat.

I didn't think she heard me, but she must have been thinking the same thing that I was, because the next words out of her mouth were, "You know, you're like the only person who can get away with surprising me. I *hate* it coming from everyone else."

"Even your best friends?" I asked, turning on the ignition.

She nodded. "God, yeah, *especially* from my best friends. You never know what shenanigans they're going to get me into—"

"Shenanigans, huh?" I raised an eyebrow over at her. What sort of *shenanigans* did a little bookworm get into with her friends? I guessed if the bar was any indication, maybe they were all a lot rowdier than I took them to be.

"Oh, shut up and drive," she said, playfully pushing against my shoulder.

"Alright, sweetheart," I said, flashing her another grin.

I turned up the radio as we drove to our destination: a cluster of food trucks organized on an empty lot together. Thankfully, for me, it wasn't a rainy February night, so despite the slight chill that still hung in the air, it was dry outside. I clipped Snowball's leash onto her collar, and then offered Noelle a hand to help her out of the truck.

When she saw where we were parked, her eyes lit up with delight. "Oh!" she said, the word full of such awe and wonder that I couldn't help but chuckle.

"Whatever you want, Noelle—it's my treat."

"You don't have to do that, Matthew." She looked up at me, and then at our hands, which were still laced together, Snowball's leash in my other hand.

"Maybe not, but I asked you to come out tonight. And I want to. So let me."

Noelle sighed, as if accepting her fate, and then pulled me over to the Mac and Cheese truck in the middle of the area. She grinned. "This smells incredible." She inhaled deeply, and I had to agree with her. Even with the smell of cheese permeating the air, it did smell delicious. The truck had the pasta dish served with all different types of toppings.

"Is this okay with you?" She turned to the guy at the counter after I nodded. "One lobster and shrimp mac and cheese, please."

"I'll have the pulled pork one," I said with a smile, before surrendering my credit card to the man taking our order. After I got the receipt and put the card back into my wallet, I slipped my hand back into Noelle's and steered us towards a table.

I tied Snowball's leash to the foot of the picnic bench and pulled out a little bowl of water for her to drink as we sat there.

"Wow," Noelle remarked, watching me pet Snowball's head. "You came prepared."

Laughing, I nodded my head. "I had to. I wanted you to meet one of the most important women in my life." I flashed her a grin, and Noelle blushed a little bit.

I ran my finger over her hand, drawing circles on her skin as it rested on the table. "You know what makes me smile?" She shook her head. I leaned in closer. "The way I've been inside of you, but you still blush over the smallest things." I traced a finger over her cheek.

Was it possible for someone to blush harder? This girl could completely, one hundred percent, dominate me in the bedroom— and I would let her— but sweet words?

And maybe I was just obsessed with her little flushes.

She swatted away my hand. "Not *now,*" she whispered back. "What if someone hears us?"

I raised an eyebrow at her. "Embarrassed of me now, Miss Hastings?"

She pouted. *"Matthew."*

"I know." I sighed. I wanted to pull her into my lap and hold her, but she was right.

Even with how I felt about her, there was still a layer of us that I felt like we had to keep secret from the world. At least until she had graduated and got another job. I didn't want the university to find any excuse to fire her—or me. Plus there was the tenure I hoped to earn one day, and I knew a scandal could ruin all of that.

But I didn't say any of that to Noelle.

Then, our food was done, and Noelle bounced off the bench in a hurry to get the dishes.

Noelle came back with two piping hot dishes of macaroni and cheese. She set mine down in front of me, and then stabbed a fork into hers.

"My God," she moaned. "Have you ever tasted something so delicious?" Noelle swirled another bite into her mouth.

I chuckled, eating my own. She stole a bite of mine. "Oh, that's good." She sucked on her fork while looking at me, and I didn't miss the heat in her gaze as she popped the utensil out of her mouth.

After we both finished eating and had thrown our trash away, Noelle perked up, leaning against me as she wound her arm around my bicep.

"Dessert?" She asked, her eyes lighting up as she surveyed the carts around us. There was an ice cream cart, but also— "Donuts?"

I laughed. "Sure, Noelle. Anything you want."

And I meant it—really. I would give her anything she wanted.

∽

WHAT WAS WRONG WITH ME? It was crazy—I had just seen her. Had just *had* her, yesterday, my mouth all over her body. Had just spent the evening with her, dinner before we strolled around with Snowball. Had watched her doze off on the ride back to campus.

Had kissed her goodnight before she walked into the dorm.

And yet—I missed her, already. I looked up at the ceiling of my living room. I couldn't take it. I was going crazy that night, sitting on my couch, throwing a ball for Snowball who couldn't seem to calm down either. It was like she could sense my anxiety as much as I could feel it. And it made my chest fill with a warmth that Noelle had liked my dog—but also, that she had loved Noelle. Snowball could be standoffish, and she often didn't like people. But Noelle? She had rested her head on Noelle's lap and laid next to her for the entire ride home.

What was I going to do with all this extra energy? We had already said goodnight. I wasn't about to show up at her apartment, expecting a booty call. It wasn't her fault if just thinking about her made me hard. I hadn't had sex in a long time before last night, and yet here I was already craving her again.

But... we hadn't even talked about what we were, officially. Maybe this *was* just a casual hookup for her. Maybe it didn't mean for her what it meant for me. I didn't want that—didn't know what I would do if that was the case, but I didn't *know*.

And I was terrified of asking and getting an answer I didn't want.

So for now, yeah... I'd just keep going with whatever this was. Whatever we had, it was good. I liked talking to her. I wanted to talk to her, even—a feeling I hadn't had with *anyone*, in such a long time. Not even my little sister. So I crawled into bed and I couldn't take it anymore.

MATTHEW
Are you awake?

NOELLE
Yeah. Just getting into bed.

I needed to hear her voice before I fell asleep.

"Twenty questions," I said as soon as she picked up.

"What?" She sounded far away, and then like she had taken me off speakerphone or came closer. "Did you say twenty questions?" Noelle repeated.

"Yes. Play with me?"

"Hmm... What do you want to know?"

"What's your favorite flower?"

"Sunflowers." I smiled. Of course, she would pick one that was as sunshiny and bright as she was. I tucked that little tidbit of information away for later. I didn't know when it would come in handy, but I wanted to surprise her.

"What's your favorite thing to do when it snows?" Noelle

asked, and I looked out the window, wishing it was a cold, winter night and we were snowed in together. That she was here with me, instead of just on the phone.

"Well, I always did like to snowboard. But I also like sitting at home with a hot drink and just watch the snow fall from the window." I eyed my dog. "I think Snowball's answer would be different, though."

She giggled. "Yes, well I rather think your arctic dog would love to run around in the snow."

I hummed. "What's your favorite book?"

"Not a fair question. There are too many answers. You can't expect me to pick *one*."

"Okay, fair enough."

"Favorite subject growing up?" she asked.

"Math."

She laughed. "Why does that not surprise me?"

"Hey," I frowned. "What's that supposed to mean?"

"Nothing." Her joyful voice made me smile, too. "Ask your next question."

"Middle name?"

"Mine is boring." She sighed. "Marie."

"Oh, yeah, try me."

"What's yours?"

"*James.*"

"Oh, Matthew. I do believe we're tied for the most basic middle name," she said, making us both laugh.

"What did you want to be when you grew up?" I asked.

"I've always wanted to be an author, publish a book. But I don't know if my writing is any good, honestly…"

"Don't say that. Noelle," I frowned into my phone as I continued to lie on the couch, staring up at the ceiling. "I've seen your projects. I'm sure you're an amazing writer."

"Yeah, well…" She sounded insecure through the phone, and I could picture her shrugging, pretending it didn't affect her. "We'll see I guess."

"Your turn," I prodded, wanting her to perk up again.

"Beach or mountains?"

"Mountains." I laughed. "Somewhere in the snow. Camping or Hotel?" I asked her.

"I've never been camping, actually," Noelle said. "But I think it sounds like fun. Hmm… Where's the craziest place you've ever had sex?" she whispered into the phone.

"Well… My office," I laughed. "With you."

"Really?" she snorted. I *loved* that sound. "Me too," Noelle added.

"What, did you peg me for some crazy sex-connoisseur or something?"

"Well, you were *impossibly* good. It was almost infuriating. Like, I'm pretty sure I was jealous of everyone you've ever been with, and you were literally inside of me."

"Honestly, Noelle." I just shook my head even though she couldn't see it. "It's never been like that for me before."

"So good?"

"Yeah."

"If you could be anywhere right now, where would you be?"

"In your arms," Noelle said with no hesitation.

"Really?"

"What were you thinking about before you called me?" she asked, her breath a little shallow.

"You." My voice sounded rougher than normal, but if she noticed, she didn't comment on it. "I just… can't keep my mind off of you, Noelle."

"Oh." I imagined her turning pink in her little apartment. I loved seeing her little blush, knowing it was all for me. "What would you do if I was there?"

I imagined her, sitting in bed, phone in her hand with her head tilted back, eyes closed as she talked to me on the phone. I liked imagining her in pajamas—wondering what little sexy thing she chose to wear to bed. But I couldn't stop thinking about what I wanted to do to her. Where would I even begin? "First thing I would do," I said, as I sat up a little straighter, "is make you dinner. Because I'm a gentleman."

She snorted. "Oh, the protective asshole act again?"

"Noelle—"

"Shush," she admonished, "I like it. Keep going."

"Then I'd eat dessert."

"Dessert? But you don't like sweets."

"Oh, I won't be eating sweets, baby. I'd be eating *you.*"

"*Oh.*" A little breathless sound drifted through the phone, and I loved that I was affecting her, even now. "What would you do after that?"

I pretended to ponder. "I'd bring you back to this big bed of mine, take my time undressing you, and after making sure you were immensely satisfied, I'd tuck you into my side and hold you till we fell asleep."

She laughed. "Alright, I think you're going to have to deliver on that."

I went back to our game. "What do you normally do for spring break?"

I could almost hear the wheels turning in her brain. "Nothing. Sometimes I spend it with my mom, but she's out of town next week."

"Do you…" I rubbed a hand over my face. "Would you want to spend it with me?"

"Does that count as a question?" Noelle asked, and I laughed into the phone.

"No. But seriously, spend it with me?"

"Yeah," she said, a little breathless. "The whole week?"

"Uh-huh. I think once I get you in my bed, I'm never going to want to let you out of it."

"Matthew—" She tried to protest, but I could hear the tone in her voice. The one that told me that she wanted that too.

I wondered if she was as affected by our phone conversation as I was. Dammit, now that I could see it so clearly, I wanted it. I wanted to take her home and learn her body inside and out. What she liked, what she didn't. What gave her pleasure. Wanted her to seek it out herself. Whatever she wanted.

Anything, everything.

I'd take whatever she would give me.

We spent another hour like that, just talking, before Noelle finally mumbled something about needing to go to bed before she fell asleep on the phone with me.

"Goodnight, Noelle."

"Goodnight, Matthew."

And I fell asleep with a smile plastered on my face.

CHAPTER 19
Noelle

A thought that slipped into my mind as I showered and readied myself for the day—a day that would be filled with editing and assignments and most definitely not thoughts of the way Matthew had taken me two days ago on his desk. Or the way he had called me last night just to ask me questions about myself. Because he wanted to get to know me. Because he cared about me.

All I could think of was how I wanted to crawl over there again and ask for a repeat. And God, I couldn't help it if I touched myself as I thought about him, if my thumb ghosted over my clit as I imagined it was *him* touching me, washing me in the shower... caring about me. *Fuck.*

I was in a haze all throughout the morning, and I tried to distract myself by cleaning up my room and doing things I had put off so that I wouldn't think about Matthew.

But try as I might, my distractions only worked so well when my phone pinged with a text, and I saw his name light up the screen. My heart jumped.

MATTHEW
Want to get coffee later?

> **NOELLE**
> Sure. 2:00?

My class gets out around then, so that'll be perfect.

> Meet you at our usual table? I have my class at 4 so I'll be free until then.

Perfect.

I couldn't help but smile for the rest of the afternoon.

~

G0D, I thought, staring at Matthew as he sat across from me, at our usual table. It was weird to think that I could even say that since we had been toeing around the lines of an actual relationship for so long, but this, coming to the coffee shop—this felt like one of our routines at this point. But today felt different, somehow, and I think it was because he *asked* me to come. *What the hell did I get myself into with you?*

His eyes caught mine as I ignored the plate in front of me—a chocolate muffin that he had plopped in front of me as he sat down at the table. Normally, I would have scarfed it down in two minutes flat, but I hadn't been able to stop sneaking peeks at him. Still, even as our eyes connected, and our gazes held, I felt my cheeks flush under his stare.

When was the last time a guy made me feel like this? Like there were butterflies in my stomach? He had fucked me on *his desk* two days before—hottest sex that I had ever had, no question about that. And I hadn't even asked what this meant for us—even after he had helped me, after dinner, after *sex*. I was scared about letting myself want more from him than he'd be willing to give me. Was it just casual for him? Did he want to see me again... like that? But no matter my apprehension, I was still filled with absolute *want* for the man.

A throat being cleared interrupted my train of lust-ridden thoughts, and I turned to find Lucas standing there, Hazel clutching an armful of books and standing next to him. I tried to clear away the rest of my less-than-pure thoughts, and I turned my attention to him. "Hi, Lucas. Hi Haze." I smiled. "You both know Professor Harper," I said, waving at Matthew, who almost had a scowl on his face. I thought I'd tease him about it later.

They nodded toward him and said hello, and then Lucas turned back to me.

"Hey. Noelle." He smiled casually like he was working up to something. "Are you going to the hall directors' event after the break?"

Oh shit. With everything going on, I had forgotten about it. I nodded to him. But still. "Yes, I told them I'd be going."

"Do you have a date?" Lucas asked me, and I knew Matthew's scowl deepened without even looking at him.

"Um... no?" I shook my head. "Besides, aren't the two of you...?" I looked between Hazel and Lucas. Hazel looked bashful like she didn't want to admit how much time they had been spending together this semester. I realized how terrible of a friend I had been because I had barely asked Hazel about him with everything going on with Matthew. I resolved to talk to her about him more.

"Not me." He shook his head. Hazel mouthed *I'm sorry* from behind his shoulder. "My friend—he's the Hall Director for Pine Hall—he thinks you're really cute and he asked me if I'd see if you'd go with him." He flashed a brilliantly white smile, and I felt bad for him—I did. But I had absolutely no eyes for anyone but the man sitting across from me. Matthew, who was currently glaring daggers at Lucas, who seemed blissfully unaware of it.

Was he even paying attention to Matthew? He didn't know about us, but Matthew was right there. Sure, we weren't trying to publicize the relationship, but it wasn't like we were doing the best at hiding it, either. I knew there could be consequences if people found out about our romantic involvement, but we had been getting coffee together all semester. As friends.

Either way... "Oh," I said simply. "Lucas, I appreciate the offer, but I think I'm just going to go alone." My eyes caught Matthew's, and I knew he was biting his tongue not to say something. Hazel just remained silent standing there, watching the interaction, looking between Lucas and me.

Lucas frowned. "You're really not interested?"

I angled my body towards him, trying to avoid Matthew's stare. "I'm sorry, Lucas. I'm just... I'm not interested."

"Noelle—He's a great guy, and I think you should give him a chance." Lucas sounded aggravated, and I gritted my teeth.

"She said no," Matthew growled before I could say anything. Hazel looked between the two of us and frowned, and I knew then that she figured out what was going on—even if I hadn't told her that we had slept together, she had pieced together a lot of the rest. But Lucas didn't know that.

"I'm sorry." I looked back at him. "I'm just not in a place in my life right now where I'm looking for that. I hope he understands." When I looked back towards Hazel, she was watching Matthew watch the two of us. Fuck.

Had she noticed the way Matthew looked at me? Like I was *his*, and he would destroy anyone who tried to take me from him? I hoped not. "Hazel, is everything all set for movie night tonight?" I asked, trying to change the subject.

Hazel nodded and her tight brown curls bounced with the movement. "I even got us a new movie. I tried for *13 Going on Thirty*, but I was sadly outvoted by the RAs."

I chuckled. "Hazel, we have already watched that one. Twice."

She grumbled. "Well, it's one of my favorites." And then she locked eyes with Lucas, who had up until that point, *still* been frowning at me. "Anyway, Lucas," she started, "your friend doesn't need a date either. Just because we're going together—"

Matthew raised an eyebrow at me, and I just shrugged.

"Okay," he began, his deep voice smoothing over my nerves.

"Now that that's settled, we're having coffee. So can we help you two with anything else?"

I couldn't help the small shiver slide down my spine just at his voice like that. All bossy, like he was in control. Oh, God.

"No—" Lucas started, and Hazel cut him off.

"We were just going, anyways. Have a movie to catch! Bye Noelle! Bye, Professor Harper!" She tugged on Lucas's arm and pulled him towards the door, and I watched them as they disappeared out of sight.

"No dates," Matthew growled at me once they were out of earshot. His hand slipped over my knee, and I could feel the possessive touch under the table—but I didn't mind. Not when it was him: this grumpy enigma of a man, this guy who showed me so much care and warmth even when he was short and cold with others. I had to admit, I kind of liked it that way. Liked knowing that *I* was the only one who he was fully himself with. I layered my hand on top of his, returning the gesture.

"Only with you?" I teased.

"God, Noelle. I don't know what I'd do if I saw you with another man."

I intertwined our fingers under the table. "You heard me, Matthew. I'm not going to date. I promise." Anyone else, that is. *I only have eyes for you,* I wanted to say. He grunted, and I shook my head fondly.

"Back to what I was saying..." I changed the subject. And then I froze, because what was I saying before? Oh. That's right. Absolutely nothing, because I was too busy eye-fucking my friend slash professor slash hookup slash maybe more in the middle of this campus coffee shop. He raised an eyebrow when I didn't continue again, and I promptly took a bite of my muffin.

There. At least now I wouldn't have to talk with my mouth full.

"Listen," he started, still a little grumpy. "I just..."

I tilted my head at him, wondering what he was going to tell me. "Yeah?"

"You know I'll go with you to any events you want, right? Even if I hate those kinds of events." I nodded because I guess I did. I had witnessed him at the last one, all grumpy till he had come over to me. "I'd go anywhere if it was with you."

"I do *want* you to come with me." Always.

"As a date?" He asked, and I nodded.

"Noelle—"

I bit my lip. "But I don't know if it's a good idea right now."

He frowned.

We still hadn't labeled it, *us*, and even if I implied to Lucas that I wasn't wanting to date... Was that the truth? I had sex with Matthew and almost ended up having phone sex with him, asking him what he would do to me if I was at his house. I *wanted* to hear him dirty talking to me because just that little bit on the phone had me endlessly frustrated. I wanted a second round. But was I ready for something more? I didn't know. Because being something more meant you had something you could lose.

I took a deep breath, but he started again before I could get a word out. "Noelle. I don't want to do anything you don't want to do, but I do want you to know how much I care about you, okay? Don't ever doubt that."

"I *want* to do everything with you, Matthew. I really do." I reached out my hand and placed it over his across the table. "I just —I need time to get used to everything, okay? But just because I'm not saying *yes* doesn't mean *no*. I just don't know if I'm ready to tell the whole world yet."

"I understand." And I knew he really did.

"It's just that if we go together to a university event, everyone will know we're dating, and if anything happens..." Everyone will know. Or worse, we start a scandal, and your future here is at jeopardy. I couldn't do that to him, I just couldn't.

"It's okay, Noelle," he said, reassuring me. "You tell me when you're ready, and I'll be here."

"No take-backs," I said, pointing at him.

His eyes lit up, the icy blue melting away into pools of crystal, and I could see the warmth in his grin. "None. I promise."

And I knew—my heart was in danger here. I wasn't sure what I was going to do if I gave it to him completely.

"We're still on for Spring Break, right?" I asked, and I didn't miss the smirk on his face. "Because I had some ideas…" I lowered my voice into a seductive whisper.

Oh yeah, I planned to keep this man as long as he would have me.

∽

I WAS LONG overdue for a catch-up date with my best friends, but with everything happening with Matthew, one thing or another had kept coming up, and I hadn't talked to them much in the last week. "And… that's what happened." I finished my story as I sipped my coffee.

"I'm sorry, you actually—" Gabbi spluttered, mouth dropping open in shock as she held her cup of coffee.

Angelina looked over at me with wide eyes, and I shrugged sheepishly.

"It just kind of… happened." I gave them an awkward smile.

"Okay… let's recap." She held up her fingers, counting them. "We told you to go get your man. You slept with him. You're now basically dating him, and you're only *just* telling us it even *happened??* Bitch, I can't believe you didn't tell us sooner! We need more details!" Angelina poked my side. "Spill!"

"Oh my god," I exclaimed, "I'm not going to tell you *every single thing* that happened, Ang. *Some* things are private, you know."

"Noelle." Angelina stared at me with a, *come on bitch, we know you* kind of glare. I sighed. "We all read romance novels. You gotta give us more than that you slept with him. When? Where? How did this happen?"

I sighed but raised my fingers. "Three days ago, his office, and I went there to talk to him and it just... happened."

Gabbi laughed. "Look at our little Noelle, all grown up."

"Please!" I shoved her arm playfully. "It's not like I was a virgin before this—"

"No, but you've also never had sex in someone's *office* before. Oh, God, was it good? I hope it was good. I hope you know I'm vicariously living through you right now." Gabbi kept going. "It's been way too long since I've been with anyone."

"It *was* good." I flushed red. "Better than it's ever been."

Charlotte groaned. "I can't believe I'm the only one here who still hasn't had sex." She buried her face in her hands.

"It's okay, babe," Angelina nudged her. "It'll happen when it happens, I promise. There's nothing wrong with waiting till you find the right person."

"I just feel like I'm *never* going to find the right person, Ang." Charlotte stared into her coffee cup. "Dating sucks. I feel like, after thirty minutes with someone, I immediately know that I don't like them. And then I have to start all over, and it's just exhausting. Noelle, you're so lucky to have found your hunky professor," she sighed dreamily against her cup.

"Cheer up, Char," I reassured her. "It's not like you're the last single one or anything. You'll find someone, I promise."

"So when are you seeing him next?" Angelina asked, looking at me over her mug.

"I don't know?" I shrugged, and then my phone pinged with a text from him. Did he have some sort of sixth sense? I giggled, thinking about him sitting there thinking of me.

MATTHEW
Come to my office after your class.

"I guess... tonight." I lifted my phone. "He just texted me." Gabbi leaned over to look at my phone, and she snickered.

"Office sex round 2, let's go!"

"Oh God," I rolled my eyes. "I never should have told you

that. And we definitely can't keep having sex in his office, because there is no way I want someone to find us on his desk—"

"On his desk?" Charlotte choked on her drink. "What sort of romance novel are you living in, and why is this not *my* life?"

"I gotta admit... It was hot," I wiggled my eyebrows at her.

"So are you *together*?" Gabbi asked, and I just gave a little shake of my head.

"Not officially. We haven't really defined anything yet. But I'm spending spring break with him at his place. I just... don't know that I'm ready to *date* yet, anyway, and I told him that. So I don't know. We're in this weird limbo between friends and something more. Maybe I'm okay with just sex for now."

"Noelle." Charlotte rolled her eyes. "I know you. There is no way you're going to be able to pull off just sex. Have you met yourself?"

I had, that was the problem. I had been a hopeless romantic for way too long in my life and look where that had got me—cheated on and left alone in New York City. "I don't know that I can do it again. The last time... it broke me. How can I put myself back together again if it happens all over again?"

If Matthew broke my heart? I wasn't sure there was a way to recover from that.

"Just... give him a chance to show you not all men are like Jake," Gabbi said reassuringly. "See where it goes. And when you realize he's the perfect man, and you're head over heels in love with him, I will totally be here to say I-told-you-so."

The other girls laughed, and I retreated further into my thoughts.

Did I want this? A relationship with him? Something more? Was I being stupid trying to protect my heart because I wasn't sure if I could survive if he broke it? Was it stupid for me *not to* at least try? "You're right," I finally said. "I owe it to both of us to at least try."

And I smiled, even though anxiety and the fear of the unknown were almost overwhelming.

CHAPTER 20
Matthew

I couldn't stop thinking about Noelle—a woman I was beginning to have feelings for. But if I was being honest... I was falling for her. Hard.

I shouldn't be spending all day thinking about her—definitely not the particularly explicit thoughts that danced through my brain. Of her naked, only wearing her skirt as she sat on my desk. Of her taste as I licked her over and over. Of—*God*, I needed to stop before I got hard at work. *Again.* I pushed the thought aside, writing 100% at the top of the paper in front of me before flipping to the next one in the stack. It was useless, though, as I was hardly able to concentrate on anything but the thought of having her in my arms again, kissing her, how she might look on her knees for me—

Fuck. She *was* mine, and all I wanted to do was prove that to her. I had declared as much. Had felt it the moment I set my eyes on her. She was supposed to be mine, supposed to be by my side. The curves of her body were the thing I saw every time I closed my eyes, and God, all I wanted was to have her like that again.

But she didn't want to date anyone. She had said so explicitly. Had looked her classmate straight in the eyes and said *I'm just not in a place in my life right now where I'm looking for that.* And fuck—I knew she needed time. She had told me as much, and I would wait however long she needed before she was ready for this. For us. Because she was my girl—had been for a while, really, and I wanted... everything from her. And when she promised me *no dates*... Well, I hoped I wasn't excluded from that list forever.

I picked up my phone, pulled up her contact, and typed in a simple message.

MATTHEW
Come to my office after your class.

NOELLE
Demanding now, are we, prof?

I want to see you.

Come, please?

Only if you promise not to keep my underwear again.

I can't promise that baby.

Steal another pair, and I'm going to make you buy me more.

I'll buy you whatever you want, sweetheart, as long as I can get you in my arms again.

Romantic today, huh, Matthew? I like it.

I snorted. Who was this girl that was making me do stupid things like keeping her panties? It wasn't like I was doing anything with them—but the thought of her walking away from me, still wet and not wearing anything under her clothes... Well, that thought may have stayed with me some nights. And in the shower.

She was there, after class, waiting by my office door, arms wrapped around some textbooks. I thought that perhaps she never looked as beautiful as she had the other day, in my arms—

"You know, I don't normally do this," I said, looking at her as I unlocked my door, feeling my neck burning at the telltale signs of my embarrassment. We walked into the office, and she quickly dropped onto the chair across from mine, waiting for me to settle into my own.

"What," she asked, tilting her head at me with a smirk on her lips, "fuck someone in your office?"

"Noelle," I groaned. "I didn't mean—" I flushed red, and I was sure the back of my neck was going to be all red and splotchy.

"You've already seen me *naked*, Matthew. I hardly think now is the time to be embarrassed about this."

"I just wanted you to know that I don't normally—I'm not..." I trailed off, not finding a suitable ending to my thought.

I wanted to say things like *I'm not one to mess around with anyone. I can't get you out of my mind. I want you again, and so help me, I can't get the sound of your little moans out of my head.* Even more embarrassing, was the simple and plain truth. *That was the best damn sex I've ever had. It's never been like that for me before.*

She paced closer to me, setting herself against the edge of my desk, leaning on it as she brushed a hand against my leg. *I've been mesmerized since I first saw you*, I couldn't bring myself to say. She had said she didn't want to date anyone, and yet, after a text from me, she was here. Sitting in front of me.

Did she just want to hook up again? Fuck that. I wanted everything from this woman—her smiles and her laughs, and sure, her pleasure and her moans, too. Still, there was more there. *I hate the way I'm attracted to you. So much so that I can't get you out of my mind, but...* But all I can do is think about you—

"I'm not trying to take advantage of you," I finally got out. "I just... I don't normally do casual relationships." Which seemed to be the wrong thing to say, because she cleared her throat, hopping onto the desk and crossing her knees as she stared at me, as if to say, well, you slept with *me*.

I tried again. "Noelle. It's just—God—you're the most beautiful woman I've ever laid eyes on. This isn't just sex for me, baby. I need you to know that. I need you to know that I've never done this before. I don't want you to get the wrong idea because that's not what this is for me." *I'm not in the habit of bringing women to my office and having my way with them. Just you. There would only ever be just you.*

"So... you *don't* want me?" she asked, brushing a hair behind her ear. "This seems like a moment where there should be a *but.*" Then she laughed, a warm sound that filled me with more feelings than I cared to admit.

"I *always* want you." I practically growled out at her, grinding my teeth. "But... We really *shouldn't* do this," I finally said. And I was being truthful, we shouldn't. We shouldn't see each other like this, shouldn't want each other the way we did.

It wasn't like I wanted to stop—it was the opposite. I wanted to take her in my arms and never let her go. I wanted to scream from the rooftops that she was mine, all mine, and no one else could ever have her. How had I become so possessive and territorial over this woman? How, in the last two months of knowing her, had she become everything to me?

But I knew if I lost her—if she walked right out of here and out of my life and never talked to me again, I knew that *I* would be the one hurting. The one with a hole in my heart, a vulnerability I had never opened myself up to until now. Until her. Because Noelle Hasting's sunshiny personality had wormed its way into my heart, and I never wanted it to find its way out. But how did I explain all of that to her? How did I—without overwhelming her, and asking her to start something with me that she wasn't ready for—tell her what I was feeling?

"Do what, *Professor*?" Noelle smirked suggestively. "We're not *doing* anything. I'm just sitting here, in your office." She crossed her knees, and I could see up her tiny little skirt.

"Noelle," I said, narrowing my eyes, with a look that I hope conveyed *I know what you're doing.*

"When I'm with you..." she breathed, and I felt a look of

surprise pull over my features. "When I'm with you, I don't think about anything. Not about my past, or my fears for the future. Because when it's just us... just Matthew and Noelle... I can finally let myself feel things I've never let myself feel before, Matthew. I don't want to lose that. I don't..." She took a deep breath. "I don't want to lose you." Of all the things she could have said, well... What was this game we were playing?

What lines were we tiptoeing because neither one of us wanted to lose the comfort of each other? The warmth and strength that simply *being* with her gave me.

"Why did you ask me to come by today?" Noelle asked, her voice breathy and low.

"I needed you," I murmured.

"Then have me," she pleaded, leaning over me, her hair falling in front of her face.

I wanted her. Of course, I did. It was ever-consuming, always present, and absolutely maddening. But... "Noelle... baby... if we're caught, if someone finds out—"

"Who said we were gonna get caught?" Noelle smirked, hand running up my thigh before it rested on my chest. Then she was leaning down into me, lips perched so close that I could feel her breath against my cheek.

"Noelle. I just—" I started, but she stopped me, placing a finger on my lips, and then she pressed her lips against mine, a sweet thing, gentle and caring. Just a peck, but the fire was already lit in me.

I let myself run my hands through her hair, burying them in her gorgeous red locks. She kissed the scruff of my beard—I needed to shave again—then the sides of my jaw, the crook of my neck, and when she pulled away, her brown eyes were alight with *mischief,* a desire that I could feel reflected in my own. The desire that was straining against the zipper of my pants. Never before had just kissing a girl made me so hard or made me want her so bad. But with Noelle...

I tilted my head at her, watching as her eyes lit up under my gaze, and I moved my hand to her cheek, thumb grazing her skin. "Noelle."

"Matthew."

I took a sharp inhale of breath. "I can't—" I stopped. *I can't what? Want her, need her, be completely enthralled by her?* But I didn't even care anymore. "I can't let you go, baby," I said, and it was the truth, the whole truth. Mine. She was *mine*.

"I'm not going to leave, Matthew. I—I want this." She shut her eyes, and I brushed back a piece of hair from her face.

"Good. Because I want you. I just want to make sure you're ready... because I just can't bear to be without my girl."

Noelle's hand was back on my thigh, and then it was moving towards my groin—her hand brushing over the part of my body that wanted her almost as much as my heart did. "Noelle," I moaned as she cupped my dick through my pants.

"Noelle," I said again, a warning this time, because as much as I wanted her, we shouldn't do this again, not here, in my *office*. Even if it was late and no one was likely to be around. Because I wanted to fuck her until she *screamed*, and these walls were not conducive to that. "We have all week," I whispered.

But, well... I also couldn't leave with this bulge in my slacks, either, and as Noelle sat in front of me, one hand on my erection and the other on the waistband of my pants, I watched her lick her lips and knew I couldn't stop her. Couldn't stop her as she kneeled in front of me, resting her legs on the back of her feet as she lowered her body under my desk.

"Let me," she breathed out as she watched me from those warm brown eyes in the crevice of my desk, her nimble fingers slowly undoing the zipper, and then my cock was bare in front of her. *Fuck*. Noelle hummed as her small hand wrapped around the base of me, fingers not fully closing around my dick, as she pumped me one, two, three times—

Her mouth closed around the tip, tongue swirling around me, hand still moving as Noelle kept stroking me up and down. I took a sharp intake of air, closing my eyes and leaning my head back against the back of the chair for only a moment as I tried to keep my voice low and breaths steady.

Then my eyes were back on the girl in front of me, on her knees for me with my dick in her mouth. "God," I cursed, "*Noelle,*" I said her name like it was the only word on the goddamn planet that I knew, like I was under her control, owned by every inch of her being. She was everything. She looked up at me, her lips forming a beautiful *o* as she sucked me, and her tongue exploring every inch of my length.

And then her hands moved to my thighs, settling in deeper before she adjusted herself to urge me further down her throat. "Baby," I warned, not wanting her to choke around me, but she shook her head, taking a few seconds to regulate her breathing through her nose as I worked to still my hips, to let her do what she wanted to me, every touch of her soft hands a curse that I would bear silently.

"So good for me, sweetheart," I praised, "on your knees, taking me so deeply." I reached down, resting my hands on her head, tangling my fingers in her hair, wanting nothing more than to yank on it and pull and pull till she was crying for me to stop, begging for me to fuck her—

The thought made me twitch under her touch and I could *feel* the smirk on her lips—knowing how she was affecting me—and so I did bury my hands into her scalp, pulling her closer to me, letting her slide down so her lips reached the base of my cock and her forehead almost rested against my toned stomach, still covered by my gray sweater.

Suddenly, I was all too aware of the way I was saying her name under my breath as she let me fuck her throat—a breathless and needy *Noelle, Noelle, God Noelle, Noelle, fuck. Noelle, Noelle*, words that tumbled out and filled the silence of the room, and an "I'm going to—" followed only by her nod as I released my fingers from her hair and allowed her to pull back slightly before I was spilling inside her mouth, pouring down her pretty little throat.

I watched her as she swallowed—God, I'd never had a woman

do that without asking before—before wiping her mouth and leaning her head up towards mine.

"Come here," I said, pointing at my desk and urging her up off the floor. I wanted to make her come again, wanted to inhale the sounds of her orgasm, and then... well, next time, we would be doing this in a damn bed.

"How do you want me?" She looked up at me through her eyelashes, her lips still shiny from saliva.

"I wanna eat your pretty pussy, baby. So get up on my desk and spread your legs for me, Noelle." She obeyed, climbing onto the wood, and spreading her legs for me. I didn't even bother taking her panties off, just pushed them aside, my fingers brushing over her entrance.

"You want this?" Noelle nodded, and I lowered myself onto the floor in front of her, licking up her entrance before I pushed my tongue inside of her, tasting my girl's cunt. I couldn't believe how much I loved doing this to Noelle—and only Noelle.

After eating my fill of her, I switched my attention to her clit, red and swollen, and worshipped it with my tongue.

She whined, wiggling underneath my mouth as I continued my relentless pursuit of her clit. I looked up as she let out another breathless little moan. "Do you need me to make you come, baby?"

I would do whatever she wanted, because fuck, I would do anything for this woman.

"Please," she begged, and I went back to worship her pussy, sucking her clit as I slipped a finger inside of her wet folds, and then another. When she started clenching around me and I could feel her come on my fingers, I pulled my mouth off of her to kiss her deeply.

"I want you," she pleaded, hand reaching for my cock, but I stopped her.

"Not here," I said, shaking my head as I caressed her hair. "The next time I fuck you... I want you in my bed, Noelle, sweetheart." She gave a little whine, and I leaned down to whisper in her ear. "I want to fuck you so hard that you scream, and I can't do that in my office here, now can I?"

She got down off my desk on wobbly legs. I knew that she wanted more, I could tell that she was still pulsing and aching for me, and I hated that I couldn't take her on my desk again. That I couldn't get her off one more time. She was wet, panties soaked through, absolutely dripping with want—but I couldn't take her here—even though I so desperately wanted to bend her over the desk and ram into her from behind. No. We couldn't do that again.

Once had to be enough for both of us for the night. So, I only sat on my chair and watched as she re-adjusted her clothes before turning back to look at me. "Matthew, I…" But she just shook her head, taking a step towards the door.

"See you tomorrow night?"

"I'll be there." She smiled. "With bells on."

"I'd prefer no underwear on," I said, pulling her back in closer to me. "But I'll take what I can get."

She smirked. "You will."

"Brat." I flicked her nose.

"Yeah, but that's why you like me." Noelle grinned. "And I expect you to make good on that bed promise," she said, before pacing out the door and closing it behind her.

"I will!" I called after her.

I sighed, then ran my hand though my hair and rested back, staring at the ceiling.

God, she was going to absolutely *ruin* me.

No, I was fairly sure I was *already* completely ruined.

I told her I wanted her in my bed—and I meant it. I wanted her in my house, wanted her in every aspect of my life, always, because she was mine. Because this possessiveness I felt for her wasn't going away.

I just needed her to realize everything I could give her first.

CHAPTER 21
Noelle

My hall director duties were finally done for the week, which meant Spring Break was officially here. I was standing outside Matthew's door, wearing a silky green dress, and not much else, with the duffel bag I had packed swung over one shoulder and my giant tote bag on the other.

We texted briefly after I got back to the dorm last night and even after a goodnight text message from him, I realized I was already missing him. But the thought that had gotten me through today was *spring break*. One whole week together. So yeah, maybe this was a dumb idea for my heart, coming to his house and staying with him, but also, all I wanted to do was see him, be near him.

I hoisted my computer bag back up my arm and then took a deep breath as I stared at the door. My hand hesitated in the air for a moment before I knocked, and when he answered, I found him dressed in a light button-down shirt, denim jeans, and dark socks. Snowball was right behind him.

"Hey, Matthew," I said, slipping in beside him, my body brushing against his side as I entered his home for the first time. It was cozy, unsurprisingly bare, but held the faintest hints of home. A painting of mountains, the statue of a wolf. He wasn't kidding at the zoo when he said he liked wolves. I smirked at the thought, and then I remembered what he called me. A little red fox. My eyes glanced over to the collection of books on the bookshelves in his living room and pictures of what I assumed were his family hanging on the walls.

"Noelle. Hi." He smiled at me, and I was so happy to see his face, that I reached up on my tiptoes and placed a small kiss on his cheek.

Moving further into the space, I dropped my bags on the chair in the living room, running my hands alongside the back of the couch. I reached down to pet Snowball's head.

"What smells good?" I asked, nose sniffing in the air.

"Oh, right. I made dinner."

"Dinner?" I said, raising an eyebrow. "Oh, Matthew, I do think you've found the way to my heart. I hope you know you're ruining me for all other men."

"Yeah, that's the point, baby." He chuckled, giving me a small smile of his own. Because he *knew* how much I loved food. How often had he watched me eat? He had seen how I delighted in it, savored every bite. And he hadn't thought I was weird, like so many others had.

"Come on then." Matthew steered me into the kitchen, setting me down on a barstool before returning to the stove, where I could see a pot of water boiling and a saucepan that he was stirring.

"Honestly, I just didn't expect you to be so... *domestic*." I giggled, enjoying teasing him. Of course, he'd cook. I didn't know why I expected anything less from him.

"What, a guy isn't allowed to cook his girl dinner anymore?" *His girl*. Oh, God. He had said it last night too, *my girl*, and the butterflies in my stomach were now back in full force. I could feel a blush threatening to overtake my cheeks.

"No," I tried to give him a coy smile, "I didn't mean that. You're just..." I gestured to his tall frame and well-built body. How did I describe all that he was? "You're *all of that*. And you can cook? *God*, you're just the whole package, Matthew. What else can you do that you haven't told me?"

Ignoring my question, Matthew gave me a small smirk before he turned to the counter and uncorked the bottle that was sitting there. "Would you like some wine?" He raised an eyebrow at me as he poured himself a glass.

I responded with a nod as he tipped the bottle into the second glass and then extended it out towards me. I had to bite back the snarky, *trying to get me drunk, are you, Matthew?*

Because, well, the way he was looking at me... He didn't need to get me drunk for me to want him if we had proved anything. And I didn't need a defense mechanism to brush away real contact, not with him.

To be honest, just as much as I craved physical connection, I had always feared the romantic intimacy that came along with being in a relationship, with falling in love.

But with Matthew... I felt safe. Maybe even safe to feel things.

I waved the thoughts away, taking the wine and sipping absentmindedly as I watched him finish our dinner. I let the taste of it run down my throat, savoring the tartness of the liquid and the way it made the world a little less sharp. A little bit fuzzy around the edges, like somehow someone had cast a glow over this dining room, and it was just us.

Matthew removed the boiling water from the sink, poured the pasta out into a strainer, and spooned out a serving of both on a plate before pouring the sauce on top. He placed the dish in front of me: garlic chicken and alfredo pasta and a side of seasoned green beans, delightful smells filling my nostrils as I picked up the fork.

"This all smells incredible," I almost moaned out loud.

"I tried to make some of your favorites," he smiled. "I noticed that you liked alfredo when we went to the Italian place. And..." he glanced at the green beans. "I figured it wouldn't hurt to get you to eat a few vegetables."

I playfully shoved at him. "I *do* eat vegetables, thank you very much."

"Mhm," he mused, looking at them pointedly on my plate. I took a big bite of them just to appease him, and then another. They were delicious. "Maybe... if you're a *good girl*, you'll even get dessert."

"Oh?" My heart pounded in my chest, and even as he sat next to me at the island and the two of us lapsed into silence, all I could think about was him. And the warmth spreading through my body, the heat pooling between my legs just from thinking about him calling me a *good girl*.

All of the food was delicious, but all of the quiet was giving me too much time to think about us, and what we were to each other. We hadn't labeled it—I had pushed the topic aside, but I didn't know anymore with the way he called me baby and texted me, and the way I cared about him, and I knew he cared about me...

Give him a chance to earn your heart, I told myself. My friend's encouragements from lunch the other day echoed through my mind. I will, I thought. I am going to give him a chance. And if it's a relationship he wants... I can try. For him, I think I would try anything.

Because seeing him smile filled me with more joy than I could explain.

And yeah, I knew one thing was for sure: I needed more wine. I really shouldn't get this attached to him, for crying out loud. Because what if it ended? But then, here was Matthew, who, yeah, had fucked me on his desk, but had also planned the sweetest Valentine's Day dinner for me.

The thought left me holding my fork in midair, staring off into the distance as I swallowed another bite of food.

"What are you thinking about, Noelle?" his voice cut through.

"Well... You," I answered, deciding to be bold instead of

holding back my thoughts. I shoveled another forkful of pasta into my mouth.

God, I should not be thinking about him like that right now. Not while we sat here eating the dinner he had so generously made me. Thinking of him like that made me feel like I was some sort of a sex-craved addict, one who had gone down him on in his office and now couldn't get enough. I ran my tongue over my bottom lip as I stared at him. I couldn't get enough of him, could I?

"Oh?" After putting his empty plate in the sink, Matthew propped his head up with his elbows, leaning onto his hands as he stared at me with bright blue eyes. I used to think they were icy, before I got to know him, but now they were so cool, yet so... welcoming. Inviting, calming. Like the ocean.

I nodded. Breaking out of my lust haze, I tried to refocus myself. Right. Important conversation needed to be had here. There were so many things I wanted to ask him, no, *needed* to ask him. Things I wanted to say to him, to clarify whatever *this* was, to make sure what he meant when he said, *you're mine.*

"Noelle." He put both of his palms on the counter as he bored into my eyes. "Is something on your mind?"

I shook my head.

"I don't want there to be anything between us. Anything that would keep us apart. Okay?"

I nodded, and he seemed satisfied with that. I needed to distract myself from my current train of thought, so I pulled a question out of thin air. "How many people have you been with?"

"Sexually? Or romantically?"

"Erm... Both, I guess." I bit my lip. Why did I want to know, anyway? "I know you said there hasn't been anyone else at the university, but I wondered..."

He looked at me for a moment, refilling his glass of wine and taking a big sip. "Well... Romantically, less than a dozen. Sexually

—five, maybe?" he said, and then I choked on my next bite of chicken and pasta.

Because while it wasn't like I had been with *that* many people either, a few hookups here and there during college before Jake, there was something about knowing that *I* had slept with more people than he had that made my jaw drop open. "That's it? With a body like *that*, you're telling me you've only ever slept with five other women—"

"I'm not some sort of sex god." He laughed. I grumbled. *You fuck like one.* "And, technically," Matthew added, looking at me thoughtfully with his wine glass paused in the air, "You're the fifth."

I shoved a final forkful of the pasta into my mouth to avoid any other thought from coming out.

"Noelle." I brought my eyes back up to meet his as he took my plate away. It felt like he was looking directly into my soul.

God. He really shouldn't look at me like this, not when all I wanted to do was straddle him right here in his kitchen. But I wasn't some sort of cheap hookup for him—he didn't do those. And I was here, in his house, for the whole week. That meant something.

"Yes?" I gulped, feeling suddenly very unsure about how I was going to tell him how I felt. Because as he stood in front of me, I knew I very much *did* want that. Wanted to be the only girl he brought over to his house, the only one he cooked dinner for. Ever. Why was I jealous of future women, already? And if that wasn't what he wanted, well... Then what was I even doing here anyway?

I left my seat at the island to hop up on the counter. My knees were parted so he could stand between them, and I felt even more satisfied as he pulled me in closer. "Matthew," I urged him on as if I could tell that the words were trapped under his tongue, and he was trying to force them out.

"God, Noelle. I don't know anything, but I know that I want you. I don't know what overcame me," he started. "You were just there, bursting into my life, and you were always making me feel like I was going to have a *heart attack* when I looked at you..." Matthew trailed off, eyes narrowing, the glint in his eyes obvious to me as I watched the emotions flash through his face. How he had always *seen* me, all of me, even from the first day we met. How he had *wanted* me. I felt powerful, magical, and beautiful in his eyes. "I don't want you to be a dirty secret, Noelle. I don't want to have to hide how much I want you. From anyone. Okay?"

I nodded. "Matthew..." I wanted to tell him how I felt, how I had been entranced by him, how from that very first day it was like he had walked over and stolen my heart right out of my chest. But the words wouldn't come to me, so I just stared at this man who was laying down all of his truths for me.

"And don't get me started on those little panties you're always wearing."

"Oh, you've noticed those, have you?" I smirked. "I wear them just to torture you, you know." I crossed my knees and readjusted the bottom part of my dress as I watched him stare at me, the slit rising so he could see right up my thighs.

"Oh, you think I don't know that, sweetheart?" His face split into a playful grin. "I also fully intend to punish you for it later."

I couldn't help but laugh then, feeling a swell of pleasure erupt through me. "And what sort of punishment do you have in mind?" I bit my lip, looking up at him with what I knew were the *biggest* eyes I could muster.

"I guess I'll just have to show you, Noelle. But some other time, because right now, I'd like to tell you something." He paused, and I sucked in a gulp of air.

"I really like you, Noelle. So much. I like your brain." He placed a kiss on my forehead. "Your heart." A kiss on my chest, over my left breast. "Your smile." His lips finally found mine. "Your body, your curves." His lips found my shoulder and he lingered there for a moment. "I especially can't get those thighs of yours out of my mind..." His hands trailed up my skirt, towards my bare skin. "I want you. All of you. Always."

"Well, are you still *hungry*, Matthew?" I purred, "Because I have some ideas about dessert…"

One of the straps of my dress had fallen down my shoulder, and I shrugged the other one down as well, pushing the dress over my chest so it would fall towards my waist—leaving me sitting with the green fabric pooled at my stomach, in just my black bra.

Matthew's mouth moved to my ear, his warm breath brushing over my neck as his tongue flicked my earlobe. "I want to *have* you right here, Noelle," he growled. "Eat you out all night on this countertop until you scream my name."

His fingers strummed over my collarbone, down over the thin straps of my lacy bra, which left nothing to the imagination. Each tap of his fingers against my skin sent shooting sensations down my spine, and I could feel how turned on I was from the liquid heat pooling between my thighs. Only he made me this wet just from a few simple touches.

"So do it," I breathed, blinking at him as I tangled my hands into his blonde locks and brought my mouth up to his. "Have me."

I wondered if my eyes were as blown out as his. The black of his irises took over much of the blue, leaving a small ring around his eyes. Because if I was looking at him the way he was looking at me, like one taste was going to absolutely *ruin* him—well, I may have been truly *fucked*.

And I didn't mean literally—though I expected that would come later.

Finally, *finally*, my lips and his met, and I knew that whatever we had, well, it was different. Because no matter how many times I kissed him, that burning intensity, that spark of passion, never subsided. Not like how it did with others. With him, something was different. Maybe it was the way his hands fit perfectly around mine or the slope of his mouth as I met him breath for breath. All I knew was I had never felt these sparks of passion with anyone else. Never felt the warm heat in my stomach from just one touch. Not until him. Until Matthew

Freaking Harper walked into that event and ruined my whole damn life.

His tongue slid into my mouth as I parted my lips for him, and I could only sigh at the taste of him—wine and sauce all swirling together with all that he was, the very taste of him that I loved—and I returned every kiss, every movement, with equal intensity.

"I dreamed about this," he panted as he pulled away and I leaned my forehead against his.

"Dreamed about what? What did you do to me in your dreams, Matthew?" Because I had, too. Dreamed about when he would take me next, how he would do it—dreamed about his lips on mine, on my neck, trailing down my body.

I had dreamed about him every damn night and he had plagued my thoughts—there was a power in knowing I had done the same thing to him. The idea of him, hard and aching in his bed alone, touching himself as I had done, night after night, making myself come as I imagined him inside of me again... was almost too much to handle.

"Everything. *Everything.*"

"Show me," I leaned in close to whisper in his ear.

So, he did. His hands reached around my back and unclasped my bra, my nipples hard and aching already, and I couldn't stop the gasp of pleasure as he bent down and took one in his mouth. Licking, sucking, teeth lightly grazing against my sensitive skin as he circled around it, fervent attention given to my breasts. I shifted my body and squirmed out of the rest of my dress, letting it fall on the floor, forgotten.

There was something about the way I felt with his mouth swiping over me that made me shut my eyes and lean back against the counter. The way he palmed and cupped my breasts with his large hands, skin still spilling out, made every part of me feel so very, very warm and *revered* as he loved every inch of my body— my curves thanks to my hourglass figure, my thick thighs I once hated, and my triple-D sized breasts.

God, and how he worshipped me.

"Matthew," I moaned, "I think I'm gonna come just from you sucking on my nipples alone, oh my *god*."

I couldn't help the noises that escaped then as his mouth switched sides, not leaving the other out, and his hand occupied the now hardened nipple. From his *touch,* from his teeth and lips and *tongue,* my arms moved from where I was braced on the counter to keep myself in place to his shoulders as Matthew continued suckling against my breasts.

I cried out loud and louder, and when Matthew pulled away, running his fingers through his hair as he looked at me, I uttered only *please* and *don't stop,* and begged him with my best big brown puppy dog eyes.

"What do you want, my sweet girl?" I wanted him. For all things holy and mighty, I wanted him inside of me and wanted him to make me come, and I didn't care if it was right here in his kitchen for goodness' sake as long as he put his mouth back on me, his fingers on my clit—something, anything.

"I want *you,*" I heaved, "to *fuck me.* Hard. Right here, on the counter." *God,* I wasn't sure if I wanted it or *needed* it anymore, just that the heat between my thighs was growing hotter, and I wanted him to quell the desire, to satisfy my needs.

And heaven help me, I wanted all of him.

CHAPTER 22
Matthew

"Please, Matthew. I need you."

God, if she kept looking at me like that, I was going to explode. Or possibly lose it in my pants before I even got her into my bed, and I certainly couldn't ignore the growing erection in my jeans. *Dammit*. I could feel myself leaking out of my tip through my boxers, and I needed to act upon that rather quickly. But...

"Noelle," I said, "Not *here*."

I told her that I wanted her on my bed, and *damn her*, I meant it. I knew that I would gladly take her anywhere —*anywhere*, but I wanted to pleasure her thoroughly, to feel her soft skin against my sheets, to watch her fingers bunch the fabric as I coaxed her over that invisible edge. And damn her because she was causing me all these feelings that I had never felt before. I had never cared about being with someone else like this—like I wanted to with Noelle. I didn't just want to fuck her, I wanted to *make love* to her, and God, if those thoughts didn't scare me more than anything else.

I nipped at her neck for good measure before scooping her up in my arms, one under her legs and one supporting her back, and carrying her to my bedroom. It wasn't much, I thought, surveying my basic room that held the bare essentials. There was a poster of a pacific northwest mountain range, one I had hiked, my bookcase full of my favorite fantasy and historical books, and then there was Snowball's bed in the corner. I sat Noelle down on top of my blue comforter, and she perched on my bed wearing only her lacy panties.

"Look at you," I said, feeling such a swell of *desire* for her in my chest. "My gorgeous girl. You look so beautiful right now." I climbed in next to her, and then we were face to face as I placed another kiss down her neck, her collarbone, on her ribs in between her breasts, before Noelle was tugging at my shirt, pulling it off, desperate for me to be as naked for her as she was for me.

Her fingers danced over my abs, solid and hard from my dedication to working out. It was my athlete's body, long after I had quit playing any sports. But the strumming of Noelle's fingers along my bare skin clouded my vision, my judgment. I could only see her, her in front of me, hungry and waiting.

I pulled her closer to nibble on her earlobe before moving my mouth down and sucking on her neck, as she moaned in response to my touch. My hands found her breasts, and I cupped them once again, massaging and gently soothing, fingers flicking over her already sensitive nipples.

"Matthew—*god*, I love how your big hands feel on me."

Shit, if I kept this up, I was going to lose it just from touching her, feeling her. I moved my hands further down her body, ghosting over her stomach, her thighs, before I slipped a finger over the lace that was the only thing preventing me from slipping inside her, and pressed down, eliciting a moan from Noelle.

"Already so wet for me, aren't you? Can't wait to get my mouth on your sweet pussy."

Noelle's voice was all breathy, a little too high as she responded, "God, *yes*, I'm so dripping wet for you, Matthew—" Another noise slipped from her throat as I pressed harder against her clit.

"You like that?"

"Yes. Yes, Matthew, *fuck*. I need you, please."

I hooked my fingers in the band on each end of her panties and pulled them down and off of her so I could see all of her as she laid down, spread out and opened for me. "Wanna look at you. My girl all sprawled out and ready for me in my bed."

"How do you want me?" she murmured, causing a slight growl of frustration, if not arousal, from me. "You can have me any way you want. On top, or—"

"*Fuck*, Noelle. First, I want to *taste you*," I said, flipping her and moving her on top of me. "Then I want you to ride me, so I can see that beautiful face of yours as you come around my cock."

Now it was Noelle's turn to whimper as I pushed her thighs apart and pulled her towards me, prompting her to sit on my face. I licked up her entrance, the lightest of touches as I teased her with my tongue.

"*Matthew!*" she shrieked from the startling, dizzying sensation of my tongue.

I moaned against her, nose bumping against her clit as I licked up and down, and again, giving her no pressure, the lightest of tongue grazing her entrance. God, I loved when she shuddered on top of me, loved tasting her pussy, spread out just for me.

"Don't—" she bit out, "tease me."

My response was muffled underneath her, and the vibrations caused a shiver to run down her body. She fisted her fingers into my hair, as if it was possible to pull me closer as she sat on top of me. I told her I wanted to taste her, and I did. I wanted to bring her to climax on my tongue, enjoying her, taking my time. The way I couldn't in my office last time—the way we *shouldn't* in my office. Because however we had met, however this tumultuous relationship had begun, during these past two and a half months with her, I had fallen for her intelligence, her sharp tongue, her quick wit. I had fallen for her mind *and* body, and there was nothing I wanted more than to show her how much I cared for

ACADEMICALLY YOURS

her. Because *fuck*, I did care about her. So much it almost scared me.

My hands moved to her hips to hold her steady as I finally slipped my tongue inside of her, exploring her. I lapped at her folds, tasting her wetness, the salty sweetness which was so unmistakably Noelle. "*Holy fuck*," she moaned. "Your tongue, Matthew. Feels so good inside of me. Do I taste good, babe?"

If I had been honest with her, I would have told her that I hadn't enjoyed going down on my earlier partners—girlfriends who had used me for my body, and not cared about my feelings.

But Noelle, my *Noelle*, I wanted to taste her every minute of every day.

"*Matthew*." Noelle's hips ground into me as she cried again, trying to gain more friction as she squirmed on top of me. "More, please," she pleaded, "Need more."

Her breathing got heavier, her thighs squeezing from satisfaction against my face as another thrust of my tongue caused Noelle to gasp. I knew she was close, but I kept my fingers on her hips, digging into her round, luscious ass, and enjoyed her anyway, knowing exactly how to drive her mad.

"Oh, Matthew, *oh*—" My tongue licked upwards and found her clit, circling around it before closing my lips and sucking. Noelle's legs shook around my head, and I was sure that if she wasn't sitting on top of me, her back would have arched off the bed against the pleasure I was giving her. But I wanted this: to give her attention where she needed it, where she would feel it most.

She trembled on top of me, crying out, "Matthew, I'm gonna—"

I just kept sucking on her clit as she found her first orgasm, her pussy clenching around my tongue as I tasted her. As I decided that there was no better place to taste her than in my bed, like this.

Finally, I pulled my mouth away from her and licked her wetness off my lips. "You taste so good, baby. I could spend all day between your legs."

Noelle shifted down off of my face, and my hands slid to her curvy thighs as she rested over my hips. She was rubbing up and down against my cock, still contained under my jeans. I was acutely aware of one thing: I needed her right this very instant, or I was going to be *gone*. I could feel the wetness through the fabric, what I knew was a combination of my saliva and her juices, and I had to grit my teeth. Focus. Breathe.

"*Noelle,*" I groaned as she rocked against me, and then my hands guided her off of me so that I could free myself from this damn denim prison, the one thing that was keeping me from taking Noelle *exactly* how I wanted her.

I stripped down out of my pants and boxers, and then my cock was free in front of her, hard and bulging with my desires. I needed her. Oh, *God*, I needed her. And Noelle clambered back on top of me— "I want you inside of me," she said. "Matthew. Please."

And I was *so* desperate to feel her clenching around my cock. As desperate as she was for me, apparently, since she guided the tip of my length into her opening, still sensitive and wet from my tongue and her first orgasm. Noelle waited a moment before lowering herself on me to the hilt. Before my brain could even think about putting on a condom.

"*Noelle—*" I warned, knowing I should pull out and wrap my dick before we continued, but *oh God* she was so tight and warm, and her hands were resting on top of my chest.

"It's—it's okay," she groaned out, sinking onto me fully, "I'm on—*oh*—birth control." I was confident that I was going to *die* right here as she settled onto me, head tilted back and eyes closed. She was taking all of me, and I had to take deep breaths and concentrate on not spilling myself inside of her right then and there, just from the feeling of her heat around me.

"You feel so fucking good, Noelle. I love your body so much." I couldn't help myself as my hips rolled up into her, sending a wave of pleasure through me as I thrust even deeper inside of her.

"Feel so good inside me," she gasped out as my hips thrust up again. "So deep. Your cock fits in me so perfectly, Matthew."

I groaned. "Yes, Noelle, yes—" She dug her nails into my chest.

Then she placed one hand on either side of me, tangled her fingers in the sheets as she began to move up and down, slowly at first. I was entranced in the way her breasts bounced from the movement, and I drew in shallow breaths as my fingers dug further into her ass, squeezing in a way I knew was going to leave marks.

I wanted to leave marks all over her—her neck, her stomach, her thighs, her ass. I wanted to see all of the places where I had touched her, where I had made her mine.

"God, you're so beautiful on top of me," I *sang*, "I knew you would look magnificent riding my cock."

"Shut," she panted out through her moans, "up."

I didn't, though, as she picked herself up and dropped back down, riding me with such intensity I was seeing stars. "*Fuck, Noelle*, you're killing me. I love your tight cunt. Like you were made for me. You fit me so well, Noelle."

"*Matthew*," she squeaked, picking up the pace even further, her fingers releasing from the sheets to move towards herself, "I need—"

I stopped her, held her hands in my own as she whined and squirmed and bounced on top of me. I rolled my hips again. "Are you close, Noelle? Do you want to come as you ride me, sweet girl?"

She nodded as she ground herself against me more, little mewls and moans that made me even harder. But no matter how close I was, how much I wanted to chase my orgasm, I wouldn't, yet. Not until I knew she was satisfied, again.

"Oh—I—God," she gasped, "I'm so close—"

I resisted the urge to thrust deeper, trying to keep my hips from the involuntary spasms as I continued to hold Noelle's hands hostage in front of her. "What do you want, Noelle?"

"Touch me," she growled, "I want to come, *please.*"

"Good girl." I relented, releasing her hands so my thumb could find her clit. And then I was rubbing it over and over, bringing her closer to that edge, that relentless chase she had been pursuing.

"*Oh*—Fuck. Matthew. *Fuck.*" She tilted her head back, eyes squeezing shut, hands curled into fists as she tightened around me, her entire body clenching as Noelle climaxed again, waves of pleasure rippling through her. Her pussy was fluttering and pulsing, squeezing me tighter.

It was glorious, and I couldn't take my eyes off of her face. I thought I might give anything to see Noelle look like that every day for the rest of my life—so full of the pleasure I gave her. "*God*, I love watching you come, Noelle."

As she came down from her orgasm, panting as she released her grip on the sheets, I flipped her over, resting her against the pillow, still buried inside of her as I peered down at her face. At her beautiful face, slightly damp with sweat so her ginger locks clung to her forehead; at the blush of her cheeks from the physical exertion that came with riding me.

"Can you keep going?" I wasn't going to continue without her permission. Even though I hadn't had my release yet, even though I had been holding on for so long if she said no, I would stop, pull out—finish myself off.

Noelle's arms clasped around my neck, and she pulled me closer, wrapping her legs around my body so I couldn't stop, even if I wanted to.

"Inside me."

"Noelle—"

"I want you to come inside me, please," she said, a little breathless, "I want you to come so hard that I feel your cock pulsing inside of me."

"Fuck. Noelle. There's nowhere else I'd rather be than inside you, sweetheart."

I couldn't stop, as I began thrusting in and out as she clung to me, forcing me in deeper, forcing me to ram deep inside of her each time I moved. I grunted with focus as I closed my eyes, rested my forehead against hers, tried to ignore the intimacy of the situation, because if I looked at her straight in her eyes as I came in her, I knew I would never be able to go back. "I'm close—"

And I did, then, open my eyes to watch her because, well... I was gone for her. So completely gone for this girl. And it was definitely, one hundred percent Noelle's fault.

Because she had sucked me in and made me feel all of these things for her, until I ended up wanting her in a way that was so unlike me.

But God, as I finally came, spilling inside of her, watching her gasp as my warm seed filled her completely—I couldn't help but lock eyes with her.

And *this,* the slow thrusts I gave her as I found my release, it felt like making love.

We stayed that way, as I collapsed on top of her, my head between her breasts, panting, with me trying to slow my breathing, for much longer than was necessary.

"God, that was..."

"Yeah," she said. "Yeah."

Finally, I pulled out of her, ignoring the whine from Noelle as I slid off of her—already missing the feeling of being inside her warmth. After I went to the bathroom to clean myself and Noelle did the same, I pulled her back into my arms and held her tight.

Because I never wanted to let her go.

We laid there, intimately, intertwined, naked together. She grew quiet in my arms, and I peered down at her. "What are you thinking?" I asked, hand trailing down to her spine as I brushed a thumb over her skin.

"I just... well. Matthew, I don't even know how old you are." Noelle's big brown eyes held my gaze, and I could feel my heart beating in my chest. Why did she unnerve me so much? Why did one look from this girl make me feel like there was nothing else in the world but her and I?

"I'm thirty." I wasn't sure what she expected, but I could tell from the shocked expression on her face it wasn't that. "What?"

"Nothing." Her eyes crinkled at the corners, and I instantly wanted to run my finger over her face to smooth her smile lines. "I just thought you were older." Now her fingers moved to my arm, trailing up my bicep slowly. As if neither one of us could resist touching the other.

"Is my age a *problem*, Noelle?"

"No. No, of course not. I don't mind you being older than me, Matthew. I want you; you know that?"

I nodded. "Yeah, baby." I buried my head in her neck. "Because I knew, from the moment I saw you, that you were mine. And I had to keep you. Had to figure out a way to have you, my sweet girl."

"Then..." There was a pregnant pause. "I... Matthew, what do you want in life?"

I blinked. "You." I didn't even hesitate. It was a shock, how fast that had dropped from my lips, but nothing had ever felt more right. "Is that... okay? I know we haven't known each other all that long but... I want you in my life, Noelle. I told you, you're mine." I picked up her hand and placed a tender kiss on the top of it. She sighed, rolling back into my arms to rest her head back against my chest.

When she didn't say anything, I added something else. Another truth. "I've never felt like this with anyone. I've never felt this much *for* anyone. It's never been like this with anyone."

Was she suddenly insecure? I had known her for almost three months, and I had never seen her be anything other than confident, loud, and self-assured, always. But now, she seemed... quiet. "I feel the same," she finally admitted, "like I saw you, and something in my heart stopped. My soul said *it's him*, and no matter what I do, I just can't forget about you. Like I... I was meant to be with you."

"Noelle," I said, pulling her up into a sitting position, cupping her face in between my palms. "If you want me, you want this—us... Then I'll do whatever I can to make you happy. To make this work."

"So, we're together, then?"

"Damn right we are, baby." I laughed, and then I kissed her again, over, and over.

I kissed her like I was starved—like she was the only thing I wanted in this world. I couldn't bring myself to worry, because she was in my arms, her lips were parting, her hands were twining around my neck, and sweet God, her tongue was in my mouth. If I could be kissing Noelle, feeling her nip at my lip with her clever teeth, feel her body fitted against my own, hear her release that little sigh in the back of her throat, why would I ever bother doing anything else?

"I think you've ruined me, Noelle."

She rolled over on her stomach, looking at me. Her arms were crossed on the pillow, and I resisted the urge to bend over and kiss her bare shoulder. Again.

"Good," she smirked. "Then no other girls will go near my man."

"Your man, huh?" I liked the sound of it. I liked it a lot. I tried not to count the freckles on her face as I stared at her, tried not to connect them into constellations across her cheeks. But I didn't resist the urge to reach out and touch them, trace them, before cupping her cheek. I needed to stop touching her so damn much.

"Yeah, my man. And I'm your girl, aren't I?"

"The only one," I confirmed.

"I just wanted to hear you say it again."

I could feel her smile as she nestled deeper into my arms. We fell asleep like that, cuddled together, arms wrapped around each other, whispering sweet nothings into each other's ears until our eyes drooped closed and no more words came to us. I fell into a deep, peaceful sleep, one where I had her for always.

I hoped the day would never come when I had to say goodbye to the sweet feisty little redhead who had taken a big piece of my heart.

CHAPTER 23
Noelle

I intertwined my fingers through his as I curled up next to him on his mattress, my messy red hair spread over the pillowcase. With his other hand, his thumb was brushing over my shoulder blade, over and over, lulling me into contentment, comfort, and warmth.

I fluttered my eyes at him, sighing as he laid there and watched me.

"What are you doing?" he finally asked.

"I'm wondering what it will take to get you to kiss me."

"That's silly."

"Why is that?"

"Because I'm always wanting to kiss you," he admitted.

"Then you should," I said, and pulled him in closer to kiss him—passionately—my tongue slipping into his mouth, intertwining with his.

God, I loved kissing him. I loved everything with him. How well he filled me, how much he cared about me in bed, in... every aspect. He was a born caretaker, a protector—something I had never needed, never wanted, yet I found that I wanted all of it with Matthew. Damn him, for making me think all of these domestic thoughts about him. All of these lovely, lust-covered thoughts as he held me in his arms. *Damn him.*

I woke with his arms still around me. I tried to pry myself out of them, but he just tightened his hold and whispered sleepily in my ear, "Stay."

"Matthew—" I tried to protest, but he just shook his head against my skin, and I sighed.

"Stay," he requested again. "I like holding you in my arms."

All I could do was agree—because I didn't want to leave his warm embrace either. I curled back against his chest and snuggled against his warm skin, the steady beating of his heart easily lulling me back to sleep.

The next time I woke, the bed was empty, except for a big white lump at the foot of the bed that I recognized as Snowball.

I rubbed in between her ears before finding a t-shirt of his in a drawer and threw it on, appreciating that it was big enough to cover all of me and brush my thighs. Then I wandered out towards the kitchen and the smell of food.

"Is this what I have to look forward to whenever I sleep over again in the future? I'm not sure I'll ever leave if you're this good to me, Matthew."

"Morning, sweetheart." Matthew smiled and leaned over to me to drop a kiss on my lips.

"Morning, babe." I appreciated his bare chest—he had only put on a pair of sweatpants, and he was leaning over the stove, flipping bacon in a pan as another appliance seemed to be cooking food right next to him. "Are those waffles?" I asked, excitedly. Waffles were the supreme breakfast food—my absolute favorite.

"I thought I'd make breakfast for my girlfriend," he said, and I beamed.

"Oh. I like the sound of that."

He pulled one out of the waffle maker, putting it on a plate for me and plopping it down on the counter before pouring the batter in for a second waffle.

"Syrup?" I asked, already poking into his fridge, looking

through the food he deemed good enough to stock. It was mostly healthy things—lots of meats, cheeses, and vegetables, but I didn't miss the small sweets he must have snuck in—things that I wondered if he had gotten just for me. Finding the bottle, I pulled it out and went to sit at the island.

"So," I said, drizzling syrup over the plate he laid out for me as Matthew took the bacon out of the pan. "I was thinking."

Matthew hummed in acknowledgement, popping a piece of bacon in his mouth as he leaned against the counter, waiting for the second waffle to get done.

I took a bite of mine and sighed happily. "These are so good. Oh my god." Matthew chuckled, and I looked up from my plate to find him sipping his coffee—black, just the way he liked it.

As we sat there, side by side, my phone buzzed on the counter. I glanced at the screen and then flipped it over after I saw who was calling.

Was I ignoring her? Maybe. I hit the side button to mute it and just kept eating my waffle as Matthew watched me.

"Are you going to answer that?" Matthew finally asked with a raised brow.

"Nope." I shook my head. "It's my mom. And I just can't deal with her right now. I have enough going on with everything." I gestured around us wildly, even though I wasn't quite sure what all that encompassed anymore. "And that's without listening to her telling me what to do or what I'm doing wrong. It's *my* life, and she just..." Matthew gave me a small frown, and I just bit my lip. "What?"

"I guess it's just... I can't talk to my mom. Even if I want to, she's gone, and I know she hasn't always treated you with the most respect in the past, but maybe you should give her a chance to change. Tell her what's bothering you."

"I don't know if I'm ready."

"That's understandable," Matthew nodded his head. "It's hard to confront the people you love. But I'm here for you, you know. If you want my help, or just moral support."

He reached out and squeezed my hand before going back to plating the rest of the food. I didn't think he realized how much I appreciated that—his willingness to do anything for me, always. I wanted him to feel the same—to know I'd stick by his side, no matter what he needed.

I nodded, and he sat down next to me. "So, you were thinking?" he said, and I just blinked at him.

I remembered the thought I had earlier. "Oh! Right. I was thinking about how you need to meet my friends."

He raised an eyebrow. "Angelina, Charlotte, and Gabrielle? I already *did* meet them, sweetheart."

"Well, yeah," I frowned. "But like, officially this time. And maybe a little more… sober, on all of our parts."

He chuckled. "Whatever you want, Noelle. I'd like that."

"Good." I nodded, going back to my waffle, happily, alternating between that and munching on the perfect, crispy bacon Matthew had put on my plate. "You're making me never want to leave here," I said, and I immediately realized what those words could mean. I looked up at Matthew, who was staring at me with a serious expression, and my mind thought the worst. "Oh. I didn't mean—"

Matthew shook his head. "No, I like it. You're always welcome to stay, even after spring break is over."

"Are you sure?" He put his cup down, coming over to stand by me, his hand squeezing my thigh in a reassuring way.

"I'm sure. Let's go out tonight. I want to take you on a date. A *real* date."

"What do you call that basketball game?" I scrunched up my nose and laughed. "Or Valentine's Day? I think those were all real dates too." I brushed a blonde curl off of his forehead.

He stared at me so reverently as I straddled his lap, resting my forehead against his. "I just… God, Noelle, I want to take you out. I want to spoil you how you deserve to be spoiled."

I touched my forehead to his. "I think I'd like that. But all I need is you, you know that?"

This is all I've ever wanted, I thought—*to just have you, all of you, with nothing coming in between us.*

"Good." Matthew smiled. "Because I do wanna take you on a proper date, baby."

"I expect to be wined and dined," I said, holding out my empty coffee mug, which he took with a laugh before filling up with coffee for me, followed by caramel creamer.

He definitely bought that for me, I thought with a smirk, because this grumpy man never drinks anything in his coffee. I grinned to myself at the thought—grumpy man—because in the last month with me, he had become anything but whenever he was by my side. It was like whenever we were together he was lit up from the inside, and it made my heart warm.

After breakfast was done, and I helped him do the dishes (also known as Matthew washing, and me sitting on the counter and drying the dishes as I watched his arms), Matthew pulled me into the bathroom.

"Time to shower," he said, tugging his shirt off my body, and even though he had seen me naked—twice at this point, plus we had spent the whole night with our bare skin touching—I still flushed as I stood in front of him completely nude. Matthew didn't notice at first, shucking his shorts off after turning the shower water on, until he turned around to find me standing there, hugging my stomach. Why did this seem more intimate than having him inside of me?

"Hey, hey," he said, cupping my face to bring my eyes up to him. "What's wrong? Why are you embarrassed?"

"I'm not—" I shook my head, clearing my throat. "I'm not embarrassed. I just..." I bit my lip. "I've never done this with someone else."

He raised an eyebrow. "What? Showered?"

I nodded. "My ex... he didn't..." I shrugged. I hated explaining to him that I hated the stretch marks on my thighs. I knew I wasn't skinny, and even though I was comfortable with my curves, sometimes I looked in the mirror and I hated what I saw. The cellulite on my thighs, the fact that my stomach wasn't flat or toned, the love handles on my sides… It made me self-conscious sometimes.

So somehow, *this* felt like it would mean more to me than just sex. Him taking care of me, loving my whole body, even when I just wanted to wrap my arms around my stomach and hide.

Matthew placed a kiss on my bare shoulder.

"He didn't take the time to worship your body every single place he could?" He made a tsk noise with his tongue. "That's a damn shame, Noelle, because I can't get enough of you."

I could feel my lips pulling up into a thankful smile, as he pulled me into his arms, our naked bodies fully pressed against each other. "Noelle. We don't have to do anything you're not comfortable with. And I mean that—for everything. But I want you to see yourself how I see you. Beautiful. Sexy. Treasured. Cared for." And the word he didn't say, but I felt, in every gentle touch and action: *loved*.

I nodded, placing my hand on his bare chest. "I feel safe with you," I said, which I knew wasn't what he had expressed, but it was what I felt, all the same.

I let him guide me into the shower, let him wash my hair, and my body, running his hands all over the places he had kissed last night. And once he was done—and very clearly sporting a massive erection, clearly as affected from this as I was from having him touch me everywhere—I returned the favor, soaping him down and touching every well-defined muscle on his body.

"Mmmm, baby," he moaned as I ran my hands up his shaft. "I love it when you touch me, but I'm gonna need you to stop that unless you want me to blow my load all over you when we just got clean."

"Or maybe," I said, kissing his chest after the soap had finished running off his body. "I could take you in my mouth, and then—"

"Nope!"

And I shrieked when he whisked me off my feet and into his

arms in one fluid motion, turned the shower off, and then carried me from the bathroom and tossed me onto the bed—still dripping wet.

"Matthew!" I exclaimed. "We're getting the sheets all wet, and now we're going to have to wash them."

He leaned down to kiss me, and I gave up my pointless protest—I wanted this as much as he did—and kissed him back with as much fervor as I could muster, holding on to his face with my hands and pulling him down on top of me.

The wet strands of his blonde hair were clinging to his face, little droplets of water falling off of him and onto me, and I giggled. "We're going to have to shower again," I said, moving my hands up and down his chest before interlocking them behind his neck.

"Worth it," Matthew said as he nipped at my neck, and then he was positioning himself at my entrance, thrusting in all the way inside of me—

"Oh *God,*" I moaned.

"Noelle, baby," he breathed out. "You feel like you were made for me."

I twisted my fingers in the wet hair at the base of his skull and kissed him again, pressing our mouths together as his thrusts became fast and erratic.

"Maybe I was," I panted, coming closer to an orgasm with every roll of his hips. I resisted the urge to close my eyes. Truly, sex had never been like this before, and with him—with this intimacy, the love Matthew showed me as he reverently washed my body in the shower. I couldn't imagine it being like this with anyone else, either.

I rested my head against his heart, listening to it beating. And I let myself go—let myself live fully in this blissful, perfect moment, connected to the most wonderful man I could have ever imagined.

All I knew was I didn't want this to end—didn't want this to ever end.

"I'm close," I whined into his ear, and Matthew leaned down to rest his forehead against mine. His thumb found my clit and he rubbed circles over it as he thrust in and out, slowing down to a painfully slow rhythm.

I think I might have whimpered, but then my mind went blank as I was overwhelmed by sensations: the feeling of his wet skin on mine, the feeling of him so deep inside of me, the way he was applying pressure to my clit, my nipples rubbing against his chest. I cried out as my orgasm hit me, feeling the blissful release as my body settled from the sensations, almost holding Matthew in deeper as my climax fluttered around his length, and then he was following close behind, spilling inside of me. I could have cuddled up next to him just like this as he almost fell on top of me, pulling me into his arms and holding me tight before he pulled out, so warm, sated, and *happy*—but I knew I didn't want to miss one moment of this weekend, of this day with him.

After we cleaned ourselves (for the second time) and got dressed, Matthew guided me outside to his truck, where he lifted me inside by the waist and buckled me in before settling in the driver's side.

I couldn't ignore the flush on my cheeks—a combination of the way he had just fucked me and how he was always so caring and considerate with me. I knew I could have done those things myself—he did too—but it felt so good to be taken care of by him, so I didn't complain.

"Where to, Matthew?" I asked him as we intertwined our hands that rested on the center console.

"Well, I was thinking we should start our *very productive* Spring Break with dinner and a movie."

"Very productive, huh?"

He nodded. "What do you want to go see? I think they have one of those girly romantic movies you love so much playing right now."

"Hey!" I protested, "They're not girly just because they're romance."

"I'm just teasing you, baby." He brought my hand to his mouth and kissed it. "What do you want to see?"

I ran my thumb over the back of his hand. "You can pick," I said, not caring what we saw as long as we got to spend time together.

To my delight, he *did* pick the romance movie that was showing, and we didn't stop holding hands the whole time we were at the movie theater. I sat with my head resting on Matthew's shoulder, like I couldn't get enough of the body contact, couldn't get enough of him. Maybe I couldn't.

Afterward, we went to my favorite pizza place, and I reminisced on all the times I had come here growing up—with my mom, for friend's birthday parties, graduations, and lots of little memories. We spent the night almost sitting in each other's laps, side by side, and sharing pizza and memories. It was the perfect day, and I couldn't have imagined anything better than spending time with him.

And we still had a whole week ahead of us.

CHAPTER 24
Matthew

I didn't think I had ever enjoyed a week so much in my entire life. We had been *enjoying* ourselves in every possible location in my house: the couch, the shower, the kitchen counter, and of course, the bed. Last night we had fallen asleep, still naked and cuddled up next to each other.

"What do you want to do today?" I asked, still lazing in bed with Noelle next to me.

She hummed, rolling over to face me, eyes still glassy with sleep. "Sleep." Noelle cuddled her head into my chest and closed her eyes.

"Sunshine." I brushed the messy strands out of her face. "There's nothing I'd like more than to spend all day in bed with you, but we only have a few more days together, and I don't want to waste them."

Noelle grumbled. I swear, trying to get her out of bed in the morning was like trying to raise the dead. "Ten more minutes," she mumbled.

I smiled, pecking her forehead with a small kiss. "I'm going to go shower." I tried to pry her body off mine.

That did it. Her eyes flew open, and she pouted. "Without me?"

I swatted at her bare ass. She had taken to only wearing my shirts to bed, and I had to admit I *really* liked it. "Come on, then."

After we were both showered and clean (showers took twice as long with Noelle, but I didn't mind), we went into the kitchen so I could make breakfast.

Noelle sat on the counter while I fried us some eggs, and bacon, and popped some toast in the toaster.

"So." She kicked her legs as she leaned back on the granite. "What's the plan for today, prof?"

"I think I asked you that, Noelle. Is there anything you want to do?"

She bit her lip. "Well, we could go to the beach, take Snowball with us?"

"It's still less than sixty degrees outside."

"Okay, point taken. Hmm..." She looked deep in thought for a moment. "Bookstore day?"

I placed one hand on each side of her as I kept the spatula in my right one. "You just want to buy more books, don't you?"

"Maybe." She stuck her tongue out at me. "Oh! What about going to the Farmer's Market? There's normally one around here on Wednesdays... and I haven't been to it since college."

"Oh, yeah?" She took her phone out, typing furiously and searching for something. Finally, she spun around her phone towards me. "Okay, that sounds nice." I nodded while reading the details. "We can get some stuff to make dinner with."

When I clicked out of the window accidentally, I realized her background photo was us from behind, holding hands at the zoo. I smiled just looking at it. It was before we were a couple—or anything, really, and she was leaning into me, and I was looking at her like I had never seen her before.

It made me realize I needed a photo of *her* for my own lock screen and background.

Noelle, oblivious to my inner monologue, beamed. "Don't think I'm letting you out of that bookstore date, though."

"Of course not." I turned my attention back to our breakfast, and after it was done, Noelle hopped off the counter and we both sat at the table, eating side by side. "Tomorrow, maybe?"

She nodded. "Let's just enjoy the sunshine today."

And we did.

The farmer's market was bustling with people who had all seemed to come out in droves for the sunny day, but it didn't bother me, even as Noelle and I weaved in and out through the crowd.

We had picked up some things to make for dinner that night, as well as various produce items, cheeses, and loaves of bread. Noelle was a sucker for bread, and well—I was a sucker for her.

"Come on," she said, pulling me over to one of the food trucks. "Let's get a snack. I'm starving."

I laughed. "We ate breakfast like two hours ago."

Noelle stuck her tongue out at me.

I got her a boat of fresh seasoned fries, and she glared as I stole one.

I smirked, dropping a kiss on her nose. "I can buy you more, you know."

She was appeased at that and popped another fry in my mouth, feeding me. I could feel the heat rising to my cheeks just from the action. How intimate it was.

"You know," she said as I chewed on the fry. "I don't share food with anyone."

"No?" I asked, wondering why she thought this would surprise me.

"Anyone," she repeated. "Ever." I watched her look thoughtfully into her fries. "Until you."

"Well." I couldn't help the satisfaction flowing through my veins. "I hope I get to share a lot of things with you, Noelle Hastings."

"As long as you keep me fed, Matthew Harper."

I grinned. "I can do that."

Noelle ate another fry before we polished off the rest of them and then we were back, bopping from stall to stall. It was incredible how many different types of products there were here. Produce, of course, and then there were the cheeses, baked goods, and wines, but also there were so many homemade goods. Soaps, jewelry, stained glass, carved wooden items, and so much more. Even if we didn't buy anything, it was fun just looking at what people had taken their time to make.

And it was also fun to point things out that we thought the other would like. When Noelle wasn't looking, I purchased some rose-scented bath stuff for her as well as a little fox figurine that reminded me of her.

As we were strolling, I looked over and saw a young family—mom, dad, and their two kids, smiling and laughing as they sampled honey from one of the stalls. The dad lifted one of the kids on his shoulders, and I could see it.

I could see us, coming here. Blissfully happy, kids in tow. It was something I had only let myself dream about in the deepest parts of my heart—a family. I had hardly let myself think about it, scared that even just the idea of it would be taken from me. But here, now? I imagined what it would be like.

To live a life with Noelle. A life full of laughter, of teasing each other. Of morning sex, shower sex, and sleeping in late. Of diapers, pancakes, and kids' art projects. I imagined watching her dote on our kids with red curly hair and blue eyes.

It was so lovely, the scene that unfolded before me. I was watching them, but it was us in my mind's eye, as Noelle sampled bread and hugged our daughter.

"Matthew?" Noelle's voice shattered the illusion, bringing me back to the moment. This moment... This was our moment. I smiled at her. I couldn't get ahead of myself, because I still very much wanted to enjoy all of this, here and now.

"What were you looking at?" She seemed to track my eyesight and then frowned at the family who had walked away.

I just shook my head, placing a kiss on her forehead. "It was nothing. Just thinking, that's all."

"Okay." Noelle gave me a little eyebrow raise before turning back to the stall with the honey. "You sure you're fine?"

I nodded, not saying anything else. I couldn't tell her I'd been thinking about our future children. We hadn't even talked about kids. Did she even *want* them? I wasn't sure. I certainly wasn't going to bring it up now. It was way too soon for talks about marriage or children or anything. We had just decided that we were *together together* this week.

"Noelle!" A female voice shouted, and when I looked back up from the table, two college students were pummeling her with hugs.

My RAs, Noelle mouthed. I realized they were the two who had gone on the zoo trip with her. I tried to rack my brain for their names.

"What are you guys doing here?" Noelle asked. "I didn't know you were spending spring break in town."

The two girls looked at each other and then blushed. They took each other's hands, and then I remembered their names—*finally*. Rachel and Jessica.

"We're—well..." The dark-skinned one, Rachel, fumbled for words, but Jessica, the little preppy blonde, just shook her head. "I invited Rach to spend the break with my family." She gave the other girl a look like they were trying to decide how much information to reveal to their boss.

I didn't say anything, but I tried to step a little bit away from Noelle, to give her privacy with her staff. I didn't know if she wanted to tell anyone what we were, especially not her resident assistants.

That was when they finally realized I was there.

"Oh! Hello Professor Harper." Jessica grinned at me, and I gave a little sheepish smile in return. Why did it feel like we'd been caught doing something we shouldn't? We were both adults, after all, and Noelle was almost five years older than these two.

"Hi," I mumbled, and Noelle's hand reached back, clasping

mine. I looked at Noelle, leaving it up to her whether or not to tell what we were to each other.

She didn't. Instead, after the girls had chatted with her for a few moments about hall business, Noelle was already saying goodbye. "Well," she started, "it's a nice day outside, and we should all get back to enjoying the market." She handed the stall owner a few bills for the items in her hand, and then pulled me back towards the trees on the other end of the street.

When we were finally alone, we both couldn't help but break out into laughter.

"I feel like a five-year-old who was caught with her hand in the cookie jar." Noelle's eyes were shining with laughter.

"Why do I feel like we got caught?" I huffed. And then I turned my attention back to the potential problem at hand. Did she even want her students to know? "Your students—"

"They're not going to say anything," she reassured me.

I had told her I didn't want her to be my dirty little secret, didn't want to hide our relationship, but obviously Noelle didn't feel the same. I frowned. "Are you sure?"

She nodded. "Did you see them?" she dropped her voice to a whisper. "They're *so* dating." She grinned. "I called it. Hazel owes me fifty bucks."

I think my jaw dropped a little. "You were *betting* on your RAs hooking up?"

She shrugged. "I've known them both since they were freshmen. I always felt like there was something more there than friendship."

"Huh." I rubbed a hand over my jaw. "And what did you feel with us?" The glint in her eyes was unmistakable as Noelle stood up on her tiptoes.

"Hmmm..." Noelle stood up on her tiptoes so she could look into my eyes better. "I felt like you were going to *eat* me. You're a wolf, after all." she batted her eyelashes. "And I'm just a little kitty."

"Noelle—" I about growled. "I *did* want to eat you. Still do."

I gave her a wolfish grin, and pulled her into my arms, even as some of her bags fell to the ground. "But you're not a little kitten, are you, hm? My little vixen."

She wasn't a kitten—she was a fox. A wicked little fox who certainly knew every possible way to get into my pants. I was glad we had the rest of the week still together because I needed to stop feeling like I wanted to jump her bones anytime I saw her.

"I'm pretty sure that I'll never get sick of eating you, my sweet girl." I gave her a wicked little grin, letting the implications of my words sink in.

She laughed, and then put on her cutest coy face. Like she didn't know what she was doing, acting all bashful and shy. Like she didn't know how this was going to end—with me on top of her. "You're sure? Absolutely, positively, one hundred percent sure?"

"Positive. I could tell you that a million times, but I don't think you'll believe me, so I'll just *show* you that instead." I wiggled my eyebrows at her and placed a kiss on her jaw before pulling away just a little.

Noelle pretended to think about it. "I think I require dinner first, and then you are free to *show me* all night long."

I nipped at her ear. "Let's get going, baby." I hoisted all of our bags back up off the grass as we finally separated, and I was glad I managed to control myself enough not to pounce on her here.

Time and place, Matthew, I reminded myself. This was definitely not the time or place.

We were going to go home, I was going to start dinner as Noelle sat on my granite countertop and watched me, munching on chips and salsa as I made us tacos, and then I was going to make love to her.

All freaking night long.

I never wanted this break to end.

CHAPTER 25
Noelle

Snowball was cuddled against me on the couch as Matthew cooked breakfast. I buried my hands in her long, white fur, and smiled as she leaned up and licked my face. I loved how soft and cuddly she was—much like her owner, who was constantly cuddling me. I smiled as Matthew came and joined me, placing a plate of French Toast and eggs on my lap. "Thank you, babe," I said as he tried to push Snowball off the couch so he could sit with me, but his dog wouldn't move.

He glared at his dog, and I laughed. "Are you going to steal my dog now?" Matthew sighed.

"Yes." I grinned. "She clearly likes me better than you, so..."

"Just so you know," he said, leaning over to ruffle my still-damp hair after our shower, "She gets attached quickly if she loves someone so..." He cleared his throat. "You're just going to have to spend a lot of time over here from now on."

"Oh?" I liked the sound of that.

He hummed in response as he nudged himself in between his dog and me.

I sighed. "I don't want to go home." I hated that it was the weekend today because that meant it all had to end soon.

After a week of being fed breakfast, lunch, dinner, and a

whole lot of *dessert*, I wasn't sure I wanted to go back to reality. I wanted to wake up next to him, take his dog for walks, and do the crazy domestic shit that I had thought I didn't want anymore. I wanted to be all tangled up in his life and interwoven into the very fabric of his identity.

Was that crazy? Maybe. Yesterday, Matthew finally took me on the bookstore date he had promised me since it was cold and rainy, and as we sat next to each other in the bookstore coffee shop, both sipping our drinks (hot chocolate for me and black coffee, as always, for him), I felt exhilaratingly happy.

Would it last? I hoped so.

"Do you want to meet my sister?" Matthew asked me as cuddled on the couch that night.

The TV was playing but I couldn't even pay attention to it. I was just focusing on the way Matthew's arm was around me, on his thumb rubbing circles over my shoulder. Snowball was laying in front of the couch, and I didn't miss the way she had looked up at us a few times, wishing she could fit on here with us, but she really was a giant dog, and the two of us already took up all the room.

I didn't want this week to end. This perfect week of *us* where no one else could ruin anything.

I was absorbed in my own thoughts, too distracted to pay attention to his out of the blue question. "What?"

"My sister flies in tomorrow. Tessa." Matthew gave me a hopeful smile. "It's her spring break, and I know it's still early, we're still so new, but I'd like you two to meet." He squeezed my shoulder. "If you're up for it."

He… wanted me to meet his sister? The only other woman in his life, the most important person to him? I couldn't help the look of surprise that took over my face. "Really?"

He nodded. "Only if you don't think it will be weird. She's only here through next Saturday, and then she flies back to New York, so…"

"I'd love to meet your sister, Matthew," I confirmed. And if I got the added benefit of hearing about Matthew when he was younger out of this, well, I wasn't going to complain. "Just tell me what day, and I'll make sure I'm free." I rested my head on his chest. "Guess this means I can't sleep over next week though, huh?"

He frowned. "Oh. Yeah. Right." He looked like he hadn't even considered the fact that it might be weird if I was sleeping in his bed every night with his little sister in his house. As much as I was excited to meet her, there was no way I was having *that* be her first impression of me.

And then there were my residents—my job. I hadn't even been worried when Rach and Jess saw me at the farmer's market. I didn't think they would spill to anyone else, but just in case, I hadn't confirmed that we were dating. I didn't really need them all to know I was seeing someone, let alone a professor on campus. I didn't think I could take all of the questions.

It was more than that though, wasn't it? Besides just my own reservations, there was still a layer of worry because of who we were. Things we had never acknowledged out loud, even when I teased him and called him Prof. Something I'd been doing a lot less of, lately.

And what would happen if we broke up, and everyone knew? I'd have to deal with all of the pity, the sorry glances, people wondering why I wasn't good enough. Because Matthew... There was no way anyone could accuse the beautiful man curled up against me of anything, ever. He was absolutely perfect.

I wanted to keep him right next to my heart, always. So that hopefully it wouldn't break if I kept it safe.

"And to think you were spoiling me so much that I never wanted to leave," I joked.

He laughed, his forehead resting against mine. "You make this place feel more like home, Noelle."

And I knew, right then and there... I was standing right on the edge of the cliff, so close to falling.

∼

I GOT BACK to my apartment on Sunday and realized that for the first time in a long time I didn't *want* to be alone anymore. After Jake, I wasn't sure I would ever allow myself to be so open and vunerable with someone again. But with him, with Matthew... it felt right. Like I was meant to be held by him—like we were twin souls, placed on this earth to find each other, be together. It felt so right, and when he held me in his arms...

"Damn you, Matthew Harper," I muttered under my breath. Just the thought of him brought butterflies to my stomach, and I knew, even more so after last night, that I was falling for him.

And I worried about everything that could go wrong—because I didn't want to lose him like I had lost Jake. I didn't want him to wake up one day and realize I was annoying, and not worth the time and effort, because I cared too much about him. And I couldn't have handled it if he decided that I wasn't enough for him. Who cared what people thought, anyway—he cared about me, and that was all that mattered. I knew by how he touched me, regarded me so reverently, held me like I was something to be cherished, to be loved.

I needed to get my feelings under control. I wasn't supposed to fall for him, to get so attached to him, and I certainly shouldn't be thinking about him after the most intimate weekend of my life.

A knock came at my door, and I sucked in a breath. "Come in!" I said, dusting my poptart crumbs off of my leggings before attempting to tidy my coffee table that I was currently working at.

When Hazel popped her head in the door, I sighed in relief. "Oh good, it's just you," I said.

"Just me?" Hazel laughed. "Glad to know that's how high I rank in your list, Noelle."

I shook my head. "You know what I mean. I thought you were a student."

She stuck her tongue out at me before plopping on the couch next to me. "So. I hear you had a fun spring break."

"Heard from who?" I asked, raising an eyebrow.

"Oh, you know... just our RAs."

"They didn't!" I gasped.

She nodded dramatically. "I'm afraid so. And they reported that Professor Hottie—their words, not mine—was even better looking this time than at the zoo. And they asked me if you two were dating." Hazel raised an eyebrow at me. "And I couldn't exactly answer them, so... Are you?"

"Haze!" I protested. "I can't believe you're gossiping about my relationship with our resident assistants! Didn't you spend spring break with Lucas, anyway?"

"Maybe." She just gave me a look. "But we at least had the good thought to not spend it in Portland."

I just laughed. "I may or may not be calling him my boyfriend now, yeah." I ran my fingers through my curls absentmindedly. "But I didn't think those two were going to rat me out to you!"

Hazel held up a dollar bill and gave me a devilish grin. "You'd be surprised what a few of these can do."

"You *bribed* our staff? Hazel!" I groaned.

She shrugged. "You've been too busy to give me all the good gossip, so..."

"I promise, I will tell you about my life," I said, rubbing my temples. "If, and only if, you promise to stop asking our RAs about my relationship."

Hazel nodded in agreement. "For the sake of disclosure, some of them have also caught you two kissing outside of the dorm."

I flushed. "Oh God."

After Hazel left and the bulk of my work for the day (and a little bit of writing) had been completed, I sat against the couch, eating Chinese takeout. I was wishing I was eating one of Matthew's homemade meals instead.

I knew that his sister was flying in the next morning, and we had decided that I wouldn't stay over while she was there, however much I wanted to, but I couldn't deny that I just wanted to talk about it—him, everything—with someone, so I sent a text to the group chat.

> **BEST FRIENDS BOOK CLUB**
>
> NOELLE
> Anyone down for dinner tonight at my place?
>
> CHARLOTTE
> I'm in, duh.
>
> ANGELINA
> I'll bring the wine. What time?
>
> 6? Whenever you want is fine.
>
> GABBI
> I'll be over after I finish my book!
>
> See you all soon. ☺

I LAUGHED. Somehow the three of them had always been capable of putting a smile on my face, and I loved that no matter what was going on, Gabbi always had her nose stuck in a book. I couldn't say anything because I normally did too. Once this semester was done, I was going to get my reading goal back on track. Grad school had definitely curbed my ability to read lately.

Hours later, we were all sitting in my living room, curled up on the couch and the loveseat, cups of hot chocolate in hand. I recapped the last few days—how I had missed seeing him, how I had gone over to his house, our date (just saying it still sent butterflies through me), and the weekend I spent at his house. Not to mention that we were *dating*. Like, actually, honest to goodness, dating.

"So you're *official*? Officially official?" Charlotte's eyes widened. "Holy shit."

"Yeah. He called me the G-word and everything."

"Oh my God. *Noelle Hastings* has a *boyfriend*?" The humor was clear in Gabbi's voice. "Why, it seems like just last week she told us she had sworn off love—" She put a hand over her heart, laughing as she pretended to tell a story. I rolled my eyes at her dramatics.

"But, for real, Noelle, how are you feeling about all of this?" Angelina asked me.

"Honestly, I don't know yet? It doesn't *feel* real. I keep waiting for something bad to happen, and I'm worried if I always expect the worst then nothing good will ever happen to me," I frowned. "And Matthew... he *is* good."

"So good," Charlotte confirmed with a sigh. I playfully punched her in the shoulder.

"It's your turn to go find one now, you hopeless romantic."

She fake gasped. "Oh, you did not!" I stuck my tongue out at her, and everyone collapsed into laughter.

"Seriously though. We're all turning twenty-six this year. Maybe it's time we *all* try to find happiness?" I looked at all of them. It wasn't like I wanted to be the only one in a relationship in the group. And I hadn't been—Angelina had a series of flings, men she left in her wake, and Gabbi had a serious girlfriend for a bit there while I was with Jake. But in the last year, somehow, we'd all gotten comfortable with our routine, not missing the presence of anyone else in our lives. Someone who would take our attention away from each other.

"Like I have the time," Angelina snorted.

I rolled my eyes at her, but it reminded me of something Matthew and I had talked about. "Also, I was hoping, maybe, that you guys would want to get together soon so you can actually meet him?" I gave my best puppy dog face. I wanted them to know him like I did, but I also wanted them to like him. To support me and my relationship with Matthew.

"I think I speak for all of us when I say we can't wait to re-meet your hunky professor boyfriend, Noelle. Do you know if he has any single coworkers he can bring along?" Gabbi joked. "As long as they're as well-built as he is, please. And maybe darker hair. You know I'm not into blonds."

I picked up my book off the table and lightly smacked her arm with it. "Stop paying attention to my boyfriend's arms, babe." I laughed. "You really need to get laid, Gabs."

She scoffed. "Please, don't remind me." Her arm flew over her face dramatically. "It's so hard to find good guys these days. I swear seventy-five percent of them take one look at you and think they're going to fuck you on the first date. No sir. Not with this body!" Gabbi wagged her fingers. And then her voice dropped lower, and she furrowed her eyebrows. "Yeah, you might be right about the whole getting laid thing, N."

I cackled, patting her arm. Angelina and Charlotte were barely holding in their laughter at Gabrielle's sudden rant, and I just grinned at my best friends. "Anyway," I said in a sing-song voice, redirecting the conversation. "We can plan something at my apartment for next week?"

They all nodded. "Just send a text in the group chat," Angelina said. "We can figure out the time in the next few days."

"Works for me," I said, and then I smiled into my coffee cup, wondering if I could keep going on with ignoring the feeling in my gut telling me everything would end badly and instead living like this. Happy.

I looked up at the sky, once my friends had left. "Thank you," I whispered to the setting sun.

I wasn't sure what I was thanking the universe for—for a sunshine-filled day in Portland, for Matthew Harper, or for the fact that after so long, I was finally feeling like I had put myself back together. I basked in the warmth of the sun on my face as I thought about the fact that a simple thank you didn't cover enough for how appreciative I was right here, at this moment.

CHAPTER 26
Matthew

Noelle had only left my house that morning and I already missed her as I pulled to the Portland airport to pick up Tessa. She was finally coming to visit me during her Spring Break from NYU. Unfortunately for me, our break schedules hadn't lined up, but she assured me she was fine to hang around my house with Snowball while I was teaching or had to do stuff on campus. More than anything, though... I was excited to have her here, for her to get a chance to meet Noelle, and I hoped she would like her as much as I did.

Because I wasn't sure what I would do if my baby sister didn't like the girl I had fallen so hopelessly for. And maybe I wasn't quite there yet—wasn't ready to call it love, wasn't ready to tell her the full extent of what was in my heart, but I knew it was there. I knew it from the way my heartbeat around her—steady and true, but always for her. I could feel it in the way she felt so right in my arms—like she was made to be there.

I found her, blonde hair tied up into a messy bun, standing waiting for her luggage to arrive. "Tess!" I smiled, wrapping my arms around my little sister in a big hug. "I'm so glad you're here." Her wavy blonde hair was tied back in a bandana, and it hit me how much she looked like our mom. I got a little choked up, just looking at her.

"Hey big bro! I'm glad this worked out." She pulled out of the hug to look for her bag on the carousel, but she must have noticed my face because she shot me a look. "What?"

"Nothing." I cracked a smile. "Just thinking about how much you remind me of mom."

"Oh." Tessa gave me a soft smile followed by a little shove. "Well, stop that. You'll make me cry, and I don't want to ruin my mascara."

"Fine," I sighed, standing behind her as she waited for her bag. When it finally appeared, she pointed at it, and I grabbed it for her.

"Ready to go?"

"Oh yeah. And I can't wait to meet this Noelle I've heard so much about."

Had I talked about her that much? Maybe I had. "I can't wait for you two to meet," I said. "I really like her, Tessa. Like, *really*."

Tessa laughed. "I know, big bro. Now come on and drive me to your house. I want to see that puppy I got you."

"Fair warning, she's a lot bigger now than when you saw her last. Not really a puppy anymore."

"I was counting on that," she smiled, pulling up the handle of her suitcase. "Let's go." Trailing behind her, we walked towards the parking garage and back to my truck.

I couldn't wait for Noelle and Tess to meet, honestly, and I was hoping they would hit it off. Because if everything went the way I hoped it would, they would be sisters one day.

And *that* thought brought a stupid smile to my face.

⁓

I shouldn't have been so nervous for my little sister to meet my girlfriend, but the fact was—I was absolutely terrified. I had never introduced her to anyone: the girls I had dated had either been for too short of a time, or I hadn't been serious about them anyway, so why would I bother?

It was nothing like what I felt for Noelle. And, because of that, it was incredibly important to me that Tess liked her. Because my sister had always been the most important person in my life, the one I had made so many decisions for, the person who I had tried to protect from everything. That was—until Noelle. My little fox had burrowed her way into my life, snuck under my defenses and found a way to snuggle herself in close—right next to my heart. So yeah, I was nervous.

And even after spending two days with my sister, taking her around Portland when I wasn't in class and doing things we used to do as kids, I couldn't help but wish that Noelle had been with us. As I got ready for breakfast that morning, I realized that I wanted her with me, now, wanted her to have been curled up around me last night. Because once I had gotten her in my bed, I found that I hated her not being in it. I was addicted to her—her sight, her touch, her taste—and I wanted to be around her all the time. I wanted to buy beach-front property on Noelle Hastings, so she was the first thing I saw every morning. So I could live every day with her wrapped in my arms. I wanted to cook for her, wash her hair, and tuck her in bed next to me every night.

And as much as I loved Tess, I didn't know what I would do if she didn't like my girl.

On the ride to the restaurant—one of Noelle's favorite breakfast cafés—we passed the time by talking about Tessa's classes, the boy she had been seeing, and her life in New York. The one topic we seemed to skirt around was her plans for after graduation, and I could tell it was bothering her, not knowing where she was going with her life afterward.

"I'm proud of you, you know." I finally said, leaning over to ruffle her hair.

"Matthew!" Tess shrieked, trying to flatten her hair back down. She narrowed her eyes at me. "I'm not ten years old anymore. Stop doing that." She slugged me in the shoulder—

hard, though I supposed she could have hit me a lot harder if she wanted to. "I was trying to look nice to meet your *girlfriend*, you know."

I shrugged sheepishly. "Sorry, little sis. I can't help it. Sometimes it's hard to remember you're all grown up and don't need me anymore."

"Matthew." She frowned. "I'll always need you; you know that right? Ever since we lost Mom and Dad—"

"I know." I cut her off, and Tess just sighed next to me.

"We can talk about them, you know. We never do. I know you miss them as much as I do…" She trailed off.

"I can't, Tess. It's still…" I just shook my head. *It's too hard.*

She turned her attention back to the road. "Tell me more about Noelle."

"What do you want to know?" I asked, scratching the light dusting of scruff on my face.

She pretended to think really hard about something. "Do you love her?"

"Tessa…" I gulped. "I've known her for a few months, and we've barely been seeing each other for a month. I think it's too soon for either one of us to be saying that."

Tess shrugged. "I don't know. Dad always said the moment he met Mom he knew he wanted to marry her. Like, you know, you know, right?"

"And do you feel like that?" I asked her. "About your boyfriend?"

She laughed. "No. But I'm young and in college. You're turning 31 this year, Matty. I don't think you want to be alone forever, do you?"

I grumbled in response as I pulled into the parking lot. "Best behavior," I glared at her as she hopped out of the truck.

Tess gave me a sly smile. "I'm not a kid anymore, big bro. I promise I won't interrogate your girlfriend." She grinned at me as I followed behind her, locking the truck and walking into the restaurant.

> **NOELLE**
> I'm running a little late! I'll be there in ten.

> **MATTHEW**
> Okay. Drive safe.

Tessa and I settled into a booth in the back, and I ordered coffee from the waiter when I finally looked up and saw Noelle rushing in, cheeks red from the morning chill outside, wearing a sundress and a chunky sweater with tights. The outfit was so very *her* that it made my heart clench a little.

"Sorry I'm late," Noelle said, sliding into the booth next to me. "My mom called, and I couldn't get her off the phone."

"It's fine." Tessa brushed her blonde hair behind her shoulder with one hand and then gave Noelle a warm smile.

I kissed Noelle on the cheek, before turning back to Tess. "Noelle, this is my sister, Tessa." I chose to omit the word *little* or *baby*, knowing Tess was likely to kick me in the shin. "And Tess, this is my Noelle."

"It's so nice to meet you," Noelle gushed. "Matthew's told me all about you, and I've heard so much about your time in New York. I lived there for a year after college, so we were probably there at the same time."

"No way!" Tess laughed. "We could have walked past each other on the street and not even known it."

Noelle shook her head. "There's no way—I definitely couldn't have seen you and not remembered you." Noelle did have an uncanny memory for faces, this I knew, but also, there was something so memorable about Tess. It might have been her height—both of my parents were tall, and at 5'10, she definitely wasn't a short little girl anymore, and she also had that face.

"Stop," my sister smiled. "You're going to give me a big head."

"Not that she needs any help with that," I added, rolling my eyes. Tessa tried to kick me under the table, but I caught her foot before she could. I gave her a smirk, and she grumbled under her breath.

"So, Tessa," Noelle said, changing the subject before my sister could attempt to kick me again. "Matthew says you're not sure what you're doing after graduation yet?"

Tess froze, and then she shook her head. "Ah... No."

Noelle raised an eye at me, and I looked at my little sister. "We don't have to talk about that if you don't want to—"

"No." Tessa insisted. "No, it's fine. I just don't know what I want to do yet." She bit her lip. "What about you, Noelle? You're almost done with your masters, right? I think that's what Matthew told me."

She nodded. "I'm still trying to decide if I'm going to stay on as a Hall Director for one more year or not. But I'm getting a master's in Student Affairs, and I'm not sure exactly what I want to do with it, but I'm hoping to stay at UP. It's like home, you know?" She glanced up at me, and I gave her a reassuring squeeze on the shoulder.

We still hadn't talked about our futures, what came next after she graduated or what either one of us wanted out of the relationship. I knew we should, but I didn't want anything to change. And I worried that when we finally had that conversation, it would change everything.

Tessa gave me a sad smile. I was sure she was thinking what I was thinking—*home*. "Home would be nice." She almost forced it out, and I could tell she didn't want to talk about this now. How much we missed having somewhere to call home. How we hadn't, ever since we had lost our parents. It had just been us, even when she lived with my grandparents before I finished college. And when we lost them, too...

Home wasn't something we had felt in a long time.

"I hope my brother has been treating you well," Tessa finally shook off her somber expression and gave Noelle another smile.

"Oh, yeah," Noelle grinned, leaning against my arm and batting her eyelashes up at me. "He's the best."

We paused our conversation as the waiter came by to take our orders, and I wasn't surprised at all when Noelle ordered the cinnamon chip pancakes with a side of scrambled eggs and bacon. Even at breakfast, she loved her sweets.

"Oh my God," Noelle exclaimed. "You have to have some good stories about Matthew you can share with me from when you were kids." She gave her best puppy dog eyes, begging my sister, and I knew she would cave. That look made me butter in her hands.

I frowned, looking between the two of them. "Hey—"

"Oh, there's the glower," Noelle laughed.

"It was permanently affixed on his face for like four *years*, believe it or not."

My girlfriend giggled in response. I think that only made my eyes narrow more at Tessa. I didn't think the Harpers would be immune to the Hastings charm—not one bit.

Tessa laughed. "When we were younger, he used to play dolls with me. He got pretty good at braiding their hair." I turned a little red as Tessa told Noelle some of my most embarrassing childhood habits. "I think he'll make a good dad someday."

"That's enough," I said, shaking my head as I wanted to dig myself deeper into my chair.

I turned to Noelle, and she was just staring at me, lips parted as if she was putting pieces together. Or maybe she was shocked, that Tessa commented on kids?

Noelle bit her lip and continued. "I don't have siblings, so for me... This is so crazy different. I never had someone to spend my time with, to play with, or just know they were there for me. The closest I have is probably my cousin, Oliver, but he's three years younger than me."

"It's okay," I said, wrapping my arm around her shoulder and pulling Noelle in tight to me. "I think siblings are overrated, anyway."

She put her mouth closer to my ear and whispered to me, "I think it's sweet. The way you are with your sister." She turned back to Tessa and grinned conspiratorially. "I love hearing about your childhood, but maybe we should do it when grumpy pants over here isn't around." She patted my thigh with her hand, and I knew she was kidding from her tone.

Honestly—it made me fill with pride, a little bit. That Noelle and Tess were getting along. That they seemed to be enjoying themselves. That I could ever hope for the day where they might be something more.

Sisters.

We could be Noelle's family, Tessa and I—we hadn't ever had anyone else, but with Noelle... I thought that maybe, none of that would matter.

The rest of breakfast was full of laughter, us all swapping college stories, Tessa telling us about the dumbass boyfriend she had dumped, and the two of them gushing over stories about me when I was younger.

I was very glad Tess did not have my baby book, otherwise, I think she would have whipped it out without a second thought.

And even if things were good, and felt so right... I wasn't sure if we were there yet.

CHAPTER 27
Noelle

The day after breakfast with Matthew and his sister, I sat around our usual table at the coffee shop and cradled a mug in my hands.

"Oh my god, you guys," I said to my best friends. "His sister is so nice. Like, so *unbelievably* nice. And she wants to be an actor and I just... I really liked her. And I think she liked me." My cheeks heated, and I buried my face in my hands as I looked at them.

"So it went well?" Charlotte smiled as she sipped her frozen drink. "See, I told you she'd love you. It's impossible not to."

"Yeah," I beamed. "It did. Really, really well." I chuckled, and the four of them stared at me. "What?"

"You're falling for him, aren't you?" Gabbi asked as she looked up from her cup.

"What?" I bit my lip. *Was I?* I just shook my head. "I'm just seeing where things are going. Sure, we're dating... But it's not that serious." I said, not really believing my own words.

"I dunno, Noelle. Seems pretty serious to me. You spent your entire break with him. You met his sister—literally the most important person in his life. How is that not serious?"

"But—It's not—We haven't even..." I trailed off. It wasn't

serious, but somehow every time I thought about the way he was with me, so tender, loving, caring, doing things like making sure I ate and calling me baby... How could I say we weren't serious? But even so. I shook my head. "We haven't even talked about the long term. We barely even decided we were officially dating. I'm not... It's not like I'm in love with him."

"Maybe not yet," Angelina snorted. I could always count on her to be my dose of reality, but right now I just wanted to live in my bubble. I needed it, because I didn't know what was going to happen and I wasn't sure what I was going to do if everything fell apart.

I hadn't asked him about the future, besides my small one-off question when we were in bed together, because I knew it was going to be the end of this lovely, happy, honeymoon phase. When we had to start answering the tough questions and had to start sharing the most intimate details of our lives with each other.

Sure, he knew I lost my dad, and I knew he lost his parents, but I had a feeling that neither one of us knew how deep our wounds ran. And I hadn't told him about Jake, either.

Not about our relationship, or what he had done to me. The real reason I had, on the heels of utter betrayal, booked a flight, packed all of my belongings up from our once shared apartment, and moved back to Portland—my home. Why I truly left the assistant job in New York—the one that I had *hated*, the one I had only got because he begged me to come with him. Not the way I had resolved myself that I was going to change my life. Not a lot of people got a second chance in life—a do-over, or a chance to start again. But I did.

Sometimes people asked me if I missed that job—the one I left behind in New York City, working as an assistant for a publishing company. I thought I had it all figured out after college: a decent job, a little apartment in NYC that wasn't much but would be the start of my life, a ring that was sure to come from the guy I thought I was going to marry—but that was before everything fell apart. And the truth was, I *didn't* enjoy the job.

Didn't enjoy living in the big city. Didn't even really want to marry the man I had once thought was my everything.

And moving home after that year had been *freeing*.

But still, there were things I hadn't communicated. Stuff I hadn't even scratched the surface on, three years down the road. My best friends didn't even know the depth of my pain. It was like there was a hole in my heart that I had never quite repaired, and this never subsided ache in my soul, even after all this time. I thought about how different I had felt at the beginning of the year, versus now.

Then, I hadn't even known how to fill that void in myself, hadn't known where the unexplained longing for rightness, stability, or care came from. But I had known that it terrified me. It scared me how much I longed for one person who could perhaps mend my heart, could put me back together piece by piece after I was shattered. And maybe I had been set adrift at sea, and I still didn't know which way was north or south. It was like I had been paddling, frantically, for the last two years, and maybe all I was waiting for was for my rescuer to pull me back to shore, to breathe *life* back into me, to hold me, warm me, and tell me that *everything is going to be okay* and to *just hold on because I'm going to save you*.

But I had known, even in the frigid ocean waters of the Oregon Coast, even as I shivered against the freezing cold currents, that this time would be different. And I had made a vow to myself right then. I didn't need a man to heal what another broke. I could—I would heal myself, put myself back together stronger than I ever was before. *I am enough*, I thought to myself that day at the beginning of the semester as I watched the world shuffle on with their daily lives. Because I had to be. Because the alternative—being broken? I didn't know how to live with that.

But right here and now, sitting in this coffee shop with my friends? I felt like Matthew had pulled me out of the icy water and wrapped a warm towel around me. And my heart. And somehow, even when I was aching and feeling this desperation deep inside of me, the one that longed for anything and everything, to feel complete and wholly loved, I knew I could do this. I knew I could survive it—*life*. Because I *was* strong enough to live, and be happy, and achieve everything I had once dreamed of. Even if love, well—that could wait a bit, couldn't it? Because I was going to find my old self again, no matter how hard it would be to do it.

And Matthew—he was the one who had showed me how much life was worth living again. The one who had shown up, day after day, and showed me what love was supposed to be like. I didn't know if he loved me—I didn't even know if I loved him, but I did know one thing: he was the cataclysm for change in my life.

He threatened to shake the foundation I had built around myself, the defenses I had created to protect myself from harm. And I knew, somehow, that if I let him, he could topple all of them.

Every barrier, every wall. He had been successfully chipping away at them for so long, that I was worried about what would happen when he finally realized how much better he was than me and left me. At the idea of being broken and so very alone, and the only person who could put me back together would be the person who had left me.

I couldn't let that happen. I couldn't let myself give every piece of my heart to Matthew Harper—even if he was the best guy I had ever met. Even if he was the only one who made me feel safe and protected but also lit a fuse in me that couldn't be quenched. The only man who had ever loved every inch of my body just for the sake of it. Because he wanted to.

Because he *saw* me in a way no one else ever had.

Fuck, I was screwed—because I was definitely, definitely on the path to falling way too deeply in love with this man.

～

THE WORST PART about Tessa staying for the week was I hadn't gotten to spend any alone time with Matthew, and since I was on duty that night, I couldn't even spend time with him and his sister.

I sat at the front desk in the dorm, working on some event stuff, when my phone buzzed. I quickly unlocked it and a huge grin spread over my face.

> **MATTHEW**
> Baby?

> **NOELLE**
> Hi handsome. I was just thinking about you.

> I miss you. I wish you were here.

> I know, but we can't, Matthew. Your sister is there, and I'm on duty, you know that.

> I just can't stop thinking about you in my bed, and I want you back in it.

> Fuck, Matthew.

> When does your sister leave again?

> Saturday.

> Not soon enough.

> I'll see you tomorrow, baby.

> You better.

> See you tomorrow. <3

When I fell asleep that night, it was with Matthew's face in my mind, imaging his strong arms pulling me in close, making me feel safe and secure in his hold.

I just hoped that feeling would last.

CHAPTER 28
Matthew

The next two weeks were a blur of activity, and then it was already almost April. After I had dropped Tess off at the airport, Noelle and I tried our best to see each other as often as possible, but even we got caught up in the middle of the semester and all of the different things we had going on. We hadn't even had a chance to have dinner with our friends yet, much to their disappointment. My friends had met Noelle, of course, and I had met Noelle's friends at the bar, but that wasn't the same.

I wanted them to get to know the girl I had fallen in love with.

I hadn't told her yet, but I couldn't forget the moment when I realized with absolute clarity that I was in love with her. So far gone that she was all I could think about.

Noelle stayed with me whenever she could—all curled up around me. Most mornings we'd wake up with her leg strewn over mine, her hair all tangled in the pillowcase, and her hand clutching my t-shirt. I had never realized how much I could love this, having a girl in my bed every night, but I came to the realization somewhere along the line that it wasn't the act that I loved—it was who I shared it with. Noelle was the only person who I could see myself sleeping beside, and she was the only woman I ever wanted to be cuddled against me like the world might end if we broke apart.

It was a chilly morning when I had rolled out of bed, thrown on a pair of track pants and a hoodie, and tried to coax my little redhead—whose face was still buried in my pillow—*out* of it.

"Come with me," I pleaded. Snowball's leash was in my hand. She was sitting at my side, wagging her tail patiently, and while I could have employed the good old 'get her' and had my dog lick Noelle awake, I preferred to do it more civilly.

It was still early in the morning anyway, and Noelle had stayed over the night before, but I had gotten used to the fact that it always seemed like getting Noelle out of bed was the hardest part of every morning. Unless…I sat on the bed next to her, rubbing a hand over her bare shoulder.

"I'll get you cinnamon rolls after," I said, hoping to entice her. It wasn't that I *needed* her to go with me. I could have gone for a run alone, sure, but I wanted her there. Not that I would ever force her to exercise—her body was perfect; I simply wanted her at my side.

"Fine," she groaned, throwing the pillow off of her head, telling me that she was, in fact, awake. "I will go on this nature hike with you to Forest Park if you pinky promise that you will buy me cinnamon rolls afterward." I nodded, and she kept looking at me. "With *extra* icing," she added.

I sighed, and she narrowed her eyes. "Extra icing. Got it." At that, Noelle hauled herself out of bed, digging through the duffel bag that seemed to always sit on the floor.

I loved every moment of her being here, staying with me, and I suddenly wanted to give her more. Something permanent, so that she had a place where she could leave things. So that she *always* felt welcome, and she knew that I wanted her here. Because I did, I really did. But I didn't want to scare her off or freak her out by moving too quickly, because this was still new. We were still so new, and I didn't want to push too much on her too quickly. Didn't want her to realize how attached I had gotten to her being in my life.

Fifteen minutes later, we were on the road. Noelle had pulled on a pair of turquoise spandex leggings and a tight black sweatshirt, and her hair was up in a high ponytail—which I loved because it showed off how long her hair was (I resisted giving it a little tug, to mess with her)—and even without makeup, she looked beautiful as always.

As we walked, jogged, and padded our way through the trails, Noelle had the slight red glow of exertion on her face, and somehow, it even put a smile on mine.

"Water?" I asked her, pulling out the metal water bottle I had packed just for her out of my bag.

She nodded, and we pulled off to the side to sit on a bench as we both drank, and I put a little bit in a bowl for Snowball, too, who was panting from exercise.

"Do you know what I'm thinking about as I'm walking the trails?" Noelle said a few minutes later when we were on our way again.

I shook my head with a small smile. "No, tell me."

"I'm thinking," she said, panting a little in the middle, for dramatic effect; I could tell the difference since I had been watching her for so long. "About all that icing that's going to be dripping down my cinnamon roll, and how I'm going to lick it off with my tongue—"

And I laughed. A pure, belly laugh that I couldn't have held back even if I tried to. "I think I can manage to find a few better uses of that tongue of yours..." I trailed off, even though there was no one around, and placed a quick peck on her cheek before leaning down to her ear. "And a few other things I'd rather have you *lick*."

"Hmm..." Noelle gave me a thoughtful look as she turned around on the path, hiding what I was sure was the blush on her cheeks from me. "I don't think that was what you promised me for coming, Matthew Harper."

"I think I would promise you whatever you want for *coming*, Noelle Hastings." I raised an eyebrow, innuendo clear in my words. She laughed, but I didn't miss her happy little blush on her cheeks, and we went back to the blissful silence, hands intertwined as we walked the trail, Snowball between us in the damp forest.

And watching her face light up as she saw the breathtaking view on the top of the mountain of the city... The thoughts that had been scattering through my brain for the last few weeks, an idea that had fully formed into a whole real *thing*, finally were illuminated just like Noelle's hair in the sun.

I loved her.

The realization jolted through me, suddenly, but I also realized I had known it to be true for a while. I loved the girl standing in front of me—every quirk, every little part of her that she had laid bare with me, shown to me—I loved every piece of her. She had captured my whole heart, and she didn't even know it yet. Didn't know how much I loved her, how much I cared about her.

She had never been more beautiful to me, and I couldn't wait to tell her how much I loved her.

∼

"You're still coming and bringing Noelle to dinner next week, right?" Bryan asked me over the phone as I buttoned up my dress shirt. I had agreed a week ago, when things were less crazy, and now I was staring at myself in the mirror, trying to tie a tie for a university event as my best friend reminded me of my plans.

The whole gang—officially meeting my girlfriend. The woman I loved. Who still didn't know that I loved her. I hadn't been able to tell her, even after we got home.

Every time I opened my mouth as I looked at her, the words just didn't come.

"Yeah, of course," I muttered into the phone.

"Good, because this is one of the last things Elizabeth will probably get to do before the baby comes, and I know how much she wants you there." She was due next month, and I knew they were so excited to start their life as a family. Jealousy raged through me before I was able to temper it back down.

I wanted to be a father. I wanted kids. I wanted a family. I wanted all of it—with Noelle. Even though I lost my parents, even if it seemed like anything good in the world would disappear if I blinked, I had Noelle now, so none of that seemed to matter.

I was more scared of a life where I didn't have her, where I didn't even try. I couldn't even imagine a life where I loved and lost her anymore. My future was just... Her. Her rosy cheeks, long red hair, freckled face, and a couple of kids that looked like us.

I wanted it.

"We'll be there." I nodded, even though he couldn't see me.

"We can't wait to see Noelle again."

I grumbled. "Yeah, yeah, can't wait to hear all of you guys tell me *I told you so* all over again in person."

Bryan laughed. "Listen, Matt, I gotta go, but I'll see you tonight, alright?"

"Sure, man," I said, saying our goodbyes as we hung up the call.

I looked at my reflection, wishing I could tell Noelle everything that was on my mind.

I wanted—no, needed—to fight for her heart. Because I needed her to love me as much as I loved her. Needed to prove to her that this—us—was worth it. Forever.

∽

DESPITE MY BEST intentions to avoid any sort of university event for the near future, here I was at the Alumni Event with all of the staff and faculty of the University of Portland in attendance that weekend. Many of them had brought their partners, husbands, wives, or significant others, and I wished I had Noelle by my side.

She would have made this dreadfully boring event a little more enjoyable. Instead, she was on the opposite end of the large dining hall, wearing a beautiful emerald dress that hugged her curves with cute little ruffles on the shoulders. And the way her heels elongated her legs never ceased to take my breath away.

When she had come out of the bathroom at my house after getting ready, I couldn't help but appreciate how beautiful she was. "Can you zip me up?" Noelle asked, holding back her hair with one hand as she stood, her bare back exposed to me.

I pulled up the zipper before placing a kiss on her neck from behind.

"Wow." Noelle turned around and I took her in—her hair down in loose, big curls with one side pinned back. I had stared at her for a full minute. "Noelle. I—just, *wow*."

A little blush had crept over her cheeks. "You said that already," she joked. "But thank you. Charlotte made it for me." She had done a little twirl for me, and I pulled her in closer.

"Damn. You're telling me Charlotte *made* this for you? Holy hell." It was *beautiful*, and it fit her like a glove, tucked around her waist and flaring over her curvy hips. "You're so fucking hot," I had whispered into her ear. "I hope I get to take this off of you later."

"Oh my gosh." She'd swatted me away. "Stop that. We gotta go or we'll be late."

"Maybe I want to be late," I told her, but I gave her a kiss on the lips before grabbing my coat and truck keys. "Ready, sweetheart?"

Noelle had basically pushed me out the door. "Yeah. Let's go get this over with." She'd made a face then.

"What?" I asked, with a laugh. "You don't want to go mingle with hundreds of alumni and faculty?"

She'd just shot daggers at me. "Like *you* do?"

I shrugged. Of course, I didn't. She knew it, I knew it. But... "At least I get to see you in this sexy dress," I said, waggling my eyebrows.

"While I do love seeing you in a suit…" Noelle pouted. "It's not *quite* the same for me."

I hummed, playfully pretending to ponder something as I helped Noelle into the car. "Maybe I could roll my shirt sleeves up later? I know you like it when I do that."

Her eyes almost bugged out of her head. "What? When did I say anything about that?"

"Relax, sunshine," I said, rubbing my free hand over her thigh. "I can see the heat in your eyes when I do it, you know?"

Noelle blushed, looking at the window, and after another pass of my thumb over her skin, she'd turned back to me. "And what do my eyes say when you roll up your sleeves, *Professor Harper?*"

If we weren't driving, I would have leaned in really close to her, looked her straight in the eyes, and told her exactly how her body reacted to mine. I didn't even need to tell her, honestly. I wanted to *show* her. But I was trying to keep my focus on the short drive to campus, and the last thing I needed was to want to have a quickie in the backseat of my car.

So instead, I just smirked, letting my hand move to her inner thigh, stroking it gently as I kept the other hand firmly on the steering wheel. "They say…" I paused for dramatic effect. "*Fuck me.*"

"Hey! I do not have fuck me eyes."

"Sure you don't."

She narrowed her gaze at me and swatted my hand away before I could get any closer to her center.

"I can't take you anywhere," she muttered under her breath, but I didn't miss the slight flush to her skin, trailing up her neck and even making her ears a little pink. I couldn't help it—I loved teasing her, loved seeing her like this.

"Come on, let's go inside," I said as we pulled into a parking spot on campus, extending a hand out to her to help her down from my truck.

"Um." She looked at me and then at the building where the

event was taking place. "We should probably go inside separately, huh?"

"What?" Her hand was slipping out of mine already. I frowned. "Oh. Okay. Yeah."

I had wanted to walk into this event together, instead of separately. Was she scared to tell people we were dating? I didn't think anyone would say anything about the nature of our relationship—after all, she wasn't my student, and we had never known each other in any sort of professional capacity. But I worried.

The university might be super conservative, but it wasn't like this was just some fling.

I couldn't help the fear that spread through me. I loved her, and she wasn't brave enough to claim me. Not yet.

We were circling each other in the room—not close enough to be *with* each other, but every few minutes, we would linger, and our fingers would drag against the other's hand. It sent sparks flying up my arm. The same way it did every time we touched, like our connection was electrifying. Meant to be.

Noelle was talking to someone, a guy, and I knew I was being jealous, but I couldn't help it. "If you'll both excuse me," I said politely to the other professors as our conversation trailed off. "I have someone I would like to say hello to." My eyes drifted back over to Noelle's.

"Go on." John's wife gave me a small smile. "It was good chatting with you for a little bit."

"Always nice to see you, Alexis."

John's wife, sweet as ever, responded with glee. "Hopefully one of these days you'll have a wife of your own to bring to these things."

I laughed, looking at Noelle. "Yeah, hopefully." One day, if I was lucky... I would be the luckiest man on earth if Noelle agreed to marry me, wouldn't I?

We said our goodbyes, and I made my way across the room, finding Noelle at the dessert table, looking over her choices. I leaned over and whispered in her ear, "I hear the brownies here are the best."

She jumped a little from my sudden nearness, and then placed her hand over her mouth to hold in a laugh. "Oh, yeah? Who'd you hear that from?"

"My gorgeous girlfriend," I grinned. "You kind of remind me of her. Red hair, obsessed with desserts, *definitely* wants to eat another brownie."

"Hmm," she smirked. "That does seem to ring a bell. But I think my handsome boyfriend will be jealous if I tell him we were consorting here at the dessert table."

"Good thing he won't know."

"Matthew!" Noelle's shoulders shook as she tried to hold back another laugh.

"God, I want to *touch* you," I muttered, my eyes trailing up her backside in her incredible dress. "This dress is—wow."

"You know, you did help me put it on," she whispered back.

I was fairly sure if we kept this up, someone was going to catch us *canoodling* by the dessert table, but I didn't care. I was enjoying this way too much.

She placed her hand over mine and stared into my eyes. "Touch me," Noelle breathed, her eyes glazing over as she just continued to stare at me. I knew that look.

And I knew how much trouble we could both get into with that look.

"Noelle," I growled, "we can't... here." Not if she wasn't comfortable telling the entire world about us. I glanced around and then leaned back down to whisper one final time. "Meet me in the bathroom downstairs in five minutes—you know, the one no one ever uses?"

There was a wicked glint in her eyes as she nodded, taking a bite of the brownie she *had* decided to pick up off the table after all. I couldn't wait to taste it on her lips. As much as I said I didn't like sweets, I couldn't resist *her,* and I loved the way she always tasted sweet. And, yeah, I might have been coming around anyway. That was the curse of having a girlfriend who loved desserts.

She blew me a little kiss as I walked out of the hall, and I was already counting down the minutes till she would follow me downstairs, and I could have my way with her. I loosened my tie as I walked down the stairs, already thinking about how magnificent her ass looked in that tight dress. How lovely her thighs would be as I kissed my way up them.

I slipped into the bathroom and flipped the lock behind me, waiting for her to join me.

After a few minutes of waiting, Noelle texted me that she was outside, and I opened the door, pulling her in.

"Hi," I said, grinning.

"Hey." Noelle smiled. "I don't think my boyfriend would be very happy with me being down here with you."

"Oh?"

"Mhm." She pushed off one of the shoulders of her dress, revealing her skin.

"I don't think he'll mind." I smiled—all teeth, feeling quite like the big bad wolf, here to eat my little red riding hood.

And when I couldn't take it anymore, the sight of her so beautiful in her dress, red curls spilling down her neck, plush skin begging me to kiss it, I pulled her towards me, crushing our lips together. It wasn't soft, sweet, or slow. It was pure desire, need, and want all bundled up into a maddening frenzy of tongues and lips.

Noelle whimpered. "I want you."

"Shh, baby," I said, pressing an open-mouthed kiss to her throat, being careful not to leave marks where anyone would see. "We gotta be quiet."

I hiked up her dress around her waist, and that was when I realized she wasn't wearing any underwear.

"Fuck." I leaned my forehead against hers. "Have you been like this all night?" She nodded, and I reached out, letting my fingers cup her, not touching where I knew she wanted it yet. "How wet are you, baby?"

"So wet," she moaned. "Please, touch me."

I plunged one finger in, and she was right—she was dripping. I worked her with one finger, pumping inside of her before I slipped a second one in. Noelle's breathing picked up, those soft little noises I loved so much, and I could tell she was trying to be quiet.

"Do you have any idea how beautiful you look tonight? How much I want to fuck you right here?"

"Please," she moaned.

I added my thumb on her clit, rubbing tight circles against it. "I'm going to get you off, and then we're going to get out there. Because when I fuck you, I'll be making a mess of your magnificent thighs, and knowing you have my cum dripping out of you is going to make me wild."

"Matthew—" Noelle cried as I made scissor-like motions with my fingers, rubbing faster against her clit. I would have loved to get my mouth on her, but we didn't have the time for that.

"I'll fuck you properly when we get home, baby, okay? Would you like that, hm?" She nodded, and I stilled my fingers. "Use your words, Noelle," I breathed in her ear. "And then I'll make you come."

"Yes," she ground out, glaring at me as I delayed her orgasm. "I want you to take me home and fuck me so hard I can't remember my name. I want you inside of me, Matthew. Please."

Resuming my pace, I kept going, and I could tell she was close. "That's it, come for me, my little vixen." Noelle gasped, and I could feel her orgasm pulsing through her as she clenched around my fingers. After a few more moments, I pulled them out, licking her juices off of me, and then planted another kiss on her lips.

"Wow." Noelle was still trying to catch her breath as I pulled her dress back down, and I just smirked at her. "That was hot." I adjusted myself in my pants, and she frowned at me. "Do you want me—"

"No." I shook my head. "I'll be fine until we get home."

"You sure?" Noelle leaned up to kiss me on the cheek as I finished resituating my coat and tie.

"I'm sure." I would have loved to get her pretty little mouth on me, but this wasn't the time for that. "Now, let's go before someone catches us in here."

"Sounds good, *prof.*"

"What am I going to do with you? Little brat." I flicked her nose.

She stood up on her tiptoes to speak directly into my ear. "Fuck it out of me," she said, and then she was opening the door, sneaking out into the night.

I needed to splash myself with freezing water. Holy shit.

∼

"Bryan?" I answered the phone, stepping outside onto the back patio to cool off after Noelle and I had snuck out of the bathroom. Thank *God* for the private bathroom downstairs with a locking door. I tried to find it in myself to feel guilty about it, that we had left the party and I had fingered Noelle on campus, but I just couldn't.

If anything, I had just wanted to shout from the rooftops, *she's mine!*, and growl at anyone who approached her. Because I *loved* her. I loved her, and I hadn't told her, and I was going crazy not saying it to her every minute of every day.

"Matthew?" Bryan sounded a little breathless, though not at all in the way I had just been. "Elizabeth... she..." He took a deep breath before starting over. "Liz's water just broke. We're on our way to the hospital. Can you meet us there?"

I drew in a deep breath. My best friend and his wife were having their baby. Oh. God. It was early—*way* early.

And where was Noelle? I scanned the outside terrace for

familiar red curls, finding her smiling and holding a wine glass in her hands. She looked even more beautiful than she had before I made her come. Fuck—*not* what I needed to be thinking about right now.

"We're on our way," I said to Bryan, asking for the details and what hospital as I was already weaving through the crowd towards my girlfriend.

"What's wrong?"

"Liz is at the hospital." Noelle's eyes widened. "She's in labor."

"Oh. Oh gosh." She turned back to the people she was talking to. "Excuse me, I have to go." And she looked up at me, calming me instantly. "Let's go."

"Are you sure?" I looked around. "You want to come?"

She squeezed my hand. "Wouldn't miss it. Now, come on, soon-to-be God-Dad. We have somewhere to be."

We walked back to my truck—hand in hand, leaning against each other, not even caring if anyone saw us. And if I was honest, I needed this connection. It was helping me not panic or freak out about the fact that Liz was in labor a few weeks early, and it grounded me back to reality. I realized how much I couldn't wait for the time in our lives when I could embrace her openly. I wanted this all the time: her leaning into me, holding her hand, feeling her body heat pressed up against mine.

Soon, I reminded myself. Soon.

After you tell her you love her, you idiot.

∼

WE DIDN'T LEAVE the hospital until almost seven am, staying up late in the night waiting for the news. I rubbed my hand over my face as I finally guided Noelle out of the hospital. I didn't realize how long labor could take with women's first pregnancies.

I looked at Noelle, wondering how she was feeling about all of this. She had been quiet, even as we gathered around the hospital bed, peering at Elizabeth and her little newborn.

They looked so happy, Elizabeth and Bryan, holding Baby Theo in their arms. They had even let me hold him, just for a minute.

"Hi, Theodore," I whispered, hoping my feather-light voice was soft enough to keep him asleep. "I'm your God Dad. Uncle Matthew." I looked up, and Elizabeth's eyes were shining with tears. "I'm always going to be here for you, okay? Even if you want to play baseball instead of basketball." I held him for a few more moments before sliding him back into Liz's arms.

"Do you want to hold him?" Liz asked Noelle, and I could tell she had frozen a little in her tracks.

"Oh. Um. Are you sure?"

Liz nodded, and Bryan placed the baby in her arms. Even though he wasn't ours, I still felt a rush of... Warmth and possessiveness over seeing Noelle with a baby in her arms.

It was insane, but something about it just felt... right.

Noelle yawned as we piled into my truck, leaning back against the seat. Neither one of us had slept all night—me, from worry, and Noelle, too focused on keeping me company.

"Thank you," I said, watching her as she buckled her seatbelt.

"For what?" she just blinked at me.

"Just... being there."

She reached out and took my hand. "I think... I would go anywhere for you." Noelle bit her lip. "Is that crazy?"

I shook my head. "I don't think so. I mean, I've never felt like this before but..." I squeezed her hand. "I would do anything for you, you know that?"

She nodded.

"God, you know that was my first time being around a newborn?" Noelle finally whispered. "He was so small, I was terrified of dropping him."

I laughed. "I still remember when my mom was pregnant with Tess. After she was born, they brought her to me, and my first comment was, *why is she so red?* And my parents couldn't stop laughing." I grew quiet, somber, thinking about them.

They'll never get to meet their grandchildren.

"Hey," Noelle said quietly. "You miss them, don't you?"

"Yeah," I nodded, throat tight with grief. "I was just thinking about how they'll never get to meet their grandkids."

Noelle looked up at me, eyes wide with some expression I didn't know how to name. "And you... want that? Kids and a family?"

I do, I wanted to say. *With you. Only you.*

"I..." I ran my hands through my hair, not wanting to start the engine. "I know we haven't talked about the future at all, but..." Noelle froze in her seat, and I tried to backtrack. "I know we've only been together for a short time." I sighed. "I'm sorry. I wasn't trying to freak you out. We don't have to talk about it right now."

She bit her lip, looking down at her lap, and then brought her eyes back up to mine. "I'm not... I'm happy where things are at right now, you know? I don't want anything to ruin this."

I nodded, finally starting the car. "Me too," I said, though some part of my heart ached, just thinking about what I wanted for us.

Was it possible she didn't want that? The marriage and the kids and the life together? *Fuck.*

I loved her, I was completely, madly in love with her, and I didn't even know if she saw us like I did: in the future, together. Always together, with kids of our own and a big porch with a hanging swing and smiles that never faded from our faces.

I focused my eyes back to the road, and we drove like that—quiet, hands still interlocked on the console, but I couldn't help the worry that had crept into my gut.

CHAPTER 29
Noelle

For the last few days, I couldn't get the sight of Matthew with a baby in his arms out of my mind. It was strange because I had never really thought about it before. What my future might look like. Because everyone I had ever loved, they had all left me. Even when I used to imagine being married to Jake, I had never thought about us having kids.

And when Matthew brought up the future, the fact that we hadn't talked about what we wanted, I kind of... shut down. I wasn't ready to have that conversation, wasn't ready to acknowledge in my mind if I even wanted that.

Was I ready? I was still twenty-five. I didn't know what I wanted to eat tomorrow, let alone how to raise a baby. Or to even think about marriage.

It was April, now, which meant the end of the semester was just a few weeks away, and Easter break wasn't far off either. We hadn't talked about what we were doing; I didn't think my mom and I were going to do anything together, either, but I didn't want to presume we would have a repeat of Spring Break without him asking.

Even so, I spent almost as many nights a week over at Matthew's place as I did at mine. Sometimes I wished I could have him stay the night, see him in my space, curled up together on my couch, but I knew that I had created this barrier, made this separation of my life for a reason.

My job—my girls counted on me. To be there for them, to be stable. And if they all knew who I was dating, and if it ended... I shook my head. It would end badly. And I didn't know what I would do if that happened.

NOELLE
> Where are you?

I texted Matthew as I walked onto campus, wanting to grab coffee or lunch before I had to go to my class for the evening.

> Want to get lunch?

MATTHEW
Still in class. Movie day.

> Right. Text me when you're out. I don't have a class for a few hours.

Or... you could meet me in the supply closet near classroom 234.

I blinked, staring down at my phone. Did he...?

> Are you...??

> I must be dreaming. You cannot seriously be suggesting a closet rendezvous.

Why don't you get your sweet little ass over here and find out?

> Coming.

You will be. 😉

Oh my God. I couldn't help but laugh at his innuendo. And

oh. I could already feel my body heat up. Damn him. I didn't wait another moment: I marched straight up the steps of the building and towards classroom 234.

I slipped into the supply closet nearby, praying no one would see me or need anything from inside, and a heartbeat later Matthew opened the door and slipped in behind me, flicking the lock with a satisfying click. "Hi." I smiled at him.

"Noelle," Matthew grinned mischievously as I eyed the small closet. "We didn't get to see each other yesterday," he said. "I had planned to take my time with you, but now that I have you here..."

I crept closer to him, placing one hand on his chest, and letting my fingers trace up one of his arms. "And what, exactly, were you thinking when you invited me to this secret rendezvous, Professor Harper?"

"I was thinking that I needed to have you, right now, my sweet girl." I nodded, already filled with lust, and guided his hand down lower, exactly where I wanted it. "God, Noelle, do you want me to fuck you in this closet while my class watches a movie?" He breathed seductively into my ear as his fingers ghosted over my clit through my panties. Wearing a skirt today had ended up being a very wise choice.

I moaned. "Yes. *Please*, Matthew."

He pressed down, rubbing with two fingers. "Are you already wet for me, baby?"

"So wet..." I moaned. I had been since I had been imagining what would happen in this room.

"You're such a vixen, Noelle," he said, fondling me a little harder as I clasped one hand over my mouth to stop myself from moaning as he rubbed over me. "My sweet temptress. So naughty."

"Yes," I agreed, gasping as he pushed the cotton aside and thrust two fingers inside of me.

"You know what bad girls get, Noelle?" I couldn't help it—I whimpered. The pressure he was creating was too good, but I needed *more*. "They get *punished*. Would you like that, hm? My little fox?"

"Oh. Oh God, yes, Matthew," I panted, and he unbuttoned my blouse, exposing my bra as he fucked me with his fingers. "Please. Harder," I cried as he brought his mouth down and sucked my covered nipple into his mouth.

"I'm gonna punish you so well that you can't walk tomorrow, baby."

I nodded frantically, so close to reaching my peak as he continued to hit that spot with his fingers. When he added his thumb to my clit, applying pressure, I almost lost it.

"I'm—I'm so close, Matthew."

"Good girl," he said, his mouth closing over mine as he inhaled the little moans I was giving into a passionate kiss. I liked him like this—commanding, ordering me around—but I liked him when he was sweet just as much. Because no matter what he said, I always, always knew that he cared about me and would put my needs before his own.

It made me feel special, even after all this time. Even after we had made love so many times in his apartment. And if it wasn't making love, well… I didn't know what to call it. It was more than sex.

But *this*, this was something different entirely. Hard and fast, sneaking around in the supply closet… it was almost hotter than doing it in his office.

"Oh," I squeaked as I hit my climax, and he kept rubbing me through it with his fingers as I clenched and pulsed around them, only pulling his fingers out when I stopped trembling. He brought them to his lips and licked my juices off of him, and then he was pulling my panties down my legs and unbuttoning his pants.

"I'm going to fuck you right here against the door, Noelle," he whispered as he pulled himself free. And thank God that I was on birth control—we had mostly stopped using condoms, but nothing could have stopped me at this moment from letting him slide into me.

"Yes, oh God, yes," I moaned as he positioned his tip against my entrance, before plunging me down on him fully. I was still sensitive from my orgasm, and the feeling of him inside me—the fullness—was almost enough to send me over the edge again. He lifted me against the door as I wrapped my legs around him, driving him in even deeper, down to the hilt.

"Noelle..." He shut his eyes as he stilled for a moment. "You feel too good, sweetheart." I clenched around him, and he groaned. "I'm not going to last if you keep doing that."

"It's okay," I whispered, brushing a strand of shaggy blonde hair off of his face and kissing his jaw. "I don't mind."

He shook his head at me, and then he started pounding against me, my back rubbing up against the door as he worked me up and down on his cock.

"Matthew—" I let out a string of breathy moans, and I knew he was close, too, just like I was. A few more punishing thrusts and I was quivering in his arms, fluttering around him as the waves of my second orgasm pulsed through me.

"Baby." Matthew's guttural voice made me whimper. He shut his eyes, resting his head against my neck as he continued to rock into me. "I'm gonna come inside you, okay?"

I nodded, digging my fingers into his back as he bounced me on his lap a few more times before grunting—and then he was spilling inside of me.

"Matthew." My voice was a breathy whisper as he continued to hold me, not moving or pulling out yet. "We gotta go," I whispered. "You have to get back to your class."

"Just..." He shook his head against my skin. "Just let me hold you for a little bit longer, okay?"

"Okay," I breathed.

And when he finally pulled out, his come leaking down my thighs as I pulled up my panties, I cradled his face and gave him a deep, loving kiss.

"I think we'll have to modify our answers to the dirtiest place we've ever had sex," I laughed into his ear. "This was definitely worse than your office."

He smirked. "If I recall, the question was the *craziest,* and I still have plans for you, little fox."

"I can't wait to find out where *that* is," I giggled, and finished readjusting my clothes before peeking out the door. "Looks like the coast is clear."

"Come over tonight? After your class?" I just nodded. "Good," he muttered, "because I want to hold you in my arms as you sleep."

Oh, my heart. I wasn't simply in danger of losing it to him anymore—he was simply taking a piece of it every day.

⁓

THAT WEEKEND, I had finally managed to wrangle the girls into an official meeting with Matthew, and I was very grateful to spend some time with them, even if it was around a giant dinner table at Old Spaghetti Factory. We went to the one near downtown, on the water, and I couldn't help but smile as I looked around at my friends gathered together.

Charlotte had even forced Daniel to come along, which was nice, considering it had been a few months since I had seen him. Even when he wasn't physically present, sometimes I felt like I heard so much about him from Char that it felt like he was actually there.

The dark-haired engineer sat on Charlotte's right where they were whispering conspiratorially, and I was still trying to figure out how they couldn't see that they were perfect for each other.

"So graduation's coming up fast, huh?" Angelina said, causing me to look up from my plate of ravioli that I was trying not to inhale.

I nodded. "Yep, just a few weeks left, and then freedom!" I

whooped. "At least for the summer. I still have to tell the school if I'm staying on one more year as Hall Director or not."

"What are you thinking?" Gabbi perked up and asked. I could tell Matthew was following our conversation, but we hadn't talked about it yet. I had told him I wasn't ready to, after all.

The future was big and scary, and if we broached the topic... it felt like it would change everything.

"Well..." I bit my lip. "I love the job, but I want to have my own place. Sometimes I still feel like a freshman, slinking back into my dorm." Especially after I would spend the night at Matthew's. But I didn't want to let on that that was one of the factors in my decision. "I started looking for student advisor jobs in the area."

"You did?" Matthew asked. "You didn't tell me that." I could see the slight frown on his face, the doubt in his eyes.

"I was going to," I whispered, placing a hand on his arm. "I promise." He nodded, but there was still a frown between his eyebrows, and I hated that I put it there. Hated that he was worried about me... What? Leaving him?

Or maybe he was thinking about leaving me, finding someone more suitable to be a wife and mother than I was. I could barely feed myself; how would I keep children alive?

Don't think about it, I instructed myself. Don't think about your children, and what they might look like. A blond-haired boy with brown eyes. A little redheaded girl with blue eyes and freckles.

I shook my head, getting rid of those thoughts. Did I even want that? To be a mother? I didn't know. I didn't have the best relationship with mine, and watching her raise me alone... I didn't want that for me. Couldn't risk being in a situation where I'd end up alone like that.

"What are you guys doing for Easter?" Charlotte finally asked. "My little sister is supposed to be coming up here, so my parents want to make a whole thing out of it this year." She rolled her eyes, but I knew she loved that her mom still did Easter Baskets and insisted on painting eggs.

"I don't know yet." I looked at Matthew and the look in his eye... I nudged him, trying to distract him.

He met my eyes. "What?"

"Easter?"

"Oh. Uh. I think I'm going out of town, actually."

I raised an eyebrow, but I wasn't going to push on this in front of my friends. If he didn't want to spend Easter with me... that was okay. I would just stay in the dorms and do things with my residents. I was sure the RAs would enjoy having me around. Not to mention Hazel, who I had barely seen lately.

But still... "Okay," I finally said, turning my attention to Gabbi, who was just pushing around the pasta on her plate. "What are you doing, Gabs?"

"Oh, I was thinking about going back to Boston and seeing my brothers, but I haven't booked my flight yet. It's been forever since I've been home..." She sighed.

I felt like all of us had grown apart from our families in the last few years. I knew Gabbi loved her parents more than anything, and her brothers were great, but she had come to Portland for a reason—to be her own person. And sometimes I wondered if going back there... If she ever felt lost in her big family's dynamic. Her older brother was married with two kids, and her younger brother was in a serious relationship. Was she the one that was forgotten?

I sighed.

Matthew nudged me. "Everything okay?" he whispered.

"Yeah. I've just got some stuff on my mind is all."

He went back to his chicken parmesan, but I didn't miss the way he didn't share more with me. And it hurt. Because I'd been falling for him, and it felt like I was standing at the edge of a cliff. And what would happen when I fell?

Angelina eyed me curiously, and I just rolled my shoulders at her. How did I share all of my fears without sounding crazy?

When we left, after ice cream and splitting the bill, I held onto Matthew's arm. I stared up at him, studying the face that I had grown so familiar with. The one I knew almost as well as my own at this point. He pulled me in tighter, and I leaned into his arms as we stood outside of the restaurant, saying goodbye to my friends.

Daniel and Matthew shook hands, promising to get together for beers soon. The girls told Matthew that he was allowed to crash exactly one book club meeting a month. Even as they all laughed and joked and everyone seemed to be so happy to get to know my boyfriend, I felt like something was off between us.

I tried to enjoy the moment with him, but deep down, I couldn't ignore the sinking feeling. It was like something in my gut reminded me those good things don't last. That this would end, badly, and I wouldn't be able to come back from this if it did. When it did. It was like I kept looking for the cracks in the ground, the signs that signaled the end. And what I worried about most was what would happen if I found them.

Like if I kept picking at the cracks, digging deeper, somehow staring at them long enough would cause the ground to fissure and swallow me whole. And Matthew and I would be just another casualty to this thing I had feared my whole life. To lose everyone I loved and cared about. I didn't know what the catalyst would be, or what would happen if we continued down this path, but I also didn't want to find out. All I knew was, I just wanted to live in this moment, with him, and ignore the irrational fear that everything would go wrong.

That I might lose the only man who ever meant something to me. The only person who was worth keeping, the only man I thought I might be able to love if I let myself. What would I do if I gave him my whole heart, all of my being, every piece of me, only for him to decide that I wasn't good enough? That I wasn't enough for *him?* That my goals weren't big enough, that I hadn't dreamed wide enough, and he would want more from me than I could give him.

I was terrified of those little cracks in my heart.

CHAPTER 30
Matthew

I knew something was on her mind, even after we had met her friends. It felt like we were so fully ingrained in each other's lives, and yet there were still things we couldn't say to each other. Were we scared? I felt like I was terrified.

We were spending all of our free time together, whenever I didn't have class and Noelle didn't have hall director duties to attend to. Sometimes that meant her sitting at my kitchen table as she poured over her assignments, trying to get all of her projects done for the semester.

Easter Break hadn't come up again since dinner with her friends, and I hadn't missed the hurt in her eyes when I said I was going out of town, but she hadn't asked any other questions. I didn't know how to tell her the truth, either.

Noelle was currently sitting at the table, growling in frustration at her laptop.

"Do you need help?" I asked, pressing a kiss to the top of her head as I moved around her, cooking breakfast.

"No," she said, just shaking her head as she typed on the keyboard.

"Are you sure?" I asked again, going to grab my travel coffee cup from the cupboard.

"Yeah," Noelle sighed. "I just can't wait till this semester is over and I've graduated again so there are no more assignments or tests or papers." She rubbed a hand over her makeup-free face.

I loved when she didn't wear any, because it meant I could count each individual freckle on her face and trace my finger over them. She was so beautiful, no matter what.

She glanced at her watch and looked up at me. "Shoot. I gotta head over to campus for a meeting." Noelle stood up, her arms stretched out as she yawned.

She had stopped bringing a duffel bag over and had just left a few changes of clothes at my house after we both realized how often she was here. I liked it—liked her clothes in my house, her toothbrush in my bathroom.

"Do you want any breakfast before you go, sweetheart?"

Noelle shook her head. "I'm not that hungry, and I can grab something later anyway."

"Okay, but only if you're *sure*." I grinned. "Don't want you to miss out on perfectly good pancakes."

"Stop tempting me," she laughed. "I'll be late, and this is important."

I noticed she didn't tell me *what* was important, but I didn't press. She would tell me when she was ready, wouldn't she?

But then, she kept standing there, twirling a hair around her finger as she looked at me. Bit her lip, opened her mouth, and shut it a few times before finally saying, "Are you sure you don't want to do anything this weekend?" Her eyes seemed to dart everywhere—to a textbook on the couch, to the pan on the stove —except my eyes. "I know you said you were going out of town, but I don't have any plans and I thought maybe we could take Snowball to the park or someth—"

"I can't." I choked out. My voice was hoarse, and my throat felt dry. It was like all of the breath had suddenly gone out of my lungs, and I couldn't speak. Couldn't get the words out, my brain completely devoid of any way to explain what the day was. What it meant to me.

"Oh," she frowned, but I could tell my dismissal stung.

"Noelle—" I started, but I froze. What could I say to explain it? *How* would I even explain it? I wanted to, and I knew she would understand, but the words wouldn't come.

"It's fine!" She shook her head, sending a grin my way but her eyes told a different story altogether. "Look, I should go."

"You don't have to," I said, but I couldn't get out the words I wanted to say. *Stay, please.*

"I uh… have a lot of studying to do, and I've been over here more than my own place lately. My girls are probably missing me." Noelle shoved her things in her bag, and I was rooted to the spot.

My girl. My Noelle. I had been so open with her about so many things—why couldn't I be about this?

I couldn't say anything, even as she put a hand over my rapidly beating heart and kissed me on the cheek. "Have a good day, Matthew," she said, and I squeezed her hand lightly, before bending down to plant a kiss on her lips.

"Bye," I whispered, nuzzling her face with mine, hoping I could show her with actions how much she meant to me, even if words were failing me. Even if the thing I was keeping inside had been eating away at my heart all this time, I wasn't sure I could even voice the thoughts. Could stomach saying them aloud, sharing the pain that I had kept at bay all this time.

∽

I LIED TO HER. I didn't have plans for Easter break—wasn't going out of town at all. But this weekend… I had always, every year, just holed up in my apartment and not let anyone see me.

I didn't want them to see me like this.

I collapsed on the sofa, one arm thrown over my face as I stared at the ceiling, holding on to my fourth, or maybe even fifth, beer. I didn't want to remember anymore. I wanted to forget. Wanted to get wasted enough that when I closed my eyes on this weekend every April, I didn't think about what I'd lost and the parents who I would never get to see again.

It hurt, more than I could ever explain, and I didn't want Noelle to look at me with the pity that Bryan, Cole, and Tanner did every time this weekend rolled around.

The first year... was the hardest. My junior year of college should have been one of the best years of my life, but instead, I had wallowed myself up in the house the four of us rented together and hadn't come out until I was numb to everything.

I hadn't cried, not really, just felt like an empty shell of the person that I used to be. And maybe I had been like this for the last ten years, ever since I lost them. Just wandering, hoping that one day it wouldn't hurt so bad. That if I could only forget it, everything would be okay again.

My phone rang, but I ignored it. Then a text came through.

TESSA
I'm here if you want to talk.

She always was. And she should have been the one person I could talk to about this, shouldn't she? But for some reason, I had never found the words. Every time I tried, I would open my mouth, and nothing would came out. No explanations, no apologies, no *I'm sorry our parents our dead.*

No, *I'm sorry I'm the reason we lost our parents. That they never got to see you grow up. That you got stuck with me, some grumpy asshole who can't even talk to his baby sister about why he's sad.* So maybe grumpiness was my coping mechanism, my safety device so people would leave me alone and wouldn't dig deeper.

Because I had never been able to figure out how to talk to anyone about this. Not my sister, not my friends, and not even the counselor my university had suggested I go to while I struggled to deal with everything over the last two years of college. Instead, I just... shut down. Didn't open up to anyone.

Hardly talked about myself with anyone.

Until Noelle. Fuck, I had been such an asshole to her.

But sitting here, downing another beer, just trying to forget, I couldn't think about Noelle. Couldn't think about the girl that I loved and that I was letting down every day by not just telling her what I felt.

My heart hurt, even as I lay there, on the couch, ignoring the buzzing of my phone. Bryan had joined Tess now. Maybe even Noelle had sent a text or two.

I couldn't talk to any of them. I shut my phone off and pulled a blanket over my face, hoping that sleep would grant me a sweet escape from reality.

Hoping that it might be enough to forget, even just for today.

CHAPTER 31
Noelle

Easter break was spent on the couch of the dorm, commiserating over a jar of starburst jellybeans while I watched whatever happened to be on TV. Which, as it turned out, was a whole lot of Hallmark movies. Hazel joined me on Friday. We sat on the couch, both in our pajamas, and we shared a bowl of popcorn, I could see the unanswered questions in her eyes.

She knew, more than anyone else, how much time I had spent with Matthew over the last two months.

I couldn't even focus on my assignments or my writing in front of me because I was so worried about him.

He hadn't responded to any of my texts since I left his house the other day. And I was worried. I had a right to be, didn't I? I felt like he was brushing me off, not letting me in, and I didn't know what was wrong. I knew there wasn't a chance there was someone else in his life—not with the way he treated me. Not when we had this crazy insane connection.

He was always so open and honest, which is why it concerned me so much that he was shutting me out now.

"What?" I finally asked Hazel, after what felt like the millionth time that she looked over at me.

She shook her head. "Nothing."

"Come on," I insisted. "Just ask whatever you want to ask."

"Okay." Hazel winced. "It's just that..." She bit her lip.

"Haze. You can say it. I'm not glass, I won't break."

"It's just that you said you weren't going to date anyone. Or fall in love. And then..."

"And then I met Matthew?"

"Right. And now you're like..." She motioned to my current attire. "I'm just surprised you're not with him right now, is all."

"Oh." How did I tell her about all my fears and worries without sounding crazy? "We're fine." Were we? "We just needed to spend a little time apart." I nodded to myself, hoping I sounded confident outside. Because I wasn't on the inside.

Hazel raised an eyebrow. "Are you sure? Because the way you're moping around..."

"Hey!" I frowned. "I'm not moping."

"What do you call eating that entire tub of jellybeans in two days?"

"Being *festive.*" I sighed. "I'm trying not to freak out, Hazel. Because I... I *really* like him, you know? And I didn't want to fall in love... Because I didn't want someone to break me again. I didn't want to put everything into a relationship only to find it wasn't as important to them as it was to me."

"And...?"

"And what?" I shook my head. "He didn't want me there."

"Maybe something else is going on, Noelle. Have you tried talking to him more about it?"

"No. He just shut down on me."

"Well... You know his friends, right?" I had told Hazel about the game—and everything else about our relationship. I gave a nod of confirmation. "Could you try reaching out to one of them to make sure he's okay?"

"I hadn't thought about that. Yeah, I probably could." Elizabeth had given me her number that day at the hospital, telling me to call her if I ever needed anything. Which was funny because she was the one who had just had a baby.

Picking up my phone and seeing all of the unanswered texts I sent to Matthew, I realized Elizabeth might have been onto something when she gave me her number. Maybe she and Bryan knew why he was being like this. And maybe if I knew, he would talk to me about it.

Because if there wasn't something wrong, why else would he push me away? He was obviously troubled by something but didn't want to share it with me. Was he shutting me out? I had thought, over and over, that we had shown each other that we could let each other in, and yet... I couldn't ignore the sinking feeling in my gut.

> **NOELLE**
>
> Good morning!
>
> Lunch?
>
> Finished my paper. Miss you.
>
> Matthew? Is everything okay?
>
> Babe. Please just answer me.

I clicked out of the chat and started a new one to Elizabeth.

> **NOELLE**
>
> Hi Elizabeth. It's Noelle. I've been trying to get ahold of Matthew since Thursday, and he hasn't responded to any of my texts or calls. Do you know if he's okay? I'm worried about him... He's not usually like this.

Instead of responding to my text, Elizabeth called me. "Hello?"

"Noelle?" Came Elizabeth's voice on the other line. I quickly moved off of the couch and into the other room where I could talk to her alone.

"Yes. Hi."

Elizabeth seemed to let out a big sigh. "I figured this would be better over the phone than text. Listen, it's not really my place to share, but I was there for it, in college, and he's never really talked about it since. Not with us. I'm not sure with anyone."

"What are you talking about?"

"His parents. Tomorrow is… it's always been a hard day for him."

"His parents?" I repeated, still confused. "He… All he told me was they died in a car accident."

"Noelle, I'm going to tell you something and I hope it doesn't freak you out. But I think you've been good for him. You've gotten him to open up again—to all of us, at least little by little. He seems so much happier whenever you're around, and I think if anyone is going to get through this wall of ice he's put up, blocking us all out of his trauma, sealing off his heart so he couldn't get hurt again… I think it's you."

"Me?" I said in a broken whisper.

"Yeah."

"But I just… I don't understand. Why is tomorrow so hard for him?"

"Noelle." Elizabeth took a deep breath. "It's the anniversary of the day they died."

Oh. I didn't remember hanging up the phone. Didn't remember it slipping out of my hands. Didn't remember sliding to my knees on the carpet, but when I looked up, Hazel was in front of me, kneeling on the carpet, cupping my cheeks in her hands.

"Do you want me to drive?" She whispered, and I think I nodded.

I didn't remember much of the drive to his place, or even navigating Hazel to the house that had begun to feel like home for me. All I knew was that I didn't want my beautiful golden-haired man to go through this alone, to isolate himself from the world and deal with his grief alone.

We pulled in, and Hazel gave me a reassuring squeeze on my knee. I nodded to her in thanks, then I got out and walked up to the door.

Matthew's truck was parked in the driveway, so I figured he was home, but I didn't see any lights on from the front of the house. It was almost weird, coming over like this. Knowing he wasn't at the door, waiting for my arrival. Sometimes I liked to wait like this, watching the windows, seeing him pace in front of the door and run his fingers through his hair in anticipation of my getting there. Today, however, there was no movement in the windows. No blonde man sitting on the couch, no white fluffy dog curled up next to him in a giant ball.

I took a deep breath before knocking on the door. I feared the worst, really—I just didn't want him to shut me out any further, to leave me standing outside in the dark. Metaphorically or literally.

I could hear Snowball running across the hardwood floor, and her bark—just twice, in familiarity—alerting Matthew that someone was there. But the sound of his footsteps didn't come.

"Matthew?" I called out as I knocked again, still hearing no response.

Frowning, I slipped the key he had given me for emergencies into the lock. I hadn't ever really needed to use it—most of the times I had come over, he had driven me, or he was waiting for me, and this feeling was *strange*. Like I was entering a stranger's home, with no permission to be there. Like I was intruding on some secret moment of his life.

But if I was his girlfriend, and we were together, then I wanted him to share every part of his life with me. And this—this grief he was holding back from me, from everyone, I wanted to be there for him. Because we couldn't heal each other, couldn't make the pain go away, but I could show him that we could get through it, together. We would get through it *together* because that was what we did. We were a team.

"Matthew?" I said, moving from the empty living room

towards his office, which was also empty. I finally landed on the closed bedroom door. I could almost hear his breathing even as I stood outside, biting my lip in thought.

I didn't know if this was crossing a line—even as I recognized the fact that he had given me a key, and I was worried about him, so it was only natural that I check on him, right? And even if he got mad at me for this, well... I'd accept that trade-off as long as he was okay.

Opening the door, I quickly realized that he was passed out on the bed, his nightstand littered with bottles of alcohol and empty glasses. And there was my Matthew—my caring, loving man, seemingly tucked into a ball, surrounded by piles of blankets. I had never seen him drink more than a beer or glass of wine, and certainly not more than one or two a night, and maybe that was why the bottles of hard alcohol concerned me so much.

That he was so broken inside, and I hadn't even realized how much grief he had been carrying. Whatever he felt... the fact that it had led him to drink his day away crushed me.

Was I going to be enough for him? Enough to pull him out of this, make him realize how much good there was still in the world? I had lost a parent too, and I suspected I knew what he was feeling. But was I... enough? For him—for us? I tried to shake the thought away—what we had was *good,* and I knew it. I suspected he knew it too, because he showed me, every day, how right we were together, and I had never doubted it.

But this—seeing him like *this*? It broke my heart.

"Matthew," I whispered, feeling the tears pool in my eyes. "I'm so sorry."

I stepped up closer to the bed, my hand brushing his shoulder. I brushed the hair off his sweaty forehead, and then I tried to give him a light shake to wake him up, but he didn't rouse. Even after I called his names a few times and shook him harder, the giant man didn't stir. I realized that his pillow was damp, and I could see the tears that had trailed down his face.

"Oh, babe..." I choked out.

After all the times he had comforted me, just by simply being there... I wanted to give that feeling back to him. I always felt so safe and protected in his arms, and I hoped mine would give him the same feeling. I slid into the bed next to him, under the covers, pushing most of the blankets he had turned into a giant nest onto the floor, and I pulled myself against him. And I held him, tucked my face against his damp shirt, and listened to the sound of his heart beating in his chest.

I didn't know how long I held him like that before the heat of his body lulled me into sleep, but later, when he woke up, it was to my arms still wrapped around his back, snuggled against him like he was my life-sized body pillow. Holding tight to him, like I couldn't let go.

"Noelle?" He murmured, pushing the hair out of my face, and tipping my chin up so my eyes would meet his. "What are you doing here, sweetheart?"

"You wouldn't answer my calls or texts," I murmured as I stared at him. At his blue eyes, rimmed with red. It killed me that he had been crying alone. "I was worried about you."

"You were—" He sucked in a deep breath. "Noelle." He squeezed his eyes shut, as though he felt guilty for my worrying. "You didn't have to worry about me, I promise."

"I can't help it, you big dummy," I said softly, letting the tears fall from my eyes. "Of course, I'm going to worry about you. I care about you too much to do anything less." My feelings for him were too big to ignore anymore, and those three words were hovering right at the tip of my tongue. I could feel them.

His arms wrapped around me, finally, and he held me tight. "I just had a rough day, I promise. Nothing you have to worry about."

"Just a rough day?" I asked in disbelief. "Matthew... *please* don't shut me out. I'm here for you. You can tell me what's going on."

He shook his head, hand running over my hair, over and over, like that gesture would calm him down. I bit my lip as I stared up at him, at his glassy eyes.

"I talked to Elizabeth, Matthew…" I said, voice so low it hardly even counted as a whisper. I could barely hear myself, even in the quiet of his bedroom.

Snowball had been curled up at his feet when I entered the room, and now she was laying with her head resting on my feet, staring up at me as if to ask, *is he going to be alright?* I knew she was just a dog, but even I couldn't have answered that question. I buried my head back in his shirt.

"What?" He stilled. His voice was rough. "What did she tell you?" When I just held him tighter in reply, Matthew sighed, planting his nose on the top of my head as he inhaled deeply. "I just—"

"Does this have anything to do with why you didn't want to spend the weekend together?" I asked, trying to force myself to breathe evenly.

"No," he said, a little too quickly, but then he frowned down at me with a little shake of his head, one that rustled his long blonde strands. "Yes. I…" I smoothed over his t-shirt, running my hand up and down his spine in what I hoped was a soothing motion. "I did want to spend the weekend together," he said, and I resisted the urge to snort.

"Funny way of showing it," I smiled. I could have told him what Elizabeth had told me, but I felt like he needed to be the one to confide in me, to share it with me. And if we were strong enough… we would make it through this. *Together.*

"This weekend… Tomorrow…" His voice got all choked up, and I rubbed my hand over his back, hoping the soothing motion would encourage him to continue. "It's the anniversary of my parents' death." Matthew finally said, and even though I already knew, the grief in his statement punched me in the gut. I didn't have to wonder why he didn't want to talk, why he was pushing me away.

"Oh, Matthew." If I hadn't been wrapped around him, my

first instinct would have been to put my hand over my heart. "I'm sorry—"

He shook his head at me. "You didn't know... and I didn't tell you."

"Will you?" I asked hesitantly, hoping I wasn't crossing a line. "Tell me now, I mean?"

He paused as if he was thinking deeply on it, trying to decide what to say. "They've been gone ten years, and I still just..." He choked back another sob, the grief engulfing his whole body. "I've never talked about it," he finally whispered. "With anyone."

"Not Bryan or even with your sister?" I was sure she felt the same way that he did, and yet here he was, alone and carrying this all by himself.

He shook his head. "I didn't want to burden Tess with my grief or put that on her. She was going through her own, losing our parents so young. And Bryan... he's always there for me, but it's different. He doesn't understand..." Matthew's eyes were rimmed with fresh tears, and I understood what he meant.

How he felt.

I rubbed gently over his shoulder blades. "No, maybe not." I took a deep breath. "But *I* do. And you can talk to me about it. You have me." We locked eyes, and I knew the realization was sinking into him. That he'd never shared his despair over losing his parents with anyone, thinking no one else would understand, and they might not. But I did. I went through the same loss. The only difference was that I had been young enough to not feel his presence so fully in my life before having it ripped away. But he had always been there, like a ghost who couldn't find his way to the other side, and I had felt his loss my whole life.

I had listened to my mom cry almost every night for years.

The tears had started flowing freely from Matthew's eyes then, and it broke my heart, but I wanted him to keep being open and honest with me.

"You know I lost my dad when I was little." I waited for the slightest nod from Matthew before continuing. "I was young enough that I didn't feel the devastation—maybe not then—but I've felt his absence in every moment of my life. I get it, babe. I would do *anything* to have one more day with him."

Matthew opened his mouth, the only sound coming out just choked garbles. I placed a wet kiss on his chest and continued, knowing he couldn't find the words yet. "He died on September 6th, in a construction accident at work, you know? And I was *three*, at pre-school when they got a call from my mom. I don't remember it, but I know what they told me. My mom was too much of a mess to even get me from school. My neighbor had to pick me up. I stayed at her house for a week because mom was a shell of herself. She didn't eat, didn't sleep, and barely said a word to anyone. The love of her life was gone. What was the point of living without him?

"I think she forgot she had a daughter for a moment there. And I just kept asking, *what's wrong with Mommy? Where did Daddy go? When is Daddy coming home?*" I could feel tears dripping from my eyes, but I just kept going. I had to.

Matthew's arms squeezed me a little tighter, but I didn't stop. I couldn't. "Mom had been trying to get pregnant again, you know? She wanted another baby. And then my dad was gone. And it was just us, and she couldn't figure out how to live without him. And I... I was too young to know what was going on, but I *remember* that feeling, Matthew. That soul-crushing disappointment when you realize that the person you love is never going to come home. And I... I can't imagine not having someone to share that with."

His breathing had finally evened out, even as the tears continued to trickle down his face. Matthew smoothed down my hair with his hand before dropping a kiss on my forehead.

I could feel it, then. The shift in him, however small. The moment he decided to tell me, sharing his burdens and grief with me. Because I was strong enough to take it—because he had made me strong enough to make it through almost anything.

"They were coming to visit me," he finally said. "To take me home for the long weekend. Easter, just like this week. We were supposed to spend it at our little cabin up in the mountains, just the four of us. We were going to get Tess after leaving my school. But there was black ice on the roads, and the-the car slipped. They slipped on the ice, and then the car rolled, and they ended up thrown against a tree." A sob wrecked his body, and I held tighter. "It's my fault. That they're *gone*. That Tessa had to grow up without them. Their *miracle* baby. They had tried so long after me to have her, and they didn't even get to watch her grow up."

"It's *not* your fault," I whispered into his heart, wanting to bury my head in the crook of his neck as we both cried into each other's arms.

He took a deep steadying breath before continuing. "I just... I shut down. I was only in my sophomore year of college and my parents were just... *gone* from this world. In an instant. And yeah, I always had Bryan, Cole, and Tanner—they didn't give up on me, even when I had all but given up on myself, but I didn't share my feelings with them. Didn't tell them what was going on in my head. I couldn't find the words, even if I wanted to. Tess was with our grandparents, and I kept my head down, just trying to make it through my last two years of college. I studied hard, focusing only on the future. On making sure Tessa knew how loved she was, even without our parents. I buried every bit of sadness and anger at the world for taking them from me, because she was more important than I was. She was eleven, you know? My baby sister. It's like you said... everything changed for her in an instant.

"I buried my feelings because it was easier than feeling... this. This agony, this grief, missing them so much my heart hurts. It was easier to not let anyone in and keep everyone at an emotional distance because that was preferable to this. Until..." He stopped and looked straight at me. "God, until I met you, and I realized that maybe I could have someone. Because before you, Noelle, I never wanted it. No one else was ever worth the effort. Not until you."

"Oh, Matthew," I let myself cry against his chest, wishing I had something more I could say, that I could find the right words to tell him how I felt. How much I wanted to mend this hole in his heart, like he was helping to mend mine. "I'm so sorry."

He pulled me in tighter. I never wanted to let him go. "Will you just... let me hold you, sweetheart?" It came out as a broken whisper, but I knew it was what he needed most right now.

What I needed, too, if I was being honest. I didn't need someone to fix me—I could do that all by myself. All I had ever needed was someone to sit by my side, to hold me while I cried—not to tell me that everything was going to be okay, but to tell me that they were here for me, in whatever capacity.

So, I nodded into his chest. "Always. I'm always here for you, Matthew."

Because I was. And because... I loved him.

More than I think I had ever loved anyone.

CHAPTER 32
Matthew

It was something about the way she was holding me—so reverently, so caring, and understanding that just shattered every defense I had in my heart. I loved her. And it was because I loved her that I couldn't give up on her—had to prove to her that I would fight for us, for this, and that we were worth it. That she was worth every risk I had ever made, every risk I would ever make.

And this—sharing my grief with her? This felt like fighting through hell. It wouldn't fix me, but maybe it would be the beginning of the road to feeling normal again.

I wanted to share it all with her.

I kissed Noelle's forehead as we continued to just lay there, intertwined in each other, her head laying against my chest. I swore our hearts were synced, at this moment where we were so open and exposed to each other.

She held me all through the night.

~

"Tessa?"

"Matthew?" When my sister picked up the phone, her voice

sounded full of shock from receiving a call from me today. "Are you okay?"

"I know we haven't talked about them enough." I frowned into the phone even though she couldn't see me. "And I'm sorry for that. It's my fault. I couldn't figure out how to live with the grief, so I just pushed it down. But I think..." I looked over at Noelle, all snuggled into my sheets, still sleeping soundly even as I talked to my sister. "I think I'm ready now. To talk about it. About them."

Tess sounded choked up when she finally responded, "Oh, Matt..."

"I'm sorry if I failed you as a brother. I'm sorry if you needed to talk about them and I was... Too focused on me to see how you were feeling. But I never wanted you to feel like you couldn't talk to me, or you didn't have me."

"I didn't," she said a bit wobbly. "I didn't think of you like that. How could I? You were my beloved big brother, and even though I missed them like hell—I always had you. You gave up so much for me, and I just—" Tess sniffled. "I'm sorry I wasn't there for you like I should have been."

"Ten years," I said with a sigh. "How has it been ten years and it still feels like yesterday?"

"I think they'd be proud of us if they could see us now."

"Yeah?"

I pictured her nodding on the other side. "Yeah. You, falling in love, finding your person and your purpose. Me, graduating from college, chasing my dreams."

"Listen, about your dreams—"

"I don't know exactly what's next," she said, "but I think that being close to you is what I'm supposed to do. And I... I started looking for jobs in Portland while I was there for Spring Break. It's not the best job in the world, but I found one leading a children's theater department, and maybe I'll get a part-time job too on the side."

"Tess," I blinked away a few tears of surprise. "Are you sure?"

"More sure than I've ever been about anything."

"What about your boyfriend?"

"Oh." She laughed. "We broke up." Before I could say anything, she added, "You're coming for my graduation, right?"

"Wouldn't miss it."

"Bring Noelle along too?"

I looked at the sleeping red lump in my bed. "Yeah," I smiled. "I think she'd like that." I smiled.

"Good. Okay, I gotta run. I love you, bro."

"Love you too, sis. Have a great last few weeks."

"I will. Bye!"

We hung up, and I couldn't help but smile as I padded back to the bed, slipping in beside Noelle and pulling her into my arms. I wanted to inhale her sweet scent and hold her just so I'd remember that she was real. That she was here.

And on the anniversary of my parent's death, for once, I didn't want to black out to not remember. I was still brokenhearted—I probably always would be—but now, all I wanted was to celebrate life instead of mourning their death.

"Morning." Noelle's smile was gentle when she looked up at me, eyes groggy with sleep as I relaxed next to her in bed.

"Good morning."

"How are you feeling?"

"Still sad, but somehow... Knowing you're here, I feel like I can get through this."

Noelle leaned up to kiss me on the cheek. "Good. I'm not going anywhere, I promise."

"Breakfast?" I asked, changing the subject. Noelle nodded. "Want waffles?"

"Oh." Noelle grinned. "Yes, definitely. You know I *always* am in the mood for waffles."

I chuckled, ushering her out of the bed as I pulled the sheets off of us. "I'll get us a table at our favorite spot. Come on."

CHAPTER 33
Noelle

A knock came on my door, and I wiped my hands on my apron with a smile, knowing Matthew was coming over that evening. But when I opened the door, it wasn't my wonderful hunk of a boyfriend who stood in front of me.

It took me a panicking minute to get over the shock.

"Jake? What the hell are you doing here?"

He looked terrible, and I could tell from the way he reeked of alcohol that he had been drinking. "I miss you," he groaned. "I want you back, Noelle, baby."

"It's been three years," I said harshly. "Three years since you tore my heart out in New York, and now you're coming back here to tell me you *miss me?* Do I have to remind you that *you* left *me?*"

"It was a mistake," he pleaded. "Come on, Noelle, don't you miss me?"

"No." I shook my head. "I was always too good for you, Jacob. And you never treated me like I was worth anything to you. Why would I want to come back to you?" My heart pounded, knowing the way he used to treat me before. How he used to act around me. How he belittled me and made me feel worthless. Made me feel like no one else was ever going to love me. Well, he was wrong.

Because I had an amazing man who... I didn't know if Matthew loved me, exactly, but the way he treated me so reverently, so caring... it was everything I could have asked for and more.

And then, just like all those other times before... Jake turned cruel, sneering at me. "When that blonde boyfriend of yours realizes how worthless you are, you're going to come crawling back to me."

I shook with anger, but I managed to snap back. "No, I'm not. Because he'll never treat me like you did."

"When he breaks your heart, you'll be lucky if I take you back after he's used you up."

"Jake," I gasped. "You... you're an asshole!" I could feel the rage pooling in my bones—I had never hated someone as much as I hated him in that moment. "After everything you did to me, I can't believe you think I would ever come back to you! Even if Matthew and I did end things one day..." I swallowed, hating to think of that at all. "I would never come back to you."

A crooked, arrogant smile twisted his face. "You will," he said, before taking a step towards me. I took a step back, but he just kept following me.

"You don't even realize how you treated me all those years, did you? I idolized you. I loved you. And you treated me like I was trash. Nothing I ever did was good enough for you, but now you're back. Did you cheat on Laura, too? The assistant I caught you fucking in our bed?" I spit out the words with such venom that I almost surprised myself. "And then you left—without a word. I didn't even get the chance to tell you what a piece of shit you were to your face, asshole. You emotionally abused me and manipulated me for years, so you can kiss goodbye any possibility in your brain of ever seeing me again. And don't you dare say one more word about the man that I love. Because he's better than you ever were or could ever be."

He was now on the threshold of my apartment, trying to get another step in. "Get out, Jacob. Leave me alone," I said, fiercer than I could have imagined would come out of my mouth. "I never want to see you again."

That was when my gaze focused over Jake's shoulders and I realized that Matthew stood in the hallway, bottle of wine and a single sunflower clutched in his hands, with a livid expression on his face. Oh no.

"Matthew—" I started, but he didn't even hear me, pinning those furious eyes on Jake.

"I thought I told you to leave her alone," Matthew growled. "What do you think you're doing, talking to my girl like that?"

"She was mine first," Jake said, stumbling as he took another step towards me, and I pushed a hand against his chest to keep him away.

"And you gave her up, fucked up the best thing you could have had in your life—something I never plan to do. You looked at her and only saw someone you could use. I look at her and I see everything," Matthew ground out as he crossed the distance between them in seconds, and then he had him pinned against the wall with only one hand.

"We'll see," Jake taunted him. "When you grow tired of her, she'll just come crawling back to me like a pathetic—" And then a thud followed by a painful cry echoed through the hallway when Matthew punched Jake straight in the jaw.

I gasped, but I couldn't lie—it gave me immense satisfaction. While Jake dropped to the floor cupping his face, Matthew came rushing over to me. "Are you okay, baby? He didn't hurt you, right?"

I shook my head, and he cradled me into his arms. Then he turned back to Jake and spoke in a threatening tone that made me shiver: "I don't want to ever see you again. If you ever make her cry again, I will find you and make your life a living hell."

His upper body muscles flexed around me—and I knew it was because he was holding himself back, but I couldn't help but appreciate his physique once again. For a professor, he kept his body in great shape, and it showed. Damn, watching him punch my piece-of-shit ex was delightful.

"Now if you don't want me to beat the shit out of you, I'd appreciate if you would get the fuck out of my girl's apartment."

Jake wiped a trickle of blood off of his chin and then gave us a toothy smile, looking more crazed than I had ever seen him. "Enjoy my sloppy seconds, Professor. She was never that good in bed, anyway."

Matthew growled. Like, full-on throat rumbling, and took a step back towards him, but Jake was quick to walk backwards to the hallway and the front door of the building, giving me one last look that made me want to be sick, before he was gone.

And my handsome, beautiful, caring man, sensing I was trembling, weak in the knees over everything that just happened—at how Jake could still make me feel worthless after all this time apart—he pulled me into his arms, locked the door and the deadbolt, and then sat us down on the couch. He brushed a hand over my hair, over and over, soothing me as the tremors in my body began to slow.

"I'm sorry," I choked.

"Why, sweetheart? You didn't make him say those awful things. I'll make sure he never bothers you again."

"Just... that you had to see that. I—I never..." My breath caught, and I shook my head as if I was trying to clear the thought. Matthew took my hand, his thumb running circles over my skin, calming me down slowly but surely. "I never wanted you to hear the things he used to say about me." I looked up into his eyes, his icy, beautiful blue eyes, and I couldn't help the few tears that escaped me. "He made me believe so many awful things about myself, and I just—"

"Shh," he soothed. "Noelle, baby, it's okay. I'm here, and if I have to spend the rest of my life proving to you that those things aren't true, I will. Okay?"

"Is this just... Why is this so hard, Matthew? Maybe... Maybe I can't do this? It shouldn't be this hard," I cried into his chest.

He leaned back to make me look at him. "Are you saying you want to end things, Noelle? End us?"

"I... I don't know."

"You... don't want to be together anymore?"

I shook my head. I *couldn't* say that—it wasn't true.

"This is what you want." Not a question, a statement.

No. I want you to fight for me—fight for us. I need to remember that not everyone is like him. "I don't know, what I'm feeling, Matthew... I just..."

The silence that followed echoed in the hollowness I felt in my chest.

"You told me months ago that you didn't want anything serious..." Matthew's voice was quiet but firm. "I thought things were different." His blue eyes were shining and I hated the fact that I was causing the pained look in his face. I didn't want to end things. I just needed a minute—to breathe. To not have this crashing waves of feelings from seeing Jake, from having him belittle me all suddenly back in my head.

"Was I wrong?" he whispered.

No, I wanted to scream. *You made me want a relationship—with you.*

"What are you saying?"

"I can't keep trying to make this work if you don't want me to, Noelle. If you don't... want me."

No. No, I loved him—but my head was a mess. I couldn't keep my thoughts straight. I was still reeling over seeing Jake, reliving all of the shit he had put me through for years when we dated in college and when we moved in together.

Slowly, Matthew disentangled from me and stood, and every quiet step he took towards the door was a stab though my heart.

I couldn't let him leave. I couldn't keep doing this to this guy. This amazing guy who I felt more for than I had ever felt for anyone, who was everything to me... I couldn't let him leave. Couldn't let my fears keep us apart.

"Wait," I breathed, and Matthew stilled. He turned around,

and the anguish in his eyes took my breath away. I hated that they weren't filled with as much hope and love as they had been just a few moments ago.

That I had done that, to him. "Stay."

CHAPTER 34
Matthew

"Wait," Noelle said, and I turned around, trying not to let my heart break. "Stay. Please. I don't—"

I loved her. Had known I loved her for weeks, but I hadn't wanted to say anything to her that might have freaked her out. But this—coming to her apartment, seeing her asshole ex telling her how worthless she was? How dare he say she was going to go back to him once I decided she wasn't good enough for me. It had made my blood boil. Because when you loved someone... you didn't do that shit to them.

I didn't want to *ever* let her go. But if that was what she wanted... If this was too much for her, I would try to let her go. I'd break myself into pieces to do it, but then again, I'd do anything for this woman. And God. That asshole. I wanted to punch him in the face all over again. I'd make sure to do some *actual* damage this time.

I knew that this was about more than just him. But Noelle's deep-rooted fears stemmed from actual experiences, and knowing how he had belittled her, mocked her dreams, made her feel worthless, day after day... I *needed* her to know how much I cared about her. That I would never do that to her.

So when she said *wait*... I did.

Because I wasn't ready to give up on her, not ever. Because I wanted her to know that she could believe in fairytales. Because she had made me believe, and I knew that she was the woman I was born to be with. I could feel it deep within my heart, that everywhere life had taken me had just been one long journey to her, and I needed her to know that she could feel the same way back.

That she could believe in us because I was never going to leave her. I would never abandon her as Jake did. I was made to protect her—her heart, her smile, and I planned on showing her that every day for the rest of our lives.

So I would fight for her, but I needed her to fight for me, too.

"Noelle..." I pleaded. "Say something, baby. Please." I stared at her as tears dripped down her face. Just a few minutes ago, I had been holding her. I itched to again.

"I'm scared, Matthew," she whispered, "that one day you'll decide I'm not enough."

I took a step closer to her. "Noelle, listen to me. I want you. Tell me what I can to do to alleviate your fears. To show you I'm not going anywhere. Because I just want you. I promise—you're worth every risk."

Noelle stared at me for the longest moment of my life, and then she gave me a little shake of her head. "I can't... I can't let you break my heart. Not the way Jake did. I don't ever want to be that girl again." She wiped a few tears from her cheeks. "You can go and find someone else. Someone better than me. Someone who's not all broken and messed up on the inside. I know you can. You deserve the world, Matthew Harper, and I want you to be happy. Please."

"I can't be happy without you, Noelle."

"You have to be." Her voice broke. "Please, Matthew. This is... It's too hard."

"I'm not giving up on us."

"But... what you said before..."

"I was upset, baby. I was wrong. I don't want to give you up; I don't want to give this up. So I'm not going to. I'm going to fight for us, Noelle." I was putting my heart out on the line and hoping, miserably, desperately—that she would fight for us too.

But she just stood there, silently, with eyes full of unshed tears. I wanted to comfort her, wanted to cradle her cheeks in my hands, to rub soothing circles on her back as I told her everything would be okay, that I loved her, that I wanted her forever and would never leave her—but I couldn't. Because I couldn't bear for her to push me away even more after I told her my feelings, and I knew, I just knew, that I had to fix this before I could say the things I wanted to say. The things I needed to say, words that had been bubbling up inside of me for a long time. Words I had wanted to say since that day at Forest Park when we walked hand in hand and I had dreamed to hold her forever.

"Noelle. I can't live without you, sweetheart."

"Why?" She sniffled. "I'm just one big complication for you. I'm making your life harder. Why are you so determined, Matthew? I'm not going to be the one to get you fired from your job. I'm not going to have you resent me over losing the thing you're most passionate about. It would destroy you, and when you left me... well, that would destroy me."

I shook my head. "That's not going to happen."

"But what if it does?"

"It won't. Because I want you, Noelle. I can't let you go."

"Why?" She whispered.

I took a final step towards her, sat on the couch next to her, and brought her hand up to mine, interlacing our fingers together. "Why what, Noelle?"

"Why can't you let me go?" It was like Noelle wasn't breathing. And maybe she knew, but I wanted to say it anyway. Needed to say it. Had to tell her the words that I had been thinking in my head for so long, I might explode if I didn't get them out.

So I spoke from the heart, and I hoped that it would be enough. To convince her that I wanted her—forever. Always.

"Baby. I told you—you're mine. I don't want to let you go. I want you in my house. In my bed. At dinner with me, so I can make sure you're not working yourself to death and that you've eaten. On the couch with me, watching a movie and giving me your little commentaries that I love. On a walk with me, so I can hold your hand and keep it warm. I want it all, Noelle. Every damn moment with you. I'm too selfish that I never, ever want to let you go."

Our joined hands felt like a lifeline in that moment. Something grounding that kept me connected to her, reminded me that this was real, and I was here—she was here.

"Matthew—" She started, but this time I gave a little shake of my head. I wasn't done.

"It's like you walked into my life and the sun could shine again, like maybe if I was holding you, kissing you..." I paused, knowing what I needed to say but feeling so overwhelmed by the love I felt for her that I was getting choked up. "If I was loving you, then everything else was worth it."

"Do you?" Noelle breathed, her big brown eyes shimmering with a whirlwind of emotions as she clutched my shirt to keep herself steady.

"Do I what?" I asked, wiping a thumb under her eye, collecting droplets of tears before they could run down her face.

"Love me."

"Yes, baby," I smiled, grazing her forehead with my lips, planting the faintest kiss there. "I do." I shook my head, in awe that this crazy girl didn't know I loved her yet. That it took me so long to tell her. "Loving you is as natural to me as breathing. I swear, Noelle, you came into my life and wormed your way into my heart. I knew the first time I saw you that there was no one like you on this planet. No one else for me." I wiped another tear from her cheek, but they kept coming. "No one but you, my sweet girl."

"You and me," she said after taking a deep breath, a small smile spreading across her face. We looked at each other for a long, beautiful moment before Noelle spoke again. "I... I can't live without you either. I can't. And I'm sorry if I made you doubt it, but you are worth it. And I just..." She pulled me into her, sliding her hands into mine. "I didn't want you to think I didn't want *you*."

I laughed. "There's no getting rid of me, baby. As long as that's what you want."

"It is." Noelle wrapped her arms around my waist, and I wrapped mine around her back in return.

"Yeah?" I murmured into her hair.

"Yeah."

Unconditional happiness washed over me. "I'm yours, and you're mine. Always and forever, okay?"

"Will you say it again?" She asked quietly.

"Say what, baby?"

"That you love me."

I grinned, placing a kiss on her lips. "I love you, Noelle Hastings."

"That's good," Noelle started, and then she flushed, her cheeks turning red as I moved my focus to kiss each individual freckle on her face. "Because I love you too, Matthew Harper. Forever and always. I'm yours, truly." As I pulled back from her face, her hands cupped my cheeks, smoothing over the stubble of my unshaven beard.

I couldn't help a smug smile. "I know."

"What?"

"I heard what you said to Jake. While you were defending me. That you loved me," I beamed.

She gaped for a moment before shoving at my shoulder. "You jerk! You were going to leave after you heard me say that?"

I laughed, pulling her body tightly into mine. "I wasn't going to let you go, I promise."

"Matthew," Noelle started. "The other day, after we left the hospital... You asked me about the future."

"We don't have to talk about that now," I said, stroking her cheek.

"I want to. I want to tell you things I've never told anyone else." Noelle closed her eyes, nuzzling against my chest again. "When I saw you at the hospital, holding Theo in your arms... It freaked me out. Holding *him* freaked me out, I think, because I hadn't been ready to think about the kind of future I wanted to have with you." I heard her sniffle.

"Baby..."

"I know it wasn't fair to you, to project my insecurities on you about Jake... and my dad. But I was terrified that you would leave, because when you did... If you decided I wasn't good enough? That was going to break my heart. And the damage would just be too much."

I opened my mouth to say something, but she just put up a hand. "You're good. And you love so deeply. I've never once doubted how much you care for me." Tears were dripping from her eyes now, and I wiped them all away. Kissed her hand and squeezed it lightly to urge her to continue. "But that fear—it was crippling. And that's not to say that I might not get in my head again... But I want it all with you, Matthew James Harper. I do. I want the house and the ring and the family and the kids and a life."

"You're sure?" My heart was beating out of my chest, and my vision was blurry as I clung to her. Because this—she was everything. My whole heart. My future.

She nodded. "Not right now, of course... But one day. Yeah. I'd like to do everything with you."

"That's good because I want everything with you, too, Noelle Marie Hastings. And one day, I can't wait to give you my last name, too." I grinned. "If you want it."

Noelle's face spread into another glorious grin. Even though her face was streaked with tears, she was still beautiful. "I do. I think. Want your last name."

"Good." I smirked. "Because I want the world to know you're mine."

She let her palms run over my shirt. "I might get in my head again—you know. Freaking out. Worrying." Noelle just bit her lip. "I don't want to burden you with my problems, but—"

"I'll always be here for you." I nodded. "Just like you are for me." I was sure there would be days where I still wanted to break down, missing my parents. I knew that she would be there for me on those instances as much as I would be there to reassure her that I loved her and would never leave her.

Noelle tugged on my shirt collar and leaned up until her lips touched my ear. "You know… we've never been completely alone in my room." She waggled her eyebrows.

My God, this woman.

"Noelle. Sweetheart. As much as I want to carry you to bed right now and make love to you until we run out of breath, someone could hear. These walls are thin." And we really don't want to be caught in your dorm, with all of your students around.

"I guess we'll have to be really quiet then," she said, nibbling on my earlobe. "Because I'd very much like you to be inside me, my sweet grumpy professor."

She cupped my cheek, and then gave a yelp of surprise as I hoisted her up into my arms. "Well, you've asked for it now," I growled, kissing her nose as I carried her to the bedroom.

"Think we can be quiet?" Noelle said, leaning against my chest as I carried her into the bedroom.

I shook my head. "Never. Because I'm afraid you're stuck with me now, and I intend to show you how much I love you all night long."

"Good." Noelle grinned, and I kicked open the door with my foot before closing it behind me.

I dropped her on the bed with a giggle from Noelle, before standing back to pull the shirt off of my body. Her eyes watched me the whole time, never drifting from mine, from my body, as I pulled off my pants and threw them off to the side, clad just in my boxer briefs. I knew she could see my erection—I was hard for her. I was always fucking hard for her.

"My sweet girl," I said, standing back at the edge of the bed and holding her face in my hands. "I hope you know I'm never going to let you go again."

"Oh, I'm counting on it," Noelle said, pressing her lips against mine as I started to tug her sundress off her body.

"I love this little thing," I said as I pulled it all the way off.

"Yeah?"

"Yeah, but I like it better on the floor."

I threw the garment on the floor, appreciating Noelle in just her bra and panties. Her voluptuous breasts. Her thick thighs. I liked that she wasn't a twig, that her body had curves and she knew how to dress them. "My little temptress," I said, trailing kisses down her neck as I unhooked her bra.

"I like your sweaters, too." I smirked as I got her bare. "But you in those tiny dresses drives me wild."

She laughed. "I wore it just for you, you know." She pulled my head down so our foreheads were resting against each other. "This definitely isn't how I thought this day was going to go."

"Unexpected visit from the ex was not on the bingo card?" I gave her a grin as I returned to her bare skin, kissing the top of each of her breasts before I brought a nipple into my mouth.

"Oh," she moaned.

"Quiet, remember?"

Noelle gave me a devilish smile. "It's just Haze on the other side of the wall, anyway. And you wouldn't believe how many times I've heard her and Lucas in there." She giggled. "This feels like payback."

"Mmm, so you're saying you *want* me to make you scream?"

"Just a little." She wiggled her eyebrows. "Now... Keep doing that."

I put my mouth back on her nipple. "Like this?" I said, blowing against it softly. She shuddered a little against me.

"*Oh.*"

And then I was sucking and nipping, taking my time worshipping her breasts before Noelle slid her hand down my boxers.

"Baby," I warned her. "If you do that, I'm going to come way too fast, and I want this to last."

She pouted. "I want you inside of me, please." Noelle shimmied out of her panties, dropping them on the floor, before she grabbed my hand and placed it against her folds. "I'm so wet, Matthew."

I couldn't help pushing a finger into her, watching the little burst of pleasure ripple through Noelle's face.

She pushed my boxers off, and a little snort tumbled out of me as Noelle flipped us over, mounting me and running her hand up my cock before she positioned it right under her—and then pushed herself down.

We both moaned. I let her set the pace, rubbing against me to give her clit friction before she moved her body up and down on my length. My hands gripped her waist as I helped her take her pleasure from me. Fuck. I was so deep in her, buried all the way to the hilt.

"Feels so good," she cried as she rocked against me.

"As much as I love you on top of me, sweetheart, I'm never going to last with you doing that." I flipped her over, burying myself in her thighs, caging her in with my arms.

"Don't stop," she pleaded as I slid out of her before thrusting back in. "Please. I need you."

"I love you," I said, thrusting into her. "God, I can't wait to make you my wife, Noelle. Watch you get round with our children. Take care of yourself the way you deserve." I dropped a kiss on her lips as I pulled all the way out before sliding back in.

I wanted to go slow—to make this last for both of us, but there was something in her eyes, in the way it felt to be connected like *this*. After telling each other how we felt, I couldn't stop or slow down even if I wanted to.

"Is this what you want?" I said with another thrust. "Us, forever? To stay with me forever?"

"Holy—*fuck*," she ground out through her teeth, "yes!"

Noelle's eyes rolled back, and I could tell she was close—and I wanted to last, wanted to make this so good for her, but just having her in my arms like this was too much.

"I'm gonna come, baby," I said, brushing a piece of hair off her sweaty forehead.

"Me too, Matthew," she moaned. "Please, make me come."

My hand—the one that wasn't holding her hip—trailed circles up her thighs. "Have you been a good girl?"

Noelle nodded, biting her lip. "Yes. Such a good girl. Please, please, *please*," she begged me.

"I love you."

She gasped as I moved my thumb down to her clit, rubbing it in circles.

And as her climax hit her, rippling through Noelle's whole body as her back arched off the bed and her fingers dug into my back, I came with her pussy spasming around me, the fluttering sensation making me see stars as I spilled inside of her.

"I love you," I said again, boneless and breathless, still buried inside of her as we collapsed against each other.

I held her like that—utterly sated and totally spent—breaths heaving, hearts beating in sync.

After cleaning ourselves off, we climbed back into bed—her bed, the one I had never slept in before—and I held her in my arms as she cried.

I told her it was going to be okay—because it was. Reassured her that I was never going to leave her, not if I had any say in it, because I meant what I said. I wanted forever. She told me about her ex, about their relationship, and how toxic he was to her.

I wanted to punch him all over again.

And maybe Noelle and I weren't fine—not completely, but in this world where I had felt so alone for so long, I had her, and she had me, and there was nothing like the knowledge that we had each other and always would, like an invisible life raft that would always stay tethered to our sides.

It was everything.

She was my everything.

CHAPTER 35
Noelle

My mom gaped at me as I walk into the restaurant, hand in hand with Matthew.

The last time we spoke on the phone, I hadn't quite told her *everything*, so it was clearly a shock for her to see him next to me. I hadn't even told her that I'd started dating, let alone anything about him. But after I had held him in my arms as he cried over losing his parents, after I had finally told him how broken I was inside—I knew I needed to do this. To conquer one of the emotional roadblocks that I always had, never feeling like I was enough for my mother.

And I had him by my side.

Matthew—my good, strong, brave, and brilliant man—had absolutely no qualms about coming with me to meet my mother for dinner. That's how I knew how serious this thing between us had gotten. And for me, the girl who hadn't been ready for another relationship, who hadn't been sure if she had wanted to attach those strings to herself... I found that all of those old negative whispers in my head were gone as I clung to him while we went to sit with my mother.

I realized it all with stunning clarity. What I needed to say. What I needed to express. How I felt.

I loved her, I did, and I knew she loved me, in a way that was too big to express. With everything she had done for me since I was a kid, since losing my dad, I owed her the world. But I was also tired of feeling like she was disappointed in me, or that I was throwing away my life. I had things I needed to say to her, and it just felt... right to have the man I loved by my side.

Somehow, in the short time that we'd been together, I'd come to rely on him for things like this. Because no matter how much I loved my best friends, there was nothing as soothing and comforting as Matthew holding me and telling me everything was going to be okay. Because when someone who looks at you with that much devotion tells you how amazing you are, you realize that you have to believe it.

Matthew would never lie to me. He wouldn't dream of it.

We were at a little Mexican restaurant for dinner, and Mom was already seated with chips and salsa on the table as we sat down across from her. Matthew dropped my hand so he could pull my chair out, and then gave me a small kiss on my forehead before taking a seat next to me. My heart swelled in appreciation because these little gestures were everything to me. I looked away from my man and back to my mother, who was sitting there studying us, margarita glass in hand.

"Hi Mom," I said, a little sheepishly. "I want you to meet Matthew." I looked at him, and I realized it felt so good to say the words out loud to her. "He's my boyfriend."

"You're *dating*?" she raised an eyebrow and looked between the two of us. Matthew grabbed my hand under the table, rubbing circles with his thumb. "I thought you said—"

"I know what I said, Mom, but the truth is... I didn't want you to try to meddle with this, too." Matthew's encouraging nod gave me the strength to continue. "I know you love me, and I love you, but sometimes you're just so... overbearing. And I needed to do this by myself. All of it." My mother looked shocked, but I knew I needed to get the words out. They had been in my head for so long, and now it was finally time for something to change.

"I'm going to stay working at the university, Mom. And I know it's not what you wanted for me, not what you pictured when you looked into my future, but it's what I really want. And I've really thought this through, so please don't try to talk me out of it."

"What about—"

"Mom. No. If we're going to have a relationship, I don't want you to try to run my life from behind the scenes." I took a deep breath, thankful for Matthew's soothing touch. "I just want you to be my mom. I want you to ask me how my day was, to let me cry when I need to, and offer advice when I ask. Okay?"

"Oh, sweetie. I was never trying to do that." Her eyes were teary, and while I didn't want my mom to cry, I also needed her to understand how I felt all these years. "I just wanted you to be happy, Noelle."

"I am," I said, not missing Matthew's squeeze under the table. "It took me a while, but I really am now."

"I'm glad," Mom said, reaching out to touch my other hand, the one that rested on top of the table. "That's all I've ever wanted for you, since you were a little girl, and we lost your dad." She wiped her eyes, and then fixed her gaze on Matthew. "Now, tell me more about this boyfriend of yours. And if I find out you're treating her wrong, or if you hurt her..." She glared at him.

He chuckled. "I promise, Mrs. Hastings, I don't plan on ever hurting your daughter." He looked at me with such conviction that I felt tears prick my eyes. I squeezed his hand, this time, and I realized it felt so true, at this moment.

Like maybe I had been wrong all along, and love could persevere in this world. Like this man—this steadfast, caring man, might be the one person who could prove me wrong.

We spent the rest of the dinner with my mom asking Matthew questions, getting to know him as I had over the past few months. And when Matthew and I finally clambered back into his truck later that night, I let out a deep sigh of relief.

"Glad that's over."

He placed his hand on my thigh and squeezed. "Better than you thought it would be?"

I nodded. "Heaps."

"Good. Now, let's go home."

"Anywhere," I agreed, "as long as it's with you."

He gave me a warm smile, and I thought I could have melted in it. In this moment, and with the strength he had given me to say the words I needed to say.

That, some voice in my head said, *is what love is supposed to look like.*

∼

THE LAST WEEK of classes passed in a blur, a whole week of studying and spending nights with Matthew and laughing and crying more than I could have imagined. When it came down to it, he wouldn't let me go, and I couldn't have been happier that he didn't give up on us even when I tried to. That last week of school was full of him loving me, caring for me, cuddling with me late at night as I stayed over at his place. Those were some of the best days of my life, and I couldn't wait for an eternity of them.

I just had to get through finals first. And accept my job offer.

"That's my girl." Matthew smiled as I hit submit on my final paper, and I sighed in relief. It was *done*. Now all that was left between me and walking across the stage to get my diploma was a few final exams. I couldn't believe how fast the semester had gone by.

"I have my final presentations tomorrow," I grinned. "You're coming, right?"

"Wouldn't miss it, sweetheart."

"Now I just have to get through finals, and then we have a whole month before summer school starts for you, right?" I asked, putting my laptop down and moving over to sit across his lap on the couch. His eyes twinkled mischievously, the beautiful blue eyes staring back at me as he gathered what I was trying to do. "A whole month to ourselves." I kissed his neck, then his jaw, before finally landing on his lips.

"A whole month just for us," he agreed, kissing me back. "You're going to stay here, right?"

I blinked at him. "Do you mean...?" Move in?

"Just for the summer, if you want... I was thinking it made sense." He caressed my arms slowly, up and down. "Just until you move back into the dorm. I just... I want you here with me, Noelle."

"Oh. Matthew, I love you." I nuzzled my nose against his neck. "But I'm not moving back into the dorms this fall."

"You're... not? I thought you said you were staying at the university."

"I haven't officially accepted the job yet... but the School of Business offered me a position as Student Advisor. So, I'll be staying there." I bit my lip, searching his eyes for something I didn't want to name yet. "I was thinking about getting an apartment..."

"Move in with me," he said, his blue eyes so big and full of delight as he gazed into mine.

And it clicked. "I... Wow. I don't know what to say."

"Say yes," my beautiful, handsome giant blonde man pleaded with me. "You're here more nights than you are at your apartment, anyway, and the nights where you're gone—"

I laughed. How could I say no to him? I didn't want to spend any time without him. We were in this—life—together. "Yes." And the word wasn't even out of my mouth yet that he kissed me with such fervor that it left us both breathless. "So... no more sleepovers?"

"No, Noelle." He flicked my nose. "It's the opposite. I want every day for the rest of my life to be a sleepover with you. I want to roll over and kiss you good morning, make you breakfast and make sure you're fed before you go to work, and then I want to be the one to welcome you back home every day." He kissed my chin, then my neck, before moving up to my mouth. "I want to make love to you every night until you come—more than once—and I want to hold you in my arms afterward. I want to spend every moment of the rest of our lives together. I want it all with you, Noelle Hastings, and God help me, I never want you to spend another night where I'm not at your side. Okay?"

"Okay." I nodded tearfully, but my smile was big and wide.

I leaned my head against his chest, fingers playing with the buttons of his shirt. "You know, I had already said yes. I didn't need a long speech."

The sound of his laugh was beautiful. "I know. But I liked the long speech. Plus, it meant I could promise you again to make you come every night."

"Did you promise that?" I tilted my head. "Because that sounds like a wicked, wicked tongue, Professor," I grinned, and he stole another kiss. I slipped my fingers through his belt loops, pulling him—and his erection—firmly into me. "So, when can I move in? Because I would like for you to deliver on all of those promises."

"Is tomorrow too soon?"

I laughed. "Maybe after graduation." I wrinkled my nose at him. "But only if you promise to help me pack. And carry my stuff down the stairs."

"Anything for you, baby."

"Now, back to that tongue…"

"Mhmm, but first…" He shifted me and placed me back on the couch, looking at the pile of my study materials. "We *do* gotta get you across the stage, baby."

"You know…" I wondered out loud, biting my lip. I pulled a textbook onto my lap as I thumbed through the pages without actually reading any of them. "I think there's gotta be a better way to study than this."

"Oh? Please, do tell, my little graduate. After six years of collegiate learning, what *is* your secret to studying?" He grinned, and I shot him a glare.

"I was just thinking that there are more *fun* ways to incentivize learning, *Professor*." I insinuated, running a finger up the spine of the book. "If you want to help me, that is."

He quirked an eyebrow, and then the textbook was page down on the floor underneath us and I was pulled back onto his lap, this time straddling his strong thighs. "Oh, my wicked girl?" Matthew nipped at my ear. "What do you have in mind?"

"I was thinking... what if you quiz me." I said, running my fingers up his button-up shirt. "And for every question I get *wrong*... you get to take off an article of clothing."

"And for every question you get right?"

"I think a kiss sounds like a good reward, doesn't it?"

The grin had fully spread over his face now, and he tugged on a loose strand of hair before leaning back towards my ear. "I think," Matthew started as he ran his hands up my back, "those terms can be agreed to."

"Yeah?"

"Mhm," he said, nipping at my bottom lip. "I think your proposal sounds very agreeable, Miss Hastings."

"Alright, Professor Harper. Do your worst."

He laughed. "Where should we start..." He picked my textbook up off the floor and began thumbing through it.

An hour later, I was a little breathless from all of the kissing and left in only my bra, having just lost my panties, and I found that, surprisingly, it was a *fantastic* way to study. Why was I even surprised? This *was* us.

"So what happens when I take that bra off of you?" Matthew asked, looking at me with a coy expression.

"Hmmm... well, I can think of something..." I winked.

"Are you admitting defeat?"

"Never," I whispered, picking up the book again. "Now ask me another one."

He did, and I answered it wrong on purpose, which Matthew *knew*—I didn't know how, but he just did—and he gave me a smug smile as his hands wrapped around my back and unclasped my bra, all in one fluid motion.

"I think that's enough studying for tonight," he mused. Then he was picking me up and carrying me—naked—in his arms, one hand on my back and one under my legs. "Now, I have more important plans with you."

I hummed, "Oh yeah? I hope part of those plans include me undressing you, because it's awfully unfair that I'm naked and you're fully clothed."

"Oh, don't worry, little fox," he smiled like the big wolf that he was. "They do." He kissed my forehead, kicking open the door to the bedroom before depositing us on the bed.

And then we enjoyed ourselves—a little too thoroughly, and not one more bit of studying got done that night.

∽

"Can I tell you something?"

We were lying on the couch, limbs intertwined, when Matthew's question broke the comfortable silence we'd cocooned for ourselves. I gave him a nod as I wondered where he was going with this. What secrets we hadn't already told each other.

"I didn't want to be there that night." I gave him a questioning expression, and he elaborated. "The night we met. The other faculty members dragged me there. I didn't want to go," he laughed. "I never would have imagined that I would have met you there."

And I think I understood, even more than he realized.

"Can I tell *you* something?" My cheeks were blazing as my thoughts ran ahead of me, a thousand miles per hour. He brushed a lock of hair off my face. "I didn't want to be there that night either," I giggled. "Hazel was the one who insisted I come. The inclusion of brownies might have sold me."

Matthew laughed, and I snuggled further into his side. "So, brownies? That's what got my future girlfriend to go to that damn mixer?"

I nodded, very solemnly, like this was a *profoundly* serious fact. "*Very* good brownies."

Matthew smirked at me and stuck his tongue in my ear, ignoring the little shriek I gave as we rolled around on the couch and he landed on top of me, caging me in with his body and his arms.

"But we found each other."

His smile was bright enough to fill a whole room. Brilliant, just like the first snowfall that coats the world in a glorious, dazzling blanket of white. Some people might think he was cold or withdrawn, but they just didn't know him like I did. They didn't know that he had just needed a bit of warmth to find himself again.

"We did. And I wouldn't trade us for the world."

"Sometimes I think that everything in my life… every moment, every decision… they all led me here, to you," Matthew said, pressing a kiss to my jaw.

"I like to believe it was fate, us meeting that night," I said, quietly. "Like the universe just knew that we needed each other and gave us a little push in the right direction."

"Is that right?" Matthew smiled as his eyes swept over my body.

I hummed in response and pulled him down on top of me so I could close my mouth over his. I nipped at his bottom lip before he let me in.

"I love you." I smiled into the kiss.

"I love you too, Noelle Marie Hastings." He held my face reverently. "More than I can put into words."

"*More* than words?"

"More than words."

I had never lacked for words—I was always talking, and then once I got my groove back, even the words had spilled out of me, flowing endlessly. But it felt like when I tried to describe the depths of my feelings for him, there were never enough of them. I thought I could write a whole book with all of the ones that were constantly running through my veins.

In some ways, I already had.

And then he kissed me again, holding me tight as he showed me how much he loved me, how much of his heart I had. And I gave it back—all of my love, all of my heart.

Hoping he knew he had all of it—all of me—forever.

CHAPTER 36
Noelle

Three years ago, I had no idea where my life would take me. I had been hurting, and alone, and moved back home while nursing a broken heart and not knowing what I wanted to do with my life. Today, however, I had survived, I had gotten my diploma, and I had found a love that taught me what life was all about. I had a guy who loved me—so much, that when I had tried to break up with him, he hadn't *let* me. And now, it was finally time for the rest of my life to begin.

In my cap and gown, with my diploma case still in my hands, I rushed over to where my family and friends stood after the ceremony. In the middle of them stood my beautiful blonde boyfriend.

My Matthew.

The biggest grin spread over my face as I saw them there, all gathered together. And as I saw the bundle of sunflowers that Matthew was holding for me.

I couldn't help but run up to him, flinging my arms around his neck as soon as I got close enough.

"So, Miss Hastings, now that you've graduated, what do you want to do?" Matthew whispered in my ear.

"I think," I said, beaming up at him, "that I'd like to kiss my boyfriend."

"Here?" he asked, looking around the quad as I leaned on my tiptoes, trying to bring our faces closer. "In front of everyone?" It wasn't like he didn't want to; no, he was asking if *I* was sure.

I looked at my mom, at my best friends—Charlotte, Angelina, and Gabbi all gathered behind him—and around us at the masses of other graduates, and I realized I didn't care what anyone thought. I hadn't for a while now.

Because he loved me, and if I wanted to kiss him in front of all of these people, I was going to. I knew he had never really liked public displays of affection, but if the way he was looking at me was any indication, he did want to kiss me senseless too.

I smiled under my eyelashes, and then nodded. "Yes, please."

"That's all? Just a kiss?" He smirked, his hands closing around my waist as he pulled me tight against him.

"Nope," I whispered into his mouth, "that's just the beginning, Matthew." I took another moment to intertwine my hands with his and then, finally, I kissed him.

I kissed him for every time I had wanted to but had held back. I kissed him for every time we had kept our relationship a secret instead of sharing it with the world. I kissed him knowing that I had a lifetime of kisses to come, but I still couldn't get enough here, now, in this moment.

I kissed him like he was *mine*, and I was *his*, and when he ran his fingers through my hair, I knew the statement was true. Like no matter what happened next—we'd be facing it together. There was no chance in hell I was ever going to let this man slip through my fingers. This beautiful, lovely man who was always there for me.

And this kiss—this dizzying, spellbinding kiss—I wanted to sink into it, pour all of my love for him into it. Wanted his tongue tracing over my teeth, tangled with mine, because everything was good and right, and we were here, finally, *finally*. Together, happy. Nothing to keep us apart ever again.

"I love you," I murmured as we pulled apart and he grazed his knuckles over my jaw.

"I love you, sweetheart."

And then he kissed me again. Over and over until I was breathless and smiling, until my friends shoved him out of the way, and my heart was so full being surrounded by all of my favorite people that I couldn't have stopped smiling even if I wanted to.

"We're so proud of you!" the girls gushed, closing in around me.

"You knew what you wanted, and you went and got it." Gabbi gave me a big hug

"And more," Charlotte said with a lovesick sigh, glancing at Matthew standing by my side.

"I couldn't have done it without you three," I said earnestly, squeezing each of their hands before pulling them all into a big hug.

"You're never getting rid of us," Angelina laughed.

"Best Friend's Book Club on three!"

"One, two, three..." We all cheered, and I looked around me. Matthew was standing close to me, holding my flowers and the diploma case that I had almost dropped earlier.

Who would have guessed that two years in grad school and three years working as a Hall Director would lead me to this moment? Not me, that's for sure.

"Thank you, love," I whispered in his ear as we took a bazillion photos and continued to be surrounded by my best friends, and my university friends who had come up to say goodbye, too. Hazel and Lucas gave me knowing smiles as they saw Matthew holding my hand, and I couldn't help but reach up and give him a peck on his cheek.

Because I loved him, and I was grateful to have him in my life.

∼

Matthew

"One more day," she said to me that morning, standing at the sink in my bathroom as she brushed her curled hair over her shoulder and touched up her makeup, "One last day, and then it's just *us*, Matthew. Just you and me, babe."

"I'm so proud of you, Noelle." I nuzzled her shoulder, burying my face in her hair as I inhaled deeply. I loved how she always smelled like roses with a hint of sweetness, like the chocolates she was constantly eating, and something that was distinctly *Noelle*.

We were both dressed up in our graduation gowns—her in her grad student robes, and me in my faculty ones—and I couldn't help but admire how good we looked standing next to each other in the mirror. I thought of how proud I was to stand by her side, and to be called her boyfriend.

God. Her boyfriend. *Her* boyfriend. Her *boyfriend*.

I liked it so much more than I ever thought I could. To be in a relationship with her, to call her mine. She was truly everything I had ever wanted but had never had. I had never found someone before who I wanted to be with as much as I wanted Noelle. There was no one else who could challenge me every step of the way, testing my brain and my wits even as she showed her love and affection for me. And I loved her so damn much, I thought my heart might burst. My heart, which once upon a time was like ice, but her warm and sunshiny demeanor had melted through every measure of defense I had built to protect it.

And I thought she had never looked as beautiful as she did that day, cheeks flushed with laughter as she stood with her group of friends. Seeing her in her cap and gown, topped off with her master's stole—it was like everything was right in the world. Here she was, my Noelle, my girl, looking the happiest I had ever seen her as she held hands in a circle with Charlotte, Gabbi, and Angelina.

Her friends that I had come to know and who had accepted

me into their lives; the friends who brought so much joy and happiness into Noelle's world that I couldn't help but smile too as she let go of them and pulled me into her side.

"I love you," I said as I kissed her temple, and she lit up like the sun.

She *was* the sun. My own special kind of sun. She was the only one that brought sunshine into my life, and I loved her more every single day. Would love her for the rest of our lives, too, if I had anything to say about it.

"Ready to go home?" I asked after her friends had left, she had said goodbye to her mom, and had talked to what felt like half of the graduates students who had walked the stage.

Noelle nodded eagerly. "I'm exhausted." She pulled off her wedged heels—I loved those things because they made her legs look long as hell, and they made it even easier to kiss her. In a heat-of-the-moment decision, I scooped her up to carry her to the car.

"Matthew!"

"What?" I feigned ignorance. "I can't have my girlfriend's feet getting all dirty."

"Fine," she sighed, but I didn't miss how she nestled into my shoulder happily as I walked the rest of the way to where I parked my truck.

She was still wearing her cap and gown as we entered my house. I had taken mine off in the car—leaving just my dress shirt and slacks on—but I loved seeing her like this. Her cheeks were still flushed from standing out in the sun so long, and even though she had been up all morning, she was still buzzing with energy as we got home.

And it *was* home, with her here. And when she moved in permanently, soon, it really would feel like it. I didn't want to spend any more nights apart. I wanted to always have her by my side.

Her gown was unzipped, showing off Noelle's red, flowy dress. She stood past the entryway, one hand on her hip, the other holding her shoes. Her toes were painted red to match her heels, and I had loved sitting on the edge of the tub just watching her paint them, stroke by stroke.

It didn't matter what she was doing, I just loved watching her and being in her presence. God, she had truly taken over my whole life, and I wasn't even mad about it.

"Hi," I said, crossing my arms over my chest as I just *watched* her.

"Hi," she whispered, tiptoeing across the wooden floor and walking into my arms.

"I'm so proud of you," I said, pulling the cap out of her hair, setting it and the bobby pins down on the table.

"I love you," she said with a sigh, a happy, contented one.

"I'm so glad I have you," I murmured against her lips as I placed a kiss there.

"I'm yours," Noelle cupped my cheek with her palm. "And you're mine."

"Forever."

"Forever is a very long time, you know," Noelle said, looking a little devious. "What if you change your mind?"

"I won't," I about growled.

Noelle started to pull her graduation gown off of her shoulders, but I stopped her. Turning her around, my erection pressed up against her ass as I massaged her shoulders. She gave a little moan in response, sending even more signals to my dick.

"Matthew!" she giggled, squirming against me as she felt my body react to her. "Hmm... Does it turn you on, seeing me in my gown?"

"Yes, baby. I want you to wear the robe," I instructed, "*just* the robe."

"Oh." She paused for a moment, and then dropped her shoes on the floor and slipped out of my grip towards the bedroom.

I growled a little, following behind her as she stripped, and then she was finally—finally bare, wearing only her little lace panties that she knew drove me crazy and her black gown, bra, and dress forgotten in a heap on the floor.

I quickly stripped my clothes off, and when I was clad in only my boxers, I pulled her in my arms. "It turns me on," I finally said, "Knowing you're *mine,* Noelle. You're all mine. Forever. So now I wanna fuck my little graduate, okay?"

She nodded, eagerly. "Forever," she said as I pulled her to me, chest to chest.

"And always."

And as far as the start of the rest of our lives went—it wasn't bad at all.

It was the opposite: perfect. Because I had her.

∽

Noelle

If you had told me three years ago where I was going to end up—living in Portland, dating the most wonderful guy I could ever imagine (a professor!), and working as an Advisor at my former university, I would have told you that you were crazy. But here I was, holding the key to his house in my hand, unlocking the door as we carried in my very last load of boxes.

I had spent most of my time over the last few months at his place, anyway, instead of my small dorm apartment, and I loved it. I loved him, and Snowball, and snuggling in his arms after he made love to me every night was just the icing on the cake. Truthfully, I had never wanted to leave.

True to his word, Matthew had helped me pack up my place. I didn't have much furniture, to begin with, and what wouldn't fit in his house we ended up donating, and now here I was—a stack of boxes in the middle of the living room, my clothes in a pile on the bed ready to put away in *our* walk-in closet.

"That's the last of it." Matthew smiled, placing the stack of boxes down in the living room. "Now, roomie, I believe I promised you some thorough loving with my tongue..." He winked at me seductively, making me laugh.

"I love you," I said as I rose on tiptoes, and he pulled me in for a kiss.

"I love you, too." He pecked my forehead, giving me one of those kisses that still gave me butterflies, and then I was in his arms, and he carried me bridal style into his room. Our room.

"You know..." I gave him a grin as he deposited me on the bed. I sprawled out, running my arms over the comforter, making angel shapes in the bed like you would in the snow. "Now that I officially live here, that means this is *our bed.*"

He leaned down to nip at my ear. "It's *been* our bed," he whispered into my ear, "ever since the first night you slept in it. I haven't wanted you to spend a single night apart from me. But I was trying to take it slow and not rush you."

I hummed, looking up at the ceiling, then smiled at Matthew who stood over me, arms bracing himself on the bed. "I think that calls for a very special kind of celebration then, huh? Now that we're going to spend every night in *our bed?*"

"Oh? And what kind of... celebration did you have in mind?" He climbed onto the bed and perched on top of me, caging me in with his limbs.

"I think you know," I murmured as I wrapped my arms around his neck, pulling him down to kiss me. I pouted when he pulled away too soon.

"I think I'm very much going to enjoy having you in *our* bed, Noelle Hastings."

I giggled as he kissed me again, on the lips, then on my jaw, my neck, before trailing down my chest. I sighed contentedly before tugging on my slouchy, off-the-shoulder sweater. "I think we have some particularly important obstacles in the way right now. Maybe we should take them off first?"

"No time," he shook his head, "I think I need to be inside my wonderful girlfriend right this second."

I laughed, pulling his shirt up from his waistband as he pushed my leggings and underwear down my thighs.

Matthew's hand dipped lower, pressing against me before he

slipped a finger inside me. "Always so wet for me, my little vixen, huh?"

"Yesssss," I cried as he stroked me deeper, exploring my insides. "I'm always so wet for you, babe." He added a second finger inside as I finally managed to undo his belt and pull it off before undoing the zipper of his jeans.

Matthew brought our mouths together as he kept working me with skillful fingers.

"I want you inside of me," I panted against his mouth, but he didn't stop pumping into me.

"I want you to come first," he said, curling his fingers to hit just the right spot. I shook my head.

"The only thing I want to come around right now is your cock, Matthew. So get inside me right now, or so help me God—"

He grinned, but pushed his jeans and briefs down his legs, finally exposing himself to me. And then his fingers were gone, and I could only mourn the loss for a second, because a moment later he was positioned at my entrance, tip just begging to press inside of me, and I gasped when he slid all the way in with one slow thrust.

"Matthew," I groaned, "move, please."

"Uh-uh. I want to make sweet love to my girlfriend on our first day in *our* house." He slid out slowly and kissed me. "*Our bed.*" He plunged back in, deliciously slow but filling me completely. "Just like this, for the rest of our lives." He kissed me again, and I bit his bottom lip as he gave me another slow thrust.

"I *love—*" I whined as he slid out again, "when we make love, babe, but right now, I really just need you to *fuck* me." I peppered his face with sloppy kisses before breathing heavily against his ear. "Hard and fast, my love."

"Oh, little fox," he muttered as he increased the pace, making me cry out. "You want it rough, huh? Want me to stir up your insides with my cock?"

"*Yes!* Please, *please.*" He gave a few more rough thrusts, eliciting a string of breathless noises that I knew would be his undoing, before he pressed his thumb against my clit, rubbing in circles, which would undoubtedly be *my* undoing.

"Are you close?" He grunted against my ear, and I nodded as he pressed down deeper.

"*Yes,* oh, *God,* yes, please—" A few more thrusts, and my cries echoed around the room as I reached my climax. I could feel it pulse through every inch of my body, pulsing around Matthew, too. He was still nestled deep inside of me when I came down from my high, and I knew my orgasm would set off his. Sure enough, I felt him stilling moments later, and he kissed me deeply as he finally came inside me.

"I love you so much, Noelle," he murmured as he collapsed on top of me without pulling out.

"I love you, Matthew," I breathed, intertwining our fingers as we just laid like that—joined together, neither one of us wanting to move or lose this closeness with the other. "I'm so happy," I added because I wanted him to know it. And I *was* happy—to be here, happy and in love, with the man who meant more to me than anything else in this world. And here, in our bed, where we would spend every night side by side together.

Through every challenge, every obstacle, this man had shown me what it meant to love someone with no limits, no expectations, or requirements. He taught me what it meant for someone to love me for *me,* to be there through every moment and never walk away, even when things got tough.

It turned out, I had always believed in love—I had just forgotten what it was like to have someone make you feel *worthy* of their love. But at the end of my story *was* a happily-ever-after, my perfect guy waiting for me, a cup of coffee and a book in hand. He had gently but stubbornly knocked my walls down and helped me heal the wounds in my heart, taught me with his words and actions how much he loved me. There was nothing on this earth I would have traded for him.

"Me too," he murmured into my hair as he kissed my forehead.

This grumpy professor had turned out to be the love of my life. There was not one single moment of my last semester of grad school that I would have changed. Because now I knew what it was like to live in the pages of a romance novel, and it felt so *good*.

And speaking of romance novels—mine was sitting on my new desk. Somehow, in the process of letting in love again, the story had poured out of me. I had slaved over it for what felt like months, but now it was done. Officially.

Looking back at Matthew, I couldn't help the giant smile that spread over my face. I had everything I had ever wanted and more. Friends who had turned into family. A man who loved me more than anything. A job I was passionate about. Dreams for the future.

And I could see it all in my head. Our lives expanding, growing, and continuing to be full of so much happiness and love together. I didn't know what exactly would happen, but I knew that we were going to write our story next.

Who knows? Maybe it would be the next best seller.

Epilogue
NOELLE

1 *and a half years later...*
I glanced up from the computer at my desk, running my hands over the edge of the wood. For an entire year, the office was mine, and I had loved every minute of advising students. We were already into the swing of my second year in the role, and I couldn't believe I had found something that brought me so much joy and just made me plain happy.

But there was nothing better than the days when Matthew showed up with a cinnamon roll and a coffee cup and we strolled around campus together, hand in hand. It was those simple actions that showed me his love every day.

Ever since moving in together after my graduation, I had loved rolling over and kissing the love of my life good morning. It turned out that loving him was worth every struggle, every hardship we had faced, because being together, being like this—it was *everything*.

And I didn't feel worried that something bad was going to happen anymore. I felt safe, content, and so sure just from his presence every day in my life. This morning, Matthew had an early class, teaching basic finance to undergrads, and then we had plans to meet the rest of our friends for dinner. We'd been trying to get everyone together for *weeks*, always running into one problem or another with either his friends or mine. But finally, *finally*, we had plans for the night, and I was going to leave work early—a shock for me, with how many students came to see me—to get ready for the evening.

I packed up my desk excitedly, waving goodbye to the Student Assistant who was manning the front desk—Nicole, a sweet undergrad who loved journaling and had bubblegum pink hair. Today, she was wearing a sweater with a black cat on it and it made me smile.

I loved it here.

"Oh! Noelle, before you go," Nicole stood up, brushing her skirt down, before pulling me into the conference room. She looked a little shifty, and I wondered what she was up to.

"Yeah?"

"I just wanted to thank you," she said with a grin, pushing a strand of pink hair behind her ear.

"Oh." I think I might have blushed a little. "You don't have to thank me."

She shook her head. "You've been so helpful to me, and I really appreciate all of the time you've taken to mentor me and help this place feel like home." She looked down at her watch and then nodded at me. "Okay! That was all. Have a good night."

Okay...? I thought to myself as she skipped out of the conference room, and then I walked out as well, coming face to face—or face to chest, really, with a very impressive wall of muscles—with someone.

I looked up. The chest belonged to a handsome blonde man holding a bundle of sunflowers in his arms. *My* handsome man.

"Oh," I breathed, smiling bigger than I once believed possible. Feeling more love for this handsome giant than I ever knew I could feel for anyone. "Hi."

"Hey, baby," Matthew said, leaning in to kiss me softly before placing the flowers in my arms.

"Let's—" I waved a hand towards the exit. Matthew chuckled,

following me out of the office. I smoothed down my plaid skirt and turtleneck sweater, my favorite fall attire. Fall was my absolute favorite time of the year. The weather, with a bit of chill in the air, watching the leaves change colors, the pumpkin patches, and the hayrides—I loved all of it.

I looked up at him, leaning against the wall as we waited for the elevator. "I thought we were meeting at home," I said, smiling into the bouquet of flowers as I took a sniff.

"I have a surprise for you."

"Oh, a surprise, Professor?"

I pulled on the hair tie of my half-up ponytail to tighten it, watching as Matthew stepped closer to me. This man, my boyfriend of over a year, the definite love of my life, someone I never thought I deserved but had secretly always wanted—he was still just smiling at me, sleeves rolled up his arms the way I loved, and I couldn't help but move closer to him till our bodies were pressed together, flowers between us. Even after all this time, it still felt like there was a magnetic attraction between us.

"So," he said as the elevator dinged open.

"So..."

"Do you think I could steal my girlfriend for a few extra hours today? I want to show her something."

I raised my eyebrow. "She's wondering if it can't wait till dinner. She was planning on going home and getting ready first."

"No," Matthew shook his head, and I could tell from the expression in his eyes that he had something up his sleeves —*besides* his lovely forearms. He smiled again as he whispered in my ear, "It can't wait."

"Well, in that case... I think she can manage to make that work," I said thoughtfully and nodded to myself just to make him laugh. The elevator opened, and we stepped out.

"Good, baby, because I'm taking you out on a date."

"A date?" I smirked. "Oh, Matthew Harper, how you spoil me."

"Only the best for my sweet girl." I stood up on my tiptoes, placing a kiss on his lips before leaning my head against his chest. "Come on," he whispered into my hair, running his fingers through the ends. "We've got places to be."

"Oh? Do tell me what these big plans of yours are."

"Nah. I think you'll just have to wait and see." He grinned, taking my hand and leading me out to the parking lot.

I couldn't help but be grateful for the thoughtfulness of this man. Over and over, he had shown me how caring he was—thinking ahead and knowing what I would be worried about, predicting my needs before I could even think of them—and it all just made my heart feel even more full.

Matthew guided me over to his truck—blue, just like his favorite color—and opened the door for me before helping me in. After getting in the driver's side and turning the engine on, his palm came to rest on my thigh.

"Are you going to tell me where we're going yet?" I asked as he pulled onto the main road, and he just smirked at me. Shook his head no. "Come on," I pleaded, giving him my best puppy dog eyes. "Can't you just tell your girlfriend where you're taking her, please?"

Matthew laughed. And God—I loved the sound of it just as much as I did the very first time I had heard it, almost two years ago. "Still no."

I huffed, slumping against my seat, and Matthew's thumb started tracing circles on my thigh. "What if I—"

"No."

"You didn't even hear what I was going to say!"

Matthew raised an eyebrow. I pouted some more. "My sweet girl, I promise, you'll see. Very soon."

"Fine." I crossed my arms over my chest, turning my head to watch the scenery out the window as we drove along the freeway before pulling off on an exit.

As we neared my favorite local doughnut shop, I gave Matthew a skeptical eyebrow raise. "What are we doing here?"

"Hold on," he said, and I stayed put in my seat as he ran inside and came out with a pink box of doughnut-y goodness. "I figured you didn't have time for lunch."

I made an appreciative sound before taking the box from his lap and opening it. Inside was a lone cinnamon twist donut, my favorite, and then I realized that something was taped to the underside of the lid.

It was a small envelope with a drawing of a heart on it, and I opened it giddily, feeling a rush of affection for my man.

Did he look nervous? I thought maybe he looked a little bit nervous.

"Clue number one," I read out loud, and then scanned the rest of the paper. "Is this... a *scavenger hunt*, Matthew Harper?"

He grinned. "I guess you'll have to play along to find out, sweetheart. Where to, my love?"

Clue No. 1:

To show how much I completely adore you, I've hidden clues all over for you. Take a sip, you will find, they are hidden in all of the spots where I have called you mine. For the next clue, try picking up a book or two.

"Oh my God. The library? Or... no, the bookstore." I read the clue again, and then nodded. "Yeah. Bookstore." I picked up my doughnut and happily munched on it as Matthew reversed the truck and drove towards our favorite bookstore where we spent our rainy days. And I knew just the place where we'd find clue number two.

Entering the little cafe attached to the bookstore, I found a cup and an envelope sitting on an empty table, as well as a hardcover book I didn't recognize.

I picked it up, looking at it closely.

"Matthew, is this…?" I stared at him dumbfounded. "You had my book bound?"

Even though I had finished writing my first romance novel around the same time that I graduated, this was somehow even more special. I had chosen to self-publish it, and I had several paperbacks sitting on my shelf, but this was somehow even more special. The words were embossed on the front, and it was clearly hand bound. It was the most recent romance novel I had written, roughly based on our story. There were a few different details, of course, but it was so us that it made me smile. Even though I hadn't published this one *yet*, the gesture was so sweet and caring that I couldn't help but wrap my arms around his waist.

"Thank you. This is beautiful. I love it." He gently wiped the tears from my eyes and then nudged me towards the envelope.

Sparing Matthew a glance, I tore this one open and read my second clue.

Clue No. 2
The first night we met, I already knew—but go to the spot where I first kissed you.

"The spot where we first kissed?" I smiled, giving him a peck on the lips. "How could I forget?"

"It was the first time in my life that I felt like all of the pieces were falling into place—it felt so incredibly right that I already wanted to do it again."

"And now?" I fluttered my eyelashes up at him.

"You know I always want to kiss you, my wicked girl." He dropped another kiss on my lips, and then shooed me out the door, back towards the truck and our next clue.

I sighed contentedly as his hand draped over my knee and rested there for the rest of our drive to that little Italian restaurant we had shared a meal at before he kissed me outside. And even though I had already known it—had felt the same that night, something about knowing he had wanted to kiss me the *very* first night we met gave me happy little flutters. I didn't think it was remotely possible to love someone more, but every single day he did something like this to prove me wrong.

"What are you thinking about?" he asked as I gave another happy sigh.

"How much I love you." I placed my hand on top of his and laced our fingers together. "How lucky I am to have found you. How glad I am that you came over and talked to me at that mixer."

"How could I not have? You were the most beautiful girl in the room. Always are the most beautiful girl in any room," he said seriously. "You messed with my mind and entranced my heart, Noelle."

I giggled. "Well, you ruined me for everyone else with your big ol' heart, Matthew, so I think we're even."

"Just my heart?" he chuckled under his breath.

"No," I whispered into his ear, "not just your heart, babe." And then I winked at him.

"Good," Matthew smirked, and I knew what he was thinking.

"No distractions," I ordered.

Matthew pulled into an open street parking spot across from the familiar restaurant. "What?"

"I know that face, and as much as I'd like to climb over this console right now and show you how much I love—"

"Noelle," Matthew gave me his best grumpy face and turned off the truck. He leaned in and nipped at my ear. "Let's go, come on."

I nodded and let him lead me over to our destination. There was a table laid out with a centerpiece of roses and another envelope. "I think it's only fair that we recreate our first kiss while we're here, don't you think?" I smiled sweetly at him. "How'd that go again?" I pretended to ponder, and then looked up at him with big eyes and slid my arms around his neck. "What are you thinking about, Matthew?"

"I'm thinking about how much I want to kiss you."

"So kiss me," I breathed, and then our lips collided, a deep passionate kiss that made me want to melt in his arms. "Matthew—"

He shook his head, laughing, and I knew what he was thinking, too. "Alright, time for the clue, sweetheart," he said, giving me one more peck before I pulled out of his arms, grabbed the envelope off the table, and opened it, tucking myself into him to read the clue.

Clue No. 3
That night, at the game, everything felt so right with you. Here, you will see, clue number four is waiting for thee.

"Moda Center?" I looked up at him, waited for his nod of affirmation, and then his hand was in mine again, guiding me back into the truck.

We got there, pulled into the parking garage, and then we were off towards the building. The next clue, he presented to me by hand, pulling it out of his back pocket after kissing me in the same spot he had after the Blazers Game all that time ago.

"I just keep getting rewarded with kisses, huh?"

"I've told you," Matthew said, brushing a lock of hair behind my ear as he continued to stare lovingly at me, "I always want to kiss you."

"Envelope, please," I laughed, holding out my hand for him to place it there.

I smiled as I read the contents.

Clue No. 4
At home, you will find, the dress and shoes I left behind.

"Home?" I raised an eyebrow, wondering why he had us driving all over town. To some of our favorite spots. It made me want to take another trip back to the Zoo, also.

He just smiled and took my hand. When we pulled up at the house I ran inside, not even waiting for Matthew to turn off the truck. On our bed, I found another envelope, as well as a beautiful dress and one of my pairs of heels laid out with it.

"For dinner," he murmured, arms wrapping around my body as I stood there staring at the outfit. "Since I whisked you away from the office early and I knew you wouldn't have time to go back and change."

"Oh, Matthew," I sighed. "I do love you."

"I hope so," he laughed. "Come on, get changed, and we still have time if you want to do your hair and makeup."

"Are you saying I look bad, Matthew Harper?" I teased, frowning at him.

"Never." He kissed my cheek. "I think you're as gorgeous wearing that dress and makeup as you are wearing nothing but my t-shirt and a messy bun. But I thought maybe you'd want to get dolled up to see all your friends."

I beamed at him. "You're right. I do." I placed a kiss on his cheek as I went into the bathroom. "Thank you."

Somehow that was more thoughtful than him picking an outfit out for me—just knowing that I would want to change and look nice to see my best friends.

I changed, mussed with my unruly curls till they were somewhat presentable, and after I had finished with a little bit of makeup—eyeliner, mascara, a bit of blush, and highlighter—I stood back in the bedroom, envelope in hand.

Matthew was sitting on the bed, legs crossed at the ankles.

As soon as I read the words, I smiled.

I knew exactly where to go next.

Clue No. 5

On every early morning run, I'd carry you into the sun. And sometimes when I couldn't drag you out of bed, I'd promise cinnamon rolls would be ahead. Into the trees now, you must go, to find your final clue with those you know.

"Where to, baby?"

"Forest Park." I smiled. "But you already knew that."

"I did." He grinned. "But I wanted you to say it anyway."

"These clues aren't very difficult to solve, you know," I muttered, and he laughed, ushering me out the door and back towards the truck.

He shrugged. "They weren't supposed to be."

I just laughed at him—my boyfriend, the love of my life.

We pulled into Forest Park—this clue hadn't required me to guess, but I loved it anyway: the fact that he was sharing something with me that he had never told me before. We had come to Forest Park together before, lots more times over the past year, but I loved that I was still learning new things about this man—my man.

He led us toward a specific patch of trees, and I followed, holding his hand tightly as I tried to keep up his pace. Sometimes, I would have to remind him that my legs were shorter than his, so he needed to slow down, but today, I felt every bit as eager to see what this destination had in store for us that I didn't even care.

When I realized we were slowing down, I saw a blonde head sitting on a bench with a white dog next to her, and I gasped. "Tessa!" I called out, smiling as I saw Matthew's sister. She had been gone for the last few months, filming a movie in LA, and I couldn't be prouder of the girl I was beginning to consider my sister.

Tessa came to meet us with a huge grin of her own. Instantly, I noticed that tied to Snowball's collar was another envelope marked with a heart, and I looked at Matthew expectantly. He nodded as I grabbed it off of her, petting his dog—our dog—between her ears the way she loved.

I opened the envelope and began reading, trying to ignore the tears pricking at my eyes as I read his words.

Noelle,

From the very first time I saw you, I knew you were the one for me. While I could never have guessed the spark that would grow between us, or how much love I would feel for you, I know it just as well today as I did then. You are my sunshine, my life, the only person I ever want to wake up next to and kiss good morning. I want a lifetime with you, Noelle Marie Hastings—a life full of laughter, kisses, a whole lot of love, and endless books read.

For the final clue, you will find... if you turn around, I'm right behind.

Matthew

Was he...?

"Oh." My breath caught in my throat. I turned around to find the love of my life down on one knee, black box in hand. "Matthew—" Tears spilled from my eyes.

"Noelle," he began, holding my shaking hands in one of his. "This last year and a half together have been the best times of my life, and I don't ever want them to end, baby. You're... you're all I've ever dreamed of. All I could have ever hoped for. The love I feel for you... It's the most wonderful thing in the world. I'm so glad to share this life with you, and I want to walk the rest of it side by side, holding your hand. And I'm never letting you go, Noelle, because I wanna give you my last name and every bit of my heart that you don't already have."

He took a deep breath and opened the box in his free hand. "Noelle Marie Hastings, will you do me the honor of being my wife? Will you marry me?"

I nodded, letting out a sob as I stared down at the man that I loved. The man who I had already known I wanted to spend forever with, and there was only one answer that I knew would come from my lips. "Yes," I cried, tears flowing down my cheeks as I smiled the biggest grin I had ever felt in my life. I was so happy—so blissfully happy. "Yes, I will marry you, Matthew James Harper. Because I want to spend the rest of my life showing you how much *I* love you, every single day."

"I love you," he whispered in my ear, kissing me gently before bringing me into his arms and holding me tight.

"Surprise!" my friends shouted, crowding around us as we stood in the park. They were all there. My friends, Charlotte, Angelina, Gabbi, Daniel, and his friends, Bryan, Elizabeth, Cole, Tanner, their girlfriends. His sister Tessa, and Snowball, of course. Angelina's husband and Gabbi's boyfriend had come too, and I couldn't have felt more loved at this moment if I had tried.

Because I was surrounded by my favorite people and the people who I knew would have done anything for me.

"Let us see the ring!" the girls cheered, and I held up my left hand.

"Oh my God," I breathed into Matthew's ear as my friends gushed over the diamond. "We're *engaged*. I get to marry you." A few more tears fell out of my eyes, and Matthew wiped them off with his thumb.

"I can't wait to call you my wife, baby." His whole face lit up as he placed a kiss on my forehead. "But first, dinner."

"After all of this, we're still going to dinner?"

"Yeah, so we can celebrate." Matthew smoothed my hair and

tucked some curls behind my ear. "Our friends wanted to mark the occasion."

"I can't believe you organized all of this with everyone but me knowing," I groaned. "How *did* you pull it off?"

"Well, it wasn't easy," he laughed. "But I had some help." He gestured over to my best friends.

My girls just grinned at me, giving me a little wave. I couldn't help pulling them all into a big teary hug.

"We're so excited for you," Angelina grinned. I knew she meant it—she had found her great love, and her old ideas about not having enough time for love in her life were long gone.

"I can't wait to make your dress!" Charlotte giggled, so excited she looked like she could bounce off of the walls.

"Oh, yes *please*," I cried, holding hands with her as we both bounced up and down.

Gabrielle gave me a mischievous grin. "I still remember when she told us she was never going to fall in love again... just feels like yesterday."

"*Oh*, shush," I said, but we all laughed about how silly I had been.

"Dinner?" Matthew asked, and we all nodded, heading back to the cars to drive to the restaurant.

Matthew had reserved that tiny Italian restaurant where we had our first date, and as our friends and family all crowded around a long table, the place was filled with so much laughter, life, and love. I couldn't have been happier.

And I couldn't stop looking at the ring on my finger.

As dinner wrapped up, I leaned back into Matthew. "Take me home, baby," I whispered in his ear, "I want to celebrate... just the two of us." I nibbled on his earlobe.

"Little vixen," he whispered into my ear as he lifted me off of my feet and gathered me into his arms.

Our friends weren't even surprised by it, considering he liked to carry me at any chance he got, and I just giggled into his chest as he held me tight. "Thank you all for coming," he announced to the table. "We're so glad we could celebrate this moment with you, but I'm afraid we're going to have to cut the night short." I could feel the warmth in my face at his implications, even though I was the one who suggested them, and I burrowed myself a little deeper into him.

"Because I'm going to do very, very wicked things to you, little fox," he muttered into my ear, and this time, when I looked up from his shirt, I found all of our friends there, smiling at me knowingly but happily.

"Goodnight," I mumbled bashfully, giving a small wave before Matthew and I were off, heading towards the truck, and then back to our house, where I was sure I would very much enjoy those very wicked things he planned on doing to me.

"Thank you," I smiled.

"For what?"

"This. All of this. My friends being here. For choosing me to be your wife."

"I wouldn't have wanted it any other way, Noelle, sweetheart. I love you."

"I love you too," I sighed, happier than ever.

Forever, we'd have this.

Each other.

Extended Epilogue
MATTHEW

1 *year later...*

Waking up every morning with Noelle by my side was one of the best decisions of my life. And driving in to work together, knowing I could walk up the stairs to her office and she would be there, helping students and giving them the care and attention they needed? I was so proud of her. And what made it all better was that I got to stand at her side through all of it. It didn't hurt that we would get lunch together most days.

My friends probably thought I was a little whipped—but I didn't care. They had gotten to know Noelle almost as well as I did after numerous dinners, game nights, and movie nights, and I knew they thought I was a sucker for the way I would wait on Noelle hand and foot. But I couldn't help how much I loved her.

I didn't think there would be anything or anyone that I loved as much as I loved Noelle Hastings. She had taken my heart and filled it with her fiery passion, her endless dedication, and her relentless pursuit of what she wanted. And yeah, I loved calling her mine.

And now, after almost three years, I knew more than ever that I was ready for this next step with her. I hadn't wanted to rush our lives, had wanted to enjoy the little moments, like sitting on our patio, enjoying the warm summer nights as we cuddled up against each other watching the stars.

I thought how lucky I was—really, truly, that this was my reality.

That this girl let me call her mine.

And even though *my* favorite story didn't start with *Once Upon a Time*, our story—one that started with my beautiful redhead walking into a crowded room—I was positive that for us it would end with a *Happily Ever After*.

I had enjoyed every moment in between. And now, it was time for the rest of our lives to begin.

Fall was Noelle's favorite time of the year. I mean, who could blame her? When the leaves were changing colors in Portland, an explosion of reds, yellows, and golds, transformed the atmosphere. But it was more than just that—the slight chill in the air, the pumpkins that we carved, her favorite color being in season (pumpkin orange, which never failed to make me chuckle when she put on that thick turtleneck sweater every year)... it was a feeling.

And when I had proposed to her last year during the fall, it had felt right. So much so that when we were planning our wedding, there was no time of year in our minds that made as much sense as Fall. We had found a little farm outside of Portland to have our wedding—one complete with a pumpkin patch and hay bales and a cute little truck to ride around the property—and we just knew.

Noelle was absolutely giddy as we planned everything, and I was all too happy to help her with all of the details as much as I could. Cake flavor? Red velvet, of course. I had grown pretty partial to it myself over the last years together, and why lie? I would do anything to make Noelle smile.

And the rest of the desserts on the table... well, let's just say I wasn't looking forward to prying Noelle away from it every few minutes. She could never seem to satisfy that sweet tooth of hers, no matter how much she ate. It still made me smile, after all this time. I still wasn't a sweets guy—except for when it came to her. There was just something about eating the things she made, knowing how much love went into them, knowing how much I loved her... that made them taste even better.

The fact that we were the third couple of her friends to get married didn't seem to bother her, and I knew how excited she was to have Charlotte, Gabbi, and Angelina by her side. Plus, Tessa and Noelle had grown even closer since my little sister had moved back to the West Coast—living in Portland when she wasn't filming in Los Angeles—and Noelle couldn't have been happier to ask her to be one of her bridesmaids. They were all wearing—you guessed it—burnt orange. I would have expected to hear some groaning. Surely, orange didn't look good on everyone—but the dresses fit the wedding *perfectly*, so really, no one objected.

Bryan, Cole, and Tanner were going to stand by my side, and, surprisingly, after over a year of becoming friends with Noelle's cousin Oliver, we had grown close too, and it felt fitting to have someone from her family on my side too. I knew it pained Noelle that she couldn't walk down the aisle with her dad—but my girl never let that detract from the bounce in her step she got every time we talked about wedding plans. It was only at night that we would share our feelings about the parents we had lost. Tears were shed, but smiles too, knowing they were looking down on us. I would kiss her head and wipe the tears from her eyes and remind her how much she was loved—not just by me, but by everyone.

Even her Mom had come around after seeing how happy Noelle was. She had done so much more than she could have ever imagined, I think, especially after she rediscovered her love for writing and she had the students that she advised, and I loved that she came home with a smile on her face almost every single day.

Even so, my strong, independent fiancée just shook her head when I suggested her mom walk her down the aisle. "I can walk myself," she affirmed. "You'll be waiting for me at the end of it, anyway, so I'm not really going to be alone, am I?"

Elizabeth and Bryan's son was our ring-bearer, toddling around at two years old, and even though we didn't let him carry the *actual* rings, I had seen the pride in his mama's eyes as he walked down the aisle at the rehearsal. It was love—pure love, and even though Noelle and I hadn't decided on *when,* I knew I couldn't wait for us to take that next step in our lives and have kids of our own to love. And it may have been a little unconventional, but Snowball, *our* beloved dog (who probably liked Noelle more than she liked me at this point), was going to be our flower girl. Yeah, I had no idea how Noelle had come up with that idea, but it was going to be a hoot watching Snowball walk down the aisle with flower petals spilling from the pouches on her back.

Bryan gave me a pat on the shoulder as I stood, looking in the mirror, remembering all of the little moments that brought us here. To the little farmhouse where I was getting ready with the guys, while Noelle was in another room with the girls. I couldn't wait to see her, to see the beautiful dress she had hidden away from me, and to declare my love for her in front of our families, our friends, and the people we loved.

"Are you ready?" my best friend asked, and I could see the happiness and pride in all of the guys' eyes as I turned to face them. To think, sometimes I wondered if this day would ever come. If I would ever find someone who I loved with a burning passion like my parents had for each other. And I had found it, a thousand times over, in Noelle.

I nodded. "I've been ready, man. I think I knew I wanted to marry her the first time I laid eyes on her," I chuckled. "To be honest, I just can't believe we're really here."

Bryan smiled. "I felt the same way the day Liz and I said I do. And look at us now. Two kids later, and I think I love her even more than the day I married her." They had a daughter two months ago—a smiling little girl Jenna, who would be bouncing in her mother's lap.

"We're so happy for you, man," Cole grinned, adjusting his burnt orange tie as Tanner tugged on his pocket square.

"You look great, you guys." I smiled. "I'm grateful to have you all by my side."

"Anything for you, Matt," Tanner said. "You did the same for us, and we're just glad we get to support you through it." Last year, Cole and Tanner—always having to do things together since they were little—married Kelly and Kaitlin in a joint ceremony. It was so very them, and Bryan and I had been happy to be their joint-best men since two was better than one. Decidedly, though, living together was determinately not one of the things they were doing together, as both couples wanted their own space, but they had managed to buy two rather large houses right next to each other. The joys of a nice MBA salary.

We weren't bad off by any means, living on both of our salaries and having a little nest egg left for me by my parents, but I couldn't have ever imagined spending as much money as they did.

I glanced at myself one last time in the mirror. My black tie looked perfect—not crooked, which I knew would have driven Noelle crazy until she could fix it. Down to the last detail, I was ready. I nodded at my friends, and Oliver ran his hand through the ginger hair he shared with Noelle.

"Ready."

"Let's go get you married, big guy," Oliver gave a little fist pump and I laughed. It wasn't like I was that much taller than him—he was still 6 feet tall, even though he didn't have the muscle that I had from years of working out. He would be with Tessa down the aisle, and I knew he was excited—I had seen that same telltale blush that Noelle had when Tessa had knocked on our door earlier to make sure we had everything. He was crushing hard on my little sister.

And I had to admit, her and Oliver would be a good fit. He was now extremely successful as a computer engineer.

The guys walked down towards the ceremony venue, and after we were all ushered to our designated spots, I realized I didn't feel the least bit nervous. My heart was beating strong and true like it always had.

Beating for Noelle.

My favorite moment late at night was when she would rest her head on my bare chest, her ear pressed over my heart, and I would hold her in my arms as she just listened. And even better, when she'd fall asleep like that, the consistent drumming lulling her to sleep.

Finally, after the bridal party began their walk down the aisle—Charlotte and Bryan, Cole and Gabrielle, Tanner and Angelina, Tessa and Oliver, it was time. The music—an instrumental version of Noelle's favorite song, *invisible string* ("By Taylor Swift, of course!") played, and everyone rose from their chairs and turned to watch as she began her slow walk down the aisle.

And there she was. My sweet girl. My little fox. My sunshine. My Noelle. Dressed in a beautiful white dress, shimmering yards of white fabric fell all around her and trailed behind her so beautifully. And she was mine—all mine, forever. I inhaled a deep breath, trying to keep the tears at bay, but it was no use. I was so in love with her, that the knowledge that I was about to marry her—that she would be Noelle Marie Harper—was enough to make a man fall on his knees. I did plan to show her how much I loved her, appreciated her, worshipped the very ground she walked on, on my knees tonight—but that was later.

Now, I just wanted to appreciate my bride-to-be floating toward me. She always joked that the first time she saw me she thought I looked like a God—finely sculpted and beautiful—but the only Goddess here today was her: ginger locks tumbling down her back, curled to perfection, freckles dotting her face, chest, and shoulders somehow even more pronounced by the white of her dress. And the look on her face... She was ethereal. The most beautiful woman I had ever seen, and the only one I would ever have eyes for.

I let out a breath as she finished her walk down the aisle, handing her bouquet to her best friend, Charlotte, who was eight months pregnant and crying over seeing *her* best friend tie the knot (she'd blame it on the hormones later, but we all knew)—and then her hands were in mine.

"Hi," she whispered, as I just stared at her. Up close, she was even more beautiful. She never failed to take my breath away.

"Hi, baby," I murmured back, taking her hand in mine and pressing a devoted kiss on top of it. Then the ceremony began, and as I admitted later—I barely heard a single word, too focused on living this moment with Noelle.

"I understand that you've prepared your own vows?" the minister asked, and we nodded.

I went first. "Noelle—you are the sunshine on a cloudy, grey Portland day. You are the best part of every day, and the only person I want to come home to at night. I know you love words, but there aren't enough of them in the dictionary, or in all of the romance novels you read, for me to tell you how much I love you. Words can't possibly express how I feel when I see you smile at the sun, or bite into a freshly baked brownie, or when you lick the spoon of a bowl of frosting." I smiled. "They can't explain how I think that my whole life—every choice I ever made—led me to you. If it wasn't fate that brought us together, Noelle, I don't know what else to call it, but I know I'm the luckiest man alive to have you in my life.

"There aren't enough words, but I promise to always try. To remind you how much I love you, every day. I promise to care for you and protect you, to always taste your newest baked creation, and to carry you in from the car when you fall asleep. I vow to help you whenever you need it and to stand back and cheer you on when you don't. I love you, and I can't wait to spend a lifetime of happiness with you."

Noelle was crying—a steady stream of tears that leaked from her eyes even as she continued to beam at me. She was glowing with joy, and I squeezed her hands as she started on her own vows.

"Matthew," she gave me a big smile, one that stretched across her face. "If you had asked me three years ago if I ever thought I was going to have my great love, the story I would be writing for the rest of my life, I would have said no. But then—I met you. And there was part of me that always knew, I think, that I would love you. I saw you, and it was like my heart knew.

"You're better than every dessert combined, and there isn't anything I wouldn't do to see that beautiful smile on your face or to hear you laugh. I vow to love you and cherish you, and I promise that when things get hard, I'll take care of you, and when I don't eat enough, I'll let you take care of me." The crowd laughed.

"He really does like that." She beamed. I shook my head softly. She was right, after all. "I promise that we'll never stop writing our love story, and I can't wait to grow old and have babies with you. I vow to never let anything come in the way of our marriage, and that through thick and thin, you're stuck with me, babe. I love you." Noelle squeezed my hands a little tighter. "I'm so excited to be your wife, Matthew."

And as we exchanged rings, pushing her white gold diamond wedding band on top of her engagement ring and her placing the smooth, metal band onto mine... All of this finally felt real. Like, we were here. We were *married*.

"I now pronounce you Husband and Wife," the minister announced. "You may now kiss the bride."

Oh, I plan to. I leaned down as Noelle stood on her tiptoes, and we shared a short, sweet kiss—before I dipped her back and kissed her harder, as the entire audience cheered loudly.

"Hi, wife," I said, leaning my forehead against hers as we both stood at the end of the aisle, facing the smiling guests.

"Hi, husband," Noelle responded, a little breathlessly, nuzzling her nose against mine. She held the bouquet in a hand and mine in the other, and then we were walking together down the aisle to the applause of our family—the one we had built.

Once at the end of the aisle, an open back truck sat, bench and all, to take us on a little ride before the reception. Noelle beamed, squealing with delight, as I lifted her up by the waist and climbed in after her.

After we were both settled and I had covered our laps with a blanket, whispered in her ear, "Do you like your surprise, wife?"

"I love it, Matthew. Thank you for surprising me, even today." She nestled into my side, and I wrapped an arm around her before kissing her forehead.

"Ready to go celebrate with all the people we love, wife?"

"I'm ready for everything—as long as it's with you, husband."

The End

Acknowledgments

Wow—my first novel is officially completed. I'm so happy that you chose to come along on this journey with me, and if you've been here since the beginning, you'll know how many changes Matthew and Noelle have gone through, but always at its heart it was about two people, a little bit broken and bruised, coming together, and choosing to love each other despite all the obstacles.

There are so many people who this book never would have existed without, and I have to take the time to say thank you to them because somehow, this wild dream for me has finally come true.

To Gabbi: you're my rock, and I cannot believe how far this series has come since I started writing it. You have been the best brainstorming buddy, reading partner, and best friend. You bring so much joy, laughter and happiness into my life, and I cannot wait to write your book very soon so we can scream about fictional Gabrielle. I love you.

To Raquel, Sol, Trini, and Veniza: I owe a lot of this book existing to you four, and all of your love and support and encouragement of me over this past year. You are some of my best friends and I am so grateful for all of our chats and all of the chaos we always share.

To Katie: Without you, I might never have started sharing my work online, and I might have never felt the push to do the thing and write this book. Thank you for being my biggest cheerleader and loving me through all of it. I'm so happy to have you in my life.

To Sara: Thank you SO much for all of your help editing this book and all of your suggestions and ideas. I can't wait to keep sharing more about these characters with you.

To Al: There are so many things I would love to say to you, my friend. Thank you for always drawing me the most beautiful art of my characters. Without you, this gorgeous cover would not exist, and I love it so much. I am so grateful for all of your encouragement, your freaking out over my characters and stories, and every silly conversation we had. Go get some Dippin' Dots—you deserve it.

To Mallory: My OG Matthew and Noelle shipper—you came into my life during a really difficult time, and I cannot express how happy I am to have you as a friend. Thank you for always letting me ramble to you about this book and universe—I hope you love it as much as I love you.

To all of my wonderful friends who beta read for me: Thank you. Thank you. Thank you. Your words of encouragement and telling me how much you loved this book helped me so much in the times where I looked at it and thought "this is absolutely terrible!" I don't know what I would do without you all, and I am so glad to have your friendship in my life.

And finally, to my Parents (who I hope are not reading this book): I love you. Thank you for always believing in me. I hope I'm making you proud.

Also by Jennifer Chipman

Best Friends Book Club
Academically Yours - Noelle & Matthew
Disrespectfully Yours - Angelina & Benjamin
Fearlessly Yours - Gabrielle & Hunter
Gracefully Yours - Charlotte & Daniel
Contractually Yours - Nicolas & Zofia (coming soon)

Castleton University
A Not-So Prince Charming - Ella & Cameron
Once Upon A Fake Date - Audrey & Parker (late 2024)

Witches of Pleasant Grove
Spookily Yours - Willow & Damien
Wickedly Yours - Luna & Zain (coming Fall 2024)

About the Author

Originally from the Portland area, Jennifer now lives in Orlando with her dog, Walter and cat, Max. She always has her nose in a book and loves going to the Disney Parks in her free time.

Website: www.jennchipman.com

- amazon.com/author/jenniferchipman
- goodreads.com/jennchipman
- instagram.com/jennchipmanauthor
- x.com/jennchipman
- tiktok.com/@jennchipman
- pinterest.com/jennchipmanauthor

Printed in Great Britain
by Amazon